I0536955

1

Heaven's Waiting Room Has Lousy Magazines

Elena Sands

Cover Art by Elena Sands

Design Consultant : Mykala Hayes

www.elenasands.com

ISBN-13 978-0692328101
ISBN-10: 0692328106

First Edition: December 2014

Chapter 1

Light

One crisp day in January Dr. Henry Hall, aged 83 years, died, though he didn't know it yet. He got up out of bed and stretched a bit. He decided that he felt pretty good considering his usual state of health these days. The heaviness in his lungs seemed to have abated. He moved towards his bedroom window and failed to notice his own pale corpse behind him in the bed.

The sparkling winter world outside his window captivated him and he let out a small 'oh'. Feeling strangely giddy, he decided to get dressed well enough to go outside. "Just for a little bit," he said to himself. He went to his chest of drawers and rummaged around for a shirt and a sweater, thick socks, suitable pants. After he had taken out a pile of things that might work, he set them down on the top of the dresser in front of the mirror. Then he looked up in the mirror and saw himself. He was already dressed, complete with hat, scarf and mittens. He stared at himself in the mirror, all bundled up like a child and let out a short, bark-like laugh. "Ha!" He turned and shuffled out of the room.

He went into the living room, but his granddaughter Becca wasn't up yet. He walked into her bedroom, opening the door as softly as he could. He tip-toed to her bed and bent down to give her a soft kiss on her forehead. "Goodbye dear. I'm going for a walk in the snow." She stirred a little, but stayed asleep.

Outside the house the air was crisp and cold. Henry smiled at the crunch-crunch sound of his feet stepping on the snow. The cold air felt good in his lungs and he breathed deeply just to feel the sting of it. He looked up and down the street and thought that their neighborhood had never looked so beautiful.

He started off down the road to see if the creek was still running or if it was frozen over. He owned the house that he shared with his granddaughter and her boyfriend as well as a 5 acre parcel of land across the street. A crooked little creek made its way through the lot and often iced over the road on that side. The neighbors had been on him for years to put in a culvert.

The creek had indeed iced over the road. Henry smiled at the ice as if it were the greatest joke ever told. He made his way up the bank on the side of the road and walked along the creek.

A freezing fog had left ice on everything. Pine needles sparkled, dark green and silver in the sun. Tree trunks and branches, desiccated leaves hanging from dormant vines, and even the yellow tips of long grasses poking out of the snow were covered in delicate ice. Henry walked along the edge of the creek taking it all in.

As he walked, something caught his attention and he stopped to listen. The air around him in the woods became very still. He felt a strange rippling effect, as if space and time were a gong that someone had hit with a large mallet. "What?" he said out loud. There was no answer. He thought he saw a light in the woods. He walked further towards where he thought the light was coming from. It grew brighter and brighter as he approached. Soon it was so bright that he had trouble seeing anything else. He tried to cover his eyes with his hands but the light seemed to be coming from all directions. He turned around and the woods and creek and trees were all gone.

Chapter 2

The Waiting Room

After blinking a few times, Henry found himself standing in a doorway to what looked like a waiting room. Gray plush chairs lined up against stark white walls. Wooden end tables sporting mellow, grey office lamps separated some chairs. Magazines appeared scattered here and there. The carpet was a silvery gray that matched the chairs. Soft muzak was coming from speakers in various places in the ceiling. There were no pictures on the walls. To one side of the room there was a white counter with a service window. Yellow light came from the window but no movement or shadow was discernible through the frosted, mottled glass. On the counter there was a red, round, ticket dispenser and a service bell. At the far end of the room there was a white door. To the left of the door, mounted to hang from the ceiling was one of those big, red-numbered, digital counters. The current number being served was 9.

People filled the seats all around the waiting room. Some of them read magazines, some were chatting quietly with each other. A few children played on the floor with balls, building blocks and dolls. An older man sat in a corner chair and snoozed, softly snoring. Henry soon realized that someone was behind him and wanted to go through into the room, so he stepped inside and moved out of the way.

The man walked past Henry and over to the counter. He took a ticket from the dispenser. As he looked at his ticket and then the number on the digital display he sighed and put the ticket in his shirt pocket. He chose a chair next to a lamp, put his briefcase down, and picked up a magazine to read.

Henry stood for a few minutes looking around the room and scrunching up his face in confusion. No one in the room paid any attention to him. He looked back into the doorway. He tried to step through it again. Again he found himself facing the waiting room. He stepped back through again. He faced the same waiting room. Henry then decided to stand in the middle of the doorway sideways, so that he faced the door frame rather than the room. He looked left and saw the waiting room. He looked right and saw the waiting room. "Oh bugger all," he mumbled.

He stepped back into the room and saw the service counter. He approached and tapped on the golden service bell next to the window. A few people in the room looked up at him but quickly looked back down. One of the children giggled. A muffled voice from behind the window said, "Coffee Break." Henry frowned and tapped the bell again a little harder. People in the room were now watching to see what would happen. Again he heard "Coffee Break!" come more emphatically from a bored sounding woman behind the glass.

"I just have a few questions about…" Henry said. The voice from behind the glass cut him off.

"We're not allowed to talk to customers…er..you. You'll be able to ask stuff later." To Henry, it sounded like the woman was talking with her mouth full. "Please go make yourself comfortable in the waiting area and don't forget your ticket." Henry heard giggling and muffled chatter behind him. A woman said, "What is with all these dumb sheep?" More giggling followed.

Henry sighed and looked at the ticket dispenser. He pulled off a ticket that read "45". The digital display ticked over to "10" as he watched. A woman sitting near the door got up, a little too quickly, and fumbled with the door knob. She went through and the door closed softly behind her with a slight click. No one in the room batted an eye.

Henry looked around for a place to sit. He chose a relatively unpopulated spot on the end of a sofa, put down his briefcase and picked up a magazine. Surprised, he picked up the briefcase. 'This isn't mine. Where did I get this?' he wondered. The briefcase was made with a lovely, deep brown leather with a gold handle and gold trim. As he turned it over and ran his hands across it he found that it had no visible lock or opening mechanism. He put it next to his ear and listened. Nothing. He shook it. Again nothing happened and no sound escaped it. He looked around the room for some sort of tool and quickly realized that there was not going to be anything helpful. A few faces turned back towards magazines. He also noticed that almost everyone had a briefcase except for the old man who sat snoring in the corner and the children.

Puzzled but resigned he sat back in the chair and picked up the magazine he had been about to look at. The name of it was "America's Favorite Well -Manicured Lawns". He thumbed through it. He thought he might see lovely gardens, or a nice patio with a trellis. Instead, there was page after page of mowed lawns in front of ordinary houses. The variety, if there was any, seemed only to do with the type of grass. In fact, the name of each kind of grass was listed on the page. He frowned and put the magazine back on the table. He picked up another one: "Stunning Window Treatments of 17th century France." "Oh you must be joking," he mumbled aloud. He picked up his briefcase and moved to another chair next to a table with a few more magazines on it. He picked up another magazine. It was entitled "Cross Stitch Designs for the 4 Seasons."

"The magazines are terrible in here," he said out loud. A few people turned their heads, but no one said anything to him. Then he began to wonder why no one was talking to him. Other people in the room were talking quietly with each other. No one sat near Henry or made eye contact with him. He began to notice that there was something on the foreheads of the people in the waiting room. Across from him there were three older ladies chatting softly with each other. They all had what appeared to be a white cross on their foreheads. The effect was subtle. He only saw it when he looked directly at their foreheads. The symbol was not so much on the skin like paint or a tattoo, but it seemed to be like a light coming from within the ladies themselves. This light streamed out of the cross shape and glowed slightly. Henry thought it was quite pretty and stared, oblivious, at the ladies' foreheads. When they noticed him staring, they glared back. It took Henry a moment to notice this. His face turned red with embarrassment. "Oh, I'm sorry," he said and looked away. The ladies sat back and looked at each other with self-satisfied smirks.

Three seats over from those women sat two old men. They both had a crescent and star on their foreheads. The man who had walked in behind Henry had a bluish white Star of David on his forehead. He sat in a chair reading a magazine entitled "100 Years of Thanksgiving Centerpieces". Henry snorted. He looked past the man to the children playing on the floor. Two of them had the white crosses while one had what appeared to be the Sanskrit letters for the syllable Aum, a common symbol for Hinduism. Henry blankly observed the children while lost in thought. After a while, he put his hand up to his forehead. He couldn't catch a glow or anything that he could see. He looked around the room for a mirror but of course there were none.

"There is nothing on your forehead," a man sitting two seats down from him said. It was the man who had come in behind him and who had the Star of David symbol. He was middle aged with salt and pepper hair. He wore a suit and tie.

"I'm sorry, what's that?"

"You are trying to see if there is something on your forehead. There is nothing there."

"Well I suppose that makes sense," Henry sighed and slumped into the chair.

"You know it's not too late," the man said. "Even now, you could probably choose and be accepted."

"Yes, my friend, but to what? To what am I being accepted? I'm not in the habit of signing contracts I haven't read you know." The man looked disappointed and turned away.

"Oh I am sorry," Henry said, "I know you mean the best. Thank you for your help." The man smiled back, but his smile faded as he turned to look at the white door. He went back to his magazine.

Feeling dejected, confused and slightly numb, Henry sat and stared at a spot in the carpet. Occasionally, a block or a ball would roll into his field of view, only to be retrieved very quickly by a little hand. 'Am I in a coma?' He wondered. 'Is this where people go when they're in a coma?' He looked around the room and saw that most of the occupants were older men and women. One of the girls playing on the floor smiled up at him. He smiled back and waited.

Numbers ticked slowly by on the red, digital countdown to judgment. People went in. No one came out. The frosted service window stayed closed. Henry tried to look when people went through the door but could never see anything beyond it. He looked back down at his blue and white ticket which blandly reminded him that his number was 45. The red digital numbers read "17". Henry yawned, slumped down in his chair, and made himself comfortable. He dozed off and slept.

Chapter 3

Three Ladies

An hour or so into his nap, Henry was woken up by the noise of several people entering the waiting room. He sat up and watched them enter. There were people of all ages; old couples, young children, businessmen in suits and even what appeared to be a whole family. They got in line and began to take tickets one by one. The room accommodated them without seeming to change. Some of them hugged each other. Some cried. Some stared at the floor.

Henry looked at them and wondered what they thought was happening. The waiting room here wasn't any less soulless and pitiful than the average airport. They might not realize that they weren't just waiting for another flight. As he watched, his sadness for them turned to awe. Almost in a wave, the forehead signs began to blink on as the passengers looked at their tickets and took their new seats. He began to seriously rethink the whole 'coma' hypothesis. His reverie was interrupted by one of three ladies sitting across from him.

"Oh no. There must have been a plane crash…or some kind of disaster. Oh how terrible," she said. The other two ladies nodded but said nothing. Henry turned his attention to her. Of the three of them, she seemed like she would be the friendliest. She wore a collared white blouse. White open-toed shoes peeked out from under beige polyester slacks. Her toes wiggled under white hose. In her lap she cradled a huge, matching beige purse which was probably stuffed with tissues, pictures of grandkids, bumble bee pink lipstick and other assorted grandma favorites. Her hair was permed white with almond colored strands here and there.

Next to her sat a slightly dour looking Hispanic woman wearing a floral print dress. She watched the people enter the room and nodded but didn't say anything. She had long, dark gray hair, swirled and bobby-pinned into an impressively tight bun. She wore a delicate gold necklace with a small cross.

"Such a terrible way to go," said the third lady who was wearing green polyester pants and a white shirt. She shook her head. She was very thin and prim looking. She wore the slightly surprised expression of someone who had had one too many facelifts. She wore small, square glasses attached to a light chain. The glasses had been hanging around her neck, but she put them on as the people came in and looked them up and down as they stood in line. When she moved her head, the chain shook a little. Her hair was cut and styled in a way which was a bit inappropriate for her age. She also carried an overlarge purse and appeared to be in her middle sixties, thus completing the grandma triumvirate.

Henry looked back around the room again and his eyes settled on the big, red counter. "Now serving number 22," it read. He slumped down in his chair and began to thump his fingers on the armrest. He looked across at the ladies and made a decision. 'Why not?' he thought.

"Excuse me ladies," he said to them, "Since it appears that we may have quite a wait ahead of us, do you mind if I ask you about um…how you got here?" The ladies looked up at him, a little surprised. The prim one with glasses pursed her lips and looked down at her ticket, eyeglass chains jingling with disapproval. The nicer one in the middle looked at the other two, one after the other, then back at Henry and shrugged.

"My name is Henry, by the way, Henry Hall."

"And I'm Diane, Diane Holman. Glad to meet you Henry." She reached out and gave him a friendly handshake. "This is Anna Cordova." She motioned to the Hispanic lady in the floral print dress. Henry raised his hand to shake but Anna nodded at him and looked away.

"And this good lady over here," she motioned to the last of the three, "is Astrid Swartwout."

Henry was shocked. Astrid was a former student of his from a ridiculous number of years ago. At one time she had even faked having a crush on him in a misguided effort to get a good grade. It didn't work of course, but she was still a holy, self-righteous terror on a good day. She had recently returned to his university to be the provost. Becca came home one night complaining about her. Henry had no idea that she'd died. He cleared his throat. Astrid glared at him over her glasses.

"Astrid…yes…I uh… My granddaughter was just telling me not too long ago about you being in hospital. She was one of your nurses you know…But I thought you were all right. They couldn't find anything wrong with you, sent you home I believe?"

"Yes and I died that night. Apparently, I was misdiagnosed. It didn't help that none of the nurses took me seriously when I told them about my discomfort." Astrid emphasized the word 'nurses'. Henry didn't know whether to laugh or apologize. Diane looked back and forth between the two of them. She appeared to be enjoying herself.

"Well, all's well that ends…er…no that doesn't work does it," Henry said. "Look, I don't really know what to say to you, Astrid. I'm sorry that…that you suffered." Astrid ignored him and looked up at the digital display. Henry was struck then by the thought that Astrid's death had occurred at least two months ago, yet here she was still in the waiting room. He turned to Diane.

"You know that was two months ago…that Becca...er my granddaughter told me about Astrid. You ladies haven't been languishing here for that long have you?" Henry began to worry about being stuck in the waiting room for eternity. It wasn't the most creative version of hell that anyone had ever thought of, but it worked all the same. Diane gave him a reassuring smile.

"Oh no. Well I don't have a watch, but I don't think that much time has passed. The line is moving…I guess…and who knows how time works here anyway. I mean isn't it all relative or something?" Diane said. Henry chuckled.

"Well I suppose it might be something like that. Perhaps time doesn't mean what it used to. So Diane, how did you get here?" Henry asked.

"Well, you know I was just telling these ladies a bit ago how it happened. I died in the hospital. …I know, how cliché, but I suppose we all die there nowadays. But you know I knew I was going to die. I was real sick for a long time, and I just had this feeling, you know. But when it comes down to it, I don't think I remember actually dying. I just remember getting out of bed, then looking at the bed and wondering who was in it, and it was me! And I looked terrible, with all those tubes and things in my nose and mouth and arms." She made a face, but perked right back up again. "But you know I wasn't surprised at all. I just walked out of the room and started wandering down the hallway. At the end of that hallway there's a big window that looks down on the parking lot. Well I went to look and see if I could see my car and I did see my car and there was Donald, that's my husband, standing there waving at me. He passed 6 years ago…heart attack. So anyway, I went into one of the elevators, trying to get down to the first floor so I could get to the parking lot, but when the elevator doors opened, I was facing this room." She motioned to the room, arms

14

outstretched. "I tried to push the 'close door' button, because you know I thought this was just another floor of the hospital, but no matter what I did to the elevator buttons, the doors always opened on this place." Her smile faded a bit. "But I'm sure I will see Donald again on the other side," she said, nervously twisting the charm on her necklace, a small cross made of diamonds set in gold. Henry stared at the charm. He thought of his wife Lauren who had died some thirteen years ago. She wore a golden cross on her necklace too. Her mother had given it to her. Memories of a dream floated up in Henry's mind; Lauren with her dark hair, Lauren young and healthy, walking on the beach. He blinked and realized that Diane was talking again.

"...so, I just said to her, no you can't do that in here. It's rude. Henry, are you alright?" she said.

"Sorry, I was just...So...I'm not just in a coma?" Henry asked. Diane laughed.

"Well, what did you think? That we all came here on a fishing trip? You're dead, silly. We all are, that's why we're here," Diane said. Even dour Anna cracked a grin. Henry turned a little pink.

"Henry, look, I'm sorry. I'm not trying to make fun of you. This isn't the easiest time for any of us I guess but most of just...we just take it for what it is. Here...why don't you tell us what happened...like what do you remember before you got here?" Diane asked. Henry cleared his throat.

"Well, just before I got here I was walking in the woods...by the creek on our property. There had been a freezing fog and everything was...it was all covered in ice and it was beautiful. I was just walking along and I felt something strange...and there was a bright light. For a little bit I couldn't see anything but that light...and then I was here, standing in that doorway," Henry said. Diane nodded.

"See, so maybe you got shot in a hunting accident or you had a heart attack?" Henry shook his head.

"I don't think so. I had...I've been sick with pneumonia for quite a while. I hadn't been out of bed for several days. My granddaughter and her boyfriend have been taking care of me at home. They're both nurses. I probably...I must have died in my sleep."

"Well, that's not so bad. At least you didn't die in the hospital. Blech," Diane said and made a face. Henry laughed.

"Oh, no. I hated the bloody hospital. I did everything I could to stay out of it. And... I knew. Just as you said, Diane, I had this feeling that this illness would...seal the deal ...and I didn't want to die there hooked up to some infernal machine. So every time they tried to take me I would make some mischief. Eventually they gave up," Henry said. Diane smiled.

"Well, a last walk in the woods on your way to heaven is much more romantic than dying in a hospital bed, it's true," her face fell, "or you know, on your way to somewhere." She smiled again, embarrassed, and then became quiet. She watched the children across the room and clasped her fingers around her imposing purse. She perked up and reached across to put her hand on Henry's arm. "You know, Henry, I was told that god's mercy is boundless...so maybe...it'll all work out. Maybe you still have time," she said as she glanced at his empty forehead.

"Well I have some thoughts about that and I..." Anna interrupted him suddenly.

"I died in my house, in my bed," she said with a thick accent. All local eyes and ears turned to her. "I lived a long time though. I am 92. But yesterday I went out to get the eggs and that damn rooster came at me again. They told me 'Don't get the eggs. Let Jorge get the eggs'. But Jorge always breaks the eggs. He is my great-grandson and he is not so smart. So anyway, I went to grab the broom, to chase that rooster away and I fell. They took me into the house and I thought I was going to be okay. But then last night I died. I don't know how. Probably I had a stroke or something like that in my sleep. But it's okay. I don't mind. I lived for a long time." She looked at each of them, then directly at Henry. She said, "You know, I'm not crazy like you. I know there is god and I believe. But I understand. I would like to meet him right now, because I have some questions too." She smiled, revealing a handful of eroded, yellow teeth.

A natural silence followed for as long as Diane could stand it then she turned to Astrid, "Well dear, it's your turn...well if you'd like to. We wouldn't push you if you didn't want to share with us."

Astrid looked nervously at the counter and down at her white and blue ticket. "I'm afraid I don't have time," she said as she stood up. My judgment is come." She turned to collect her purse and briefcase.

"It was nice to meet you ladies. I'm sure I will see you again soon." She turned and faced Henry. "Good-bye, Dr. Hall. More than any of us I think I need to wish you good luck. We all have sins to atone for, but your one sin is greater than all of our…little ones combined." Her voice faltered but she recovered quickly. "For your sake I hope you use what time you have left in here carefully." Henry looked up at her and shrugged.

"Well thank you for concern, Astrid. I'm sure you mean well." She frowned at him and turned to walk to the door. Grasping the handle she took a deep breath, opened the door and went through. Henry tried to catch a glimpse of what lay beyond again, but couldn't see anything. He turned back to his travel buddies. Anna whispered a prayer, eyes closed. Diane was teary eyed and dabbed at her cheeks with tissues. She took out her ticket and looked at it then at the counter.

"You know I'm leaving soon too," she said while folding a tissue.

"Well, I'm sure you will do just fine, a lovely lady as nice as you are, no worries at all." Henry smiled. She smiled back, but looked back down at her purse, a little quiver visible in her chin.

"Oh Henry, aren't you scared, hon? I'm scared and I don't know if I have half as much reason to be as you might. I mean what if all that fire and brimstone stuff is true?" Diane said. Henry looked around the room, at the people and the variety of religions and cultures they represented. He looked at the magazines and chuckled.

"I really don't think so, Diane. This place is more like…a government office. It certainly doesn't look like the door to Hades…and look, everyone is here. No separate waiting room for the various faiths."

Diane looked around the room and then back at her purse, her face drawn with sadness. Her expression changed and she began to rummage around in it. She pulled out a small device and began to work the buttons.

"Henry, would you like to see my grandchildren?"

"Why of course I would." He didn't really want to, but he knew this was her way of calming herself down. For him all children under 10 looked exactly the same. Diane's grandchildren were no exception. Several cute little people with messed up hair and missing teeth were displayed on the screen in various silly poses. They looked like they needed bathing. He imagined that their hands were sticky with that ubiquitous substance that seemed to make all children's hands sticky. Diane told a story to go with every photo. Henry grinned and bore it with grace.

After a time the counter approached Diane's number. She gathered her things together and sat waiting and watching. Henry sat with her and held her hand. When the big, red numbers digitally shuffled into her numbers, she and Henry stood up. She gave him a brief hug and thanked him for being so kind.

"Well, that's me. I'm going now." She turned and waved once more before going through the door.

Henry sat back down. Anna was whispering another prayer. He looked around the room. People continued to read magazines, or sleep or chat. Anna's prayers had turned into a nap. Her head drooped and she snored in short, little bursts. For the first time, he noticed that she didn't have a briefcase. He looked at his own case and smiled.

Chapter 4

Dr. Marc Cabrera, Physicist

Having nothing interesting to do, Henry sat and watched people as they entered or left the waiting room. Here was sadness, there a shock that slowly faded; some were even happy. There were Muslims, Jews, Christians, Buddhists, Hindus. Some forehead signs he didn't recognize at first until he discreetly managed to get a better look. Henry played this game in his head: spot the religion. Hindu? No. Zoroastrian? Are there any left? Jains? Goodness, what's the symbol for Scientology? Do they come here too? Interesting. I wonder where they go next. He snickered at this out loud. There were a few disapproving stares, but they always dissipated quickly. Anna suddenly got up, nodded to him, and left. She knelt and made the sign of the cross on her chest before opening the door and going through.

Henry looked back across the room and saw a man enter. He was tall and big around the middle. He wore dark pants and a very ugly, multicolored sweater. His brown and grey hair was sculpted into a high and tight like he had retired from the Marines five minutes ago. His heavy, brown eyes surveyed the waiting room. Henry's heart leapt as he recognized his friend from the university. He jumped up out of his seat and walked to him.

"Marc? Marc Cabrera, is that you?" Henry asked.

"Dr. Henry Hall. Dr. Philosoap himself! Why you old codger!" He reached out for a handshake and jerked Henry's hand up and down. "I didn't think I'd meet you here....well actually...Dr. H., my friend, I am glad to see you, but I just realized I don't know where the hell I am," he said as he looked around the room. Disapproving frowns popped up from behind magazines. One of the children wagged her finger at Marc, and shook her head 'no'. Marc was a big man with a voice to fit. Even his whispers were loud. His loud use of the word 'hell' probably didn't help.

"Doc, what the he...what's going on here?" he whispered loudly.

"Come and sit down with me, Marc. Oh but do get a ticket first." They passed the counter.

"A ticket?" He looked over at the counter and smiled. "Will I get a sandwich for this?" he said as he took his number. "87. What does that mean?" he asked as Henry directed him to his previously held territory.

"It means you might want to take a nap," Henry said. Marc sat down opposite him and fiddled with his briefcase. He put it down when he realized he couldn't open it.

"There's probably not a crowbar in here, is there, Doc?"

"Ah no. There isn't really anything helpful to be honest." Henry watched Marc as he picked up a magazine from the adjacent table, grimaced, put it back down and picked up another only to roll his eyes at it. Marc patted his hands on his legs, sat back in the chair, and looked at Henry.

"So…I know I'm dead, and I know why too. I was a big fat bastard. Clogged arteries, heart trouble and all that." He gave a slanted grin and shrugged his shoulders. "Funny too. I was there looking at myself. I stood there and watched them put the paddles on me…..Nothing. I couldn't leave until they quit though. And that was kind of annoying because they worked on me for a long time. Then they called it." Marc rubbed his hands together in front of him. "And I ended up here. Though I get this feeling that it didn't happen right away. Like I didn't just die and walk through that door. It feels like I died a while ago….Weird. So how long have you been here, old man?"

"Well, just like a casino there are no clocks in here because I suppose they want you to spend your money and buy drinks rather than go home," Henry said. Marc chuckled.

"Still a joker even when you're dead, eh Doc?" Marc said. A man nearby ruffled his magazine and coughed. Marc looked at him and dismissed him at the same time.

"You know, Doc, I went to your funeral," Marc continued, "mmm, but that was six months ago or so. Yes, yes it was. Damn nice funeral. I hope mine was good like that. Everybody and their brother liked you. You know that."

"Six months? Well it doesn't feel like I have been here quite that long. I imagine Diane was right when she said it was all relative or something," Henry said as much to himself as to Marc.

"Diane?"

"A rather nice grandmother whom I met earlier, before she went through the door," Henry explained. Marc nodded and looked around the room.

"So this is where everybody comes before they meet god… or whatever happens? Hmmm. Oh and it looks like you get branded while you're at it. Did you see those light things on their foreheads?"

"Mm, yes I did," Henry said. Marc examined Henry's forehead. "Well you don't have one. Do I?"

"No, old friend, you don't."

"Not even a big green question mark?" Marc asked. Henry laughed out loud.

"No, no, not even that, but that is what it should be." Marc surveyed the room again and brightened.

"Hey I wonder if the laws of physics are the same here." He took one of the magazines, held it out at arm's length, and dropped it. He watched it flutter to the floor. "Well, there's gravity." He looked around the room and spied the children playing on the floor. He crouched down and asked a little girl, "Can I play with this ball, pretty please?" The girl smiled and handed him a yellow, billiard-sized ball. Marc knelt on the floor in a straight-line path to the main entrance to the waiting room. He rolled the ball towards the opening. It went through and immediately came back through, rolling into Marc's hand. He caught it and looked at it in wonder. He held the ball up to show Henry.

"Did ya see that, Doc? That was cool as hell. This room is like a …a closed universe!" Marc said with excitement. Several more frowns appeared above magazines around the room like popcorn and disappeared just as quickly. Marc ignored them. Only the children watched with rapt attention, waiting to see what he would do next.

Marc, oblivious to the audience, performed the experiment again. Again the ball came right to him. Caught up in the mystique of these new rules, Marc tried curves, banks off the door frame, and then started playing catch with himself through the door until someone came through it. The ball bounced off the bosom of an elderly black woman as she entered the room. She was not amused.

"Hmm, well maybe I shouldn't throw it through anymore, if it's just going to bounce off angry old ladies, but I'm sure I can find other things to do." Marc got up off the floor and sat down on the sofa next to Henry. He held the ball and stared at it.

Henry watched while Marc conducted his trials. Marc occasionally said, "Oh," or "Will ya look at that," though Henry did not always understand why. As time passed, he became aware of a nagging worry. The big red counter on the wall next to the other door was approaching his number. It was already at 40. With each passing number, unease turned to disquiet and disquiet then to nervous fear.

"Oh let's have more fun with gravity," Marc said suddenly. He grabbed one of the magazines and loudly ripped out a page. Even more loudly he crumpled it up in his hands. With the yellow ball in one hand and the crumpled magazine in the other, he stood up, held his arms at length, and dropped both objects at the same time. The ball appeared to fall faster than the paper, in fact it hit the ground a full second before the magazine ball.

"You have got to be kidding me!" Marc said. Several eyes looked at him over magazines. This time, they weren't so much disapproving as they were curious. "Doc, gravity is wrong here. The ball falls faster because it has more mass."

"Are you sure it doesn't fall faster because it is less pious than the magazine?" Henry quipped. Marc laughed, examined the ball, and then looked at Henry and shrugged. Marc performed the experiment again and got the same result. He returned to the sofa and sat next to Henry.

"You need to have someone else do the experiment," Henry said.

"Huh?" Marc said as he returned from deep thought.

"The observer affects the outcome of the experiment, user created reality and the like. Have other people in the room do it, then you can see…" Henry caught sight of the digital counter and looked at the floor. "I'm sorry, Marc. I would love to experiment in this room with you. It's a good bet that physics and philosophy unite here in interesting ways…but…I'm afraid I haven't much time left."

"How close are you?" He looked at the counter and back at Henry.

"My ticket is 45. It's at 42 now. Earlier I felt all right but I am becoming more and more unsettled. I guess I'm just nervous really." Henry looked down at his ticket. Marc looked at the yellow ball in his hand, running his fingers over its smooth surface.

"There are no marks on our foreheads, Marc. So I don't really know what's to become of us." Marc sat silently as he watched someone in the room get up and go through the door. The counter now proclaimed, "43".

22

"Well Doc, I reckon I should have all the same worries and fears and I do… I do, but you know…we lived our lives well. We didn't hurt anyone. We opened the eyes of one out of every …hundred of those numskull kids, or less," a grin spread across Marc's big face, "but anyway, if the afterlife starts with a crappy waiting room that everybody goes to first, I think even if we do go to some place for delinquents, the worst they would do to us is post a really strongly worded memo, or ask us to come in on Saturday." Marc chuckled. "Oh you know I kid, but still, we are good people you and I, Doc. Damn good people. You go through that door and give 'em heck… or better yet give 'em truth. You can't go wrong with that."

Just then the big red counter flipped over. Henry had not been watching and realized that it now displayed "45".

"Well, that's me," Henry said. He stood and grabbed his briefcase. He and Marc shook hands. Marc pumped Henry's hand up and down, even more vigorously this time, and clapped him on the shoulder. Henry turned and walked to the door. He grasped the handle, turned back towards Marc, smiled and walked through.

Chapter 5

Judgment

Henry closed the door behind him and found himself standing at the entrance to the great hall of what looked like a grand, gothic church. The walls were made of soft pink and orange sandstone. There were large fluted columns that flowed up and spread out into a stone ceiling with many decorated and painted vaults. The whole place was lit with tall candelabras placed here and there, on the sides of the hall, and in between large wooden pews. He noticed that only one side had pews, the other side had large, multicolored woven rugs, layered and laid down over a large space. There were no people, either on rugs or pews or anywhere he could see. Beautiful, tall, stained glass windows glowed on either side of the galleys, projecting their green, blue, and yellow lights onto the pews and the rugs. The light was eerie. He could tell that it was not sunlight as it shown equally on both sides of the room and was not at a natural angle. The room itself, rather than cavernous and filled with echoes, was soft and quiet. He thought he heard the sound of someone turning pages in a book, but that was all.

Henry walked slowly down the center aisle looking back and forth at the stained glass windows. In one panel he immediately recognized Moses coming down from a mountain and carrying the tablets. The mountain itself was stormy with a frosted glass flash of lightning here and there. Moses held the tablets, showing them to stained glass people. The tablets glowed a bit more brightly than the rest of the scene. It was art so beautiful, Henry imagined that Michelangelo himself had been commissioned for it.

In another window, Jesus gave the Sermon on the Mount. Little, silver glass fish and brown, glass loaves were passed among the listeners. In another, Jesus hung on the cross, a golden, glowing crown on his head. Another window was intricately colored and decorated, but contained only lines of Arabic script.

"Ahem! If you are done sightseeing we'd appreciate it if you'd join us over here." A loud, impatient voice bellowed from the end of the center aisle, in the front of the church where a pulpit would be. Henry walked forward and found, instead of a pulpit or a dais, a long wooden table. Seated at the table, opposite from Henry, was an older gentlemen. He wore brown monk's robes and an irritated scowl. His face was wrinkled in such a way that made Henry think he had been sporting that irritated scowl for many years. His head was shaved with 4 or 5 days of salt and pepper stubble grown in. His face carried the same stubble.

The table was long and a dark brown. Most of it was covered by stacked file folders filled with cream colored papers. Individual papers also littered the desk. To the old monk's right there were a series of wooden handles. Henry didn't know what they were until the old monk grabbed one and pressed it into a black ink pad.

Behind the old monk at the table there were several filing cabinets that served as a wall. A space between cabinets made a door into what Henry thought might be a labyrinth of filing cabinets. The cabinets were tall enough that he couldn't see anything beyond them except an extended ceiling. Standing next to one of these cabinets nursing a cup of hot something was a young man wearing the same style of brown robe as the old monk seated at the table. This young man had brown hair cut into an unfortunate bob. He turned to put his coffee down and Henry spied a shaved bald spot on the back of his head. At that moment, another young monk came out of the filing cabinet labyrinth with a cup of coffee and took up position, leaning against another of the filing cabinets. He wore the same brown robes but had dark hair. He also held a clipboard and a pen. He looked bored. Henry approached the table and stood waiting. The old monk picked up several papers and put them down in succession.

"Todd, where's his damn file? It's not one of these is it?" The old monk asked, picking up files near him and stacking them. Todd, the young monk with brown hair, rolled his eyes and exchanged a look with the other young monk who smirked. Todd looked at his clipboard, picked up a file from the top of a short stack of them right next to the old monk's right hand, and put it in front of him. The old monk scowled at him but said nothing. He put on glasses and opened the file then read the first page.

"What's this…why do they call you Dr. Philo…soap? Dr. Philosoap? What's that nonsense?" the old monk asked, still scowling as if he smelled something bad.

"Well," Henry cleared his throat, "I am a professor …of philosophy, and my colleagues would say that I take my soap box with me wherever I go. Once I was at a lunch, at a café' that we frequent, and I lectured Marc about..."

"Enough, I understand now," the monk said, still reading. He looked up from the file and looked Henry up and down. His eyes lingered on the briefcase.

"You know, we hardly get any one through here anymore without some kind of baggage." He sighed heavily again then grabbed hold of the stamp he had previously set on an inkpad, jammed it down into the pad then held it up over the paper in the file. He took a deep breath and spoke.

"Dr. Henry Hall, do you believe in the all-merciful, the all-wise and highest of the high, the heavenly father our Lord and do you submit to his will in humility and admit your love for the holy spirit and all his creation and do you further believe that Jesus Christ is his son and your savior and that he died on the cross for your sins and finally do you further accept that Moses, John the Baptist, Muhammad, George Pearson etc., etc. from the list of consigned messengers of the book are his prophets unto you O' mortal?" The old monk's voice had taken on a sing-song tone as if he were tired of saying the same thing over and over again. He held the stamp over the file and waited, looking down at the paper. When no answer immediately came he looked up at Henry over his glasses. "Well?" he said impatiently. Todd and the other monk looked at Henry. Henry looked at all three of them, one after the other, cleared his throat, and spoke.

"Well...it appears that I have been wrong...about some things but I...still have some questions for you gentlemen."

Todd and the other young monk looked at each other. Todd shrugged. The old monk, his hand still holding the stamp and hovering over the document, rested his head on his other hand and gave Henry a look.

"Just say yes," he said, exasperated.

"I'm afraid I can't do that," Henry said, gathering his nerve. "I have some questions. I am not saying any oaths or ...signing my freedom away until I know what's going on." The old monk raised his eyebrows.

"Freedom?" He laughed a coarse, bitter laugh. "You want your freedom, do you?" He laughed again. "Well, Dr. Henry Hall, educated as you are, you should know better. You must have faith." He pointed his finger down at the page in the file. "That is the key to this one door…faith. So, I ask you again, Dr. Hall, will you take the oath?"

"Can't you just tell me what my options are and then I chose?" Henry asked. The old monk smirked.

"Does this look like a coffee house to you? Am I a damn barista now? No, I won't tell you anything. You must have faith. That's the whole point. Now, will you take the oath or not?" The old monk glared at Henry over his glasses, his eyes on fire.

Henry shook his head. "No, I will not take any oath blindly and a good and just religion would not require me to do so." Henry stood still and eyed the old monk who eyed him right back. His expression changed.

"So be it," he said. The menace was gone from his voice. He put the stamp down on the black ink pad and picked up a different one from the row of stamps. He quickly stamped the paper, closed the file folder and handed the file to the dark-haired monk who accepted it and disappeared into the file cabinet labyrinth.

"Bye now," the old monk said as he gave Henry a sarcastic little wave. Henry looked at him and then at Todd. Todd shrugged his shoulders and took a nonchalant sip of his coffee. Henry was confused.

"So, does something happen or…do I go somewhere or what?" Henry asked. The old monk ignored him and began sorting the stacks of files on his desk again. He took a sip of coffee. Todd came around from behind the big table and motioned for Henry to follow him. Todd walked Henry down one of the outer aisles of the church almost until the end of the room where he had come in. Todd stopped in front of one of the stained glass windows. The scene here was silver and gray and showed people, masses of them, huddled together and reaching up towards the sky. As Henry stood looking at the scene, Todd shoved him into the window, practically picking him up by the back of his shirt and tossing him in. Just before he went through he heard the old monk shout behind him, "NEXT!"

Chapter 6

Elysium

Henry landed face down on a floor with grey carpet. For one terrifying moment he thought he was back in the waiting room. There had been no breaking glass or crashing sound. He had felt only a strange, enveloping feeling, as if he had walked through a wall of light syrup. He stood up and checked himself over. Other than a bruised ego from being tossed like a rag doll by a smaller, younger man, he was unharmed. He looked around and realized that he was in a place that looked a lot like an airport terminal. He stood in front of a doorway that led out into the terminal and behind him, into something that looked like a walkway connected to an airplane. He turned and walked down the ramp. At the other end he faced the terminal again. He shook his head.

"Not this shite again," he mumbled to himself. He stepped out into the terminal and surveyed the scene. The place did in fact look just like an airport terminal. Neat rows of seats spread away to the left and across a center aisle in the building. Several of these seats were occupied. Various people sat here and there looking as if they were waiting. One person lay on a row of seats sleeping under a large woven hat. He walked forward cautiously, taking in the scene. There were also rows of windows. The window directly across from him showed nothing but cerulean blue sky and tan sand. Henry said, "ooo" and walked to the window. He was standing and admiring the view when a lovely, lightly accented voice spoke from behind him.

"Hello, Dr. Hall." Henry turned around and his jaw dropped. A gorgeous woman was walking towards him with her hand extended. She took Henry's hand and shook it. "My name is Ra-Neferu and I will be your guide here. Welcome," she said. Henry stared and stammered.

"Uh…ah…uh…Hello. I uh….you're…you…please pardon me." He took a moment to collect himself though he decided, when rational thought returned, that he could not be blamed for his moment of astonishment and confusion. Before him stood a beautiful, caramel skinned woman dressed to the nine's in either the best costume he had ever seen or the real deal in ancient Egyptian royal fashion. She wore a pleated white dress made of fine, semi-transparent linen. Every available and appropriate space on her body was covered in jewels of some sort. She wore golden bracelets, golden bands around her upper arms, a light gold belt cinched at her waist. A large, wide, jeweled, golden neck plate rested on her chest from which turquoise, red jasper and lapis lazuli gleamed. On her head she wore a delicately braided, jeweled wig which was topped by a small, jeweled crown and behind that an odd, off white cone-shaped thing that looked like soap. She smelled faintly of flowers and her skin shone with some sort of oil. Henry was mesmerized. Ra-Neferu took his hand and said, "This way please." He did not resist or protest. They walked together toward the center aisle of the terminal.

Ra-Neferu led Henry down the wide center aisle of the terminal towards an end of the building that was open to the air. He looked around in wonder at the windows along the side of the building, at the blue sky and sand outside, ahead to the open walkway and behind him at the rows of chairs and the other, closed end of the terminal. To Henry's surprise, every so often along the walls of the terminal there was a vending machine. He couldn't make out whether they contained drinks or food.

They passed by some people sitting in the chairs or standing in various places but they all ignored him and his beautiful guide. Henry's mind observed and worked, observed and worked as it always did but he kept silent. Ra-Neferu led him along without a word as if in a wedding march. At the end of the terminal she stopped.

The terminal ended in the open air, onto a large, round, stone staircase. The steps led down to a narrow stone path and sand. Ra-Neferu paused on these high steps to look at Henry and get his attention. She held her arms out and gestured to the vast landscape in front of them.

"Welcome to Elysium." She smiled. Henry stood and took in the view. He looked out on an ocean of sand. Brown and tan waves undulated away towards the horizon, basking elegantly in the sun. In the hazy distance to the right he could see the dunes subside and the wide, dark swath of a river emerged, bordered on either side by a deep green that was muted by the dusty haze in the air. In the distance something shimmered; a glint of something white in the sun and the barest impression of mountains or was it pyramids? A cloud bank obscured them and he could only see tantalizing bits and pieces through holes in the passing clouds.

Henry stood and watched in awe and silence. His mind cleared. He felt lifted, his feet only barely in contact with the stones of the stairs.

In his immediate surroundings, he saw two stone paths leading away from the stairs in opposite directions. One curved off to the left beyond a stand of palm trees and bushes. The palms and bushes were suspicious in their location. It almost looked as if they had been planted to obscure the view from the top of the steps in that particular direction. The other path wrapped right around the side of the terminal. He wondered if it led to the river. It seemed a safe guess.

As he stood taking everything in, his rational mind began to recover from the shock of recent events. Questions rose up from the depths and breached the surface of his mind. He turned to Ra-Neferu, almost afraid to look at her.

"Ra-… I'm sorry. I'm having trouble with your name. Will you say it again please?" Henry asked.

"Ra-Neferu."

"Ra-Nefellu," Henry repeated, not quite right. Ra-Neferu nodded. "Um…So you are my…guide did you say?" he asked.

"Yes. I am here to help you through these difficult first days. Many people struggle with the transition," she said. "You may come and stay at my villa and be my guest there. I will help you to adjust." Henry snorted. Anger began to rise inside him.

"Adjust," he said bitterly. "Yes, that will take some time, won't it? That will take…Say, how do I even know that I'm dead? Was I ever dead? Or am I in some… damn hospital bed, hooked up to machines and pumped full of drugs…and where the hell is this place? What exactly is going on? I just want some bloody answers for a change," he said.

"Henry, just give it time. It will be alright," she said. Henry looked at her, at the terminal and the people around them. Nearby a woman was bawling. Another woman held her and stroked her hair. He saw a few others wearing masks of sadness, fear, and despair. His sudden burst of rage subsided. Weariness slowly replaced it.

"I don't know you," he said softly. "I don't…I'm so bloody tired." Ra-Neferu nodded and put her hand on his shoulder.

"Come. It will be alright. If you do not want to come with me, you may choose not to. I will not stop you from going as you please," she gestured at the distant river. "I do, however, offer you my help." Henry looked at her again. She seemed genuine. He detected no small gestures of deception. He sighed, and nodded his head. She gently took his hand again.

She led him down the stone path that led to the right along the side of the terminal building. As they walked Henry heard someone shouting his name. It came from behind them. Ra-Neferu kept walking. Henry stopped.

"Ra…Ra-Nelellu…I hear my name. Someone is calling me," he said. Ra-Neferu stopped and looked back at the terminal building. She pursed her lips.

"I was hoping to avoid this but they are always so quick. Come on." She led him back towards the terminal and along the stone pathway that led away to the left, past the obscuring palms and bushes. Henry was confused.

"What's going on?" he asked. Ra-Neferu frowned.

"It is the missionaries," she said, "they are trying to save you." Henry detected the slightest hint of sarcasm. "You will see for yourself. Do not worry though. You have nothing to fear," she said as they walked. This did not make Henry feel any better.

"What exactly are they trying to save me from?" he asked as they passed the terminal steps.

"From staying here in the land of the godless pagans, outside the presence of the One God. They will offer you another chance to get to Heaven. I was hoping to avoid this but I suppose it does not matter. They will compel you to repent and enter Heaven." Henry's eyebrows rose but he did not respond. The thought also crossed his mind that Ra-Neferu walked very briskly for someone weighed down with so much gold and jewels.

The mystery that lay beyond the obscuring palms and bushes in front of the terminal stairs involved a lovely fish pond, appropriate accent plants, salmon colored paving stones, and velvet bank ropes on brass stands. There were also three missionaries and a door to nowhere. At least that was what Henry decided to call the unattached, white door frame that stood atop a set of three wooden steps.

Three men stood behind velvet bank ropes. The door to nowhere was behind them. When they caught sight of Henry, they beckoned.

"Henry, come to us! Repent your sins. Accept the One God! Come to the Kingdom of Heaven with us. This is your chance!" They continued to shout as he and Ra-Neferu approached.

One of the men wore a white robe. He had short, dark hair and a beard and looked like he might be from somewhere in the Middle East. A second man wore the distinctive white shirt, black tie, black pants combo of the Utah Mormon missionary, circa the 1980's. He was blond haired and blue eyed, with cheeks pink from the heat. The third man looked like Jesus, or at least he looked like what many North Americans pictured Jesus would look like, with Caucasian features, light brown, wavy hair and sporting a golden yellow robe, tied at the waist with a cord. Henry stood and listened. A few other people came along the path and gathered around the shouters.

"Henry and ….and Jeff. Jeff you too. Will you repent? Will you be saved? Come to Heaven with us! Reject the heathens who have rejected the One True God," said the Mormon.

Jeff, wherever he was in the crowd, did not respond. Henry passed through the crowd and stepped closer to the men.

"Excuse me, gentlemen," Henry addressed them. The Mormon had been about to shout something again, but stopped, finger still in the air.

"Are you Henry?"

"Yes, and who are you?"

"That is not important right now. You must repent and come with us to Heaven. The Kingdom awaits you," the Mormon said. Henry raised his eyebrows.

"If I go with you to the Kingdom, could I also return to this place if I chose to?" Henry asked. The men frowned. The one who looked like Jesus spoke:

"No way, dude. Once you go to Heaven, you can't hang with the Heathens. That would be like…wrong." The Jesus man sounded like a California surf bum.

"Are you meant to be Jesus?" Henry asked him, knowing he couldn't actually be Jesus. The Jesus man laughed.

"No way, dude. I'm not THE Jesus, I'm just a really, really big fan, ok." He smiled and tucked a bit of golden hair behind one ear. In spite of himself, Henry chuckled. Everything was so unreal. He could not believe what was happening.

"Well how about this then, gentlemen, I am new here and I have many questions. Would you like to come with us," he gestured towards Ra-Neferu, "and we could have a chat somewhere?" He looked over at Ra-Neferu for confirmation. She looked worried or annoyed, Henry couldn't tell which. He continued. "We might have some tea or other such drinks and food which people have around this place. You could then tell me all about Heaven and why I should go there, and what it's like, and answer all my questions. What do you think?" The Jesus guy started to talk again but the Middle Eastern looking one cut him off.

"No! We will never enter the abode of Heathens. It is god's will. In his abundant mercy he gives you this chance, to come here, repent and be accepted into the Kingdom. And if you do not, if you choose this place over the Kingdom, it is a grave and unforgivable insult to the highest. Repent! Repent now!" He held a book high and kept shouting.

"Sir, sir, please," Henry interrupted, "Would you just…answer a few of my questions?" The three men stood staring at him.

"We shouldn't need to explain Heaven," the Mormon responded. "You just have to accept it and come with us."

"On faith?" said Henry.

"Yes, exactly," said the Mormon, who smiled. Henry turned to Ra-Neferu.

"If I go with you, may I return here and attempt to enter Heaven?" Ra-Neferu nodded.

"Yes. You can always come back here if you like. They say you only have one chance but in reality they will take you if you change your mind, but you will have to perform serv…" she was interrupted by the three men who starting shouting names and their other stock phrases. Henry turned to Ra-Neferu.

"I've seen enough. Let's go." They walked away down the path towards the terminal and around the corner. As they turned around the side of the building Henry was glad to see that the path did indeed lead down to the river. Near the edge of the river there was another door to nowhere. This one was different from the missionary door in that it was a stone arch rather than a wooden frame and it was level with the ground. There were no steps. As he watched, two people walked through the arch and disappeared. Henry's breath caught in his throat.

"What happened to them? What is that?" Henry pointed.

"That is a portal. We use them for travel. Before you enter you state your destination and then…you are there," she said with a flourish of her hand.

"Amazing. How does that work? Is it a stable wormhole or some such thing?" Henry asked. Ra-Neferu frowned.

"I have not heard these words before. Wormhole?" Ra-Neferu asked.

"Oh well, it's a…it's actually hard to explain. It's a folding together of time and space so as to…bring two distant points together," Henry explained. She nodded.

"The truth is, we do not know how the portals work," she said. "They contain no machinery that we can discover."

"Oh." Henry looked down at his feet. Disappointment fluttered in his chest. Ra-Neferu took his hand and they walked.

"Travel through a portal is instantaneous. However, there is something to be said for a comfortable barge and a nice view. Look." Ra-Neferu pointed towards the river at a strange boat. It was made of long stalks of something lashed together. He knew it was not wood. He thought it might be stalks of papyrus but he was not sure, never having seen such things during his life. As they walked closer, he saw that the craft was actually quite large with plenty of deck space and a small, open cabin at the aft end. Several men sat waiting at oars. They were completely bald and tanned. They wore only a white, linen sarong-like garment about their waists. They waited and made no noise. Henry thought it odd that they didn't chat, but imagined that there might be several unsuspicious reasons why they wouldn't. One of these men waited by the entrance to the barge and bowed as Ra-Neferu and Henry approached. She barely acknowledged him as they walked past him and onto the barge. This bothered Henry a bit but he said nothing.

Ra-Neferu led him to the open cabin at the back of the barge. The cabin was not much more than a shade. Two entrance ways and windows on either side were open to the air. Inside there were two wide benches along the inner walls and across from each other. They were covered with fine red and orange pillows. In the center of the cabin sat a low table with a bowl of fruit; mostly grapes and figs with a few dates and a fat plum or two. Ra-Neferu motioned for Henry to sit. He picked a spot with a good view in most directions and gratefully sat down. He felt tired down to his bones. They sat quietly for a few moments. With a lurch, the barge began to move. Henry looked out at the dark water, the vegetation along its edges, and the more distant sands. Along the path of the river he could see more evidence of habitation; the dust obscured shapes of houses, arch shapes that were probably portals and a distant and extremely large glimmer of white. The dust haze obscured large, murky shapes in the distance. 'Are those mountains?' he wondered.

As he sat admiring the view from the boat, the missionaries floated up in his mind with their pink, angry faces and clenched fists. He grinned then began to chuckle. Ra-Neferu gave him a questioning look.

"I'm sorry, Ra-Neferulu," he still didn't have her name right, "I just never expected that the afterlife would have so much bloody comedy attached to it. I mean that awful waiting room…those stupid, stupid magazines…" he continued to chuckle. "Bloody missionaries," he mumbled and chuckled some more then scratched absently at his chin, an old habit. He turned to her, "Ra-Neferulu…I um…so is this all real? I am having trouble coming to terms with all this strangeness…beautiful strangeness to be sure" he gestured at the river, "but... also, am I saying your name correctly yet?"

"Not quite, but you are getting better." She smiled. Henry returned her smile but it faded quickly.

"So, are you sure I'm not just in a coma or something like that?" Henry asked.

"Quite sure." She paused to look out the window, her face serene. "Sometimes I forget what a shock it can be, especially in these times." Henry nodded and stared at the bowl of fruit without really seeing it. She turned and saw him staring.

"You are welcome to it if you like." She gestured to the bowl. This caught Henry off guard.

"Huh….I'm sorry what?" he asked, his trance broken.

"Fruit, Henry. You may help yourself if you like."

Henry looked at the fruit, really seeing it for the first time. He wasn't really hungry but he loved dates and the bowl was brimming with them. These dates looked fresh and delicious, not like the gummy, stale things in grocery stores. He wondered to himself if he ate this fruit, or swallowed any seeds, would he be forced to stay here in this world for as many months as seeds? Would he be forced to marry a dark man who goes about on a chariot stealing virgins and springtime? 'Well, 'that's just silly', he thought to himself.

"Henry?" Ra-Neferu asked. He looked up from the fruit.

"Er...yes?"

"You may eat it. It will not harm you."

"Well, it looks harmless enough, but...there are stories about such things you know, and now I am thinking that anything could be true. You're a lovely lady but I don't want to spend so many months of the year married to you if you turn out to be some angry, dark god," Henry said. She laughed.

"Oh, Henry. You are funny! What a delight. No, please, please, have no concern. Tricking people into eating our food is not how wedding vows are made in my country." She laughed again. "You have nothing to fear." She picked a date from the bowl and ate it. "If it makes you feel any better I will give you my oath that I will not poison or drug you."

"No, no, that is not necessary... I think...I suppose, I will just have to trust you." Ra-Neferu smiled. Henry smiled back took a handful of dates from the bowl. He popped one into his mouth. It was delicious.

Chapter 7

Questions and More Questions

Henry's mind would not let go completely of his wariness but nevertheless he sat silently in the boat, munching dates and watching the scenery go by. He wanted a bit of silence and Ra-Neferu did not try and engage him. He was very grateful to her for that.

The river was wide and dark. He could not see the bottom or any distinguishing marks beneath the water. A flashing glimpse of silver sometimes made him wonder about fish, or any other such creatures as might be in an afterlife river. However, the fish, if that's what he saw, remained very fish like, elusive and quick. He saw no other creatures, fantastic or mundane. The banks of the river were quite a ways off and were a scrubby green color. Abruptly, at a certain distance from the river on both sides, the green ended in sand. The rhythm of the oars went on though the rowing men were silent. There was something wrong about those rowing men. They did not act like people. They didn't talk or sing or look around. There was no one to call out the rhythm and yet, they rowed in perfect unison. Henry frowned at them through his window.

As he looked out the window he could also see a building not far off. It was large and white and looked vaguely adobe. It sat near to the river, but not right on it. The building had several large windows, some of which gave hints of color.

"Henry, we will arrive shortly. Are you ready?" Ra-Neferu asked.

"Yes." He smiled politely, wondering what crazy thing would happen to him next. One of the oarsmen appeared at the door. Ra-Neferu nodded. He nodded back and left the cabin again. Henry felt the barge glide, slow down, then catch and stop, gently rocking. The man appeared at the door again. Ra-Neferu rose and left the cabin. Henry got up and followed her. They were led by the man to a ramp that joined the dock. This dock was very similar to the dock that he had first seen at the terminal. It was simple and wooden and appeared weathered. At the end of the dock, Henry stood in front of a stepping stone path that led to an open courtyard area of Ra-Neferu's palatial home.

"Welcome to my home, Henry. You are welcome to stay as long as you wish." She turned to him and smiled. Henry nodded and said a quiet 'Thank you'. He stood and looked over the house. It was almost a strange collection of cubes. Most of it was adobe and had no indication of bricks or seams. The second floor hung over the first. Stone columns supported the overhang. The columns were painted to look like palms, with long, light brown, crisscross patterned trunks and the impression of green leaves at the top in relief in the stone and extending along the wall. Henry stood on the edge of the dock, with his back to the river and with the shore on either side. Stepping stones lay here and there on the sandy shore, some in the water, and some leading to it. The main stepping stone path led straight from the dock into a courtyard in the center of the structure. The courtyard was paved with creamy, tan and orange colored stones. In the center, a stone fountain with a large shallow pool around it gurgled and bubbled. Exotic palms and plants grew all around, either planted or in pots. Large windows of the house looked out over the river. Henry also noticed that the roof was flat and that leaves and fronds of plants were visible over the sides of the roof. He smiled at the idea of a rooftop garden. His reverie was disturbed by the sound of things hitting the water behind him. He turned and saw the oarsmen jumping in the river. They did not make a very large splash, as just before they entered the water, they appeared to transform into little, silver fish. Henry walked to the end of the dock and stood looking into the water behind the barge. Several fish milled about there, patiently treading water. They were all oriented towards the dock and Henry. He waited. The fish also waited. Ra-Neferu came down the deck and spoke to the fish.

"We will not need you for the rest of the day. You can go." The little school separated and the fish went darting away into the shadows of the barge or the depths of the river. Henry stood upright and frowned. He looked at Ra-Neferu over his glasses.

"So apparently…in Elysium…you have made slaves of the fishmen. Is that right?" Ra-Neferu laughed.

"Henry, you jest, but I know how you feel. Please, do not worry. You will understand. I know it is overwhelming, but it will be alright." Again that smile. Henry couldn't help but return it. "Now," she said in a business-like tone, "you have several choices. A room has been prepared for you and you may go there and rest if you like. If not, my home is your home and you may enjoy it freely. Food or drink can be prepared for you. You are my guest and the choice is yours."

"Well, I…I would love a cup of tea. I would also really like to know why you have enslaved the fishmen of Elysium. Can we sit somewhere and talk a bit?" Henry asked.

"Yes. Let us go up to the roof and enjoy the view and some tea. I will explain to you about the …fishmen. Please follow me."

She led him through the courtyard and into the house. They briefly passed a living room area with cushy chairs and couches facing a large fireplace. She turned and led him down a wide corridor with large, wooden doors on either side. The corridor was two stories tall with a second set of rooms above the first on either side. The far wall of the corridor contained a large, long stained glass window of vibrant colors. Henry realized that this was the window with the hint of color he had seen from the barge. The scene in the glass showed a large river with many ships and barges, some similar to or larger than Ra-Neferu's barge. In the foreground grapes and figs grew on trellises. In the distance a white pyramid gleamed. The same scene glowed on the floor and on Henry's clothes. Ra-Neferu led him slowly past the window so that he might have a good look, and then up a staircase along the wall. They passed the second floor rooms and kept going up stairs until they reached a wooden hatch in the ceiling. She pushed it open and they walked right up the stairs out onto the roof.

There was indeed a large garden of potted plants on the roof. Pots of all sizes; royal blue, ivory white, pink sandstone; contained plants of all sizes, even up to small trees. He was struck at once by cool shade and moisture, quite a change after the glare and warm breeze on the barge. She led him to a sitting area under a large, tan, fabric shade. There were chairs and a table of some lovely red wood. She motioned for Henry to sit down as she sat in an opposite chair. Henry heard water running somewhere, but could not see it.

A servant appeared from amongst the plethora of pots and bowed.

"Henry, what would you like?" Ra-Neferu asked.

"What do you have? Do you have tea?"

"Yes, is there anything else you would like? I can also have food brought out, some pastries?"

"Yes, wonderful but can you add cream to my tea?"

"Of course. Dala, bring out the regular tea service, but with a serving cup of cream."

Henry watched as Dala nodded and turned away, disappearing somewhere in the rooftop forest. She had been wearing a simple, off-white, linen looking garment without sleeves or even straps. Her arms and legs were bare, youthful and caramel colored, similar to Ra-Neferu. She wore no adornments and her small head was completely shaved, almost polished. Henry wondered what her voice sounded like.

Henry turned to Ra-Neferu. "Ra-Neferu, I uh…haven't had the best manners so far so I must apologize for that and also…thank you for having me here in your home," Henry said. Ra-Neferu smiled and nodded. "However, I do have a problem though…I feel I can be honest with you and I must tell you that I won't stay in a place where people are enslaved. I don't understand how this could possibly make sense. I mean why? Why do you have slaves here?"

"We do not have slaves. No one is enslaved here, Henry."

"Then who or what is Dala? And the fishmen rowing the boat? I never heard their voices. Aren't they slaves…or at least paid servants of some kind?"

"No, no. They are not paid servants and they are certainly not slaves because…they are not people. They just assume this form. Henry, let me explain. The people you see as servants are not people. They are…oh I forgot the word that most of you know, most westerners…um" she paused to think, "golem. Yes, that is it. They are golems."

"What?" Henry asked, raising one skeptical eyebrow at her.

"They are servants made from stone or clay and then animated. Golem is the Hebrew word. The Greeks call them andrapodon. We call them ushabti. In the Living World, they put them into our tombs to serve us in this life."

"So that girl who just came and took our tea order…was made of stone?"

"Not of stone, *from* stone but yes she is animated stone. Everyone likes to be served, but no one really likes to do the serving." She shrugged delicately. "It is the human condition. Here, the gods have blessed us with ushabti to do our bidding."

Henry kept frowning. He didn't know whether or not to believe her. Dala looked like a real person, warm and tan and

40

fleshy. She didn't speak and had strange mannerisms, but that could be explained in many ways. Ra-Neferu interrupted his thoughts.

"Would it make you feel better if she was a robot instead…or if she looked less human?"

"Perhaps, …yes it probably would." Henry rubbed his chin. "It's just strange. It's a kind of magic or something." He looked up at her. "So, have I entered a world where magic works? Is that it? It's difficult for me because…the mind I spent so long cultivating in the real world does not accept such things. That mind is telling me that she is a robot, or has a hidden power source or that you are not being truthful, that she is a real slave." Ra-Neferu smiled like she was full of secrets.

"This transition is difficult, but it is even more so for those who have received so much education. You spend your life learning how some part of the world works and then..."she snapped her fingers, "the rules change. You must learn new rules now, Henry. After you accept that, the possibilities are endless."

Henry sat back in his chair and looked around, content but not quite happy. Dala appeared with a large silver platter which looked too heavy for her to carry. She set it down on the side of the table and began to set out cups, a pot of tea, a creamer, and a tea tray containing varieties of small pastries and sweets. As her arm came near Henry, he snatched it and held her firmly. She did not move or make eye contact with him. She said nothing. He quickly let go of her arm. It felt wrong. It had a fleshy give to it, but was also too solid and dense. She was not a person. Dala continued to set out the tea things as if nothing had happened. When she was finished, she waited. Ra-Neferu nodded and Dala turned and walked away.

"I believe you," Henry said. "She is not a person." Ra-Neferu said nothing but motioned to the tea and sweets. Henry poured himself tea and cream.

After a minute or two, Henry heard a little splash from somewhere in the foliage. He made a face.

"Oh, for Pete's sake. Is she a fish too?" he asked. Ra-Neferu laughed and nodded. She sipped her tea. Henry hesitated again before sipping his tea, still thinking about pacts made with dark gods over food. He took a small pastry with glazed pecans and decided to go for it. Of course it was delicious.

"So, ushabti," he asked between bites, "how do you tell them apart from people…I mean without touching them? Is it the uniform or?"

"Ushabti do not have hair, that is the most obvious thing, and they do not speak."

"Ah well, that would do it," Henry said, still munching.

It was early evening and as he ate, he felt the tea and sweets were having the opposite effect from what he had wanted. He was feeling more and more tired. Questions still went through his mind but they had slowed down from a frenzied run to a lazy backstroke in warm water. Presently he said:

"Ra-Neferu, I'm afraid I'm very tired. Is that normal?"

"Yes. It is normal. A room has been prepared for you. Come." She got up and began to walk towards the hatch that opened out onto the roof. They walked down the stairs and directly to one of the rooms on the second floor. She stopped in front of a large wooden door and opened it for him.

"If you need anything Dala will help you. There is a bell on the dresser that you may use to call her."

"Oh…well…, yes, thank you." Henry gave a weary smile as he entered the room.

"Good Night, Henry," Ra-Neferu said.

"Yes, good night."

Henry watched her walk away briefly before closing the door. He turned and saw a small, tan room with a wooden floor. There was a sandy brown, wooden dresser with lots of drawers and a large mirror. There was also a large, cushy looking recliner and a low bench, to one side of the room. Central to the room was a large bed, dressed in shiny cottons and a thin, blue and white blanket. It looked quite normal except that it was lower to the floor than the beds he was used to. The bed was angled so that it faced a large window. From there he could see the wide swath of the darkening river, the spreading green clinging to its sides, and then the vast and distant expanse of dunes and mountains. Puffs of dust were rising in the distance as if a car was driving on a dusty lane. As he waited to see what it was, two chariots became visible, tethered to white horses. Two small figures stood in each chariot, holding the reigns and shouting animatedly, though he could not hear them. They appeared to be racing. As they went by, Henry could see that they were young boys with shaved heads, except for one dark lock on the side. He watched until the boys were puffs of dust in the distance again. He went to the dresser and opened a drawer to look for something to sleep in. In one of the top drawers there was a comfortable looking pair of striped, cotton pajamas. He put them on, yawned and clambered down into the low bed. He fell asleep immediately.

Chapter 8

Being Dead Ain't So Bad

On what he thought was his second day in the world of the dead, Henry woke up very late. There was no clock in the room. It was the sun angle that told him that it must be some time after noon. Feeling guilty and ashamed he got up quickly and looked around the room hoping to find an attached bathroom. He thought he must look an absolute mess. Catching his image in the dresser mirror he gasped. There stood his younger self, tanned and toned from summer farm work. He had never been bursting with muscles, but he had been fit and trim at one time. This was his body at his best. He took off his pajama tops and looked down at his chest and arms. There was no loose skin and wrinkles, no age spots. His surgery scars were gone and replaced by smooth muscle. He even felt taller.

"Well, hello, handsome fellow!" he blurted out at the mirror. He flexed his muscles in various poses. "Ha, ha! Is Arnold Schwarzenegger around? We should have a pose down. Grrrrr." He growled into the mirror and erupted in laughter. "I think I shall never get used to this," he said to his reflection. "Well, if we are beautiful then we must also be clean. That is the rule." He turned to investigate the door in the corner of the room, hoping it was a bathroom. It turned out to be a very nice bathroom which included, to his relief, a toilet. Henry chuckled at the idea of an afterlife with toilets and then at the idea of an afterlife without them. 'Curiouser and curiouser,' he thought.

He found everything he needed for a shower and even a shave if he had needed it. He also found fitting and appropriate clothes in the dresser; a white, cotton, short sleeved shirt and blue jeans. He had not worn blue jeans in years and was happy to put them on.

Later when he opened the door to his room and poked his head out, Dala was standing there. He shut the door and came out into the hall. "Uh, hullo...Dala." She looked up at him and then turned to walk up the stairs to the roof. She stopped and turned towards him again and waited. "Shall I follow you?" Henry asked. She nodded. Henry followed and she led him up to the rooftop garden again, directly to where he and Ra-Neferu had sat previously. Ra-Neferu sat at the table. Her attire was less formal than it had been when they first met in the terminal, but she was still highly decorated. She wore no wig, but her own dark hair contained braids and beads. She wore large earrings and a delicate golden necklace woven with shells. She wore another light dress of linen, one made for more for comfort rather than for looking like a goddess. Of course she was still gorgeous.

"Henry, please join me." She gestured to the chair. "Feel free to have Dala bring you food or drink."

"Please forgive me for sleeping so late. I am very sorry. I hope I haven't ruined any of your plans," Henry said.

"No, no, everything is fine. I have been busy these past few days." She looked him over. "I see you have recovered your young self. You look well." Henry made a face.

"I'm sorry, did you say days? How…long have I been asleep?" he asked.

"You slept solidly for two days and have woken up this afternoon." She turned to Dala. "Dala, please bring out tea for us both. No sweets, but bring out the cream for Henry." Dala nodded and walked away. Ra-Neferu turned back to him. "If you feel the need to eat, when she comes back I will instruct her on what food to cook for you." Henry scratched his chin absently and stared off, thinking. "Henry, it is normal to feel tired, as you did. It is also normal to sleep for a few days. Most people sleep for 2 or 3 days."

Henry nodded in response but quickly slipped back into his thoughts. Questions were floating up and bobbing around in his mind. 'Why did I sleep so long? How do they prepare food? Do they have meat? I did not see any chickens. What do people do here? Do you need to sleep? Why was there a toilet? Without thinking he blurted out "Why is there a toilet?"

Ra-Neferu began to speak but Henry waived his hands. "Look, I'm sorry. I am just feeling a little overwhelmed. I am someone who…I like to understand things. Everything used to make sense and now nothing does. It is like you said before. The rules have changed and I am feeling…untethered."

At that moment Dala returned with a small silver tray with teapot, cups and cream. She placed everything on the table and then waited. Ra-Neferu nodded at her and she walked away. The light sound of her footsteps was followed by an audible splash. Henry made a face. Ra-Neferu looked at him with detached concern, as if he were a patient in her hospital.

45

"You will feel this way, untethered as you say, for some time, but it will pass. In all the ways that it can happen, being born is painful, terrifying and then filled with wonder. The pain and terror will subside." She poured tea into his cup. Henry stared at it.

"Not that I am complaining, but why am I young again?" Henry asked.

"One of the gifts of this world is that every morning we are resurrected to our full health and most perfect fitness from our former life. If you get injured, the next day you will be restored. The first time this happens, it takes a few days."

"What happens if I die? Is that, is that even possible? How does that work?"

If you injure yourself enough to die, at sunset you will become a kind of spirit, transparent a little bit. You spend the night in that form and then are resurrected at sunrise."

"What, really?" Henry asked. He sat back in his chair and imagined ghost Henry, an amorphous white sheet, two black holes for eyes, and no feet, floating around and saying "Ooooo" like a bad cartoon. "So...can you go through things? What's that like?"

"When you become a night spirit, or take ghost form as some call it, you must imagine that the whole world has become like...liquids with a different thickness to each...perhaps surface tension is a better way of thinking of it. You may walk or sit or lie down on something, if it is large enough, but you cannot really pick up or use things that are small. Your hand will go right through it. When you experience ghost form, you will learn the rules very quickly." Henry gave her a look.

"So, you expect me to die soon, do you?" he teased. Ra-Neferu smiled.

"Everyone dies eventually." Henry sat back and thought about it. "It sounds like...It's just like I'm in a video game. How many lives do I get? Three? Five? Are they laying around in the desert for me to pick up? Like little hearts or coins?" Henry chuckled. Ra-Neferu sipped at her tea and made no response. Henry decided that she was just not going to get many of his jokes. He wondered how old she really was, how long had she been here. What could her perspective be like if she had been around for a few thousand years. What was Henry to her but an infant, practically larval.

"So, is this what life is like here?" Henry asked. "The ush...ush...golems do all the work and we live a life of leisure?"

"More or less," Ra-Neferu answered. "People are free to do whatever it is that they love."

"Well, except for doctors, right? Because everyone is healthy. A doctor wouldn't have much to do…or a house painter. I'm sorry I'm just joking. It's how I deal with terror…apparently." Ra-Neferu nodded. Henry felt the conversation spiraling quickly towards awkwardness. He tried to recover it.

"So, Ra-Neferu, um…tell me about Elysium. Who comes here and how does that work?" Henry asked.

"Elysium is the home of all those who lived before Christ, some Jews, and anyone who is not a Muslim, Christian, Zoroastrian, or Bahai," she said.

"And fence-sitting agnostics apparently," Henry smirked.

"Yes, but that does not happen very often. Henry, people like you are rare. Even the most ardent atheist, upon seeing the Waiting Room and the signs of faith on peoples' foreheads, will take some faith before being judged." Henry nodded. He thought about the Judgment Hall and its stained glass windows, the old monk at the big wooden table, the Waiting Room and the newly dead with crosses and stars and crescents on their foreheads. He admitted to himself that he had been tempted to just take the oath.

"So really…anyone who says yes to his…to the old monk's question goes to Heaven, no matter what the religion of his birth? That can't be right?" Henry asked. Ra-Neferu nodded.

"It is true. That is actually a recent development. It started after the Water Wars."

"Oh," he said and nodded. During the Water Wars, Henry had been in Hawaii with his wife Lauren, far away from the bombs and the fallout. He stared at his tea cup.

"What do you call Earth…I mean what does everyone here call it?"

"You can call it 'the Living World' and people will know what you are talking about or …many people refer to it as the 'the Plane of Sorrow' or the 'Sorrowful World'. That is what people in this area call it. I am sure that there are many other names."

"Oh. Well, I suppose that makes sense." Henry felt a bit defensive about the Earth having such a sad moniker. He had loved it well.

Ra-Neferu produced a small bell from some hidden pocket and rang it twice. Dala appeared promptly. Little beads of water could be seen on her smooth head and a few drops here and there on her arms. Her linen shift, however, appeared dry.

"Henry, I am going to have food prepared for us. Do you have any requests?" she asked.

"Surprise me," Henry said. She nodded and spoke to Dala in a language Henry did not recognize.

"It won't be long," she said. Henry cleared his throat.

"Ahem, so… what about Heaven? Is it beautiful? Do they have wi-fi?" Henry chuckled.

"Well…yes, I assume so. I have never been there…well once, a very long time ago and not for very long. Our information on Heaven comes from defectors who have managed to escape. Leaving Heaven has become more difficult in recent years. Once there were doors…portals between Elysium and Heaven, but most of them have been destroyed or hidden. As far as we know, Heaven is just like Elysium, with the same rules and gifts."

Dala arrived with food. She brought out the huge silver platter again, the one that looked as if it weighed as much as she did. The laws of physics decreed that she could not lift the thing, and yet she did. She set out dishes of what looked like roasted lamb, bread, butter, a green vegetable of some kind, a pot of honey, fried bits of dough that looked like they might contain cauliflower and several, small containers for sauces. Henry's eyes lit up. He looked up at Ra-Neferu.

"Help yourself," she said. And he did. They feasted together and Henry was happier than he had been in a long time. He recounted for her his experiences in the Waiting Room and told her the stories that the three women had told him. She was delighted and laughed easily.

Later, towards evening, Henry wanted to walk along the river. Ra-Neferu agreed and walked along with him. After he asked whether or not there were good fish to eat in the river, she described how food was made in Elysium. They did not grow crops or raise animals to eat. Food was made in much the same way that the ushabtis had been made. Any sort of food or drink was modeled in clay. It didn't need to be a perfect likeness, or the correct size. Brief ingredients or instructions could be written on the clay with a stylus. As the clay baked it became what it was meant to be, even gaining its correct size, volume and temperature. As Ra-Neferu talked, Henry imagined Dala shaping small loaves of bread out of clay, putting them in an oven, and pulling out hot loaves of bread. It made him giggle.

*****

In the evening they came back to the roof and sat in a different area, one made for nighttime use. The chairs were soft and cushy. The view was unmolested by plants and there was a fire pit, stacked neatly with what Henry thought must be dried palm, or the brown stalks of some desert plant. Dala brought them a pitcher of sweet wine and then bent to light the fire with a candle. She sat on the other side of the fire from them and tended it.

Henry sat savoring the alcohol, which was another thing he had not had in quite a while. He looked at Ra-Neferu who watched the fire. The wine loosened Henry's tongue.

"Ah Neffie, can I call you Neffie?" he asked. Ra-Neferu paused a moment to consider it.

"If you would like to."

"Well, always saying the two parts…it sounds so formal…as if you were calling me Dr. Hall, or some nonsense. May I ask you another question?"

"Yes, anything you like."

"I don't know…well I don't know whether it is polite or not to ask people about the manner of their death. I would like to hear your story, but is it rude to ask?"

"No, it is not rude. It is a common enough question among new friends. Actually, I drowned. I was pushed off of a boat by a jealous cousin. She only meant to shame me, but I couldn't swim."

"Oh," Henry said, eyes downcast. "I'm so sorry."

"It was a long time ago." She sipped her wine and watched the fire.

"What about after? I assume this was long before the time of Christ or even of Moses. Was there still some sort of waiting room?"

"No, things were very different then. When I died, exactly what I thought should happen, happened to me. I was trained for it in life, told what to expect. So right after I died I remember suddenly standing on the sand in front of a large boat. A walkway was put down and other ka's, …souls, were getting on the boat. This was the Mesektet Boat of Re which traveled to the Hall of Osiris. This hall was the place of judgment for us. So we sailed

49

through the skies and came up beside this Hall, which looked like a palace. We were taught in life to know the name of the door keeper of the palace so that he would let us pass into the hall and also to answer correctly his other questions, which I did. Then we were greeted by the god Thoth and led to the throne of Osiris to be judged."

"The god of death, Anubis, stood by the scales used to judge our hearts. One by one we approached. He reached into my chest, with no resistance or pain, and pulled out my heart. He then weighed it on the scale against the feather of truth. I saw the beast Ammit, the eater of hearts waiting to devour it if I failed the test. I was terrified. But then, he said my heart was pure and that I could enter the Fields of Peace. Those of us who passed this test were sent through a…portal. When I stepped through I was here, next to the river. I walked along the shore and found this house. Everything that had gone into my tomb was waiting for me in or near the house. Dala was sitting on the edge of the fountain in the courtyard."

"My, oh my," Henry said, looking at her with awe. "Fascinating. So…I must assume that for other peoples…does this world contain all the other pagans, for lack of a better term?"

"Oh yes, the old Greeks are here and the Romans. Any pre-Christian group that you could think of is here as well as modern people that you might call pagans, like Hindus. The land spreads on endlessly and the people with it in their places," she said. Henry stared into the fire pit as Dala poked at it with a stick. After some time he said,

"So, is there a place, like hell?" Ra-Neferu sipped her wine.

"Yes," she said finally, "yes, there is. Let me explain. There is quite a bit of mercy in the moment of judgment. So long as one accepts the oath, many sins are forgiven. However, after accepting the oath, people enter Heaven and are subjected to more …government, like what you described. Did you have a briefcase in the Waiting Room?"

"Yes, yes I did. I couldn't get the damn thing open. I don't have it anymore. It disappeared when they tossed me through the portal to Elysium."

"Upon entering the Kingdom the briefcase opens and it contains papers that list and describe sins that must be atoned for either by punishment, service or both. If a sin is bad enough for punishment, then a person is sent to hell for a time. There, they atone for their sins and then are offered mercy in the form of service. They become workers, laborers, servants to the more sinless residents of the Kingdom. It is said that they are made free eventually, but only through good service."

"What do they do though? Don't the ushabti do everything menial?"

"They will not use ushabti or works of clay. They dislike anything …magical."

"Do they have portals? Do they use them?"

"Yes, they have portals. They only do not like ushabtis or works of clay. They say that is wrong to have a living being with no soul and to eat transformed food."

"But water into wine is ok, I imagine," Henry said as he swirled the wine in his glass. "Another trait all humans seem to share…hypocrisy." Ra-Neferu nodded but didn't comment. She gazed at the fire, far away in her thoughts. Her eyes had become dark portholes into an immeasurable ocean of time. The extended silence made Henry nervous. He cleared his throat.

"Neffie, you don't live here alone do you? Don't you have some family here?" The question seemed to catch her off guard.

"Yes, I have family here and normally they live here as well. They are staying in the city now. We will join them tomorrow and see the city as well."

"Ah, Excellent. Good fun. What should I expect there? Is there anything I should or shouldn't do?"

"No, no, just…be you Henry, be who you are. That is enough." She said this last sentence with what looked like mixed emotions. There was a hint of sadness in her face. She stood up. Henry, more slowly, stood up as well, feeling the wine swirl in his head.

"Oh my, well…wine still works the same way it did before," he said, finding his balance.

"Good night, Henry. We will leave in the morning." She walked away towards the roof hatch.

"Good night," he called after her. Henry sat back down. He looked at Dala who still sat cross legged by the fire, poking it with a stick. "Dala, I have had a little too much wine." She put the stick down, got up and walked over to stand in front of him. She extended both her arms towards him and waited. He took her hands and she pulled him to standing. Then, to his great surprise, she

51

picked him up and carried him, as if he weighed no more than a bag of flour, and began walking towards the roof hatch.

"Whoa, whoa….put me down. Stop lady!" She stopped and gently put him down. Henry wobbled until he stood up straight. "I'll take myself to bed, thank you kindly. You might want to give a man a kiss before you carry him off like that." She turned and went back to the fire. Henry sauntered off to bed.

"May life go to immortal life, and the body go to ashes. Om. O my soul, remember past strivings, remember! O my soul, remember past strivings, remember!" Isa Upanishad

Chapter 9

The Flood

Henry stirred as he lay in bed, fingers spreading across soft, cream colored sheets. He opened his eyes slowly to the light of the room. The sun was low on the other side of the house. Out his window, river and desert were just beginning to take form and color. A shadow of a dream was trying to hang on, trying to break into his waking memory, but he was distracted by a mural on the ceiling which he had not noticed before. He let go of the dream.

In the center of the mural, on a background of deep violet, was a bright, golden, fiery sun with yellow and orange flames stretching out from the center. Surrounding the sun the orbits of the planets were represented by silver lines, with a phosphorescent planet adorning a spot on each line. Earth shimmered, crystalline blue and silver white. Henry blinked and realized that there was motion. It was subtle, but he could discern it if he watched carefully. The sun rotated slowly. The planets moved along their orbits. Earth's white clouds gently swirled around the globe and its moon dutifully revolved around it. Saturn's rings shimmered. The Jovian moons of Jupiter danced like fairies around the great orange and cream ball. All around this little solar system against the deep violet space, stars twinkled. The mural seemed to radiate its own soft glow. Henry lay there for a while, mesmerized by the subtle motion, the illusion of depth. As he watched, a shooting star graced the edge of the mural.

Henry rose and went to the window, hoping that he had not slept for two days again. The long shadows told him that no, it was indeed morning and suitably early enough as to not be embarrassing. He showered and dressed, smiling as he slipped again into blue jeans. He also couldn't resist a quick muscle pose in front of the mirror before he put on a pale blue light cotton shirt he had found in the drawer. There was a light knock on the door. Henry buttoned up his shirt the rest of the way and answered.

"Yes?" he said as he opened the door. Dala stood there. "Have you come to retrieve me, stony girl?" She nodded and began to walk towards the roof hatch. "Hang on then, let me get my shoes on," he called after her. He bustled around his room, tucking in his shirt, awkwardly putting on socks and shoes. Out in the hall, Dala stood waiting, unperturbed. Henry followed, shutting the door and mumbling. "Good morning Henry. How are you today? Will you please follow me? Would you like some tea and cream that used to be mud a few minutes ago? Good I thought you might." He followed her up the stairs to the roof.

Ra-Neferu sat waiting for him at the table. Tea, cream, croissants and butter were laid out and ready to eat. Henry's eyes went wide. In the last few years of his life, his grand-daughter had tried to keep him on a strict diet. To see a butter dish out in the open was cause for celebration. Henry sat down, greeted Ra-Neferu, and dug in.

When the appeal of fresh croissants and butter had faded, he noticed that something was not quite right with Ra-Neferu. She was dressed down, her gown little more than a drab shift. Most of her jewelry was missing. When she wasn't busy being a gracious host, sadness showed in her face.

"I thought we might go to the city today, Henry. Does this appeal to you?" she asked.

"Oh yes, absolutely. From the terminal I thought I saw a city. I thought I saw white pyramids in the clouds. And if it's anything like that wonderful mural on the ceiling of my room, I'm sure it will be beautiful there," Henry said in between bites and chewing. Ra-Neferu nodded and sipped her tea. She appeared to be avoiding eye contact with him.

"Neffie, are you alright? You seem …off this morning."

"Oh no, I am well. We should get going soon though. There is much to do in the city, but the first thing that I need to show you is how to use a portal." Henry raised his eyebrows at her.

"Do I have to? Couldn't we take a boat or a chariot or something?" Henry asked. This surprised her.

"You have nothing to fear from portals. They are safe."

"I know, I just…call me old fashioned but instantaneous travel makes me a bit uneasy. On Star Trek, transporter accidents are always bad. I wouldn't want to…" Henry looked up at her. She had no idea what he was talking about. "Portals uh…they make me nervous."

"We will walk part of the way, but at a certain point the portal will be necessary," she said in such a way that made it clear that the matter was settled. When he finished, they rose and walked towards the roof hatch and down through the house.

They walked together in the morning sun along a stone path not far from the river. Ra-Neferu, if it was possible for her, actually looked sullen. Henry was brimming with questions but stifled himself for her sake, not quite knowing what to do about the change in her.

The ever-present dust haze hung in the distant air, and silver heat shimmers danced on the path ahead. The sun shone without restraint or obstacle, though Henry thought he saw some clouds in the distance. The distant city sparkled in the sun and Henry tried to imagine the wonders he would find there. He felt his heart lift in anticipation. They walked in silence for some time until he couldn't take it anymore.

"Oh, Neffie. I am excited to see this city of yours, I must admit. I can't remember the last time I was excited about anything so...this has all been truly wonderful."

She nodded but said nothing and looked down at the path while they walked. Every so often she turned and looked behind them. Clouds were gathering on the horizon. She continued walking at a faster pace. Henry followed, wondering what was going on. He looked at the dark bank of clouds on the horizon.

"Is there a storm coming? Should we be worried?"

"No, no. Everything is fine. If it does rain, it is nothing to fear. Rain is a gift from the gods." She trudged on and wouldn't look at him. Henry stopped.

"Ra-Neferu, please tell me what's going on. I know something is wrong here. You are not yourself and I know when..." his voice faltered as he saw them.

In the distance he saw tan colored, hooded figures on white horseback galloping at full speed in their direction. Dark clouds spread quickly across the sky, dulling the sand. He thought he heard a distant rumble of thunder but realized that it was the horses' pounding hoof beats. Ra-Neferu turned to him, pulling up a hood on her own robe which was the same tan color.

"I am sorry Henry, but it has to be done this way." She touched his arm gently. "You will understand later."

"I will understand what...what's going on?!" The horsemen were nearer now. Henry looked around for a weapon. He saw only sand and the edge of the river nearby...no rocks. He started to run. The horsemen were almost upon him. He ran towards the river and sloshed in until he thought it was deep enough to dive but the horses charged right in behind. He hit the water but was pulled from it by his arms. The robed figures took him out of the water while he struggled and dug in his feet to no avail. They dragged him to a small sand dune near the water's edge and pinned him down. Ra-Neferu stood nearby and looked down at him with pity.

"Ra-Neferu, please..." The robed figures took him by the arms. She stood watching, her face drawn with sadness. Two robed figures approached carrying four large wrought-iron spikes. They were long and pointed with a thick metal loop at each top, like the eye of a needle, but completely round. The length of each spike was slightly curvy with a barb near the tip. Henry looked at them in fear and panic and wriggled violently in the sand. The figures drove in the spikes, two near his arms and two at his legs. They bound his arms and legs to the spikes with ropes tied many times around and pulled tight. When he was completely bound, Ra-Neferu came forward and knelt by his side.

"Nef..Neffie, what are you doing? Why are you doing this to me?"

She almost whispered, "See now the many lives you have lived before."

Henry looked at her and started to say something when it happened. In a flood, images of his past lives swirled around him and through him. Though he felt the bonds holding him to the spikes and the sand under him, he couldn't see Ra-Neferu or the desert anymore. He saw his lives, himself being born and dying hundreds of times. He felt like he was traveling through them all. He had been women, men. He had died as a baby and as a child many times. He died in battle. He was a sailor who drowned. He died in childbirth. He had lived many, many lives and the perspectives of all these lives saturated him. On the sand as he lay tied there, his body shifted and changed into all the people he had ever been, faster and faster, until there was just a blurred, twisting, vaguely human form. He phased in and out faces and lives at terrifying speed. Birth, life, death, birth, life, love, death.

"Lauren," he whispered.

He traveled further and realized that he wasn't human anymore. Lives flew through him that he didn't understand until through all these lives, seemingly at the end of a tunnel there was a light. Henry abruptly entered the light and he felt that he was the light. He opened his eyes and looked up at a clear sky above him. He blinked in the sunlight.

"I was light," Henry said.

"As were we all," said the robed figures all at once.

Henry blinked and looked around. The robed figures began to pull back their hoods. Ra-Neferu approached and knelt next to him on the sand.

"Henry, are you still you?" she asked. He thought about it. A part of his mind had been unlocked and a vast history of lives became available to him. He reviewed these lives and personalities, like skimming the pages of a book. After a few moments, he decided that he preferred the last chapter or so, at least for now.

"Yes, yes Neffie. I am still me, I will still be Henry…for now anyway." Her face lit up and she smiled. Around them, more people knelt on the sand and began to undo his bonds. He sat up and rubbed the sand from his hands. Someone nearby helped him to stand up. As he looked around at the people, now unhooded, he felt that he recognized some. He walked forward to a man in the crowd.

"I know you…except....you were my sister," he said with awe. He reached out to shake the man's hand. The man smiled and said, "And you were also my sister. It is good to see you again." They embraced. Henry looked around at the other people who were there. He searched their faces for his wife, half daring to hope, but he knew in his heart that Lauren wasn't there. There were only 4 or 5 of them but for each one there was some history. There in that small group was a woman who was once his mother, another woman who was once his uncle, and two men who had been his aunt and nephew respectively. He went to them all and embraced them.

"Who knew I had such a family," he said as tears threatened to break their banks. He turned to Ra-Neferu.

"I don't know you. I have no memory of you..."

"And I have never known you," she replied, completing the ritual. She smiled happily, all traces of her worry and sadness gone. "We have found that when people arrive here, if they meet someone who they have known before, it triggers the Flood. We also must be careful not to even mention past lives or the memories will be triggered. There is no way to prepare for it here. It just happens like that. However, we found that if we connect you to the earth in this …very dramatic way, that even through the Flood you will remember where you are and not get...lost."

"Is that why you were worried, Neffie? Were you afraid you'd never see this Henry again?"

"Yes. Yes, I was worried. Henry you are an interesting and charming man. I was hoping that you would continue to choose to be this person rather than some other life of yours. One person is bound to the earth, but you can never really tell who will rise after. About half the time, a person will choose some other life."

"Choose?"

"Yes, you can choose at any time. Most people choose a single person, though under any guise you will still be known as …you. That is how you recognize your family in these people. In the past things were different, but it is the fashion now that…to change form often is rude…and never in public." Ra-Neferu took his hand. "Now, there will be plenty of time for learning new rules later. You have been out of these worlds for 83 years and many things have changed, but first we must celebrate. Today is like, your birthday Henry. We will go into the city and celebrate. You can meet the rest of my family. You have already met one member. Here." She beckoned to a dark-haired woman who came forward. "This lady who was once your uncle was once my sister Bent-Reshet." Bent-Reshet came forward and embraced Henry again.

"I am happy to see you again," Henry said to her, "but I must say it is a bit disconcerting. I remember you as a big, strapping young man. You used to chop wood and I would....help you stack it...in Russia... or what would become Russia, I suppose. Yes...that was it." He shook his head. "You know this is so odd. Do you ever get used to it?" he asked Ra-Neferu.

"Yes, eventually. It takes some time but you will get used to it all again. Come. We have so much to show you."

Henry took her hand and looked south towards the distant city. Around him his lost family mounted their horses while chatting happily. There was something comforting about it, something familiar. Henry was also given a horse which he remembered immediately how to mount and ride. He sat in the saddle looking towards the city. 'Bittersweet.' He thought. 'Life is bittersweet and so is death.' Happiness and pain mixed in him, up and down convection currents of joy and sadness, fulfillment and longing.

Now he knew where Lauren was.

58

Chapter 10

Heaven

Lauren swam in the shallows, through sea-green, yellow and blue shimmering light. She knew this part of the reef so well. She knew all its nooks and crannies, all its hidden places. She began to swim out to one of her favorite spots. There was a sort of clearing in the reef, a small area, about 15 feet deep and 8 feet wide which was encircled by reef all around but the bottom was sandy. It was shaped more like a shower from top to bottom but she nicknamed it the 'bathtub'. She would swim down to its bottom, stirring up whispers and small waves of sand, and then float slowly to the surface along one of the edges, hoping to spy a goby or a puffer fish hiding in a crevice. If she spied one, she would hold on to the rocks and watch it as long as she could before going up for air. Yellow tang would often school there in the bathtub, sometimes surrounding her in a cloud of golden yellow and spiral motion. It was disorienting and wonderful.

As she swam farther out towards the bathtub she vaguely heard her mother's voice, distorted by the water flowing past her ears. She stopped and swam breast stroke back towards the shore.

"Yes, mama?" Lauren's mother walked down the beach until her large bare feet and ankles were submerged in passing wavelets. She waddled more than walked. There never had been any time in her life when she was not quite fat.

"Lauren, don't go so far, crazy keiki! Remember the party tonight for your uncle's birthday. Don't get yourself drowned again like at Kawika's party! Plus you need to help me make the soup. Come back in one hour okay baby? The soup!"

"Okay", Lauren shouted and waved. Her mother waved, turned and walked back towards their villa. Lauren turned in the water, still lazily swimming the breast stroke in the direction of the bathtub. 'No matter how old you get, you are still a child around your parents,' she thought. Like a resentful child, she was tempted by the idea of drowning herself again. She did this sometimes so that she could stay out all night in the ocean as a night spirit. She would go out on purpose near sunset, drown herself, and then wait for the evening transformation into ghostliness. Then she was free from the limitations of lungs and could enjoy the depths of the reef without interruption. It was definitely a no-no and made her mother quite mad. She said it was resentful of the Makana, the great gift of the One God and that she would get in trouble if anyone found out. So today she would be good and come back in time to help mama with the soup.

Through her goggles she soon spied the lip of the 'tub' and was gratified to see a flash of yellow fins. The water got a little shallower close to the lip and she gingerly pulled herself along so she wouldn't get scraped or snag her swimsuit. She didn't really like wearing swimsuits and would have preferred to swim nude, but one, it horrified her mother and aunties and two, getting her boobs scraped on coral was not fun. It didn't hurt, because nothing really hurt in Heaven, but it was still a bloody, unsightly mess that could attract sharks.

She swam across the lip and let her legs sink. The yellow tang there moved away from her, seemingly annoyed at her interruption. She turned back toward the edge and stuck out an elbow on the side to support herself and rest a little. She always smiled at this small luxury. It was ok to touch the reef here when it never was in the Sorrowful World. Touching the coral didn't harm it in the Moana Lani, Heaven's Ocean. There were things she couldn't touch of course, poisonous things, spiny things, but she knew to avoid them. And in the end it didn't really matter if she got stung or bitten or even died. No matter what, the next day she would be fine.

She pushed off the wall out into the center of the clearing and then dove straight down towards the sand. As she approached, she thought she saw something golden in the sand, a bit of yellow metallicity in the tan grains. It became clouded though as her momentum in the water followed her down and shifted the sands, swirling them a bit. She wanted to swim back down to the object, but she knew so much movement would stir up the sands too much. So she waited, floating slowly back up to the surface. She came up and took some breaths. Then she swam down again, trying to swim more gently if such a thing were possible. Just looking at the sand showed nothing, so she waved her hands lightly over the top of the sand, trying to stir the thing up. Nothing. Frustrated, she went up for air again. This time she waited, floating a bit in the sun. The yellow tang were quite offended by her intrusions and had swam off through a small hole in the coral wall. A solitary goatfish hovering near an edge was her only obvious company now. Looking down at the sand from the surface through her goggles she spied the bright speck again and this time she was well oriented on her target. She dove down and grabbed at the object and its surrounding sand. She then allowed herself to float slowly back up, swimming the last bit for lack of air.

In her hand lay a golden coin that looked vaguely like gold bullion from some lost ship wreck. It was bumpy and worn. She judged it to be between 3 and 4 centimeters in diameter. On one side there was a Star and Crescent, raised in relief against an intricate background of geometric shapes. On the other side, over a background of more interlaced geometric shapes, was an inscription: "Let them see."

'Well, that's odd,' she thought to herself. She looked around, though she knew already that no one was anywhere nearby. If she came out of the water a bit she could see her villa in the distance, but there were no figures on the shore. She looked back down to the sandy bottom. It was empty; tan grains settled back nicely into their little hills and valleys. She wanted to dive back down and really dig around in the sand but the lowering sun reminded her of the passing time. "Oh, the soup!" she said aloud. She clutched the coin in her hand and awkwardly swam a side stroke back to the shore.

*****

Lauren stood at the kitchen counter chopping potatoes she had just finished peeling. At an island in the middle of the kitchen her mother kneaded buttermilk dough on a big brown cutting board. Though they didn't need it, a fire burned on a nearby stone hearth. Lauren's mother, Mahina, worked the dough and then scuttled around the kitchen gathering spices and getting out spoons and vegetables. She would knead the dough a little and then get a spoon, knead the dough more then get something from the fridge, knead it more and then poke the fire. She did this while chippering and chattering the whole time.

"Oh this dough is turning out good. The bread will be soft. I better put some more wood on the fire. I think it's dying down. We have fresh clams don't we? Oh, I know we do. I put them right here. I wonder if Kawika will bring that new girl he found. It's just not right you know, but I guess it's ok if they all think it's okay. How are those potatoes coming Lani Lani?"

61

"Almost done. Is this enough?" Lauren tipped the pan so her mother could see.

"Oh yes, that's plenty. Don't do that last one, oh never mind you have to, 'cause we peeled it already, well I guess it's okay."

"Put this one in too?"

"Yah, yah. It's okay. It won't be too much." Lauren continued to chop while Mahina moved a pot of clams to a gas burner on the stove.

"Mama?"

"Yes?"

"Why do we still celebrate birthdays?" she asked, continuing to chop. Mahina looked up from her clams and came back to the island, kneading the bread.

"Well, why not? I guess any reason for a party is a good reason right?" Mahina chuckled.

"It seems like…every day is a birthday here. We don't age so…so anyway how old is Uncle Joseph?"

"Oh that's a good question. Well he was 62 when he passed and that was…"Mahina looked up at the ceiling counting, "oh he's going to be 107, I think. Hmmm." Mahina looked down at the floor shaking her head. "Well, that's not so much. Your great-grandma Ihilani is 203…at least I think." Mahina laughed out loud. Lauren gave a weak smile, finished her chopping and was rinsing the potatoes. Mahina looked at her and frowned.

"You are not your usual happy self, salty girl. Did you get stung by something nasty in the bathtub?"

"Oh no, I'm fine. I just feel kind of…I don't know…actually Mama I found something strange in the bathtub."

"Oh? What some pirate treasure?" Mahina laughed.

"No…well kind of… I found a coin and I think it's gold. It's weird though. It has a …" Lauren was interrupted by a great knocking at their open door and the entrance of several relatives.

"Oh you tell me later, Lani. Everbody's here!" Mahina scuttled to the open door with arms open hugging everybody that came through with great energy. After all, she hadn't seen them since last week.

Lauren watched and smiled. She was suddenly startled by the pop, pop, pop of the clams opening in the pot. She came over to the stove and inspected them. A few more popped while she watched. She turned the heat off just in time to dissolve into a flood of chattering, hugging, relatives.

*****

Mahina's kitchen opened right to the back garden of the house which faced the beach. White and tan sand came almost right up to her low stone fence. There was an outdoor dining area attached to the yard in a low stone-wall enclosure with a long wooden banquet table and many chairs of the same chestnut colored wood. There was an outdoor kitchen range at one end. Lauren walked around this table, straightening the long white tablecloth she had just rolled out. She had candles and bundles of silverware and napkins to set out, stacked and ready on the low stone wall. She smiled as she set the pillar candles at intervals along the table and lit them, one by one. There was a slight breeze ruffling the white table cloth and the setting sun made it look orange and pink. Waves crashed on the shore with a pleasant booming sound. She looked out to sea, at the setting sun and the crashing waves.

"Lauren! Quit moping around that table! Come and get the soup!" Mahina shouted, beckoning with her big hand out the back door. Lauren walked back to the house and into the kitchen. Mahina was picking up various dishes, trying to decide what to take first. Other family members milled around in the kitchen, poking the fire, having a drink. Uncle Joseph was roasting a marshmallow on a stick.

"Oh Joseph, do you really need to do that?" Mahina scolded.

"It's my birthday," Joseph said while shoving a marshmallow in his mouth. Mahina sighed and grabbed two plates. "Lani, grab the soup please and Maria, will you get those rolls and the butter?"

"Oh yeah," said Maria, another of Lauren's Aunties, who had been pouring herself some wine.

They walked together out the back door, all in a line, Mahina in the front, then Maria, and Lauren in the rear, carefully carrying a huge pot of soup, whose destination was the range top in the outdoor kitchen. Some bit of light, some little sparkle from the direction of the ocean caught Lauren's eye and she stopped and turned. Expecting to see phosphorescence in the waves or the light of some night fisherman she was quite surprised to see the diaphanous, pale blue shimmer of a night spirit, a man, walking away down the beach. Her eyes followed him until he disappeared and she turned and continued to lug the soup to its home.

"Why are you stopped, what are you looking at?" Mahina looked and saw the ghost walking down the shore. "Oh ahah, somebody did something stupid didn't he eh? Ah well, god is kind to him too. Here bring the soup, lady."

Lauren brought it and handed her the large pot. Mahina took it and placed it on the burner.

"There now, let's set it to warming and …voila…Mahina's clam chowder. Mmmm you can't beat it." Mahina smiled and clapped. "If you want it done right you have to do it yourself." She smiled broadly. Lauren sat on the stone wall looking out to sea while her mother bustled around. Maria went back to get more dishes.

"Okay, keiki, now you tell me right now what is wrong with you? What's going on? You are moping around here, staring at the ocean, what is it, baby?" Lauren looked up at her with tears flowing down her cheeks.

"I had a dream…we walked on the beach. We talked. He made jokes like he always did. In the dream, I said that he would come here soon…because he was dying. He said he knew it too, but…" she paused to wipe tears from her cheeks. "That was months ago." Lauren stared out at the ocean while more tears flowed down her cheeks. She looked back at Mahina. "Henry should have been here by now, mama."

Chapter 11

Pirate Treasure

Lauren swam in the shallows, enjoying the feeling of the warm sun on her skin contrasted with the cool water. She was heading out to the bathtub again, thinking she might find more pirate gold, or at least some normal treasure, like a neon goby or a spotted puffer. She smiled at the thought of a puffer fish. She arrived and floated peacefully in the center for a bit. No yellow tang today. The bathtub was empty. She dove down to the sand and let herself slowly rise. A sudden shadow across the sun caused her to look up and see the silhouette of a head, a man, which quickly disappeared. Lauren came up out of the water and looked around.

"Hello? Is someone there?" She turned to see a man sitting on the coral, submerged up to his bare chest, wrapping a strip of brown fabric around his head. He was brown and lean and not dressed for swimming. He wore loose brown pants and the fabric he was tying around his head appeared to have come from a shirt that he had ripped up. Any remains of this shirt were nowhere to be seen. He smiled a warm, slow smile. His features were clearly Middle Eastern of some sort, though Lauren didn't know enough to pinpoint a country. The man steadied himself against a passing wavelet.

"I am sorry if I disturbed your swimming here. I assure you I didn't mean to. Again I am very sorry."

"It's okay." Lauren looked at him suspiciously while treading water. There was an awkward pause.

"Well, then, I will go. Good-bye." He smiled and gave a little wave and then turned to swim away.

"What are you doing out here?" she yelled out quickly. He turned back and sat back in his spot.

"I lost something out here last night. I was looking for it. It is nice to meet you, by the way. My name is Burhan," he said politely.

"Oh, well…" Lauren was taken off guard again, "Hello. I am Lauren. I live…right over there in that villa. …I swim here, just about every day."

"It is a pleasure to meet you." He nodded his head as they were too far away to shake hands. Lauren nodded back. 'Why am I so tongue-tied?' she thought.

"Well, it was nice to have met you, Lauren. Now I will leave you to your swim." Again he turned to leave.

"But what were you doing out here at night in the first place?" she asked him. Again he sat back down. His slow smile returned.

"Well, I thought I would have a night swim. I wasn't up to anything, I was just walking along the beach. I am…new here…and I never got to do these things in life. I was curious." He paused and chuckled. "I was also very naïve. I thought it would be safe but I was stung by something. I don't know what it was. I went numb and then I couldn't move. I sank like a stone and drowned." Lauren caught her breath.

"It was you! You were the ghost we saw at the party. We saw a night spirit walking."

"It may have been me, yes," he responded.

"So what did you lose?" Lauren asked, her fright and suspicion wearing off. She moved to the side of the tub to stick an elbow out and rest. She put her goggles up. The man reacted a bit at the question.

"Ah well….I don't expect to find it out here, it was very small…but it was a coin. I…my father gave it to me. I always carry it with me and it must have fallen out when I was stung by that…creature." He pursed his lips. "It didn't hurt but…drowning…I was terrified." He stared off at the water remembering. Lauren lit up.

"I found a coin!"

"What?"

"I found a coin here in the bathtub, a few days ago. Wow! It's probably your coin. Unreal!"

"What? Bathtub?" Burhan looked confused. Lauren laughed.

"Oh sorry, you don't know…I call this," she gestured to the walls, "I call this area the 'bathtub'." Burhan looked around.

"But, it looks more like a shower." He looked up and smiled. Lauren smiled back.

"Here, walk with me, and swim I guess, to our villa. Let's see if it is your coin, then you can get back with your family. Will they worry about you?" Lauren asked. Burhan looked down.

"No, my people, most of them serve."

"Oh…and you don't?" she asked.

"No I don't. I never have." He smiled. She returned his smile. She began to swim off towards the villa and Burhan followed.

Chapter 12

I Don't Want To, You Can't Make Me

Lauren and Burhan walked together up the beach towards the villa. The back door was open. For an instant Lauren caught Mahina's big face looking out the door towards her as she bustled, then coming back into view with wide eyes. She came out the back door walking towards them.

"Well, keiki, instead of pirate treasure, did you find the pirate? Who is this one then?"

"Mama, this is Burhan. I met him out swimming." Burhan walked forward smiling, hand extended. Mahina grasped it with two hands, pumping Burhan's hand up and down while she looked him up and down, not so subtly.

"Welcome, welcome," she said smiling, "Please have a seat, Boohan." She gestured to a nearby patio table and chairs. "You want something to drink, ya? Some tea?"

"Ah," Burhan looked at Lauren and back at Mahina, "Yes, okay, that would be very nice, thank you."

"Okay, good, I will be right back. Go on, sit down. I will bring you some towels too, you wet doggies." Mahina giggled cheerfully and motioned to the table. Lauren turned to Burhan and motioned to the side of the house.

"We have an outdoor shower on the side of the house, for rinsing the salt off if you want to," she said. She suddenly felt timid and nervous. Inwardly, she chided herself.

"Oh no, thank you, I am fine right now…maybe later," Burhan said, his slow smile never quite leaving his face. "I would like to sit down though, I am quite tired. I am not such an experienced swimmer as you." He sat down and looked up at her. He was quite handsome and Lauren stood there looking at him for a few seconds like a moony school girl before she remembered herself. She felt her cheeks flush.

"Um, excuse me, I will be right back. I will go and get the coin I found." She went into the house. Burhan sat up a little bit.

"Oh, yes, thank you," he called after her.

In the house Mahina was boiling water and filling glasses with ice.

"Oh salty girl, I didn't have any tea made and now I have to make some. So who is this handsome man that you pulled up in your fish net huh? Oh, he's a nice looking one."

"He was swimming near the bathtub. He said he lost a coin. Maybe it's the one I found! I put it on top of the hearth here…." She stepped up on the stone fireplace and stood there looking at all the brick-a-brack on top of the fireplace hearth. It was her favorite place to stick shells, sand dollars, sea glass and any other interesting things she found. There it was. She took it down. The coin was cool and heavy in her hands. Mahina came over to look at it.

"Oh well that makes sense. He looks like some kind of Arab," Mahina said looking at the side of the coin with the moon and crescent.

"Mama, please don't say that. He might be Persian and then if we said he was Arab he would get really mad...or he might be…we don't really know."

"Well does he serve?" Mahina asked.

"No. He said his family does, but that he never has. Actually, he's new here."

"Oh…well then he must be good. No worries. Anyway, I knew right away. He's a good one. I just can tell these things you know." Behind her the water began to boil. "Here, you go out and talk to him and I will fix this tea."

Lauren walked out to the table and extended her hand to Burhan with the coin on it. Oddly, as Burhan got up from the chair, he seemed to be looking at her forehead. He looked at the coin in her hand and back at her forehead quickly, then away, as if afraid he might be caught. His attention returned to the coin and with visible relief he picked it up and examined it. He smiled.

"Yes, yes. This is it. Oh, I am so relieved. Thank you, thank you so much, Lauren. You have saved me. I am so happy." He put the coin in his pocket and moved in to embrace her. She returned his embrace and patted him awkwardly on the shoulder. They moved apart. Lauren brought her hand to her chest in a subconscious effort to slow her fast-beating heart. She smiled at Burhan then looked down at her shoes. This made her angry at herself as well. She felt like a little girl.

Mahina came out just then with tall glasses of iced tea on a tray and they all sat down at the patio table. Burhan unwrapped the thin fabric from his head and shook it out. He folded it carefully and set it on the table. When he looked across at Lauren her eyes were drawn to the moon and crescent on his forehead which appeared faintly, as if a light had swept across it and then was gone. She touched the side of own forehead absently.

"Here we go. I made it sweet. I hope you like sweet tea, Boohan," she said as she brought the tray to the table. Lauren and Burhan both gave their thanks.

"So what is this pirate coin that my Lani found for you, Boohan?" Mahina asked.

"Ah," Burhan handed her the coin. Again, Lauren saw his eyes dart to her mother's forehead but slowly this time. His wide smile seemed more relaxed and easy. "It is from my father. He gave it to me when I was very young…well one like it. This one he gave me here…a heavenly replica. I keep it with me always…as a token of faith but also of family." Mahina nodded at him and turned the coin over. She read the inscription aloud.

"'Let them see.' What does that mean? Is it from your holy book?" Mahina asked, handing the coin back to him.

"No, it just means…it means that… by the coin people will know my faith, that's all."

"Ah." Mahina and Lauren nodded together, though some small butterfly of doubt fluttered in Lauren's chest.

"So, Boohan, would you like to stay for dinner?" Mahina asked smiling.

"Yes, thank you. That would be wonderful." He smiled and Lauren felt her cheeks warming again.

*****

Burhan stayed with them for two weeks. During Lauren's long swims, Burhan would go walking. He was often gone for hours at a time, but he was always back at the house before dinner. He helped Mahina cook and collected driftwood for the fire. He would do any little chore or run any errand that she asked. At dinner, he would tell them all stories of his childhood or of interesting things he had seen on his walks into town. He was charming, funny, humble and sweet. He would often meet Lauren as she came up the beach from swimming, holding a big towel out to her and taking her goggles and snorkel so she could dry off. Every successive time he did this, Lauren felt her heart melt just a little bit more.

One day Lauren sat on a high edge of flat coral, waist deep in water, staring at nothing. She felt sad, confused, lonely and stubborn. She would not go back for dinner. She would drown herself and stay out here all night, wandering around in 30 foot water, taking refuge in the sublime underwater world, forgetting everything, but she didn't. She just sat there unmoving as the sun made its way to the horizon. She watched the light change in the air and in the water. She watched the shadows lengthen. First one star, then another began to twinkle. Darkness spread and engulfed all under the water until there was only a barely discernible difference between dark rock and sandy shallows. As she turned in the water to swim home, her movements disturbed enough bioluminescent plankton to produce a soft, intermittent blue glow. It was beautiful and it only made her heart sink farther into sadness.

She arrived in an open sandy area which was only a little above waist deep. In the glow of the lights of her villa she thought she could see a silhouette, a person standing near the water's edge.

"Lani?" Burhan called, straining to see in the variable darkness.

"Yes, I'm here, I'm coming," she answered. She walked out of the water and towards him. He held out a towel and wrapped it around her shoulders.

"Are you alright Lani?"

"No," she looked up at him and dissolved into his arms and his lips, into a long awaited, long dreamed of kiss.

Chapter 13

Theft

Early the next morning Lauren crept quietly out of the guest bedroom where Burhan was sleeping and returned to her own room. Before she left, he embraced her and said that he wouldn't let her go. They talked together about getting a new place, just for themselves. It was easy, happy talk, the talk of lovers. She left sadly, but she knew she couldn't stay in bed with him all day, at least not here. Her own villa was there waiting for her, but she had never stayed there because she was still waiting for Henry. Henry. Thinking of him made guilt rise up from her stomach and coat her throat.

She showered and dressed. She didn't want to arouse suspicions in her mother so she kept to her normal routine. She went out to the beach and walked among the rocks at low tide, looking for hermit crabs. She hadn't been out there long when she saw Burhan coming down the beach to her. She walked to meet him. He smiled his charming smile and embraced her then kissed her.

"Your mother is awake. I didn't say anything to her, other than I would pick up some fresh oysters for her when I went to the town center today. Oh Lani. I wish…" He squeezed her tight. She returned the embrace.

"Burhan, let's not…let's not tell her, or anybody yet. Let's wait a little while. I don't…"

"Lani, it's okay. I understand. There is no reason to rush anything…especially here." She smiled up at him and they walked along the beach together.

"She will know though," Lauren said. "She will know as soon as she sees me. She knows everything. I don't know how she does it."

"Then she may already know from my smiling face this morning," Burhan said, chuckling. "I don't hide things well," he paused. "In which case, it doesn't matter. The secret is out." He smiled again and stroked her hair, the side of her face. "Well, I had better go and get those oysters. Do you want to go?"

"Oh gosh no. I better not. Then the whole town would know. I am…not ready for that yet. I had…I was…." She gave him a sort of pleading look.

"It is okay, crazy keiki," he said jokingly. "I get it. I know what small towns are like. Sometimes it seems like the whole of Heaven is a small town, in a way. Don't worry. I will see you later and…" he said as he walked away backwards, "I hear there will be fresh oysters." He smiled broadly and waved, then turned and walked off down the beach towards the town center.

*****

Around lunch time Mahina came walking down the beach calling for Lauren.

"Lani, where are you? Come on salty girl. Ah ha. There you are. Lauren!" Mahina cupped her hands around her mouth and yelled out to sea. Lauren had seen her and was walking back to shore, half wading now where earlier she walked on bare rock. She waved.

"Lani, come into town with me. Let's go to Herbert's. We will meet your boyfriend there." Mahina smiled with her whole face.

"Dammit," Lauren said under her breath then she shouted. "I'm coming. I need some dry clothes and shoes though. Let's go back to the house for a minute."

"Okay then, I will go and you catch up." Mahina shouted and waved and started walking away.

"Mom, wait…" Lauren shouted after her but Mahina had already scooted off down the beach and didn't turn around. She walked really fast for someone so chubby. Lauren noticed that it had gotten breezy and the waves were a little more serious. She made her way out of the water with some difficulty and back to the villa.

At home she fussed over what to wear and dressed in a rush. 'Why am I so anxious?' she thought as she finally settled on a blue and white beach dress and threw it over her head. She ran a brush through her hair and examined her teeth in the mirror. It made her think of the dentures she had worn when she was alive. She smiled at herself in the mirror now, a real smile, not a checking-teeth-for-cereal smile. She quickly put on some sandals that she had left by the door and walked out leaving the inside door open.

'Mama will tell the whole stupid town,' she thought as she walked. 'When I get there he will be in a tux standing on the steps of the church and she will be waiting there with a wedding dress.' She sighed. A sad thought crossed her mind. Why get married in Heaven? It's not like you can have children. And 40 or 50 years maybe but forever? She pushed these dark thoughts away and tried to empty her mind. 'Just be here.' She told herself. 'Just clear your mind and exist and accept whatever happens with grace.' She walked on.

As she approached the center of her little beach town she saw Mahina through the window of Herbert's, sitting at a booth and talking animatedly to Maria and Sandy, another of her aunties. Both ladies sat still in rapt attention, listing to Mahina. As she approached, Mahina caught sight of her and waved. Her two aunties also waved coyly, flaunting knowing smiles.

"Dammit" Lauren said under her breath.

Suddenly there was a commotion. The town courtyard was full of people shopping, eating, standing around and talking. Off to one side she heard several "Oh!"s and other expressions of fear and surprise. Someone was running through this crowd toward the center of town and other someones were in pursuit.

As Lauren watched, she saw the signature silver and gold helmets of several knights of the Guard bobbing in the background, on the chase. Their quarry burst out of the crowd into an opening and headed directly towards the Missionary Well in the center of town. Lauren's heart sank when she saw that it was Burhan. He was holding the hand of a boy of about 12 years. They looked frantic, their faces masks of fear and haste. Burhan headed straight for the Missionary Well, a recessed portal that missionaries used to visit the underworld.

Time seemed to slow down. Lauren watched with horror and shock as Burhan led the boy towards the recessed stone steps of the well. At the same time, three missionaries were returning up the steps from the portal at the bottom. As Burhan and the boy raced to the steps, he just happened to look her way. He paused to look back at the approaching Guardsmen, and again at her. His face showed sadness, fear and longing. He raised one hand to her, as if to say 'I'm so sorry' and 'Good-Bye' all at once. He then rushed head long into the missionaries who were now trying to

74

block his way and grab at the boy. There was a scuffle and Burhan and one of the missionaries seemed to be fighting over something. The missionary held the object away from Burhan and he reached for it, grasping at the man's arms and hands. Finally, Burhan wrenched the thing out of the man's hands and knocked him down. Lauren saw the object glint in the sun but couldn't make out what it was. There were shouts and cries. The Guardsmen also arrived and rushed headlong down the staircase. Lauren couldn't see what was going on in the well and couldn't get through the crowd to get closer. A few minutes passed and the missionaries and Guardsmen came up out of the well, red faced and angry, waving their hands and pointing into the well. There was no Burhan and no boy.

She walked slowly to the edge of the well and looked down into it, grasping the golden rail that surrounded it. The well was empty. The stone staircase ended at a cement floor, grey except for a mural of a silver cross painted directly after the last step. She rushed down the stairs and dropped to her knees on the mural, banging her fists on it as she began to cry. One of the missionaries, a woman, approached behind her on the steps. Gently, she took Lauren's arms and lifted her up.

"Come on now. Don't shed tears for sinners. He will pay. Don't worry." The woman led Lauren up the stairs. Mahina met her at the top and swallowed her up in a big hug.

"Oh, salty girl, I'm so sorry." Mahina walked Lauren in the direction of home.

Chapter 14

The Awkward Truth

Henry and Lauren Hall sat on tan and white sand watching their 4 year old daughter play. Willa, in a pink, orange and yellow baby two piece, was running around throwing big clumps of wet sand into the rising wavelets and giggling as they dispersed. Lauren sat up to her waist in a water pocket in the sand, rinsing handfuls of collected pebbles and shells, looking for something interesting. Henry sat near her, making a sand castle with a plastic cup. Willa ran by and threw a wet sand clod at her dad's chest and ran away giggling as if she were fit to burst.

"Why you little rascal! Come back here and I'll get you," Henry called. Willa stuck her tongue out at him and did a 'nah nah nee boo boo' dance. Lauren laughed and splashed water up on his chest, washing away the sand. As they sat, the sun was getting lower in the sky and the horizon was turning pinkish.

"Red sky at morning, sailors take warning. Red sky at night, sailors delight," Henry said and smiled coyly at Lauren. She raised her eyebrows and flirted back.

"You were never a sailor."

"Ah yes, but why should I be denied any delight just based on that silly technicality?" he learned forward and kissed her. She smiled. Her eyes lingered on him a happy second before she turned to look out at the sea. Her expression changed.

"Henry, I have been meaning to tell you something." She fiddled with the worn shells and small pebbles she had collected.

"Oh?" he said as he watched little Willa gallop around.

"Yes, I ....this is hard for me." She had his full attention now. He reached for her shoulder to give her a supportive squeeze.

"I want...to go to church on Sundays, with the rest of my family." Henry chuckled.

"Ah well, that's not so terrible. Why should that bother me, dear? I don't want to stop you from spending time with them. They may not approve of me but I certainly...." Lauren was shaking her head.

"That's not it," she said. She let out a heavy sigh, gathering up her strength. "I need to tell you this and you need to accept this about me...I know how you feel about religion....but I....believe,

Henry. I have faith. You don't know about it but I...pray sometimes." Henry was surprised. He had never believed her to be anything but a secular academic like himself, viewing religion as just another facet of sociology. She looked out at the reddening sky again and Henry caught the sparkle of a tear on her cheek. She turned to him.

"I know what they mean when they say that someone ...hears the call. Henry, I feel it in my heart," she started tearing up in earnest now. Henry moved to hold her and kiss her on the top of her head. Through her sobs he heard her say,

"Do you hate me? "

"Oh no, no, why on earth, why would I ever hate you for that....or for anything....silly girl. I could never do anything but love you, you know that."

"Yes, but will you think I'm weak?...because you have said that before Henry, you even put it in one of your books. You said that religion is the crutch of the weak minded....that it's a… an evolutionary mental illness." She implored him with her big, brown eyes. Henry sighed and held her close.

"Look at that sunset. Gorgeous isn't it?" he said, gesturing to the horizon.

"Yes, but what does that have to do with..."

"Lauren, I have never told you this before, but I will now. I have....come to a conclusion over the years, an impasse." She looked up at him, puzzled. "I believe fundamentally that the world as we see it, is not the world as it is."

"Have you become Buddhist now?" she asked, wiping away tears.

"No, not at all. No, no, I believe that the world as we see it, is the world as it is translated for us, through our minds. All, not some, but all of the information we receive is an interpretation made for us by our brains. You see this glorious sunset, but our eyes only see a small portion of the electromagnetic spectrum. Our ears are similarly limited. And what's more is that, this translation device of ours is not a perfect machine. Brains can be faulty; they can be tricked, they can be damaged subtly and terribly. I wouldn't trust a brain as far as I could throw it." He chuckled a little at his own joke. "So what is religion? Is it real? Is god real? I don't know because I find the only device through which I might find these answers to be fallible. And as for religion, well, religion is what it is and serves its purpose. I don't blame anyone or think less of them for their participation in it. And you my daft bird, I would love no matter what you believed in. From Allah, to Krishna, Buddha to Scientology, Bahai to ....oh the flying spaghetti monster...whatever....I don't care...I would think it was strange....but I wouldn't stop loving you because....above all things...systems of beliefs, family traditions what have you....I do firmly believe in love and its bonds...because...they hold me. Believe and do as you like. I am here for you."

A giggling, screeching little girl came running up at that moment.

"Oh mommy, did you get an ouchie? Lemme kiss it and make it better." Willa kissed her mother's knee and went running off again. "See, all better now," she called back as she went running back towards a sea bird. Lauren smiled and sniffed and Henry held her like that for some time.

Chapter 15

Rebel

Henry and Ra-Neferu strolled through the stone streets of the White City. They were headed to the town center where there were several fountains and beautiful statues. The old gods themselves stood there and gave out blessings, food, and flowers. Never in any of his lives had Henry felt so strange and so out of his element as when he shook hands with green-skinned Osiris and accepted a delicate blue lotus from Isis for the first time. He said 'Thank you' quietly and stepped back, overwhelmed, all his questions dissolved. They weren't just people. They weren't in costume. Being in their presence caused a feeling he struggled to describe. He wanted to know more, to investigate, but when he approached them, words floated away into an abyss of peace. Even that bothered him but he had no idea what to do about it.

Now as they walked and chatted, Henry was familiar with the sights and smells of the city. The gleaming white pyramids dominated the view to the west. He no longer stood gawking at them like a child. The city had become normal, home. The streets were lined with the blocky adobe houses of the city dwellers. These houses were not crowded together, but were spread apart, sprawling along the wide streets, separated by gardens filed with grape vines and fig trees. Date palms dotted the landscape, always heavy with fruit. Men and women sat on the roofs of these houses on beautiful carpets and cushions. They reclined under potted plants and half tents of colorful fabric. Children ran back and forth in the streets laughing and chasing each other. People were all around, walking down the street, carrying food, and busying themselves in their gardens. Ushabtis were everywhere as well, running errands, washing children in tubs in the gardens, carrying packages. They were easily recognizable with their simple white robes, bald heads and vacant expressions. Henry had still not quite gotten used to that. Every once in a while he would come up behind one and poke it in the back of the arm or some other soft spot. Once he even pinched a female's behind. Nothing. They never jumped or were offended. Every single one, without fail, would turn slowly towards him and wait until he gave them an order. Normal conversation produced no response. Finally he would give up in exasperation and tell them to bugger off. The ushabti would bow and then turn and continue along its way. He had since given up on conversation but he still liked to poke one every once in a while.

"Henry, what are you thinking about?" Ra-Neferu asked as they approached the tan and ivory paving stones of the center courtyard.

"Ushabtis."

"Oh, not that again," she said.

"I know. I know. If they just didn't look so real. Though I think I understand now why it has bothered me so much," Henry said, scratching at his chin absently.

"Oh?"

"When I went to school we had history classes of course and they always made it a point to spend some time on slavery and the evils of it. It was pounded into our heads that slavery was evil and wrong....and that's fine. That's as it should be...but these stone servants of yours look like people so...I think those lessons nag on my conscious. It's not rational, I know."

"No, it may not be rational but it is...expected...but the more you interact with them the more you will come to see them for what they are, just a tool in human form. Also, there is no rush, Henry. I keep telling you this but you fail to hear me." She poked at his chest playfully. Henry smiled. "But..." she continued, "...that is also something else that people struggle with for some time when they first arrive here, that feeling of pressing time. In the Sorrowful World, the clock is running, but not here."

"Well, maybe I will get used to it...eventually." Henry grinned at her.

"You know, there are other places where the ushabti do look like robots, or other things that are not so human. Other cultures choose...appropriate façades. Were you never pagan? Did you never come to any part of Elysium before?" she asked. Henry thought about it a moment. He was still finding it a bit difficult to access all his memories. Sometimes he would ask Ra-Neferu a question and then remember the answer while he was asking it.

"Yes...I was...but I don't remember anything like golems...in any façade. For most of my recent lives I was Christian. I went to Heaven, got bored after a while and went back to Earth through the Lover's Door. Last time I was in Heaven...well...there were no golems and there was no clay. The food was real…or I guess, grown. I never really knew who grew it. I suppose that's a bit sad, isn't it?" Henry asked. Ra-Neferu shook her head 'no'.

"No, no. We are all blind at one time or another. We are not always good or smart or…having a conscience. No one can alter the circumstances of his birth." Ra-Neferu paused to look at one of the many fountains in the City's central courtyard. "Henry…maybe that is why…we are given so many chances…so we can find that person who is…most comfortable for the soul to inhabit," she gave the smallest of shrugs.

"Is that what happened to you? One life and you knew it would never get any better?" Henry asked. Ra-Neferu laughed.

"Oh Henry, no, no." Her smile lingered. "There were many before. Now…I am just stubborn."

"I can believe that," Henry said and grinned at her.

Ra-Neferu was still Henry's friend and guide after these many months. He thought it was probably months that had gone by though he hadn't really been keeping track of time. He still stayed with Ra-Neferu at her mini-palace. After his Flood he had met others who lived in Ra-Neferu's house and had stayed away until he was ready. Ra-Neferu's sister, Bent-Reshet, lived there as well as her husband, two adult children of theirs and two more people who were of no close relation, but who had been introduced to Elysium by Ra-Neferu. For many of the newly dead it was a good bet that she had never known them and was called upon often to be a guide. Though she would never give her exact age, Henry calculated that her last life on Earth must have been at least 6000 years ago.

They entered the central courtyard which consisted of a large fountain and pool centered in and surrounded by a large square of paving stones. All the stone here was tan or white or ivory and arrayed in geometric patterns. Water shot up in the center of the pool in several jets. The pool was large enough to walk around in and was tiled with small, alternating light and dark blue squares. Children and adults sat on the edges and submerged their feet or waded around in the water. Some children jumped through the jets of the fountain or blocked them with their hands.

The entire square of this courtyard abutted a mountain on one side. Down the side of the mountain streamed a waterfall. The water disappeared under the square and presumably into tracts and pipes to various houses and watercourses through the city. Carved directly into the side of the mountain, on either side of the waterfall, there were several statues of the gods; Osiris, Isis, Horus, Set and others. Stone steps led up to the entrances of temples in the mountains. For each statue there was a corresponding temple within the mountain. Each temple was the home of that particular deity and he or she could be found there or down in the courtyard or sometimes just walking around the city. It was overwhelming and astonishing to look up at those giant statues, to hear the roar of the waterfall, to know that the old gods themselves stayed there. One day Henry saw green-skinned Osiris take a seat on his own stone big toe. He nearly fell over as he laughed.

Now as they entered the square they found an unoccupied stone bench and had a seat. Ra-Neferu had dispensed with her more formal clothes and jewels in favor of simpler ones. Henry noticed that she was fond of jewelry and used it to good effect. She wore a headpiece of oval pearls which lay in elegant lattices across her hair and culminated in a single pearl at the top and center of her forehead. They sat and watched the children playing in the fountain.

"Henry, I think it is time that I told you something," she said. "I felt that I needed some time to know you, to know if we can trust you."

"We?" said Henry. She looked up at the cascading fountain.

"Even though it does not appear so, though things appear peaceful, there is a war going on. Right now it is a cold war, but be assured that we are under attack."

"Mm…well, I suppose that is not a surprise, considering." He stared at the fountain and through it, lost in thought. Finally, he said, "So the missionaries are the overt attempts at conversion, are there covert attempts, spies among us and that sort of thing?"

"No, not as such. They really do believe that they will be corrupted if they come here and stay …and indeed, some of them have been. There have been heavenly spies and they have either turned or returned. They lose too many spies sending them among us so they have abandoned that path for the most part. Their propaganda falls apart quickly here."

"So it is you who has spies in Heaven. What a strange profession." Henry pictured a man in a ninja suit, slinking down a dark alley and peeking in at a room full of angels playing poker. He stifled a giggle and cleared his throat. "Anyway, what leads you to believe that you are 'under attack' as you say? You are right Neffie, it is hard to believe sitting here looking at all this," he waved his hand vaguely towards some children playing in the fountain, "that anyone is under threat. It's just so damned …pleasant here, isn't it? Oh maybe 'damned' pleasant wasn't the right word…or maybe it is now that I think about it." Henry chuckled at his own joke.

"Are you done making jokes today, Dr. Hall?" she teased.

"Probably not, but do continue, though Neffie," he sighed, "I think I already know what sort of thing you are going to tell me and I already don't like it." Ra-Neferu pursed her lips and looked down at the stones beneath her sandaled feet.

"Heaven does not like us, Henry. This is…no surprise. They consider it an affront that we continue to exist outside their…dominion. When I say us, I am talking about all of the places for religions which are not Jewish, Christian, and Islamic. The Bahais are welcomed there and so are the Zoroastrians but not the Hindus, Buddhists, Daoists, Animists, Pagans and anyone who has no religion."

"So, what do they want?"

"To first destroy our way of life, then force us to convert to their way. They would destroy the ushabtis, forbid works of clay…and destroy our temples and statues. They would make us slaves." Ra-Neferu looked up at the mountains.

"Don't you have…couldn't you raise armies? Couldn't the gods protect you?" Henry asked.

"Were you here during the third war?" she asked. Henry thought.

"Uh…no. I was a coward in that one. I died, woke up in Heaven in the middle of a battle, and immediately ran for the Lover's Door again." Ra-Neferu nodded her head in understanding.

"At that time I would have called you a coward but now…" She shook her head. "In this sense, I understand why they have chosen to forget in Heaven. A long memory is not always a good thing." She sighed and sat silently for a time before she continued. "Henry, we have been trying to avoid this for so long, but negotiations have failed. Now there is no communication. Their ambassador went back over a year ago. They control all the portals. They can come here through their "Islands of Sanctity", where the missionaries stand but we cannot use those portals. We would fight of course, but being only on the defensive…there would be no way to stop all the destruction …and the kidnapping. This is what they do now, Henry. They take hostages. They have captured some of our spies. They first send them to Hell to be tortured, then they force them through the Lover's Door. Most of our people have been here for centuries. When Christianity took hold and began to spread in the Sorrowful World, our people stopped going back. Now on Earth, there is a better chance of being born into one of their faiths than at any other time. More than anything else, people here are afraid to go through the Lover's Door and undergo the life conversion. In Heaven, the people don't remember their past lives. The…" Henry interrupted her.

"What? How is that even possible? They can't…that wasn't true before…at least…" Henry sat trying to remember if he could remember his past lives when he was in Heaven the last time, and he wasn't sure. It was as if he just never bothered to think about it. That was even scarier. "Neffie, I don't…I can't remember…from when I was there. I didn't even think about it." Her face saddened.

"This is what we have heard. Even from people we send there now. When they step through the portal, the memories of other lives are just gone. They only remember…the life of the form they inhabit." She paused to wipe a tear away from her cheek. "We cannot forget our gods, Henry. We would sooner face a true oblivion than that kind of hell." Henry put his arm around her shoulders and hugged her.

They sat quietly together, watching people wading in the fountain. Henry thought about the Lover's Door at the terminal. He had been back a few times to wait for some people who had started their Flood in the terminal. While they waited, he stood in front of the large portal at the closed end of the terminal, Elysium's Lover's Door. He had been tempted to walk through it in much the same way a person standing on the roof of a tall building might be tempted to jump. It was a morbid thought. If he went back to the Sorrowful World he would most likely become someone who would, at judgment, take the oath and go happily into a pleasant tyranny. Henry and everyone he had ever been would be gone.

"Do you know what they think of us now?" Ra-Neferu continued. "They tell their people that Elysium is just another part of Hell. They say that we are cruel barbarians, that we kill each other daily and rejoice; that women are raped constantly and that we are cannibals. The loudest message of their propaganda is that unspeakable things are done to unbaptized children, most of whom come here when they die. They are going to justify their invasion with this…to save the children of heathens, whose sinful parents on Earth caused them to come here. Henry, things are getting serious. Not everyone in Heaven supported these plans, but something happened recently which spread anger and fear in the masses. A child was stolen from Heaven. One of our people went back as a spy but he happened to find his brother. He was forced to make a hard decision and he brought him here rather than leave him and risk never seeing him again. This plays right into their propaganda. They announce to the citizens of Heaven that the savage heathens will come and steal children unless something is done. We expect retaliation soon."

Henry was angry now. He watched Isis across the courtyard as she handed out flowers, shook hands with people, hugged them, and smiled. For a second he saw Lauren there instead of Isis, passing out flowers and smiling, wearing her favorite blue and white Hawaiian dress. What must her life be like now? What must she think of him? Henry consumed these thoughts, chewing on them like tough meat. Ra-Neferu interrupted his thoughts.

"Our need for information is critical now. We must be able to respond to their invasions. Henry you are an intelligent and perceptive man. If you don't want to do this you may walk away and no one will think any less of you. If you would help us though, I think you would do well," she said. Henry hesitated. He didn't quite know what to say. His confusion was apparent to her. "We think that you would make a good spy." Henry made a face. "Really?...but I…" she interrupted him.

"Look, you do not need to decide now. Just think about it." She smiled and patted his back reassuringly. She stood up from the bench. "Come on. I want to introduce you to a friend of mine. You will like him. His name is Burhan."

Chapter 16

Café on Main Street

"Neffie, where are we going?" Henry asked as he followed her through the town center, past the fountains. They turned down the stone path that led to the river walk. Shops and cafés lined the waterfront, their windows glinting in the sun.

"We are going to meet Burhan at a bake shop."

"A bake shop?...How exactly does that work?"

"Well there is a bakery, staffed by ushabti. There are tables and chairs on the upper balcony. You can get fresh bread or sweets and drinks," she said as she bustled along.

"Ah," said Henry.

"You seem disappointed?"

"Well I uh…seeing as how we are…what we're doing. I just thought it would be more clandestine. I pictured an abandoned warehouse filled with illegal weapons or a secret cave in a canyon, something like that."

"Oh I see. And was your friend Arnold Schw…I still cannot say that name. Was he there too?" she asked. Henry laughed.

"Why not? I suppose he could have been. Is he here?" Henry asked. She paused a moment.

"I do not think so."

"Ah well, bad luck," Henry said.

"Anyway, Henry, part of being a spy is about being ordinary. A bake shop is ordinary. Strolling along and shopping with your friend is ordinary. Ordinary is not suspicious. What is normal is easily overlooked. You need to learn this before you go. You want to be as ordinary as possible."

"So are you saying that you and your lot think I will make a good spy because I am ordinary?"

"Of course not. Most people take the oath. However, there is a precedent for lost academics seeking redemption so that they might see their families again. You could fall into this category. Most Britons are Christians of some sort, so are most Americans." Henry's face fell a little bit.

"Oh," he said sadly.

"Henry, I am sorry. I did not mean to cause you any pain. I should have thought more before I said this."

"No, it's alright. It... makes sense." They walked in silence for a few minutes.

"Are you going to look for Lauren when you are there?" she asked.

"I don't know. I would like to, but she...probably wouldn't come here anyway. She was a Christian. She wasn't when I first met her. She was a secular academic like me...but after our daughter was born.... She finally told me one day that she wanted to go to church. She thought I was going to be angry. Can you imagine that? How could I be angry with her for that...or for anything really?" Ra-Neferu put her hand on his shoulder and squeezed. She gave him a sympathetic look but stayed quiet.

They passed several shops and cafes. One store was filled with ladies' shoes. Henry wondered if they made those out of clay as well. The shoes looked normal to him, but he wasn't exactly an expert. The clothes in another shop looked normal as well. Henry supposed that someone's version of the afterlife must include shopping.

Ra-Neferu stopped in front of a shop. Breads, pastries, pies and other deserts were displayed prominently just in the window. Henry's eyes lit up. He loved sweets.

"Here we are," Ra-Neferu said. She entered the shop and Henry followed. Inside, there was a long counter containing a display case filled with more sweet treasure. The air smelled of baking bread, yeast, cinnamon and cloves. Henry closed his eyes and drank it in. It was wonderful.

In front of the display case, a tallish man with dark hair was peering in at the various desserts. Henry thought that the man was on the thin side and it was probably a good idea for him to consider doughnuts as he was. An ushabti stood behind the counter. Oddly, the ushabti was wearing an apron which had splotches of flour on it. Some flour had even been splashed across part of her face and not wiped off. Through a door behind the ushabti Henry saw machines and heard the sound of something running, like a blender. The man stood up and saw Ra-Neferu. He smiled and held out his arms.

"Ra-Neferu, there you are." He embraced her enthusiastically, practically picking her up off the floor.

"Hello, Burhan. It is good to see you too. Here, come and meet Henry." Burhan approached Henry smiling and extended his hand. They shook hands.

"It is very good to meet you." He paused briefly and examined Henry's face. "I have never known you," he said.

"And I have never known you." Henry was now accustomed to the polite responses. "It is good to meet you as well...for the first time ever." Henry chuckled. Burhan turned to them both.

"Let's go upstairs. We can sit and catch up, have some tea and dessert if you like." They all nodded agreement and headed up the wooden staircase near the back of the shop.

Chairs and tables dotted the wide balcony. Each table was accompanied by a shade or overhang which was pleasantly translucent and serenely blue. The sunlight shone through the fabric and left cut-off, faded, blue geometric shapes of light, sometimes on tables, sometimes on the tiled deck. Some of the deck tiles were painted with geometric patterns or plants and flowers. Henry stood admiring the scene while Burhan selected a table and sat down.

"Is every place here so damned beautiful? I am starting to be wistful for ugly. Has someone got a gruesome poodle I could cuddle with? Honestly, Neffie." He shook his head as he sat down with Burhan. She laughed.

"It took me some time before I got your jokes, Henry. Months ago I would have brought you an ugly poodle, if I could find one." She smiled her full-of-secrets smile then turned to Burhan. "Now, Burhan, how is your brother settling in?" she asked.

"He is doing just fine but..." Burhan looked embarrassed, "he has chosen another form, an adult man that he was once. I don't think he has any trouble with this but I keep expecting to see this boy. This man he was, was some sort of Viking, I think. Anyway, he's huge and has blond hair. He enjoys sneaking up on me in this form. It's quite frightening."

An ushabti appeared and took orders. They ordered tea and the house specialty dessert platter, which was apparently a selection of small bars, cookies and petit fours. When it was brought out to the table Henry's eyes lit up like saucers. He rubbed his hands together in anticipation. Ra-Neferu laughed.

"Henry has a most serious sweet tooth, Burhan. His eyes grew wider when she brought out the tray. I saw it!" she teased.

"Oh yes, it's very true," Henry said as he perused the platter. "I am not shy about it either."

They sat and leisurely ate, drank and chatted. They talked of past lives, families, and local happenings. Henry's heart lifted a bit and he forgot for a while. The sun sank lower and lower towards the horizon. An ushabti girl came upstairs and lit several lamps on the balcony with a small torch. She still had flour on her face. Henry laughed.

He enjoyed himself as much as he was able. He liked Burhan and found him to be intelligent and charming. The small voice of conscience nagged, but he set it aside.

"Burhan, shall we talk of anything serious tonight or shall we wait?" Ra-Neferu asked him after a lull in the conversation. Burhan furrowed his brows and thought for a second.

"Well, let's ask our guest." He looked at Henry, who blew a blustery puff of air though his lips and sat back in his chair in response.

"I'm in," he said to them both. They exchanged surprised looks.

"Henry, please don't think that we expected you to pledge this night. You can think about it. There is no rush," Burhan responded.

"Look, I already knew I would do this. I knew when Neffie took me downtown and told me what was going on. I might have known before that, honestly. I didn't need to think about it." Burhan and Ra-Neferu exchanged glances again while Henry fiddled with his empty tea cup. "My wife is there," he said still looking at his cup. He looked up at them both. "I will go." Ra-Neferu reached over to touch his arm.

"Henry, are you sure?" she asked.

"Yes, I'm sure," he lied.

Chapter 17

Osiris

Henry walked alone down the streets of the city. It was quite late so only a few people were out and about. As he passed the city center and the fountains in the courtyard, he saw a couple embracing on one of the benches.

The stairs up to the temples were enormous and he expected it to take him a good while to get to the top, though he hoped he was wrong. He stopped at the bottom step and looked up at the distant door to Osiris's Temple. It was open and a soft glow spilled out. 'Ah good,' he thought. 'He's home.' Henry began his climb.

He had to stop once or twice to rest for a little while and to enjoy a stunning view. He could see the whole city, lit up like a golden constellation. This glow bounced prettily off the pyramids and some sparse, nearby clouds. In the distance stars glittered.

Finally, he approached the door at the top and peered inside. He didn't see anyone so he gave a polite knock. A young, dark-haired woman exited a side doorway and approached. She wore a pretty, white dress and had a pink ribbon tied around her delicate waist. Her skin was light brown; she could have been Egyptian, but she didn't quite fit with the surroundings in the temple. Her dress was too modern.

"He's waiting for you. Please come with me," said the woman. Her voice was mellow and pleasant. She led him through the temple, past statues and colorful carpets and cabinets filled with scrolls and books. The academic inside Henry squealed with delight and wanted to run over to the scrolls and start rummaging through them, but that was not what he was here for. He soldiered on. Leaving the main room, the woman went into a hallway and then opened a door for him. He entered and found himself in a small, white room which had many shelves and alcoves, all out of the same stone of the walls. There were candles here and there which cast a friendly orange glow over the room. At one end, there was a large wooden table. Osiris sat there in an elaborately carved wooden chair. He smiled at Henry and motioned for him to sit in another of the chairs at the table. Henry complied as if in a trance. He sat down and cleared his throat, struggling to think of what to say. 'How do you break the ice with a god?' he thought nervously. Osiris spoke:

"Dr. Henry Hall, among others, you do not need to feel guilty." Osiris's voice was moderately deep and pleasant, his manner kind. Other than having greenish skin he looked like an ordinary, handsome, thirty-somethingish man. There was something about his presence, though, that filled up the room. Henry needed a moment to process what he said. The statement caught him off guard but then he realized it was true.

"I….uh…but I do. I feel guilty. I also feel conflicted, nervous, and I…" Osiris put up his hand.

"What did you tell yourself you came here for, Henry among others?" he asked.

"To ask you what you are," Henry blurted.

"Why?" The word hung in the air. Henry's mind danced around the truth at the center and then he said it anyway, almost in spite of himself.

"Because I want to know that I am on the right side. I want to know if I should be a spy. I want to know why all this is happening and what god's role is in this, or who god is or just something that makes sense. I don't understand any of this. Sometimes I think I'm still in a coma somewhere." Osiris gave a hearty laugh then sat back in his chair, watching Henry.

"And what did you think you would discover, Henry among others, when you came to talk to me here?"

"I thought I might find out that you are …that you're a charlatan or fake somehow…that you are an ushabti or something else and that I should …convert… or better yet go live on some deserted island. I'm sure if I said, "remote deserted island" and stepped into a portal something interesting would happen." Henry sighed.

"But I am an ushabti," Osiris responded jovially.

"What?" Henry asked, shocked.

"What are ushabti, Henry among others? They are servants made from stone, animated for some purpose. I am a servant made of flesh, animated for a purpose and so are you. What you must ask is, what animates?"

"I don't know." Henry shrugged and looked down at the table. He felt like a small child who had somehow disappointed his father.

"Henry among others, who am I?"

91

"Osiris?"

"You are wrong and you are correct. Try again." Henry was puzzled.

"I don't understand. Are you Osiris?" Henry asked.

"Yes."

"Are you also another god?"

"Yes."

"Which one?"

"All of them." Osiris smiled. "Henry among others, just as you are now Henry, but you are also others, I am Osiris and I am also others. I am Isis also and Zeus. I am Poseidon. I am Odin and Freya. I am Brahma, Vishnu, Shiva, Sarasvati, Lakshmi and Ganesh. I am in Nirvana and I am Nirvana. I am the One God who your enemies revere and fight for and I am the other gods whom they denigrate and despise. I am all of them. Those who worship any god are in truth addressing me. I shine through all these guises. I am the illuminator of all avatars. I am the source." He said this in such a congenial manner, such a friendly, conversational tone that Henry was taken aback. He sat staring at the man in stunned silence.

"Henry among others, I am also Dala and the ushabti who row the boats and work the clay. I am the clay itself as it transforms into food. I animate all."

"Then...then what am I?" Henry asked, suddenly afraid.

"Another avatar through which my light shines. I am the spark which animates you, but you are also your flesh and your experiences and your lives. You are yourself but you are also me, though I am separate from you. I am that which animates you."

Henry sat in silence, staring at a candle. After some time he smiled and then he laughed.

"I still don't know...I still don't know what to do?" Henry laughed. "As astounding as this all is, it doesn't really help me much. I suppose I could go sit on a rock on some island, couldn't I? It doesn't matter. None of it matters." Osiris grinned.

"You could go sit on a rock, but you won't. You will spy and you will fight. You are there on the field of battle even now and I am by your side. It will happen, it is happening now, it has already happened. I know how it ends."

Henry stared at him blankly. Osiris gave a broad, reassuring smile.

"You are still evolving. Your minds are still primitive at this point. You can only experience time in a linear way." He sat back in his chair and closed his eyes. "Mmm…Growing pains, growing pains."

"And you…what do you…experience?" Henry stammered.

"I am at all points in time and space at once. I am here in this room with you but I am also your brother on the field of battle. Of course, where else would we be!" Osiris smiled and reached over to grab Henry's shoulder. "I see the singularity become the universe. I watch as the universe dies. I am watching as Ra-Neferu drowns while her cousin looks on in guilt, terror and despair." Osiris looked a little sad then. "Free will is a tricky thing, Henry among others…but necessary, oh so important." He paused. "It all works out in the end though, don't worry." Osiris' broad smile returned. Henry sat in a daze, trying to process everything he had just heard.

"Do I even … have a choice?" Henry asked.

"Of course you do. Every one of you does, but I know you, Henry among others. You are a good man. You have seen the world and made your conclusions. In your heart you want people to know the truth and to be free. This is what you fight for, not for me." He smiled again as if he were having a great time at a party. He stood up and motioned to the door.

"It was good talking to you again, Henry among others. Now, go and do your thinking. Just remember, to gain passage, you must have the right coin. Remember that." Osiris winked at him, which was frightening rather than reassuring. Henry nodded and walked around the table, heading towards the door. Osiris came behind him, clapping him on the back like a football player going out to the field. Remembering his manners, Henry turned around and said, "Thank you", to an empty room. Osiris was gone. Henry turned again to the door and the same woman that greeted him initially was standing there waiting for him. He noticed that a blue and white lotus flower, the kind that Isis gave out, was tucked into the pink ribbon around her waist. He followed her out into the main hall of the temple.

"Thank you…um miss. I will see myself out."

"Good Bye," she said cheerily and walked off. Henry turned and walked out, stepping out onto the stairs and the cool night. He walked a few steps down the stairs and then sat looking at the city. He sat there unmoving until finally the sun began to rise. When the first rays of light began to reach across the landscape he started to cry.

Chapter 18

Ambustus

Burhan and Henry stepped out of a portal to find a small lake. Sandy shores gave way to green grass and deciduous trees with wide green leaves. There were bushes and plants that Henry recognized, even a wild rosebush lazily brushing against a walnut tree. From somewhere he heard the chattering of a squirrel.

All this pleasant woodland ended abruptly in desert. The White City was visible in the distance, resting above silver heat shimmers and slightly obscured by the ever present dust haze.

"How does that work?" Henry said as he gazed all around the lake.

"What?" asked Burhan.

"The plants. I know these plants. That's a walnut tree. That's a wild rose. I recognize those bushes too. How does that work?"

"Well, the truth is anything will grow where you plant it. People just like what they like." Burhan shrugged his shoulders.

"Really? You mean if I planted a banana tree in Neffie's back yard it would grow and thrive?" Henry asked. Burhan nodded.

"Actually, have you looked back there? She might already have one."

"Curiouser and Curiouser," Henry said as they walked along the small shore.

Burhan lead Henry around the edge of the lake to a set of buildings at one end. One of the buildings was a three sided enclosure, open to the lake side. The inside was obscured by shadow except for a faint orange glow. The other buildings appeared more or less normal except that they were made of wood instead of the adobe of the city.

As they approached, a man came out of the enclosure and walked up to them.

"Hullo, Burhan!" He reached out and shook Burhan's hand vigorously. "Burhan, my friend, good to see you, good to see you." Burhan responded happily, shaking the man's hand and patting him on the back.

"Ambustus! Good to see you. Here, come meet my friend, Henry. Ambustus, this is Henry, our new friend. Henry, meet Ambustus, our famous metal-smith." They shook hands. Ambustus was shorter than both Burhan and Henry. He was dark haired and looked vaguely Italian or Spanish, Henry wasn't sure. His hair was close cut and he was clean shaven. He wore only a leather apron and brown trousers, no shirt. Thick, muscular arms protruded a little awkwardly from his frame. Every part of him was smudged with black soot and grey ash. Even his face had a large black soot stripe across it. Henry and Ambustus looked at each other.

"Good god!" Henry said. "I know you. You were my cousin. Ha ha! Cousin, I remember you, I remember you just like this, Ambustus the burnt, the scalded." Henry embraced him.

"Yes, yes it's true. I see it. Aha! Family. This is good, what a good day when lost family arrives. Come, come, let's go inside and sit and talk."

They walked together up to the largest building, presumably Ambustus' home. He held the door open for them. "Come in! Come in. Make yourself at home. Sit down there, relax." He pointed to a table and chairs near the front window. "Let me clean up a little. I will be right out. Concreta! Concreta, we have guests." Ambustus shouted as he disappeared into a back room. An ushabti came out carrying a tray with cups and a pitcher of iced water. Henry and Burhan waited while she served and poured.

Ambustus' home was large and airy, in a kind of Roman style. The living room was a large square with various chairs and tables and lounge chairs around the outside. In the center, there was no roof and sunlight spilled onto a fountain. On a perch on one side of the room sat a large green parrot. It eyed them suspiciously. When the ushabti passed by again the parrot jumped up and deftly landed on her head...and shat. Runny, white bird excrement ran down the ushabti girl's bald head. The parrot squawked. Henry burst out laughing.

"Oh my goodness, Burhan. Sometimes...I just don't know." Henry shook his head. Burhan smiled.

"So, I guess I don't need to tell you who Ambustus is?" Burhan asked.

"No, no, I remember him well. He was a slave as was I, though I was a woman in that life, well a girl really, I didn't live that long." Henry sighed. "I was a kitchen slave. Ambustus was...he made coins; this was in Rome by the way, and at the height of the empire, I believe. Anyway, I was a maid in a patrician home and he worked all day making coins. When he was young he would heat the coins for the others to stamp with the dies. That's why they called him that, Ambustus. He burned his hand once and it scarred badly." Henry paused, thinking. "When I died I think he was just starting to learn engraving."

"Yes, he does that for us. He is actually quite skilled in many ways. He can make superior weapons and armor also," Burhan said. Henry nodded and scratched absently at his chin.

"Well, good. You know I think we were from Spain, originally but..." Henry made a face.

"What is it?" Burhan asked.

"I suddenly remembered how I died. I was beaten to death by the son of the family I served."

"Why did he beat you?"

"For fun most of the time, but the day he killed me I had really made him angry. Up until then I had been too young but when I was 13, I started to look more like a woman and less like a girl so he tried to rape me...but I said no and I fought. I was in the kitchen so I grabbed a knife and cut him right across his eyebrow and into his cheek." Henry smiled. Ambustus came back out then, looking not that much different from when he had left. He had put on a shirt under his apron, but even that was stained. He sat down with them.

"So, so, what's new with you? I haven't been to town in a few days. How is my gorgeous girl?" Ambustus asked.

"Which one?" joked Burhan. Ambustus laughed.

"What can I say? I'm popular. No, no, my Egyptian queen of course. She sent you, yes?"

"Yes she did. She sends her regards. She also sends you this and requests that you make it for her." Burhan handed Ambustus a long, rolled up paper. Ambustus unrolled it across the table and had a look. The paper displayed design instructions and a drawing of a jeweled cross made of gold.

"Just one?"

"To start with, yes."

"Clay?"

"No, she wants it forged, from native gold and jewels. She already tried clay herself. It didn't work."

97

"Work? It's a cross. What else should it do?"

"We think it might be the key to the missionary portal."

"Ahhhhhh, ok… Really?" He said looking up from the design. "Wow…So, do you have one? The real one?"

"Yes, but…she wants you to try and make one from raw materials."

"It would be better if I had that one to play with." Ambustus rubbed his hands together and smiled.

"Well, Ambustus, that's why she didn't send it. She knows that you have a habit of …melting things down," Burhan said. Ambustus laughed again, a single loud burst.

"HA! Smart woman. She's right. She's right. Of course she's right. She knows me too well. Well, this is no problem. We will get to work straight away."

"Good, thank you, Ambustus."

"Anything else?"

"Oh yes, we need more coins."

"Oh? What flavor? I have several. Do you want to try something else when you go back in?"

"Oh no, it's not for me. It's for Henry," Burhan said.

"Oh, ohhhhh. Alright, cousin. So you are entering our dangerous little game, eh?" Ambustus asked. Henry grinned.

"Yes, I suppose so."

"Ah, well, if you are going to continue to be this British guy here, you need a Christian coin. I will give you one, two extra in case you lose one, like our friend Burhan here, who loses coins in the ocean and then has beautiful young ladies find and give back to him." Ambustus laughed and clapped Burhan on the back. Burhan actually seemed embarrassed and turned a shade of pink.

"What's this Burhan?" Henry teased. "Were you putting the moves on those Heavenly ladies?" Burhan looked down at the floor, cheeks still pink.

"Here, let me go get the coins. I will show you how it works." Ambustus shuffled off, yelling for Concreta all the way. Henry turned back to Burhan who was staring out the window and looking wistful.

"Burhan, is something wrong?" Henry asked. Burhan seemed reluctant to answer.

"I know he's just teasing. He means well, but…it wasn't just some affair. I was falling in love with her. I didn't mean to of

98

course. It was stupid of me to stay there in the first place. I should have left but…" Burhan trailed off.

"Do you think she would come here with you, if we got her out?" Henry asked. Burhan looked down at the floor.

"She saw me go through the portal, saw me wrestle the cross away from the missionaries, watched my brother and I disappear into what they think is hell….No, I needed more time but even then, even if that hadn't happened…she was very invested in her family there. She might not have come, even if she loved me. I mean, I chose family and that's why I'm here now." Burhan rubbed his face with his hand. "I just want this all to be over. I'm so tired of this East Berlin, West Berlin, Iron Curtain bullshit. I'm sorry, Henry. Please forgive me. My heart is still broken." Henry stood up and gave him a friendly pat on the shoulder. He walked to the window and stood, looking out at the lake.

"I understand, Burhan. I know just how you feel. I am certain that my wife is there as well. I feel that, even if I do find her, she won't come back with me. She will chose family and faith and I…I honestly can't say that I blame her…but it doesn't hurt any less."

Ambustus came back in, jingling with coins. He came up to Henry and put a coin into his hand. It was about 3 centimeters in diameter, maybe a little more. The coin had a pleasant heft to it. On one side it showed a cross in relief. On the back, there was an elaborate border and within the words, "Let them see." Henry was surprised as the coin seemed old and bumpy. It was worn.

"Is this an old one Ambustus?" Henry asked.

"No, not really. A few weeks maybe. Oh, because...okay. No, I make it like that. When you make it look shiny and new…it looks like money. Then people say, 'why do you have money?' It gets too much attention. This way it looks like an antique or a token. Do you see?"

"I suppose so. How does it work? Do I need to always be touching it or …?" Henry said but Ambustus interrupted him.

"Oh, no, no, no, no, it is too easy, nothing like that." Ambustus shook his head vigorously.

Burhan looked up at Henry. "There it is," he said, looking at Henry's forehead. A cross of light had appeared briefly on Henry's forehead, a wispy mark that appeared and disappeared within a few seconds.

"Is there a mirror in here somewhere?" Henry asked Ambustus.

"Oh no, no, Henry, you will not be able to see it, not even in a mirror and it won't...show up in the mirror. Please, stay away from mirrors while you are there. Burhan here learned that lesson the hard way. But, people, people will see the cross, just for a second or two, like they all do."

"You mean, it's not there all the time?" Henry asked.

"Ah, no, just when you meet people, or in public prayer, in the church, things like that. It's like a sign to everybody...this guy's ok, he's a Christian too, don't worry... like that...Now, let me explain." Ambustus took the coin from Henry's hand and demonstrated. The same wispy cross of light appeared and disappeared on Ambustus' forehead. Henry drew in a breath. "Oh my," he whispered. Ambustus continued.

"You can put it in your pocket." Ambustus put the coin in the pocket of his apron with a small flourish of his hand. A faint wisp of the cross appeared on his forehead and then was gone. "You can put it in your shoe if that's what you like ... whatever, as long as it is in your control. You can even hand it to someone to look at. So long as it is in your control people will see the cross. But," Ambustus held up his finger. "if you lose it or it is taken from you, you're done. Just like that. Burhan, what did you do? Wrap something around your head I think you said?"

"Yes, my shirt. I was doing okay until I ran into someone and had to think fast. I was out swimming, looking for the coin, so I ripped up my shirt and put it around my head. I could have said that it was from the glare, or to stop sunburn but...they never asked." Henry frowned.

"Burhan, you say you lost your coin?" Henry asked. Burhan smiled in embarrassment.

"Yes, I...I was being pursued. I ran through a portal without saying anything and I came out of one that was submerged. If you go in without naming a destination, apparently it is random. There are many submerged and ruined portals on the ocean floor near the Castle, which is great if you are a good swimmer, but me...not so much. I came out into probably...30 feet of water and didn't make it." Burhan smirked at Ambustus who was laughing at him. Henry chewed his lip and frowned.

"Burhan, you say that a woman found your coin so…she picked it up, took it home. Didn't they figure out how it worked? Your coin was for Islam, how did that work?"

"I don't know. Nothing ever happened. She had the coin in her hand and nothing was on her forehead. I looked carefully," Burhan said. Henry turned to Ambustus with a questioning look.

"Don't look at me," Ambustus said, still chuckling, "I don't know how they work." Ambustus laughed heartily. This seemed to be the way that he ended his sentences. Henry smiled up at him. "Anyway…you were lucky." Ambustus poked Burhan in his chest. "Next time, you take an extra coin. Service isn't the worst thing they can do to you, you know." Ambustus turned to Henry and handed him the coins. Henry picked one up and looked at it carefully. The cross of light appeared on his forehead. Ambustus frowned. "So, unless you want to be like this guy over here, you be careful with it, okay?"

"Sure," Henry said while examining the coin. "So, as long as it is under my control?"

"Yes, yes," Ambustus said as he walked off to look at the cross diagram on the table.

"I think I can handle that, Ambustus. Thank you. Say, Ambustus?"

"Yes?"

"Do you have a lot of these lying around…in different flavors as you say?"

"Sure, why?"

"Can you spare some for me…several in different denominations?" Burhan raised his eyebrows. Henry grinned.

"When I get back up there, I think I know just where I want to go." Henry flipped the coin up in the air, caught it, and smiled.

Chapter 19

Burhan

Henry and Burhan parted ways with Ambustus after a tour, lunch, and some crying from Ambustus after Henry told him why, in their Roman life, he had died. He was very angry. He swore that if he ever found that patrician son, no matter how many pious lives he had lived since, Ambustus would kill him the same way every day for a week. Henry accepted this politely, as a show of familial love. Other than that, it was a pleasant afternoon. Henry and Burhan walked towards the portal. Henry's pockets jingled with the coins.

"Burhan?" Henry asked as they walked.

"Mm?"

"How far away do you judge the city to be from here?"

"Maybe 10 miles."

"If we skipped this portal and kept walking, how long do you think it would be before we came upon another one?" Burhan frowned and looked around the lake.

"I imagine that a branch of the main river empties into this lake. If we walk around the lake and then follow that river back towards the city, mmm…a mile or two. It would be different if we walked out into open desert. The portals tend to flank water ways. Are you going to take a walk?" Burhan asked.

"Yes, I think so. It's one of my habits. I like to walk things out, if you know what I mean, though not for ten miles, of course. One or two will be sufficient. You are welcome to walk along if you like. I don't need to be alone." Burhan considered it and nodded.

"Sure. I've never walked out this way. I should know it," he smiled, "just no swimming, alright?" Henry chuckled.

"I never said I liked to 'swim' things out. You are safe, Burhan." Burhan laughed.

"Good," he said.

They walked along Ambustus's lake in silence for a while, enjoying the fresh air and exercise. Henry delighted in the scurrying and chattering of the occasional squirrel, the smell of grass and trees. He thought he saw a deer once and began to wonder about animals, green parrots, and ushabtis. Were the animals real? He looked over at Burhan who looked deep in thought.

"Say, Burhan?"

"Mm?"

"How did you end up here?"

"That's...kind of a long story," Burhan said. They stopped in the path and peered into the distance along it, looking for the next portal. There was no portal in sight. Burhan shook his head.

"Well," Henry said, "You might as well tell it." Burhan grinned.

*****

Burhan was born in Islamabad, Pakistan, the son of a professor of environmental science at the University of Bahria. His mother had been a nursing student at the university but she became a homemaker when she married. Burhan did well in school and sport. His younger brother Jasim followed him around and tried to emulate him. Their family life was more or less normal. They identified themselves as Muslims but weren't particularly devout.

Burhan was 12 when the wars started. Eventually, they became known as the Water Wars. The dependable and boundless waters of the Indus became more sporadic. Years of drought were often followed by years of catastrophic floods. The governments of Pakistan and India struggled to appropriate water use rights fairly, to restrict its use, to help displaced farmers but it was too little, too late. The struggles in Kashmir became a convenient excuse. The war began and Islamabad was bombed, strafed, and burned. Burhan's mother and four year old Jasim, were lost, crushed under rubble.

Burhan and his father eventually fled the city after a week of anxious hand wringing in a hotel room. There was a rumor going around that India was going to use a nuclear missile to destroy Islamabad completely. It wasn't true, but it didn't matter. Everyone believed it and people began to flee the city. One day the hotel staff abandoned the hotel. A few days later Burhan and his father became refugees.

Thirteen year old Burhan found himself living in a tent city with his father, scrounging to find food. His father became thinner and weaker and finally died of a heart attack. Burhan used their tent tarp to cover the body and drag it away from the other tents. Two boys tried to steal the tarp but he fought hard and they ran off. He buried his father as well as he could with a chunk of metal that he believed had come from the side of a car. He marked the spot in his memory vowing that he would come back when he could and give his father's body a proper resting place.

Feeling like he had nothing left, Burhan left the refugee camp and headed south along the dwindling river. A few days later, as he was walking he heard the sound of a truck coming up the road behind him. He hadn't heard or seen any vehicles for a few days so he turned and stood staring, hoping they might either shoot him or give him some food. At that point he didn't really care which. The truck came to a stop and four men wearing fatigues and carrying automatic weapons stared at him and talked animatedly with each other as they approached. They looked him up and down and without a word grabbed him and hauled him into the back of the truck. Burhan didn't resist or say anything. He just didn't want to walk any more.

*****

Twenty year-old Burhan stood on the marble steps in front of the Lincoln Memorial in Washington D.C. It was a sunny day in July, bright but not as hot as it could have been. Over three weeks he and Hassan had been there a few times already doing dry runs. Walk up the steps. Hassan puts his half-eaten ice cream container in the trash. Burhan puts a fast food bag and drink in the trash as well. Walk into the gift shop. Leave the book. Browse for 1 minute 45 seconds. Buy something. Walk out. Take a picture of the statue. Leave the camera if you can. Walk out down the steps into a crowd. Call. With just the explosives on their bodies they expected to take out 20 people. The building would not come down, but most of the people inside would die. Burhan smiled.

Three days later the weather was perfect and they expected big crowds at the memorial. This would be the day. In the morning Hassan inserted the mini-bombs carefully into the book and the camera. Burhan went out for fast food and ice cream. Hassan was very quiet that whole morning. The only thing he said was, "Burhan, I am sick of ice cream." Burhan nodded but didn't respond.

Bombs ready to go, they drove to the Mall and parked in one of the metered spaces right on the park. Often they couldn't find one of these spaces open and had to drive around for a while or give up and go park in one of the garages. They were lucky that day and came across an open spot almost immediately.

They walked along the reflecting pool, just two brothers on vacation. They talked about parties, girls and classes. Hassan would occasionally take a bite of his ice cream. If he really hated it, he hid it well.

As they approached the memorial, Burhan saw that it was very crowded. People stood by the reflecting pool, sat here and there on the stairs. Inside near the statue of Abraham Lincoln, people were packed in together taking pictures. He saw camera flashes bouncing off the white marble walls.

Burhan's eyes were drawn to a little girl down by the reflecting pool. She wore a white dress with a pale pink ribbon across the front. Her brown hair was cut in a bob. She held something white in her hand. Burhan wondered about her. Her dress was a little too formal for modern children. Most kids ran around in shorts or blue jeans, t-shirts and tank tops. Girls and boys both dressed this way. Their clothes all looked the same. Burhan thought that maybe that was why she stood out.

They walked up the steps. Hassan put his half-eaten ice cream container in the trash with visible relief. Burhan put his fast food bag and drink in the trash and patted Hassan on the shoulder. They walked into the gift shop. It was so crowded that it was difficult to get around and the shop itself was small anyway. Burhan made his way to the cabinet where the books were and pretended to browse. He picked up a book, read a little and put it back. He took his book out of his back pocket and put it on the shelf as well. He turned and realized he was at the back of the checkout line, so he just stood there and browsed while the line moved forward. He picked up a metal keychain and a pen. Hassan made his way to Burhan and stood near him. Burhan saw a single tear trickling down Hassan's face and became angry. He gave Hassan a look with daggers in it. Hassan quickly wiped his face.

They paid for their souvenirs and made their way out. It was so crowded that the going was slow no matter what they did. They waded through people towards the statue. Burhan posed by the statue while Hassan tried to find a good angle. He pretended to take several pictures. Looking around, there wasn't really anywhere to stash the camera so they made their way to a second trash can and discreetly threw it away. They walked down the steps towards the reflecting pool. The crowd outside had thinned out and Burhan was disappointed. They walked toward the edge of the pool and stood looking around.

"We need to wait until it gets thick again," Burhan said. Hassan did not answer. He stared at the water. Suddenly his face hardened.

"Burhan, we should not do this. This is mad. These people didn't do anything. Most of them are foreign…"

"Shut up!" Burhan whispered harshly. Around the corner a large group of people, probably a tour group, was moving towards the memorial. Burhan watched them, waiting. From the corner of his eye, there it was again, that flash of white. He turned and saw the little girl. She was still there by the pool. In her hand she held a flower, a large one. She placed it gently in the water and watched it float. Burhan was becoming overwhelmed with rage, with a sense of urgency, with fear and growing doubt. He took out his cell phone.

"Burhan," Hassan said, grabbing Burhan's arm, "we don't need to do this. We don't need to die." Burhan looked into Hassan's eyes.

"We are already dead," Burhan said as he turned and headed into the crowd. Hassan screamed as loud as he could, "RUN, RUN. HE'S GOT A BOMB. RUN!" and then tackled Burhan. They struggled and fought for the phone. The crowd dispersed around them and ran. Cell phones came out and someone began yelling for the police. Burhan hit the button.

*****

Burhan blinked and stood looking at a stone path in a walled garden. The path was flanked by soft green grass. Here and there were flowering bushes and trees. Butterflies flitted and birds chirped. Mild sunlight was filtered through the wide green leaves of the trees above him. The path on which he stood led straight to a wooden door in the side of a stone tower. The ivy covered walls of the garden attached directly to the tower. Burhan couldn't see anywhere else to go so he went to the door and entered.

Inside there was a pleasantly furnished round room. A padded bench ran along the round edge of the room except for a fireplace. An intricate red and gold carpet covered the floor. In the center of the room there was a polished, carved wooden table on which sat a large bowl of fruit. There was another door on the other side of the room. Burhan tried it and found it locked. He turned and sat down on the bench. Now he felt like he could and should relax, but something nagged at him and made him restless.

Along the wall he noticed a small sign in Arabic which read, "Please be patient. Someone will be with you soon." Burhan shrugged and walked back out into the garden. It was actually smaller than he thought. Walking the other way down the path led to the intersection of the garden walls. Along one edge there was a wooden door. It too was locked. As he was about to climb up the fence and have a look on the other side he heard a door open and swing shut. He walked back to the round room.

Inside the room a man stood waiting for him. He was silver-haired and wore a brown robe. The man nodded and motioned to the bench. Burhan sat down.

"Burhan...you have martyred yourself in the service of god," he said in a mild tone. Burhan knelt on the floor.

"I only wish to serve," Burhan said. The man nodded.

"But, you have also sinned." Burhan looked up at him, surprised. The man continued. "You have taken the life of innocents."

"But I thought..." The man sat down on the bench and shook his head.

"Things have changed in the world, Burhan. The taking of lives must be paid for, no matter the cause." He put his hands on his knees. "Here is what will happen. To pay for your sins you will further serve god here in Heaven... You may be an office worker, a cook, maybe a missionary...we'll find you something suitable. You will perform this service for a time. Then you will be allowed to enter Heaven, freely. You will be held in the highest esteem, as all those who give their lives in the name of god are held. You are the Jihadi, the warrior for god. You must serve him a little longer before your reward. That is all. Now come with me and I will show you where to wash your hands and feet. Then you will begin your service."

*****

The three missionaries stepped through the door into the Island of Sanctity. Chad, a young, blond-haired, blue-eyed Mormon, held the golden cross in front of him so that the portal would open. A rush of warm wind and bright sunlight enveloped them as they stepped out onto the salmon colored paving stones of the Island. Steve, dressed like Jesus as portrayed in an elementary school play, walked over to the pond to put his iced coffee underneath some of the leaves of one the potted plants there. Burhan held a clipboard. They waited behind red velvet ropes on brass posts. After a few moments a small crowd coming from the terminal walked by. Chad launched into his typical sermon. One or two of the people in the crowd stared at them and frowned as they walked, but they never stopped. Steve sighed and started waving his robes around in an effort to cool his legs.

"Hey Chad, let me know when more come. I'm going to stick my feet in the pond," Steve said. Chad sighed heavily and rolled his eyes.

"Steve, we are not supposed to do that. We're supposed to be professional. Besides, this job does come with some sacrifice you know. "

"Yeah, but dude, it's hot here." Steve dragged out the word hot until the "o" became an "a". "I don't think the big man would mind if I cool it a little." Steve brushed a blond strand of hair back behind his pink ear. Chad harrumphed but didn't say anything else. Steve sat at the edge of the pool and slowly dipped his feet in, holding his robes out of the way.

"Ahh, that's it," he said with obvious relief. Chad looked sternly towards the terminal trying to see through the palms. From their vantage point they could not see directly into the terminal. Someone had planted a row of bushes and palm trees which blocked everything except for the corner of the rounded stair that led out of the building. Burhan stood quietly checking the names on his clipboard and looking at the terminal. After a few minutes more people came walking by, heading down the path to the wide river beyond the terminal.

"Steve, come on. Get your feet out of that pond and get over here. More are coming," Chad said. Steve jumped out of the pond and came over, leaving wet, red footprints on the salmon paving stones. The three stood waiting behind the ropes. As soon as the people were in sight, Chad began shouting.

"Houng Lee! Houng Lee! Come to Heaven and glory in the splendor of the One God! Repent and experience salvation! Eternal paradise waits for you! Houng Lee!"

One of the men, presumably Houng Lee, looked at them in confusion, but another man pulled him away, talking the whole time. Steve sighed.

"Is there anybody else coming through, Burhan?" Steve asked. Burhan looked down at his clipboard and frowned.

"What name does it say?" asked Chad.

"It doesn't, it just has a...." Burhan looked up toward the terminal, "Do you hear that?"

All three men turned to listen and heard the sound of light steps, skipping along. Burhan caught sight of a child, a little girl of seven or eight years, hopping down the steps of the rounded staircase. She wore a white dress with a pale pink ribbon on the front. Her bobbed brown hair bounced prettily as she hopped and smiled, hopped and smiled, zigzagging her way down the stair. Her skin was brown, like Burhan's, but her features were difficult to sort into a particular race. She held a large, delicate blue flower in one hand as she bounced. As she reached the end of the steps she saw the three men and smiled. She came over and stood before the red velvet ropes.

"Hello," she said. Steve and Chad stared at her, mouths open. Burhan answered.

"Hello little one. Are you lost?" he asked.

"No," she shook her head and looked at her flower.

"That is a pretty flower," Burhan said.

"Yup. It is," She agreed. "I was just at the temple this morning. Isis gave me this flower." She held it up to Burhan. "You want to hold it?" The petals were white at the center and then gradually blue towards the tips. Delicate strands in the center were yellow with pollen.

"No, that's ok. You hold it and keep it safe. Did you come through the door over there, in the building?" Burhan asked her. The girl looked over at the terminal.

"No. I never came through that door. I've been here for a long time. I came here on a boat." She smiled and lightly touched her flower. "Isis said that this flower never wilts. I can carry it every day." Chad burst in.

"Little girl, would you like to come with us to Heaven?" he said enthusiastically. Burhan frowned and touched Chad's sleeve. He shook his head 'no'.

"No thanks," she answered "I like it here." She skipped over to the pond and set her flower afloat. "It looks pretty in the water too." She crouched at the edge of the pond and watched it for a little while. The men watched also and were silent. Abruptly, she plucked the flower from the water and walked past them towards the river.

"Well, good-bye," she said. She skipped off down the path that led to the river. Chad turned to Burhan.

"Why didn't you let me save her? A child? Have you lost your mind?"

Burhan looked down at his clipboard. In the briefest moment before the girl came down the steps, a small flower had appeared on his clipboard on the "name" line and then faded away. Now, the line was empty. He looked back up to watch the girl skip along towards the boats. He cleared his throat.

"She was not on the list, besides I don't think she..."

"So what! We still could have saved her," said Chad.

"And take her away from her family here? No, the list is empty. Let's go," Burhan said.

"Finally, dude, I am baking. Phew." Steve rubbed has hand across his sweaty forehead.

"Don't you mean baked?" Chad said.

"Dude, no," Steve answered defensively, "Why do you always say that Chad? You know I don't do that....at least not when I'm working. The things you say man, can be pretty hurtful sometimes."

"Whatever. Let's go get an iced coffee," said Chad.

"Agreed," said Steve, suddenly perking up.

Chad brandished his golden cross and they walked through the white door into Heaven.

*****

Chad, Steve and Burhan stepped out from the white door into the Island of Sanctity.

"Oh geez. I think it's like extra-hot here today, if that's even possible," Steve said as he slurped loudly on an iced coffee.

"Steve, you are not supposed to bring that down here. We're supposed to be professional." Chad looked down and shook his head. "You'll be doing this job forever if you can't straighten up."

"Whoa, really? Forever....you really think so?" Steve said. Chad wiped sweat from his forehead and nodded.

110

"Yeah, friend, forever."

"...because of an iced coffee? Doesn't that seem harsh to you?" Steve asked.

"No, not because of one iced coffee..." Chad made an exasperated noise. "Look here comes somebody....just hide it....like over by that bush near the pond like you always do."

"Oh, okay." Steve crouched near the pond and gingerly placed his iced coffee under the leaves of a lily-like water plant on the edge of the pond.

Two people left the terminal but they walked right by all of Chad's shouting and Steve's gesturing. This happened several more times. When it was quiet, Steve would retrieve his iced coffee from the shelter of the plant. Now it was all but gone and he noisily slurped the last lukewarm drops at the bottom of the transparent plastic cup. Chad's cheeks were flushed and pink with the heat. He tugged at his tie.

From their 'island' they had quite a view. To their right was the terminal and it's grand, circular stairs, mostly hidden by bushes and date palms. The masts of riverboats could be seen above the terminal building and beyond it. Opening out to the right from behind the building was the big river. It wiled away, off towards the south, becoming a thin dark strip as it passed by distant mountains and white pyramids. Boats moved slowly along its length, large and grand with bright red sails. Farther along the river, the boats looked so small that they reminded Burhan of toys.

To the left of the island there was nothing but what looked like miles and miles of butterscotch sand and azure blue sky. A silver heat haze constantly shimmered there. Burhan never saw this place in anything but bright daylight and often wondered what it would be like out there at night. Would there be stars? moonlight? Would there be poisonous snakes or lizards? His eyes ventured out toward the city. Today was a good day to almost see it well. Often a dust haze or distant clouds interfered. White pyramid peaks poked up out of the tan haze and silver shimmer. Mountains, their sides carved into the likenesses of the gods, wavered lazily. How could a place that looked so beautiful and reverent to their gods be filled with violent barbarians and murderers? Was it a sin to even wonder about that place? To imagine that its grandeur might at least parallel that of Heaven's Great Castle? As he scanned, squinting in the sunlight, something white caught his eye. There was some motion, a dancing, a skipping. As he watched, she came into view. It was the same little girl, the one with the white dress and pink ribbon. Her skipping, white form shimmered and gradually solidified, until the heat shimmer was only at her feet and she became clearer. She seemed to wave to him, to beckon him to go to her. For some reason that he could not grasp this made Burhan feel profoundly sad. His heart ached. He put his hands to his face in a grimace of sadness and pain. Chad and Steve noticed and asked him what was wrong. As Burhan turned to look at Steve, he saw floating on the surface of their fish pond that same blue and white flower that she had offered them. He went quickly to the pond and carefully plucked the flower from the water. He held it up to show Steve and Chad.

"Whoa, hey, isn't that the flower that little girl tried to give you that one time? It looks just like it," Steve said.

"Yes, I think it is," Burhan said, "Except that this time, I think I will accept it." He handed Chad his clipboard and golden cross and marched briskly off towards the desert. Chad and Steve stood staring, dumbfounded until Chad found his voice and began shouting at him.

"Burhan, come back. Don't be a fool! It's a trick. You're walking into hell!" Chad stepped out and yelled. He looked down and realized that his foot was over the line made by the velvet ropes and quickly withdrew it.

"Dude, it's not really hell," Steve said. "It's like purgatory or something. I mean hell is downstairs, right?"

"Shut up, Steve."

*****

Burhan soon came to where the desert began in earnest. Dunes spread out before him like ocean waves, frozen in time. He looked back at his missionary colleagues, Chad, face red with anger as he shouted, and Steve, sweaty and long faced, with his hand over his eyes to block out the sun. He turned back to the desert. In the distance he could see the outlines of the wavering mountains and the hints and shapes of pyramids and other structures. He stepped gingerly onto the sand. Nothing happened. Chad had always made it sound as if something terrible would happen the second they left the island. Burhan smiled and started walking.

He walked for hours in the direction of the mountains. He saw no sign of the girl or of anything else, just sand and sky. The day settled into something hot and quiet. Burhan, joyful as he was, was not prepared for the deep desert. He felt the heat. He ripped part of his shirt to cover his head and give his eyes a bit of shade. His legs felt heavy and slow from walking in the sand and a persistent, scratchy thirst was building. Sweat dripped into his eyes. His thirst became more persistent. 'Why didn't I follow the river?' he thought, angry at himself for behaving so rashly.

The mountains seemed no nearer at dusk. As the sun set, stars began to pop out of the darkening sky. There, at least, was one question answered. There were stars.

Weary, he found a comfortable edge on a dune on which to lie, propped up, and look at the sky. His mind was empty. It was as if everything in it had leaked out of his ears onto the sand. His whole body felt emptied in this way, buoyed up by this ocean of sand, weightless. He plucked the blue flower from his head wrap and looked at it, running his fingers over the edges of the petals. He had carried the flower all day and at some point had put it in his impromptu hat. The petals were as fresh as if it had just been cut. He smiled and slept.

Sunlight striking his head over the top of the next dune woke him the next morning. He stood and stretched. Feeling refreshed, even his need for water having abated, he walked with a brisk step and stomped directly onto a horned desert viper which bit him cleanly on the leg through his cotton robe. He stepped back quickly, backing away from the snake. It slithered away. He didn't feel any pain but he had a sinking feeling.

He sat on the sand and drew up his robe. There were two small holes, oozing blood and …something else? water? venom? He took off his improvised head wrap and ripped a small strand. He wiped at the small wounds, squeezed them. He was not flexible enough to suck on the bites and spit, not that he thought that would do much good anyway. He held the shirt on the bites, sitting on the sand and hoping. He didn't feel too bad. Maybe the snake wasn't that poisonous. What did he know about snakes anyway? He stood up and started to walk, and stumbled. He sat back down and became aware of a subtle paralysis, creeping its way up his legs.

In Heaven, Burhan had never died and resurrected but it was a common sort of thing to do. Some idiot always swam out too far or fell off a cliff. Accidents, due either to stupidity or bad luck,

113

continued to happen in any plane where there was space, gravity and a measure of free will. However, the next morning said idiot would awake to find himself whole, healthy and the same age. This was so ingrained, such a given, that no one bothered to tell Burhan. Forced missionary work was not so treacherous or difficult. It was mostly disappointment and boredom. Now, sitting on the sand and feeling his body slowly shut down, Burhan was terrified.

He lay back on the sand. Thoughts and emotions swirled through his mind in a maelstrom. 'What have I done? What happens if I die here? This can't be it. Were they right? Did I walk into hell?' Burhan's thoughts became muddy. Eventually the paralysis began to affect the muscles around his lungs and he stopped breathing. His body died and the world faded from view. It was almost as if he slept.

A sunset in the desert is usually beautiful and often red, pink, and orange. The dust suspended in the air absorbs blue light and scatters red. As the blue sky was gradually replaced by pink, purple and orange, Burhan became sentient again and slowly rose up a ghost out of his body. He stood looking down at his body on the sand, at the stiff limbs and glassy stare. A creature that looked very much like a scorpion rested on his dead face. Burhan looked down at his own, new form. He was a translucent shade; a shadowy, faint blue glow with the impression of structure.

"Fuck me," he said. His voice sounded like the sand grains blowing over the dunes and trickling down the side.

He looked around and then up at the sky. The sun had completely set now though there was still twilight. He looked towards his destination. The city was still there and all aglow, like a golden constellation on the dark ground. Burhan, numbed by crisis or the lack of flesh, had no coherent thoughts. He began to walk towards the city.

He walked for what he thought was many hours. The city slowly grew in his vision. Around him the desert was quiet. Eventually the moon came up, painting everything with silver. Nocturnal creatures, mostly mice and insects, skittered here and there. He wondered if a snake would bite him now. He thought not. He did notice that he wasn't tired anymore and that he felt no pressure, heat, cold, or thirst. He thought of stopping for a rest, because it was the normal thing to do, but he found he did not need it.

A slow glow in the east caught his attention. He was not far from the city now, maybe a mile or two. He could see its tan adobe houses and the colossal white pyramids which had steadily grown along his journey. Little lights twinkled here and there. As he approached, the sudden intrusion of sunlight caused him to catch his breath...in his lungs. He looked down. There he was, back in his body again, feeling refreshed and wearing ripped clothes. He reached up to his head wrap and felt the blue lotus, still tucked into the folds. He smiled and kept walking towards the city. Soon he caught up with the river where it entered the city. People walked along its banks. A woman carrying a basket walked past him and stopped. She turned and approached him, reaching out for his shoulder. Their eyes met.

"Mother, mother!" she said as she embraced him, tears streaming down her face. "I'm so happy you're here. I never thought I'd see you again." Burhan felt weak and dropped to his knees. He looked up at the woman. "I, I remember you..." He fell over onto the sand and began to phase though his past lives. Another thing they did not mention in Heaven was the flood.

Chapter 20

Something's Wrong Here

The newly deceased Lauren Hall stood in the Reception Garden in Heaven's great Castle surrounded by family and friends. She and her mother hugged and cried and hugged again, joyful at seeing each other after so many years.

"Oh Lani, Lani. I'm so happy to see you! I missed you so much," Mahina said through her tears.

"I missed you too, mama," Lauren managed to croak, her voice breaking into little pieces. Unknown women brought her flowers. Her Aunt Rosie, who Lauren only remembered as elderly, appeared in the peak of youth and health. She approached Lauren and put a lei around her neck.

"Welcome home, baby girl!" Aunt Rosie said as she smiled and jumped into the group hug. Somewhere nearby a man cleared his throat.

"Welcome to Heaven, Lauren Hall. You may now go and enjoy your eternal reward." The speaker was a dark-haired man who looked and sounded bored. He was giving them the wave-through like the whole thing was a Disney ride and they needed to keep moving.

"Alright, Alright!" Mahina said, still clutching Lauren. "Let's go. Let's go home. Oh, you will love it, salty girl. We live next to the ocean. You can swim every day!" Mahina said, still talking through her tears. Lauren paused and looked confused. She looked at the bored man and all around the garden.

"Wait, mama…Where's…where's god?" Lauren asked. Everyone went silent. Mahina suddenly looked worried.

"Oh, Lani…" Mahina looked nervously at the attendants who stood against the walls of the enclosure. "Let's go and we'll see…we'll see god later."

"No, mama, this is Heaven… and I should be able to…" Lauren saw Mahina's face go hard with fear and saw the subtle shake of her head as if to say, 'No, not now. Don't ask that now.'

"Lani, let's go home because you know what I made for you? That's right! Mahina's famous clam chowder. It's ready right now. Let's go." Mahina winked at her. Lauren nodded and followed Mahina, surrounded by her huge, colorful, Hawaiian entourage.

They walked out of the reception garden through a large, wide tunnel, past open, golden gates and into a grand courtyard. Lauren paused to look around and stare at the immensity of the Castle and the city of New Jerusalem around it, but Mahina pulled her along, chattering the whole time about soup and the ocean and fish. They continued in this way until they reached a portal.

"Take us home!" Mahina practically shouted at the portal and they all walked through. When they stepped through onto the beach Lauren looked down at her body and moved to wipe away whatever that stuff was, that membranous, metallic, stretchy stuff that must still be on her body as they walked through the portal. There was nothing there but her favorite blue and white Hawaiian style dress and white sand under her sandals. Immediately, Mahina and the others started to shuffle her along in the sand towards somewhere, but Lauren broke through them and headed straight for the ocean. She stopped long enough to kick off her sandals and ran for the water. She fell to her knees in passing little wavelets and wet sand. Her heart sank like a stone in her chest as she pressed her hands into the sand. She couldn't understand or escape the sadness that now descended on her and filled her to her core. Her mother came walking up and sat down next to her in the wet sand. The others waited in a small, dense crowd.

"What's wrong, Lani Lani?" Mahina asked. Lauren could hardly answer. She looked out at the ocean. Wind whipped her long, dark hair around her face.

"Mama, I…I'm happy to see you…" Lauren raised her sandy, wet hand and clapped her mother on the shoulder awkwardly. Globs of wet sand went all over Mahina's dress. "Oh, sorry, mama, I didn't…"

"No, it's okay. It's alright. It's just…sand." Mahina wiped away the sand and smiled, though worry permeated all the little lines of her face. Lauren sniffed and tried to calm herself down.

"Mama, I feel…why do I feel so sad? Where's god? Where's Jesus? Why didn't Jesus come to meet me there?" Lauren asked as new tears rolled down her cheeks. Mahina shook her head sadly.

"Oh, Lani. We have a lot to talk about. First, let's just go home, yah? Let's go home and have some soup and just try and rest. It will get better. I promise, salty girl. I promise, I promise.

Now, let's go." Mahina stood up and then held her hands out to Lauren. "Come on." Lauren reached up and took her hands. The family entourage escorted her to Mahina's sprawling beachside villa down the coast of Heaven's Great Ocean. She wondered if there was a word for being the happiest she'd ever been and the saddest she'd ever been at the same time. She didn't think there was.

*****

"You have got to be kidding me," Lauren said to Aunt Rosie as they sat at Mahina's big outdoor dining table several days after Lauren arrived. Mahina, Rosie's cousin Lolo and his wife Olivia sat nearby. Rosie was shaking her head.

"No, it's true. He only comes out at Easter and Christmas. He stands on that balcony up there and gives a speech, like the Pope. All you can see is a dark-haired guy. He has a nice voice, I guess," Rosie said while she smirked at her reflection in the wine in her glass. Lauren frowned.

"Have you ever seen him close up? Or like…with wings or something?" Lauren asked. Rosie laughed.

"No. He just…sometimes he wears a crown, but that's it," Rosie said.

"So how do you know he's really Jesus…and not just…some guy?" Lauren asked.

"I guess we don't really know that, do we?" Lolo said. He shifted and put his arm around his wife. "I saw him up close once." Lolo shrugged his big shoulders. "He just looked like a haole to me." Mahina frowned.

"Lolo, you don't call your lord and savior a haole. That's disrespectful," Mahina chided. Lolo shrugged and drank his wine.

"Well, what about god? Is he…is he there somewhere? Can we see him? Because I thought…I thought that being here in Heaven meant that we would get to …" Lauren paused and frowned, "Well, I guess I don't know what I thought would happen."

"Did you think you'd get a bear hug from an old haole with a long beard?" Lolo asked and then laughed out of his big, barrel chest.

"Lolo!" Mahina said. "You watch it. You're going to get in trouble." Mahina continued to frown at him.

"Not here," he said. He waved his wine glass around to indicate the house and the beach. Mahina sighed.

"Lani…in New Jerusalem there is a church…it's open to all. You can go there and they have a…like an eternal flame kind of thing. That's all. We are supposed to know that we are in the arms of god because of his gift of eternal life, daily resurrection, the way things grow, how we don't feel pain, how everything is so much easier here for us. We don't need to struggle and fight. Everyone gets a place, has enough food. Nobody's sick or hurting…all that good stuff is from god," Mahina said.

"What about Henry, mama? Will he come here too?" Lauren asked. Mahina pursed her lips. She had never really liked Henry.

"Mm, well, only if he makes the right choice at judgment. He better. When his time comes and he sees those people in the Waiting Room with the signs on their heads…he'll figure it out," Mahina said. Lauren stared out at the ocean and shook her head.

"No he won't, mama. He'll ask a bunch of inappropriate questions and get in trouble like he always does," Lauren said.

"You think he'll end up in service?" Rosie asked.

"God knows where he'll end up," Lauren said.

Chapter 21

Eternal Flame

The center courtyard of New Jerusalem bustled with people. Most walked, a few rode bicycles. Cars buzzed by on nearby streets but were not allowed in the courtyard. Lauren walked along looking at everything with wide eyes. The courtyard was dotted with small fountains, flowering plants, and large trees around its edges. To the west, there was just city; city as far as the eye could see. From north to south, the Castle filled up the world. Beyond it, to the east, there was no way to see the coastline of the eastern ocean that allegedly lay on the other side.

Lauren walked down the street that ran along the Castle wondering if she would ever find what she was looking for. Somewhere along this incredible building there was a holy inner sanctum where god's eternal flame was kept. Somewhere else in the Castle, lived a man who everyone thought was related to god. Lauren had already seen him and she was not impressed.

Two days earlier, New Jerusalem celebrated the Feast of the Nativity of the Blessed Virgin Mary. Aunt Rosie told Lauren that for this Feast, Jesus would be part of the parade. She came to the city and stood with the vast crowds, more people than she had ever seen in her life, assembled in one area. A grand parade went along the Castle and around the courtyard before continuing down one of the main streets. Parade floats went by, elaborately decorated with flowers. People stood on the floats and waved. She might have recognized them, had she been catholic, but her family had always gone to a non-denominational church that focused on the Bible. She didn't know any saints.

The parade of saints seemed to go on forever. Lauren noticed that the floats were supported and moved by ordinary cars that were carefully concealed. They couldn't conceal the exhaust and the street smelled more and more heavily of the products of combustion. Finally, as twilight settled over the courtyard, in the distance she could see the largest, grandest parade vehicle. There on the float, on two elaborate thrones, sat a woman who she assumed was the virgin Mary, and a young, dark-haired man. As the float came closer, she knew right away that something was wrong. The man was not Jewish. In fact, he looked almost exactly like an actor she remembered named Jim Giordano. He waved and smiled. Once, he even blew a kiss to a group of fawning women. Mary frowned and tugged on his arm as if to say, "Cut that out."

Lauren looked around at the faces in the crowd around her. They seemed oblivious. They cried and shouted. They proclaimed their undying love and devotion. She watched the man in the float go by and knew, knew in her heart, that he was just a man, probably an actor. The real Jesus would not have stood for all this pomp and circumstance. The real Jesus would have been among the crowds, touching people, talking to them and washing their feet. The real Jesus wouldn't sit on a cheesy parade float and blow kisses at girls.

Today Lauren was in New Jerusalem looking for god. She had no idea which direction to go. There were no signs along the street that paralleled the Castle. Finally she broke down and approached a member of the Guard, New Jerusalem's famous and feared heavenly law enforcement. He stood next to one of the ubiquitous unlabeled doors to the Castle, resplendent in gold and silver armor.

"Excuse me…sir, but you could tell me how to get to the Holy Inner Sanctum?" Lauren asked. At first the Guardsman looked confused.

"Ma'am, what exactly are you looking for?" he asked. His armor made him imposing, but his voice was friendly and his manner kind. Lauren relaxed a little.

"I'm new here and I'm looking for the Eternal Flame? " The Guardsman smiled and laughed.

"Oh I see. Who told you it was called the 'Holy…never mind. NJ is a big place." He smiled broadly. "The Eternal Flame is housed in a mini-chapel down the way you are going, though it's more than two miles down the road. Step up to that portal over there and say 'Eternal Flame'. You will pop out right in front of it."

"Thank you," Lauren said. She hurried off towards the portal and turned to say thank you one more time as she walked. The Guardsman waved good-bye.

She said the words 'Eternal Flame' and stepped through the portal. After stepping through she soon realized that she stood in front of a ruin. To the right the Castle still sprawled, but to the left it crumbled away into the distance until there was nothing but the road and the distant shore of the ocean. Broken walls and errant plants stood in front of her. It looked like part of the Castle here had been crushed. There were still big blocks of granite spilling into the street. There was, however, a stone path that was subtly indicated by a small sign.

She followed the path as it twisted through the blocky ruins. Eventually it opened out in front of the remains of a small chapel. Only the back half of the place was left. There was a curved plaster wall, yellow with age and smoke. There were a few nooks in the wall where candles sat unlit with tiny, wax stalactites still extending down and away from them.

In front of this wall, 3 or 4 steps led up to a raised area of sandy-tan granite. In roughly the center of this strange altar, concentric circles were carved right into the surface. From the outside to the center of the shape, the circles increased in number, becoming indistinguishable from each other until they reached a small, dark opening. From this opening emanated a ragged, orange flame.

At first glance the whole place was unimpressive, dingy and disappointing. Rough, jumbled stones sat in piles against broken walls. Water-starved weeds poked up from between rocks on the dusty ground. An old woman in dirty clothes sat limp against a nearby wall. She snored softly. Lauren sat down on the granite dais, near the flame. Disappointment settled into her chest.

As she sat staring at the flame, something changed in the air around her. Everything became very still. Silence descended on the ruined place like falling snow. Time slowed down. Every dust mote in the air swam past her in the sunlight, turning slowly like little planets. All of her worries and emotions evaporated into a calm peace. The flame continued to burn, unchanged. Motion caught her eye and she looked up at the old woman who had been sleeping next to the wall. She was suddenly beautiful. She no longer lay awkwardly against the wall but stood, bright and tall in the sun. Her white, gauzy clothes flowed around her as if she was underwater. The long end of a pink ribbon wrapped around her waist floated in serene coils. Her chestnut brown and silver hair seemed to be settling slowly onto her shoulders. In one hand she held a blue and white flower. She raised her other hand to her lips as if to say, 'Shh'.

And then it was over. Time flowed normally. The ruined chapel was ruined and dingy again. The small flame whipped in the erratic breeze. She thought she could hear the gas line that fed the flame somewhere nearby. The sleeping woman was gone.

Lauren sat there for a little while longer, looking at the flame. Slowly, she smiled. Then, she got up and headed home.

Chapter 22

Government Work

Henry left Ra-Neferu's barge and stepped onto the dock at the river by the Terminal. He turned to Ra-Neferu, Burhan, and Bent-Reshet who stood in a line, waiting to say good-bye and wish him luck. He hugged Bent-Reshet and shook hands with Burhan. "Good luck, Henry," Burhan said. Henry hugged Ra-Neferu, lifting her off her feet as he did so.

"Thank you so much, Neffie. You've been wonderfully kind," Henry said. Ra-Neferu smiled.

"Are you ready?" Burhan asked.

"Well, I have everything." He patted the pockets of his suit coat and smiled. "As to whether or not I am ready…" He shrugged.

"Henry, if anything happens, use the cross and come home. If you feel you are suspected, don't wait for them to come knocking down your door. Get out fast," Ra-Neferu said looking worried. Henry squeezed her shoulder.

"Don't worry, Neffie. You will see me again." Ra-Neferu smiled. Tears formed in her eyes. They hugged once more. "Well, no time like the present…see you soon." Henry sauntered off towards the terminal. His friends stood and watched him go.

Inside the terminal, the place was almost empty. One or two people could be seen sitting and waiting quietly in the banks of chairs. The Island of Sanctity was also deserted. Henry took a seat on the rounded stairs that led out of the building, careful to sit on the edge where he could see the missionaries enter their Island. In his pocket he turned the coin over and over nervously. He almost jumped when he heard voices behind him. As he heard those voices, in front of him three missionaries popped out of their portal and took up their positions behind the velvet ropes. Henry thought he recognized two of them. Behind him in the Terminal, a few people were coming toward the stairs. As they walked by Henry and down the path, the missionaries started shouting.

"Sanjay! Sanjay! Rejoice in the light of the One God. Repent and enter Heaven! Sanjay!" Sanjay and his female escort kept walking. Sanjay looked at them with that same surprised and confused look that Henry imagined he must have given them when he first arrived. He got up from his spot on the stairs and approached them. The men fell silent and looked at him suspiciously.

"Can we help you?" one of the men said. Henry shifted on his feet nervously.

"I want to repent. I want to go to Heaven." He looked at each of them and they in turn looked at his forehead. The white cross of light swept across his forehead. The blond one who was dressed in black pants, white shirt, and tie raised his eyebrows and exchanged surprised looks with the other two. Another of them, that same surfer-Jesus-guy that Henry remembered, said, "Well, alright." He nodded his head happily. "Come on dude! Welcome, welcome to the like... abode of god. Alright. Let's take him back Chad." Chad looked back towards the terminal and down at his clipboard. He shrugged his shoulders. The other man, dressed almost exactly like Chad, remained silent. Chad pulled a slender golden cross out of his back pocket and they walked up the two steps and through the portal.

*****

Henry and the missionaries emerged from a recessed set of cement stairs in the ground and onto a busy courtyard. Henry stood looking around and realized that he carried the briefcase again. He followed the missionaries across the yard, past a stand that looked suspiciously like a Starbucks coffee stand, and then through a small wooden door in the side of what Henry could only describe as a huge castle. The elaborate stone structure filled up as much as he could see and seemed to extend indefinitely in both directions as well as in elevation. The structure was truly colossal.

Henry didn't have time to really look around as he was shuffled through a door and into a room that looked like any cubicle ridden, corporate gray office room complete with water cooler and copier. Henry had to stifle the urge to start giggling. When he entered, missionary heads popped up from inside cubicles and eyed him curiously. Steve grasped his elbow and led him through the office and through another door into a hallway.

"Alright dude. I'm so happy for you. So, follow me and I'll drop you off in the assignment room."

"Assignment room?" asked Henry.

"Oh right." Steve stopped in the hallway and looked at Henry. "Um, like, because you didn't come here the first time, and like maybe there's something in your case…you know…the case worker will look at your files and decide what kind of job you will get. It's like…um…well you have to earn Heaven you know? But don't worry dude. It's not so bad. It's still Heaven. You just have like…a crappy corporate job for a hundred years or so. No biggie." Steve smiled and patted him on the back. He turned and opened a door that led to another large waiting room.

"Here you go. Good luck, friend," Steve said. Henry stepped through and Steve closed the door behind him.

Henry stood in front of a waiting room that looked almost exactly like the one he remembered except for a few small details. There was still a counter with a ticket dispenser. The window on the counter remained shuttered and light could be seen through the frosted window. Instead of a single white door and a number counter, there were seven doors with an electronic sign next to each. To the right of each door there was a window into an office where a case worker could be seen talking to a person, writing things down, drinking coffee. Henry sighed and went to the counter. He took a number and chose a comfy looking seat next to a lamp. He didn't even bother to pick up any of the magazines, but the title of one caught his eye, "A History of Double Glazed Windows". 'You have got to be kidding.' Henry said under his breath.

*****

After 20 minutes or so, Henry's number came up on the counter next to one of the doors. He got up and started towards the door when it opened and a short, pudgy, curly-haired woman opened the door and smiled at him, motioning towards her office. He walked in and she closed the door behind him.

"Hello, Dr. Hall, please sit down. I'm Catherine and I'll be your service assignment counselor today. Lovely to meet you," she said in a happy, lilting Scottish accent. She smiled broadly and motioned to a single chair facing her desk. Henry sat down. Catherine turned and sat down at her desk, clasping her hands in anticipation.

"So, let's see what we've got!" She reached out both hands expectantly. Henry looked confused.

"Your briefcase, silly goose, let's have it." The fingers on her extended hands wiggled at him. Henry nodded and picked the briefcase up off the floor and handed it to her. She pulled something out of a desk drawer and opened the briefcase with a click. Henry could not see how or with what she did it. She pulled out a stack of papers and gently tossed the briefcase to the floor behind her. Her eyes grew wide as she read. She nodded and whispered softly to herself.

"Oooooo," she said, drawing her breath in as if she was looking at pictures of kittens. Henry was getting agitated.

"Are you supposed to be reading..." Henry asked and was interrupted.

"Oh, you've got some juicy ones here..." she said, her eyes bright. Henry frowned.

"Shouldn't that be private, I mean...."

"Vanity, gluttony....mmm wouldn't have thought that about you...some sloth....oh, daddy issues, mmm. It's always the way with you English isn't it?" She giggled and then sighed loudly. Henry was getting upset. Her punctuated sighs were becoming like nails on a chalkboard to his ears. Catherine continued, oblivious to his distress. "Coveting, lying...," she paused and made a face. "You stole a policeman's helmet? Do they even do that anymore?" She wagged a finger at him, "Tisk, tisk Dr. Hall, you naughty man, you." She continued to read and sigh or gasp while Henry sat frowning. Finally, she let out a great, final sigh.

"Well, this is pretty normal, really. Everybody does the little things don't they? And the ones who do the big things, well, they don't come here do they?" She giggled. "Well, Dr. Hall, most of this wouldn't be enough to put you in service but unfortunately you did the one thing that always does..." she looked at him expectantly.

"I said no?" he said, unsure.

"Yes, you did say no, and right to Saint Pete himself didn't ya? And started to ask him questions as well. Aren't we high and mighty and the bees knees and all that?" She put the papers down and looked directly at him. "Yes, you will have to serve. But don't worry your head too much. It won't be so bad. It's just like having a crappy corporate job for a hundred years or so, no biggie." She smiled as she rummaged around in her desk drawer.

"You know you're the second pers...," Henry said and was interrupted again.

"So, I can put you in a variety of places. Do you have anything that might…make me want to help you a bit?" Her eyebrows danced up and down.

"What, I'm sorry, I don't…"

"Well, you are a slow one aren't ya?" She held out her hand and rubbed her fingers together. Henry understood and nodded.

"Oh, yes, yes I do, in fact…" He reached into his jacket pocket and pulled out a carefully wrapped parcel with some barely discernible grease spots. Catherine's eyes lit up.

"Oooo, what's that then?"

"Um, a fritter…apple I think." Catherine clapped her hands together with joy.

"Oh, yes delightful, wonderful, can't wait. Careful now, no, no, no, under the table, yes mind the window, in front of your body, that's right." She hastily took the package under her desk and put it in a drawer which she opened and shut quickly. She then opened the drawer again and peeked at the package, then closed it again. "That will do just fine." She turned to face her desk and picked up a piece of paper.

"Dr. Hall, what sort of job would be appropriate for you? Do you have anything in mind?"

"Yes, actually I…wouldn't mind working in the Waiting Room," Henry said. Catherine's face fell. "Which one?" she asked. She wrinkled her nose in disgust.

"Well, the main one, when you first come in," Henry said. Catherine continued to frown.

"What, really?" she asked.

"Yes, I think…I think, I could be of use there," Henry said. Catherine shook her head.

"I could get you something so much nicer….missionary work in a small town, nobody around to complain if you want to get a lunch or something…or you could be a groundsman in the gardens…I mean the Waiting Room Department is," she made a face. "Are you sure?"

"Yes, that'll be fine," Henry said. Catherine eyed him for a second. She looked at his forehead and the cross appeared briefly, a reassuring flash of light. She shrugged her shoulders.

"Alrighty then, Dr. Hall. To each his own, to each his own. Are ya sure though? We just had something open up among the shepherds….the sheep and the mountain sides, lovely views?"

"No, thank you," Henry said, though it was tempting. He could sit out on the side of a mountain somewhere, minding sheep and scratching his beard while other people spied and fought wars. He shook his head at the thought. It was too late now.

Catherine busied herself with the papers and things on her desk. She wrote something on a particular paper, stamped it with a big, black stamp and put it in a box labeled "out-going" along with the other papers from his briefcase.

"Okay, now you're all done. Get going you," Catherine said. She stood up and pointed to a door, opposite the one he came in. "Now you go and have a great eternity." She giggled. "That's my little joke." Henry got up and walked to the door. She patted him on the back and shut it behind him. He thought he heard a drawer open and then a little giggle behind him.

Henry stood in front of yet another grey, corporate waiting room. He sighed and looked for a seat. Before he could sit down a woman entered the room and approached him.

"Dr. Hall, please come with me. I'll take you to your room in the dormitory." Henry smiled, thinking that his first mission as a spy went well. 'Well, I'm in it now!" he thought.

Chapter 23

Lauren the Spy

Lauren sat on the warm sand looking out at the waves. This was her new spot. She did not frequent her old haunts; the bathtub and the other named places with relatively shallow water and sandy bottoms. She sat there and looked at the waves, fins and goggles next to her on the sand, unused. Her mother occasionally came to yell for her to come eat some meal or other. She wasn't really interested. Two of the nights since Burhan left Lauren had drowned herself at sunset and walked along the dark sea floor as a ghost until sunrise.

In her mind she kept replaying the scene in the town center; Burhan's frightened face, how it changed to sadness and longing when he saw her, the glint of gold as he struggled with a red faced missionary and disappeared down the steps into…what? Hell? Purgatory? Did Burhan come here and seduce her all so he could bide his time and kidnap a child to take to hell? It did not, could not make sense. He was not evil, he was not. He was sweet and kind. He was gentle. Lauren got lost for a moment in a sensual memory, a lovely moment of skin and breath. She shook the memory away.

"Laauurrenn, Laurrrrrenn," came her mother's call. Mahina saw her sitting in the sand and shuffled towards her. Lauren actually stood up to face her which made Mahina step back a little. "Oh, salty girl. Want to have some lunch?" Mahina asked, trying to sound cheerful.

"No, mama I think I will go into town today for lunch, to Robert's…you know for some real comfort food," Lauren said. She turned and started to walk down the beach towards town still in her swimsuit and loosely carrying her fins and goggles.

"Oh, crazy keiki, not in your swimsuit. Come inside and change first ya?" Mahina led Lauren back to the house and she did not resist.

That day and for several days after, Lauren had lunch in town. This meant that she went to Robert's, ordered an iced tea and then sat at a table on the second floor deck, overlooking the town center. Nobody sat up there very often so she wasn't bothered. Even the waitress would forget about her sometimes. She would eventually reappear and apologetically refill Lauren's tea. Lauren sat, sipped her tea, and spied on the missionaries. From her viewpoint, she could see the whole of their well, the steps down into it and the painting of the cross on its cement floor.

Robert's Bistro, though everyone just called it Robert's, was right on the main street next to the town's missionary office. The side of their brick building actually formed part of the enclosure where Lauren sat. She liked to imagine that one of the missionaries was snoozing in his room, right on the other side of that wall.

After the first day Lauren nicknamed them Larry, Curly, and Moe or just 'the boys'. The boys were very predictable. One of them, who was pudgy and dark haired, carried a clipboard and seemed to be in charge. She called him Moe. He always went down into the well first. The other two were rather nondescript. Larry was skinny with close-cropped , blond hair. Curly was a bit on the thicker side and taller than the other two, with brown hair. All three of them always wore khaki pants and a short sleeved buttoned shirt of a single color. She saw them once on a Friday and Moe was wearing a Hawaiian shirt. 'Aloha Friday, nice,' Lauren thought.

Every day Moe would emerge from the missionary office followed by Larry and Curly. They would cross the street, go down the steps of the well in the center of the courtyard, and disappear. It seemed to Lauren that right after they went down, it was somehow quieter in the town center. Lauren wondered if it was just her imagination.

The boys would go into the well at around 10: am. They would reappear close to noon, sometimes looking a little pink and sweaty. Most of the time they would just go back across the street to their office, but some of the days they stopped at the food truck in the square and stood around eating burritos like it was the best food they'd ever had. One day it looked like Larry was licking his fingers clean. They had the body language of the guilty. They looked around nervously like naughty kids trying to see if a teacher was watching before or during the deed. Lauren did notice that the burrito truck faced exactly opposite the window to the missionary office, so if someone was watching from the window, they would not be able to see them enjoying their burritos.

A little while later, always before 1pm, they would go back down into the well. Lauren knew from previous experience that they would go down for a while, come back, go down again, come back, and then finally knock off at around 5pm. There was one other missionary, a woman. Lauren only saw her once when she came out of the office and walked around like she was looking for the boys. The boys did emerge shortly from the portal and the four of them walked together to the office. Larry was holding something over his eye. Their faces were long and unhappy, but they said nothing.

The day after Larry's eye incident Lauren decided that she might like to have a burrito for lunch. She was sitting up on the second floor deck and saw them come out of the well and make a b-line for the burrito truck. Lauren hopped up from her table and went downstairs as quickly as she could without attracting attention. Robert hollered at her as she left.

"Hey, are you gonna eat somethin' today, ya?"

"Uh, yeah, I'm gonna go get a burrito," Lauren said absently as she left. Robert made a face.

"Dat wahine is crazy," he said to a couple of bar patrons. They nodded.

Outside, Lauren slowed down and tried to walk casually to the burrito truck. She couldn't help but smile a little when she got in line behind the boys. She pretended to ignore them and to look bored while she waited. She listened to them talking.

"Well, let's get a celebratory burrito. We failed to meet our quota again," said Moe. "Woo hoo," he said sarcastically. Larry snorted.

"I didn't know we 'ad a quota. We don't get no ova numba than zero." Larry's accent was British and thick. The third man, Curly, chuckled but didn't say anything. Moe reached up to get his burrito, smiled at the vendor and said thanks.

"Anyway, they'll never change, those old pagans," Moe said. He dived into his burrito. Larry stepped up to get his. He rubbed at his eyebrow and whistled.

"I just 'ope they don't hit me again. Pagans don't pull punches. I swear I 'eard me eye socket crack," Larry said as he stepped aside for Curly. Curly, grabbed his burrito, stepped out of the way for Lauren. Curly said, "Yeah that guy clocked you pretty hard. Does it still hurt?"

"No, stupid. Nuffing hurts here…and I rezzed this morning, didn't I?" Larry said with his mouth full.

"Oh, yeah…sorry," Curly said.

Lauren felt sorry for Curly. He must be new. She eyed him, wondering what he did to get service. Lauren stepped up and ordered her burrito. No one was behind her so she stood there waiting. She made eye contact with Moe. The wispy cross of light made its appearance on his forehead and faded. Moe nodded his head at her just slightly, a polite sort of acknowledgement with a hint of 'we won't talk because our social statuses are incompatible'. Then he turned to face the other two who were leaning on a picnic table that was wedged right up next to the burrito truck.

"Eh boss, s'pose one day we could go up in Robert's and get somethingk real? Eh, no offense, mate," Larry said to the burrito truck guy who was sitting on a stool in the truck. The man nodded. He was a service worker as well. Moe shook his head no.

"Mmm, she might not be able to see through this truck, but I think she would see us hoofin' it over to Roberts." Larry and Curly nodded and chewed. "Maybe at Christmas we could get away with it." The other two brightened up. Larry swallowed an over large chunk.

"It's easier out here anyway…to get away with it, in'nit? I'd 'ate to be one of 'em in New J, can't never eat, smoke, drink, get away with nuffing really…with all those eyes all 'round. And anyway, office bitch might squawk at us for 'aving this, but what's she doin' while we're down there? Shoving donuts down her gob, betcha," Larry said. Curly sighed. Moe just chewed and nodded.

"Everybody cheats as best they can," he said after a few moments. "That's how it's been since they started this whole mess," Moe said.

"So, it used to be different? Before you could eat?" Curly asked, hopeful.

"Well, yeah, but people never got anything done. Have a leisurely breakfast, do a little work, have a long lunch, afternoon donuts, leave early to meet somewhere for a nice dinner. If you know you won't get fat…or fatter anyway… or get diseases, people love to eat, drink…smoke. Plus, it's not like we're getting paid or not getting paid. It's kind of like communism; there's just not much motivation to work," Moe said. Larry gave a short, sharp laugh. Curly looked sad. Moe continued, "In the big city they get one thing that we never will…converts. Sometimes some dumb sheep says no to Peter and then they go south. When they figure out what it's really like down there they'll come begging and

133

repenting." Moe smiled. "But we, my friends, will not be so lucky." He sniffed and looked around. "Ech, we're going to smell like these…delicious burritos," he said, eyeing the man in the truck. "We can wash off in the pond down there. Hopefully, that will be enough. You guys done?"

"Yeah," Larry answered as he threw away his trash. Curly shoved the rest in his mouth and threw away the wrapper. One of his cheeks puffed up as if he were a giant chipmunk.

"Owlright," Curly said with his mouth full.

The three of them walked off towards the portal. Curly was wiping his hands on the back of his pants, leaving greasy finger lines. That's when Lauren spied the golden cross in Moe's back pocket. It wasn't a gaudy thing, just a simple, flat golden cross with pearls or some other white looking gems at the top and on the two arms. Was that it? Just a cross? Would any golden cross work? She watched them. When they got to the well, Moe took the cross out and held it in front of him. She lost sight of him for a second, then in procession, Moe, Larry and Curly went down into the well. Lauren started walking away, headed towards the nearest portal.

*****

Crickets chirped lazily as Lauren walked in the dark from her mother's villa to the nearby portal. It was quiet. The only noise was from her sandals on the fine gravel path. In her pants pocket she nervously felt the little crosses she had found in her jewelry box. Two of them were tiny with little gems, diamonds on one and an opal on the other. One of them was bigger and gaudy. Auntie Rosie had given her that one. 'No one that was young in the 70s ever quite recovered,' Lauren thought and smiled. She wondered if they would work. She wondered if she was an idiot, going down into hell, level 1. 'Those missionaries didn't look so tough,' she thought. 'That guy Curly was practically weepy, poor guy.' As she approached the portal, she did not slow, but just walked right through as if it wasn't there at all. She had gotten used to it, but going through a portal always left her with a sticky feeling, but only if the sticky stuff were liquid metal, like mercury. She felt enveloped in it as she walked through and that it clung, ever so briefly to her, as she walked away. There was nothing there, nothing visible or tangible, but the sensation happened every time.

It was late enough that the town center was quiet and dark. The bars were closed though she knew people might be over at Petey's ocean bar, drinking until morning. She kind of wanted to be at Petey's bar drinking until morning, but she charged ahead. As she approached the well she grew more cautious, looking around, stopping at any sound. There was nothing and no one around, so she relaxed a little. She walked down the steps of the well and sat on the bottom steps looking at the cross painting on the cement floor. She took out her three crosses. The largest one looked most promising so she held it out in front of her and stuck her foot down onto the mural as if she were checking the water in a pool with her toes. Foot and mural made contact but that was all. She sighed and put the big cross back in her pocket. She took out the other two crosses, still attached to their chains. First she would try the one with diamonds. She held it out in front of her and dipped her foot. Again, nothing. She put it back in her pocket. As she drew out the last cross her heart sank. She held it out in front of her and dipped her foot, nothing again. She sighed. 'Well, now what?' she thought. 'Can I tackle Moe? I think I could take him.'

She looked at the little cross on its gold necklace in her palm. The cross slid down and swung gently. It glittered prettily in the dim light of a nearby street lamp. She looked down at the cross mural. The cross there was painted so that it looked silver and was plain. No jewels. Around it were curves of soft colors, almost giving the impression of ribbons or fabric, in velvety red, mellow orange, ivory, and a faded light green. She reached down with the cross charm on the necklace and touched the end of the mural cross. She dragged the tiny end of the cross charm along the outline of the mural cross like a child drawing in the sand with a stick. The cross brushed the surface and then went into it with a slight tension. Lauren gasped. She pushed her hand straight down and felt that portal feeling, the softly broken tension of some membrane that followed her hand through. She scooted forward and put her feet through and felt another step below the mural. She stood up with her shoes and ankles unseen beneath the mural. The mural itself had taken on a watery, metallic cast with a hint of motion. Lauren kept going down and once completely through, stood blinking in dim light in front of a door frame with two steps.

She was standing in a small area covered with paving stones and roped off with what looked like velvet bank ropes held up by brass stands. Behind her there was a small pond and some plants. It was quite dark but she thought she could hear the ocean in the distance. The glitter of yellow light caught her eye and she suspected that she was looking at a distant fire. Shadows moved there. The shadows transformed into running, shouting men with angry faces. They were coming toward her. Ceased up with fear, she turned around and tried to go through the portal. The men kept shouting. She stepped through, nothing. Back through, nothing. She fumbled with the cross and held it up in front of her, then brought it forward to the plane of the door frame. The air in the door frame took on that same watery sheen and she ran through. She heard the men behind her yelling angrily in some unknown language. She tumbled out into her familiar world and ran for the nearest portal home.

*****

A few days later Lauren sat on the stone extension of the fireplace in Mahina's kitchen. Mahina bustled around the kitchen chopping things, getting stuff out of the fridge, putting it back, cracking eggs, and boiling water. Her cooking style was chaotic and noisy and yet always seemed to yield good results. Lauren sat holding a light pink scallop shell. She ran her fingers over the lines and edges and said nothing while her mother prattled.

"No, now what did I do with that…oh here it is," she went back to her cutting board and begin to chop a carrot with gusto. Suddenly Auntie Rosie burst in to the kitchen through the screen door. She was out of breath.

"Oh thank god," she said when she saw Lauren. "Lauren, come on. Come with me. They are coming for you. We've got to hide you…for a few days maybe…come on." Mahina and Lauren both stared at her.

"What are you talking about?" Mahina asked. "Why? Why would they come for her? She hasn't done anything." Mahina looked at Lauren. Lauren looked at the floor. Mahina frowned. "What did you do?" she asked more worried, than angry.

"I went through a portal," Lauren answered. Mahina frowned.

"I ate a muffin for breakfast…so what! Everybody does that every day," Mahina said.

"No, I went through the missionary portal in center of town…to the underworld." Rosie and Mahina both gasped. "But

136

mama, I don't know how they knew! No one was there. I went at night. No one saw me, I know it!" Lauren pleaded.

"Well, someone saw you. Go, go with Rosie then." Mahina motioned to Rosie. "Go hide for a couple days and they will forget about it or give up or maybe find someone who looks like you, just for show. It's ok, keiki. It's good luck for us that the cops here are so lazy. Go now. Go." Mahina shooed Lauren towards the door. Lauren looked back at her with watery eyes. Mahina grabbed Lauren and hugged her. "It will be ok, but you have to go." Rosie and Lauren walked out the door.

Rosie led Lauren along the beach, north and away from town. They walked briskly but did not run.

"Where will we go?" Lauren asked, looking behind her.

"We'll go to the water portal, the one that is out on those rocks, you know? The tide is out, so it should be dry enough. They probably won't be guarding that one. We'll have to swim to it otherwise we'll be easy to spot. We'll get wet, but oh well."

"How do you know…how do you know that they will give up?" Lauren asked. Rosie shrugged.

"Look, this shit happens sometimes. Before you came, they tried to take Rudy one time because he got drunk downtown and said some stuff. Idiot. Anyway, somebody heard him and reported it. The police came for him so we hid him for a week. It all blew over. They don't really care, they just have to make a show of it right? Just…we need to make sure they don't get you, 'cause if they do…there are people who do care and they are not like the local police. They will hurt you," Rosie said looking at the sand as she walked forward.

"How will they hurt me? We don't have pain and how did you find out?" Lauren asked.

"Because Lolo is in the police…my cousin, you remember?" Rosie said. Lauren didn't. "Look it doesn't matter. He called me and said they were coming. He said he told them you went to NJ to go shopping. That will buy us some time then they will come and search the houses, all the families' houses." Rosie kept looking in the distance for the portal and looking behind them for the police.

"Where will we go?" Lauren asked.

"Far out. There are some old ones. They don't know us but if we speak a little Hawaiian they will accept us no question. They are from the time when Queen Liliʻuokalani was deposed. They are Christian and all but… they don't really don't like haoles. Don't worry. You look Hawaiian enough. They will hide you good," Rosie said.

The wet portal that Rosie was looking for was about 400 feet off the coast on a long, rock peninsula that stretched out from the sandy shore. At low tide you could walk right to it if you hopped over a few puddles. At high tide, the water was 4 or 5 feet deep. Just then the tide was coming in. Lauren could still see the path but it was getting patchy. Large rocks stuck up out of the water here and there. They walked up to where the rocks started to stick out of the sand.

"We better get in the water. Maybe we should have been swimming this whole…" Lauren interrupted her.

"Stop, do you hear that?" Lauren said. She thought she heard a rumble, like distant thunder. In the distance she saw horses, men on horses coming for her.

"What the hell?" Rosie said. "Run. Now!" Rosie pushed her. "Lauren, run!" Rosie yelled. Lauren ran.

The thunderous hoof beats got louder and louder. Lauren did not look back as she bounced from rock to rock, splashed through higher areas and ran as best she could on exposed rocks. The hoof beats stopped and for a moment she looked back. The horses were there on the shore and two of the Guard, not the local police but the actual Castle Guard, were dismounting to follow her out. Rosie was running away from them towards the water. Looking over her shoulder caused Lauren to miss her step and she fell, crashing into some rocks. With her knee bloody and shaky from the impact, she stumbled forward. Just before she got to the portal and was about to say "Kahoʻolawe" she was grabbed, and jerked upward in the steely grip of an angel.

Chapter 24

The Lady is Not a Tramp, She's a Bitch

Henry's life took on a new strangeness. His days had become the endless stream of grey fabric and white copy paper that defined a crappy corporate job. He rose each morning at 7: am, showered, watched the morning news over a cup of tea, and then went to work at 8:45. He worked all day and knocked off around 5pm.

The service workers were confined to certain sections of the castle. Henry had access to the gardens, a library, and a stretch of beach. He would walk on the beach or in the gardens. He got books from the library or watched his TV in his room in the dormitory until bedtime. He expected great things from the library and after some time it did prove to be the one source of joy in his life. There were unbelievable gems there, true histories written by witnesses or the great people themselves. He relished those books.

His small room was reasonably well equipped. He had his own toilet and shower and a microwave with a faucet nearby so he could heat up water. His single bed was comfortable enough. There was a colorful quilt over the top which he was sure was sown by some charity or other who did nice things for service workers. He had a set of drawers with a mirror and of course the TV on which he watched the church approved news.

Television shows in Heaven were dull, vanilla, and controlled by the Castle. There were some interesting nature shows that Henry would watch from time to time. They were well done but it brought to mind nagging questions. Why did Heaven's world have an ecosystem? Where does the food and power come from? Solar panels? Is there coal? Natural gas? Farming? There must be oil with all the cars around. How did that work? These questions bothered him but the television and newspaper gave no answers. The one time he actually tried to ask a person at the office she just looked at him and said, "I don't know. Who cares?"

This made Henry even sadder than he was willing to admit so he became determined to investigate the real workings of the place. 'The stars' he thought, 'I must remember to look at the stars.'

To Henry's great disappointment he learned that service workers were not allowed to eat during the day. They were allowed one small meal in the evening in the New Jerusalem Central Government Service Worker Cafeteria or the S-Caf as people called it. This was supposed to remind them of their sin and to serve as part of their penance. The food they served there qualified as a penance all by itself. Henry rarely went there. Drinks were allowed, however, and all workers drank throughout the day; tea, coffee, water…that sort of thing. Sodas and fruit or ice cream drinks were not allowed as they were considered indulgent.

Outside the missionary office of the New Jerusalem Central Government building, which was part of the vast, sprawling Castle, there was a coffee shop that was very similar to a Starbucks. The coffee and tea they served there was decent and to Henry's great relief they had milk and cream. They also had cappuccinos, espressos, machiattos and all such nonsense as went on in coffee places in the Sorrowful World.

Henry was the low man on the totem pole in the office, so he spent a lot of time getting coffee for people. He also made copies, filed folders, acted as a courier between departments, distributed mail in the mail room, and cleaned rooms when necessary. He was the office gopher. He would do whatever anyone needed him to do and as he did it with a smile and a friendly manner, he was well liked. It wouldn't have been so bad, actually, if it hadn't been for Astrid.

Yes, Astrid Swartwout, spoiled, self-entitled college student in her youth and ruthless, self-important provost of his former university in her middle age, had insinuated herself into the workings of the Waiting Room. Henry had no idea what she'd done to get service but now, here in Heaven, she was the "Director of Primary Entry Operations". Henry wondered how she had risen so quickly through the ranks when they had sat next to each other in the waiting room. It didn't matter though. She was the director and she made sure everyone knew it.

When Henry first came to the office, he was indoctrinated into the job by the previous gopher who was now moving up to the East Asian Regional Coordinator position. Everyone in the office was friendly and helpful enough and Henry never even saw Astrid until the second week he was there. She came through one day leading a Pope and his entourage through the spaces. She was young and beautiful again. He had forgotten how beautiful she had been and was a bit taken aback. Astrid saw Henry, paused only just, and delivered the most devilish, most threatening smile Henry had ever seen. From that moment, it was on.

After that her daily goal became to torment Henry in some way. She would order coffee and then say the order was incorrect when he got back with it and toss it in the trash. She enjoyed coming up with complicated and improbable orders. She apparently enjoyed tormenting the baristas as well. Every day she found some new way to twist the thorn in his side. One day she made him sharpen a box of 1000 pencils with an old fashioned hand crank pencil sharpener. If she was in a position to do so without it being obvious, she would trip him, but only when he was carrying coffee. It started out small like this, but of course as such things do, it escalated.

Death not being an issue, or at least not permanently, makes people with a tendency towards cruelty a little more bold than they might otherwise be. This gave Astrid leave to torment Henry in ways that might otherwise have killed him. On more than one occasion she poisoned him. When he became ill, everyone assumed he had eaten something that had gone off from some secret store of food. One time he actually did die, sweaty, feverish and dazed in his room. Because it was nighttime, he rose as a ghost out of his body. With nothing better to do he went up to the roof and lay there looking up at the stars until morning.

That was his first 'death' in Heaven. Yes, there wasn't pain as such, but the fever, fatigue, sweatiness, and disorientation were discomfort enough. He remembered something Burhan had said, that ghosts made the best spies. He wanted to snoop around but was apprehensive. He also wasn't too keen on dying again.

Each time that Astrid managed to cause him some public torment, she would write him up. She filled out disciplinary paperwork on him for arriving 1 minute late, leaving 2 minutes early, causing a nuisance by dropping pencils, ruining carpet with spilled coffee and for hiding and consuming food, the proof of which had been his very public and embarrassing illnesses. (He had thrown up in an office trash can). She liked to tell him, with a gleam in her eye, that if he managed to accumulate several of such notices, he would receive a more severe punishment. She wouldn't say what it was, but she said the word 'punishment' as if it were delicious.

Finally, it happened. Astrid called him in to her office one morning and handed him some papers. "Go put these in the shredder," she said absently. Henry took the papers and left. He knew better than to do exactly what she said. He stopped in the office and examined them. They appeared to be the approval for three pardons. Henry had never seen pardons before but that was what the language seemed to indicate. Two cafeteria workers and a barista would leave service and enter Heaven in light of their excellent service. Rather than shred them he took them to Katie, an assignment secretary.

"Oh, I've been waiting for those. Thanks, Hank." She smiled. "Good news is rare enough around here." Henry tried to conceal his grimace. He hated being called 'Hank'. It was something only Americans did and it annoyed him to no end. He had told her twice not to do it, but she never appeared to listen much.

"Ahem, yes…well for some reason Astrid told me to shred them, so I brought them to you thinking it must be a mistake." Katie's little face hardened. "Thanks for bringing this to me," she said and picked up her phone.

Henry didn't think much of the incident until it blew up in his face a few days later. He knew that anything and everything that he did, good or bad, would probably be used against him in some way, but he had given up trying to predict anything. He also couldn't do much about it. As much as it pained him, he had to keep up his cover: mild mannered professor, penitent and helpful. With Astrid in the mix it complicated things. Now while the iron was hot, she dealt her first real blow.

In the morning Astrid called him into her office.

"Henry, you have caused a lot of problems since you arrived, but this time you've gone too far," she said. Henry waited. He was accustomed to her tirades. "On Monday I told you to copy some paperwork and take it to the assignment office. You told the secretary there that I said to shred them."

"You did tell me to shred them, Astrid," Henry said.

"How dare you lie to me! Those papers were pardons Henry, pardons. Now because of your lies those people will have to wait to get them until we get this straightened out. I mean really, Henry, it wasn't even a good lie…ridiculous. I just can't understand why you would want to hurt those poor people just to get at me. You're practically a tyrant. It's so hard to work here

142

every day with you hurting me in all these ways. I just, I have to do something about it. I can't let your disrespectful and disruptive behavior continue without redress." She sighed as if pained. "I didn't want to do this but…" She sat at her desk, opened a drawer and pulled out an orange half sheet of paper. She filled out some lines and then signed it. "Here, Henry. You will get an appointment in a few days. Now, go back to work and…I expect to see improvement." She turned and picked up her phone. Henry took the paper and walked out of her office.

Henry walked past the cubicle of the North American Regional coordinators desk, a nice Hispanic woman named Chloe. When she saw Henry's paper she gasped.

"Oh Henry, she didn't," she said sadly.

"Chloe, what is level 2 penance?" Henry asked. Chloe stood up and moved close to him. She put a hand on his shoulder and half whispered.

"It's pain, Henry. They'll give you back pain," she said. Henry frowned.

"How? Is it permanent? More importantly is there an appeal of some kind? Astrid's bullying is getting ridiculous…actually we passed ridiculous two weeks ago when she poisoned me." Henry sighed.

"You can take it above her head to the VP but it won't do any good. Word is, he's totally in her pocket…and HR always defends the Castle, not the worker. They will do whatever they can to make you look like the bad guy, even if your complaint is legit. Oh Henry, I am afraid for you. Please be careful." She squeezed his shoulder.

"I will try, Chloe. I will try," Henry said.

*****

Henry was making copies when Astrid came in to the spaces. "Henry, take everybody's order and get coffee. You should know by now what I want." She left and had seemed distracted when she spoke. Henry took his copies and picked up a yellow notepad and pen from a nearby table. He walked around to all the regional coordinators, taking their orders. Next he went down the hallway and went into a dark closet. He opened the next door very slowly and carefully, trying not to make any noise. He listened at the crack for what was going on in the Judgment Hall.

"Can't you do anything right?" Peter said. "I told you to put that folder in the red outbox." Henry knew he was safe if Peter was openly berating the two monks. It meant they were in between judgments. He walked in. As soon as Todd, one of the two monks in brown robes, saw him, he brightened up.

"Henry, I'm happy to see you, friend. Are you taking coffee orders?" Todd said.

"Yes, I am. Go ahead."

"Ok, I will have a caramel macchiato, decaf. I don't want to get all jittery," Todd said.

"Sure thing," Henry said as he wrote. "So that drink gives you the jitters?"

"No, I just already had a regular coffee this morning and I don't want to push it. The office coffee at our station is bitter and way too strong," Todd said making a face. With his hand concealed in front of his body he jerked his thumb towards Peter. Henry nodded.

"Ah, I see. And what about Brad?" Henry asked. Brad shouted over.

"Hey Henry, I want a Columbian Dark, cream and 2 sugars," Brad said. Henry nodded and wrote.

"Quit shouting, boy. It's undignified," Peter grumbled at him. Brad rolled his eyes. Henry turned back to Todd.

"What about..." he looked at Peter and back at Todd.

"Oh him...oddly enough he likes a fat coffee lately, 3 sugars and double cream," Todd said.

"That is odd," Henry agreed. "Alright then. You gentlemen are all set. And I will have it back for you soon." Henry smiled.

"Ah thank you, Henry. You're a lifesaver," Todd said. Henry nodded and left through the same dark door he had used to come in. Before he left, he stole one wistful glance at the stained glass section that he knew was really a portal to Elysium. He could just walk through it right now and be done with all this silliness, with Astrid and her bullying. He sighed and left the Judgment Hall, shutting the door behind him.

A thought struck him then about St. Peter. How or why did he look old? He was one of the few people he had seen who actually looked over 35. He was paunchy and had salt and pepper hair with more salt than pepper. He still looked reasonably young and healthy, maybe 50 or so, but it was obvious that he was no spring chicken. Had he really been doing that job for over 1900 years? Did he ever get a holiday? Why was he so mean and condescending? Perhaps 1900 years of the sins of humanity would do that to a fellow. Henry chuckled. He walked out of the castle into glorious sunlight and the open street. He stepped up to the coffee stand. He handed the paper to the friendly barista he knew there, Jared.

"Jared, I need a favor…and it's not a small one," Henry said. Jared grinned.

Chapter 25

There is No Berry Cobbler in Hell

Henry carried a ream of paper and some file folders as he went down to the basement of the Castle where the penance office was. It too had a small waiting room. It was not like any room he had seen as the walls of the room where a rough, tan stone, like the outside of the castle and the chairs were all of a dark wood. There were two pictures awkwardly hung on opposite walls. One was of a beach at sunset. The other was of a kitten, hanging on a branch. The words "Hang in there." were printed in white at the bottom of the poster. Henry chuckled. 'Any time you see that poster, you know you are nearer to hell,' he thought.

He checked in at a sliding window and then sat down and waited. There was only one other person in the office, a woman who looked like she had been crying recently. Henry left her alone. After 10 minutes or so they called in the woman. Another 10 and they called Henry's name.

A pleasant brunette opened the door and said, "Henry, please come with me." They walked down a hallway that seemed normal enough except for those rock walls and a strange, faint odor, as if something had been burning.

"What...what is that smell?" Henry asked as the woman led him into an examining room. She wrinkled her nose.

"Oh that, I don't even smell it anymore. Here you go. Someone will be with you shortly." She closed the door and Henry thought he heard a file being placed in the door shelf, just like at a doctor's office. He looked around the room. There were some cabinets, a sink, a doctor's stool with wheels on the bottom, a couple of small "waiting" chairs, and one bigger chair, like an examination table at the doctor, but not quite. The chair was upholstered with black leather and did not look like it reclined. A tinge of apprehension made its way into Henry's stomach. He picked up a magazine from the table and tried to relax. He read the title and immediately put it back down. It was entitled "101 Sin Free Ways to Deal with Boredom: A Self Help Primer." 'Will I never learn', he thought and sighed.

There was a small knock at the door. Henry said, "Come in". A man entered, or at least a humanoid entered. He wasn't exactly a man. Henry blinked and realized he was looking at a demon…a demon in a white doctor's coat, a powder-blue collared shirt and tan slacks. His feet were bare because the claw-like structures that were his feet would not have worked in human shoes. The demon had a relatively normal face except for the reddish brown skin, dark horns, and fangs. He smiled. One of the longer fangs was golden.

"Hello, Henry. What can we do for you today?" His voice was deep, but surprisingly normal. He took a seat on the wheeled doctor's chair and rolled over to him. He looked through Henry's chart. "Oh, the gift of pain, eh? Somebody's mad at you." He wagged a finger at Henry and chuckled. "Did you do anything or does your boss just not like you?" he asked.

"She just doesn't like me. Or actually, I think she just doesn't like anyone. She torments everybody in the office somehow or another." Henry sighed.

"You know it's amazing how many people like that end up in leadership positions in the administration. We could use them downstairs, that kind of talent, but they always get mad and say, 'That's offensive' and 'I don't belong in hell and blah , blah, blah…It's kind of funny…so anyway are we going to do this or…?" he asked. Henry nodded. He still had his folders and ream of paper. He brought the ream to the top and ripped the paper off. Instead of paper there was a cardboard box under the wrapper. He lifted the lid and showed the demon a lovely cobbler.

"Oooh! A whole cobbler. Wow! That is great. You are slick my friend, slick. Hand it over. Is it babies?" he asked expectantly as he looked at the cobbler and reached out for it.

"Ah NO, no no. It's not …that. It's berry I think…like a mixed berry." Henry handed it to him. The demon sniffed at the cobbler.

"Ah yes. Mmmm, wonderful. Yes, that will certainly do it, my friend. Who doesn't love a baby…I mean a berry cobbler. Excellent." The demon smiled at him. Henry peed a little. The demon lowered his voice and moved in closer to Henry. "So, now I won't really do it, you understand, but we need to keep up appearances. So, I'm going to burn your forehead a little bit, but not with my thumb like I normally would; I will use a cigar instead. I'm sorry about this, especially since you went to so much trouble, but make-up just won't cut it. Ok?" he asked. Henry nodded, feeling surreal. This man…er demon…was frightening to look at, but his demeanor and body language had all the hallmarks of a good bedside manner. Henry fought the urge to giggle.

The demon turned around and from out of a drawer he pulled a big cigar. He cut the end off with a cigar cutter from the same drawer, lit it with a silver lighter, also from the drawer, and inhaled deeply. He smiled as smoke billowed from his nostrils. "Smooth," he said as he appeared to enjoy himself. Henry frowned.

"You know um…doctor…a friend told me that I could do this…bring you something…but I still don't really understand why? I mean, can't you have anything you want to eat?" The demon was busy loading a syringe with some clear liquid from a small bottle while he smoked. He talked around the cigar, holding it in his teeth.

"Well, yes and no. It's not just about the food. The food is good, but uh …I like to game the system too, if you know what I mean." He winked at Henry. "But…it's true that they don't have stuff like that downstairs. It's all charred meat and blood…not much variety." The demon puffed and smiled around his cigar. Smoke streamed from his nostrils. "No, my friend, there is no berry cobbler in hell." He put the syringe down and fumbled with some blue laytex gloves. As he was putting them on, one of them ripped over one of his claws.

"That happens a lot." He chuckled and got a replacement glove from the box and put it on.

"Alright, Henry, hop up in the chair and let's numb you up a little." The demon patted the seat of the black chair in the center of the room. Henry climbed awkwardly into it. The demon carefully and gently injected Henry's forehead with some sort of numbing medicine. "Little pinch…there that's it. Now, let's let that take effect." Henry was frowning. "Is there something bothering you?" the demon asked.

"Well, if you don't give me the …gift of pain as you call it, why will the burn hurt…and why did I feel that pinch?" Henry asked.

"It's just because I'm a demon. If I touch you at all with my skin, it will burn you and you will get the gift…and just being around me makes it so that you can feel pain again, temporarily. Sorry man, I can't do anything about that…it's a hellfire thing." The demon shrugged.

"How does one, remove the gift of pain?" Henry asked.

"Oh, then you just have to get an angel to touch you. They can remove the pain. They uh…they don't like cobbler though, if you know what I mean." The demon winked at Henry and then sat back puffing on his cigar. Little bits of ash would fall to the floor when he moved. "Now, Henry, it's still going to hurt when I burn you, but it won't be near as bad as the real thing so here's the deal…you gotta make this look and sound good. Ok? When you really get the gift of pain, you have pain again…so if somebody pokes you, if you stub your toe, if that bitch boss of yours jabs a pitchfork in you…whatever…you've got to remember that it hurts and then act accordingly, ok?" he asked. Henry nodded. "Ok, good. Now also, when I do burn you, I want you to yell…got it? I mean it will hurt a little, but don't be stoic….yell loudly so they can hear you out there. One of those office bitches is a snitch. Got it?"

"Yes, I think so," Henry said.

"Ready pal?" he asked.

"As I will ever be," Henry replied.

"Alright then." The demon puffed on the cigar so that it was good and hot then he jabbed it right between Henry's eyebrows and held it there for a few seconds. It didn't really hurt that much.

"Yell," the demon whispered.

"Ahaaahahahooooahaahaahahahaha," Henry yelled.

"More, more," the demon whispered.

"AHHOOOOahahahaooooooo," Henry yelled.

"More, go high, like you're a girl," the demon whispered. Henry screamed and yelled and generally over did it.

"AHHHHAHAHAHEEEEEEEEEOHOHOOHAAHAHAA HEHEHEEEOOHOHOHOHAAAAA!"

"Awesome…awesome….good…enough…enough you're done," he said.

A black and red, raw, bleeding, smoldering mess was left on Henry's forehead. The demon looked at it, nodded and smiled at his work. He held his hand up in an A-OK signal. "Oh, hey can you make yourself cry?"

"Well, I could probably work myself up if…." Henry said. The demon interrupted him.

"Ah, no problem. I've got something for that too," he said. He reached into a drawer and pulled out a metal box. He opened it up and held it in front of Henry. Immediately Henry's eyes began to water and burn. He choked and coughed.

"What…what is that?" Henry asked.

"Just a little bit of brimstone I keep around," he said.

"It's awful," Henry coughed.

"Yup, does the job every time." The demon smiled. "Ok, now you can go but remember what I said about keeping up appearances. Don't make me look bad, ok?"

"No worries," Henry said and smiled. He grabbed some tissues from a box and held them up to his forehead. He gathered up his folders and walked out, head hanging low. The demon held the door open for him. Henry walked out through the empty waiting room, sniffling and crying. The desk attendant watched him go, shaking her head. For her benefit, Henry let out a sob on the way out.

Chapter 26

Inquisition

Lauren was unceremoniously dropped out of the sky next to a portal closer to town. Two members of the Guard were waiting for her with handcuffs. They restrained her and led her through the portal. The angel followed. They came out of a portal in the center of New Jerusalem, right across the street from the sprawling Castle. As soon as they stepped through the portal, the angel flew up and quickly out of sight. The Guardsmen, each with a hand on Lauren's arm, led her past a stand that looked a lot like a Starbucks. A man was getting coffee there. He looked very familiar.

"Henry!" she shouted once. It was Henry and he turned, staring. The Guardsmen dragged her as she began to struggle. One of them backhanded her.

"Quiet, whore," he said. Henry ran over to them, walked along with them while Lauren struggled to look at him.

"Stop, please, stop, just a minute, please stop," Henry said. The Guardsmen stopped and glared at him.

"Do you know this woman?" One of them asked. Henry looked at her. Tears began to fill his eyes. He started to speak,

"Ye…

"No…" Lauren said quickly. "He's not…he's not who I thought he was." She shook her head 'no' subtly as she looked into Henry's eyes. The Guardsmen merely grunted and dragged her away. Henry stood staring. Lauren looked back at him, tears streaming down her face. She mouthed the word "wait". Henry nodded and turned back towards the coffee stand.

The Guardsmen held Lauren's arms and walked her through a wooden door in a rock wall fence. They traveled through one section of garden with roses and then through another door in a wall. Lauren had never been in this part of the Castle and had no idea where she was. She had only ever seen the Waiting Room, the Judgment Hall and then the reception garden where people who were going directly into Heaven were welcomed.

The trio traveled down two flights of stairs into a barren looking basement and then through a portal right next to another set of stairs that went up. Neither Guardsman said anything before they entered the portal. As they exited the portal, Lauren was surprised to see sunlight. The Guardsman led her into a large, round room with stone walls. Cells made entirely of metal bars sat on either side of a short walkway to the other side of the room. The room looked like empty storage and the cells, a discarded afterthought. High windows on either side of the room showed blue sky and nothing else. Instead of a door or a window, the other side of the room ended in a hole in the wall through which the wind steadily flowed. It smelled like the ocean. Clues floated up in her mind and solidified into an unhappy realization. She was in the tower, Heaven's notorious prison. Her heart sank.

The Guardsmen took her down the walkway to the very last cell and for a moment she thought they would just push her out of the tower through the hole. Instead, they opened the cell door and shoved her in. From inside her cell she could look down through the open wall and see ocean waves crashing on black rocks below. The height was dizzying. The Guardsman turned and left through the portal without a word.

Lauren looked around the little cell and then sat on the bare mattress of the lower bunk bed. There was a sink, but it was rusted out and looked dry. There was a seatless metal toilet attached to the wall but it also had no water in it. The wind whipped in and out of the cell, mussing her hair and pulling at her dress. She sat down in the corner, farthest from the hole in the wall where the wind wasn't quite so direct. There she huddled in a little ball and cried. For a while, she slept.

*****

After an unknown amount of time she woke up to the squawking of a large sea bird.

"What?" she said out loud as she woke with a start. A large, grey bird that looked almost like a pelican was standing outside her cell, squawking at her.

"What do you want?" she said to the bird. The bird turned its head and trained one large black eye on her. It seemed to look her over and then, with a final loud squawk, it flapped away through the hole. Lauren began to look around her cell for something she could use to kill herself.

"Come back here and kill me you dumb bird," she said aloud, "then I could get out of here." She continued to look but there was nothing useful in the cell. Her own breezy, sleeveless dress was not long enough to hang herself with. She tried to squeeze through some of the bars, but they were two close together, even if she managed to break some bones. She sat back on the floor in her corner and began to pick at the rock wall with her finger.

Later, towards evening, two Guardsmen came through the portal and marched down to her cell. It was not the same two Guardsmen but it might as well have been. They wore the same cheesy, silver and gold armor and had the same hard, disinterested stares. They opened her cell door and came in. One of them grabbed her, turned her around roughly and handcuffed her again.

"Seriously?" she asked. The men did not respond. They led her again through the portal and stepped out of the one in the basement that she had seen before. They escorted her down two, quiet, semi-dark hallways of the same rough, tan stone that the castle walls were made of. They stopped in front of a door and knocked twice. The door opened and she was led in and seated in a chair facing a grey, metal table. The Guardsmen left and Lauren was left alone with a dark haired, brown-eyed man wearing a grey suit and matching tie. He turned his head to shut the door and she saw that he had an earpiece connected to a transparent wire tube that curled along his neck and disappeared down the back of his suit. In the room there was just the one battleship grey table and matching uncomfortable chairs. The four walls of the room were white except for a large one way window on one side. In one corner, near the ceiling, she saw a video camera. The whole thing was a little silly. She suppressed a rising giggle.

"Lauren Hall of New Waialua, we have security footage of you going through a missionary portal." He waited for her to react. Lauren remained silent.

"You approached the well at 2:37am. You sat there for a few minutes. You entered at 2:45am and came back out at 2:46am. Then you ran off like you were afraid for your life. Mrs. Hall, would you care to explain this?" he asked. Lauren continued to sit and watch him, careful to keep her face expressionless. She got the impression that he didn't really want to be there, like he was acting intimidating instead of actually being intimidating.

"You see, we don't really get why anyone would go down there. First, it's forbidden, but that's just for your own safety. Our missionaries are trained to deal with the hazards down there. It's very dangerous as you must have seen," he said.

Lauren snorted. She thought of Moe, Larry, and Curly going through "special training" to be missionaries. She couldn't help but smile.

"Have you recently been in a relationship with a Muslim man named Burhan?" he asked. Lauren's smile evaporated as she envisioned Moe, Larry and Curly being replaced by Burhan; Burhan with his face full of love and sadness as he looked back at her in the courtyard before disappearing forever into the underworld.

"I should tell you, Mrs. Hall that Burhan is not what he seems. He's actually a spy and a rebel. The Heathens are trying to start a war with us. They are spying on us, stealing our children. They are trying to steal our women too and one…one almost succeeded, didn't he? At least that's what your mother said." Lauren shot him an irritated look and then immediately regretted it. 'I've got to keep my cool,' she thought. 'What can I tell them that will make them let me go?'

"Well, that hit a nerve," the man said, rubbing his hands together. "Oh yes, mom spilled the beans about your boyfriend. So, I guess my next question for you is, are you just a stupid whore who opens her legs to every man who happens to swim by your house? Or are you one of them?" He got right down on the table and came too close to her face. He whispered, "What's worse than a whore? Well, a Pagan whore of course. All of you down there are whores aren't you?" He was trying to make her angry. He backed off and stood there looking down at her. He raised his eyebrows at her as if to say 'yeah, that's right. I said it'. She looked back at him, looked him up and down. Then she sat back in the chair, looked at her nails and sighed.

"WELL?" he yelled, red faced. "WHAT ARE YOU?"

"Bored mostly. I mean are you serious? Is the good cop going to come in and offer me a cup of coffee and a cigarette while you go out in the hallway and 'cool off' or something? You're the lamest interrogator I've ever seen. Were you a D list actor? Reality TV maybe?"

"Hey," he said in a hurt voice.

"Mm hmm, thought so. You need to work harder on being intimidating. I could tell the whole time that your heart wasn't really in it." Lauren turned directly towards the video camera and started talking.

"Look, this is what happened. I met Burhan. He was a nice guy and he stayed with our family for a few weeks. When I watched him go down the well with that boy I was just as shocked as anybody. I had no idea. He never said anything about the underworld or plans or anything. He never said anything bad about the government. He talked about his family and his youth in the Sorrowful World. He was…" She almost said 'He was sweet,' but thought better of it. "He was friendly and kind and the mark of Islam was on his forehead. I believed he was good and never had a reason not to. We all did. That was it. We all got taken," she looked at the floor. The interrogator pressed his finger to his earpiece.

"Did you know the boy he took?" he asked.

"No, I never saw him before that day."

"Why did you run from us?" he asked.

"My family was afraid for me. I think they thought…I'd be tortured or something. They just wanted to protect me."

"Why did you go through the missionary portal?" he asked.

"Would you believe I was just curious? I mean, I heard the rumors about it, like everybody does, but the missionaries in our town didn't seem so tough…not like the Guard anyway…they just seemed like regular guys. I thought it couldn't be that bad if they could handle it," she answered.

"What happened? Why did you run out?" the interrogator asked. He wasn't trying to be intimidating anymore.

"As soon as I came through, some angry, half-naked men starting running towards me and yelling. I was scared so I came back through." He paused a minute to listen to his earpiece.

"Did you see anything?" he asked.

"No, it was dark. I think I heard the ocean and I saw…like a campfire."

"How did you figure out how to get through the portal?" he asked.

"Jesus, it's not that hard. I just watched the missionaries and saw them pull out the cross. They don't hide it or anything." When Lauren said, 'Jesus', the interrogator's eyes widened and he waved his hands in front of his body as if to say 'don't say that'. He listened to his earpiece. "Yup, okay," he said. He flashed her the 'A-Okay' sign with his hand. He knocked on the door and said to the Guardsmen "Take her back up."

The two men came in and lifted her up and out of her chair.

"Wait, why? I told you everything. That's all I know. Wait…why can't I just go home?" she asked.

"Oh don't worry, they probably just can't let you go until they finish up your paperwork," said the interrogator.

The Guardsmen manhandled her again, out into the hallways, through the portal, and up into her windy cell. They shoved her in but did not remove the handcuffs.

"Hey!" she called. "Hey, take off the cuffs! Come back!" Without a word, they stepped through the portal and were gone, replaced by wind and the distant sounds of waves.

*****

Lauren lay on the mattress in the cell, scrunched up her legs, and struggled until she managed to get her handcuffed hands in front of her. There were four bunks in the cell, each with their own dingy, bare mattress. She sat cross legged on the one closest to the hole in the wall and watched the sunset. If she got down on the floor and sat in the corner that was closest to the open wall, she could look directly up and see the rest of the tower above her. She could also see a cloud swept shadow high above that did not move as clouds passed by. She knew that on the other side of that dark shape was the abode of the angels. Their world was always sunny and always lit with stars at night. She thought if she stared long enough she just might see one flit by. Looking back down toward the blue ocean, a shape caught her eye. A little ways out from the black rocks at the very bottom of the tower she could just make out a shape of dark rock under the water. It looked like a big 'U'. The water looked shallow from her altitude, the way that lakes and rivers look like puddles and streams from an airplane. There were no other visible rocks around the U shape. It was just there. Feeling bored, angry, silly, and a little tired she started naming things that started with U.

"Useful…Ulysses…Usurper…Ugly…Unguent…Underwear," she giggled. She sat looking out at the ocean and sky until it was too dark to see much. While she still had a little light, she pried one of mattresses up from the metal support on the windy side, lay down on the other bottom bunk and used the freed mattress as a kind of blanket. It was too thick to cover her or bend much, but it did protect her from the wind enough so that she could sleep. She didn't sleep well or for very long, but when she did, she dreamt of large, grey seabirds squawking at her and flying away from the tower over the open ocean. In the dream, she turned into a sea bird. She knew she could fly away, but she was still in the cage and couldn't get out.

No one came to her that evening, all night, or most of the next day. She picked at the rock wall some more and even tried kicking the toilet for a bit to see if she could break it. Some rust fell off, but that was it. Mostly she sat in the corner of the cell closest to the open wall and watched. When the tide was fully out, the U shape was more clearly visible. 'How deep was it?' she wondered, '20, maybe 30 feet?' It was difficult to tell. Tide in or tide out, she could see it.

Near sunset, someone did come. Lauren was sitting in the windward corner of her cell watching the sun's descent through some stratified clouds, when two people came through the portal and walked to her cell. There was a funny smell in the room. Lauren suddenly became aware that her legs were stiff and sore from sitting in one position for so long. Her stomach burned with hunger and her lip was sore from when the Guardsman backhanded her. 'How in the…' she thought to herself as she realized she was feeling aches and pains. She touched her lip. "Ouch", she whispered and pulled her hand away.

One of the men took a seat on a stool near the portal and the stairs. He sat in shadow. Lauren could not see his features. She heard the flick of a lighter and saw an orange glow. Soon the smell of cigar smoke floated her way.

The other man walked down to her cell, opened it, stepped in, and closed the door behind him. Lauren began to feel truly scared. She got to her feet and said, "Where …" but her question was interrupted by a backhand to her face. Pain radiated from her cheek and around her head. She reeled and fell back into the bars of the cell. The man didn't really look like much. He wasn't muscular or tall. He was thin faced and skinny. His skin looked a bit pale in the red light of the sunset. He reached down and grabbed a handful of her hair and yanked her up from the floor. She cried out and swung at him with her handcuffed fists. Contact

157

was made with some part of him, but when she looked up she saw only the thin line of a smile.

"Now," he said with a quiet, breathy voice, "you will tell me everything."

"I already did," Lauren pleaded. "I told them everything. I didn't really know..." again he backhanded her. She fell to the floor. Something was wrong with her eye. It felt funny. She tried to open it, but wasn't sure it was open. Everything there was black. After a few seconds a blurry image returned but she struggled to see anything on that side. She looked up at him with her good eye. As soon as she did, she was hit again.

The man punched her. He backhanded her again. She felt something crack in her jaw. She tried to fight back but he just laughed. She began to feel woozy. On her knees in front of him she retched but only yellow bile came out. Her throat burned. He hoisted her up by the neck and said just as softly as he did before, "Tell me about Burhan." He pushed her down onto her mattress.

"I already told you. I met him. He stayed with us. He was my," she coughed, "boyfriend. I didn't know he was...I didn't know anything about him," she said slowly, trying to find the words through the daze and the pain in her jaw. The man grabbed her arms and pinned her down on the mattress with one knee. He reached into his coat pocket and brought out a pair of pliers. His eyes gleamed. He began to pry out her thumbnail. Lauren screamed.

This sort of thing went on for some time, though Lauren had no real concept of time in the process. He pulled out more nails, asked questions, used the pliers to break the small bones of some of her fingers, asked more questions. Lauren threw up a few more times. She began to wish she had something in her stomach to throw up. She answered every question with her increasingly scratchy and useless throat. Every time she said she didn't know the answer she was punished somehow so she began to make things up. She said that Burhan was a terrorist, that he loved to drink and curse god while he drank. As she got more and more punch drunk she started to say that he was a sailor in the deep blue sea and that he knew where all the mines were.

Finally, he stopped. Lauren lay on the floor, bleeding from her nose and mouth. She heard footsteps.

"She doesn't know anything else. She's just a stupid whore who got taken advantage of," said the man.

"Well, did you have to beat her up so bad? She's been saying that the whole time," said the other man. The air still stank of cigar and whatever that other, acrid smell was.

"It always works. When they start making things up, you know you've got it all. We're done here," said the man. He walked back to Lauren's cell and opened the door. He dragged her by the hair over to the edge where the wall was missing and then kept going, dragging her right through the hole in the wall and over the edge. Lauren was only barely aware that she was hurtling towards the ground. "Good," she whispered and landed on the black rocks at the base of the tower.

*****

Lauren rose up out of her broken body, a wispy, night spirit. She sat on the rocks near her body and sighed. Waves gradually lifted it up and she watched it float away slowly. She decided to wait there until morning as she wasn't sure what would happen if she tried to rez through a portal. She had never died this far from home before.

With her head finally clear of pain and concussion, she decided to walk underwater. She didn't want a ghost-hunting angel to find her, catch her, and drop her back at the tower. Auntie Rosie had told her that the angels can rez by touch and that if criminals escaped in ghost form at night, angels would be on patrol.

Given the inefficiency of the Castle, it was also not so far-fetched that they had already lost her paperwork and would make her do the whole thing over again, including interrogation and torture. She had to hide and get home.

She walked downhill into the ocean darkness as if the surface wasn't even there. 'Don't go too far or too deep' she thought to herself. She didn't want to resurrect into 50 feet of water and drown. As she walked there was some movement that caught her eye. She turned and looked up to see her own battered body floating above her. It didn't look like her. It didn't even look human. Her left eye was swollen shut. Some of her teeth were missing. There were cuts above both eyes. A dark shape on her jaw might have been a bruise. She looked away and kept walking. Her thoughts turned to Henry. Through all the pain and haze of her beating, she had almost forgotten their brief meeting.

She wondered about him. Where was he? Was he looking for her? How did he end up in service? Was it the agnostic thing? That seemed a little harsh, though who knows what he said to St. Peter. He could have really stuck his foot in it. It would be just like Henry to say the wrong thing to St. Peter and end up in service for a hundred years. Service workers in the Castle were practically sequestered. It would be difficult to see him. 'Oh Henry' she whispered, 'what have we gotten ourselves into?'

These thoughts and more swirled around in her mind. She wondered if it was really over. Would they just get her again, torture her again? She found some rocks on the sea floor and absently walked on them like a little girl walking on a curb. The perfect curve of an arch made her realize that this was it. She was walking on the big U that she had seen from her tower cell. Here it was right under her feet. She walked its full length, back and forth and back again. She sat down on the edge of the rock. Her legs came down into the interior of the u-shape and with a ghostly gasp she felt the mild, metallic resistance of a portal. Her feet came through and she wiggled her toes in dry air that she could not see. She lay down flat on the rocks and reached her arm through. Through the portal, her hand and arm felt remarkably solid. She felt around. Her hand came to rest on a handle of some sort. She pulled. Gently through the portal came a long handle and the floppy, stringy head of a mop. As soon she pulled it through the portal, she couldn't grasp it anymore. The mop slowly floated up and away, its grey cords swaying gently. 'What the?' Lauren thought. 'Portals don't make you rez.' Suddenly, she felt a familiar tingle. The sky had grown lighter and she was beginning to resurrect. She headed back towards the shore. Almost as soon as she came out of the water and sat on one of the rocks, she was completely back into her body. She took a deep breath, relieved to be whole again. She pinched and poked herself on her arm, roughly, to make sure she wasn't feeling any pain. Thankfully, it was gone.

Lauren realized that she was not alone. A brown haired man in khaki pants and a light blue shirt came stepping from stone to stone towards her. He stopped and looked at her.

"What'd you do?" he asked.

"I...I got drunk in town and said some bad stuff about the government," Lauren answered.

"Ah, yep. That'll do it."

"What'd you do?" Lauren asked him.

"Oh nothing. My boss just doesn't like me. She likes to have me thrown out of the tower," He sighed.

"Where do you work?" Lauren asked.

"Assignments," he said. "Speaking of, I better get back to work. Have a good one," he smiled at her and sauntered off down the beach. She watched him go. When she turned her head in the other direction she saw another man, naked, walking along the beach and holding a brown shoe over his genitals. He disappeared around a corner.

Lauren got up, looked herself over, and started walking along the beach where she knew there was a portal she could use to go home. She walked along until she saw it in the distance. Then she began to run.

Chapter 27

Sex, Lies, and Webcams

Henry walked back up from the demon's office to the Waiting Room offices on the first floor and started going about his duties as normal. His eyes continued to water. They also felt scratchy. Henry thought they must be bloodshot. He walked into the mail room and came back out with a wheeled cart. Someone gasped and the room became very quiet. Heads popped up out of cubicles like gophers, wide eyes centered on Henry's forehead. Henry stopped by Chloe's desk to pick up some outgoing mail. She grabbed his arm.

"I'm so sorry, Henry," she whispered. Henry patted her on her arm. He had thought, leaving the demon's office, that he might have trouble behaving correctly, but his coworkers sad faces and teary eyes made him feel so bad that it didn't matter. Just then, Astrid came out of her office and addressed Chloe.

"Chloe, do you know if Henry is back yet?...Oh there you are, Henry. I need you to..." She stopped. Henry had been facing away from her, but he turned around. Her eyes went to his forehead, to his face. Henry glared at her.

"Yes, Astrid, what did you need?" Henry asked. He tried to sound as normal as possible but he couldn't keep the anger out of his voice. She stuttered.

"I...uh....I want you to..." She kept looking back at his forehead, looking away again, and then back. "You should...take the rest of the day off and we'll see you in tomorrow," she said. Henry nodded and wheeled the mail cart back to the mail room. Behind him he heard Chloe ask with barely suppressed rage, "Are you happy now? Does that make you feel better?" Astrid turned away quickly and went to her office. She shut the door behind her.

*****

No one had to tell Henry twice to knock off early so he left. He went home and took a hot shower. He sat on his bed and watched TV in his pajama bottoms and a thin, white undershirt. He had a bottle of black market booze stowed away under a floor board. He didn't know what it was but it tasted very similar to

Southern Comfort. He nipped at the bottle a few times and put it away. Eventually he nodded off.

Sometime later there was a knock at the door. There were no locks on the doors so people could just enter if they wanted to, but so far people had been polite and still knocked. Henry woke up and went to the door.

"Yes," he said sleepily. He jumped. It was Astrid. She looked almost remorseful.

"Henry, can I…can I talk to you? Can I come in?" she said.

"Well, I can't really stop you, there's no lock." He walked away from the open door and sat on his bed. He pointed at a nearby desk chair. Astrid entered the room, pulled the chair away from the desk, and sat down primly. She looked around his room and then at his forehead. The open wound there was about the size of a quarter. It was pink and orange and red and crusted over with dried blood and pus. The skin around it was either bright red or charred black. As she looked, the faint wisp of the cross appeared, even over and through that charred mess of flesh. She looked away.

"Henry, I am so sorry. I wanted to tell you that. I know I've been horrible to you. I know I went too far. I didn't know. I thought they just touched you and then you could feel pain again. I didn't think it burned…" at that she began to cry. Henry slid over and sat closer to her on the edge of the bed. He felt conflicted. He wanted to help her, to comfort her, but he still didn't trust her. Her remorse looked real, but was it part of some twisted game? She took some tissues out of her purse and dabbed at her face. "I don't blame you, Henry. I wouldn't trust me either."

"Look Astrid, maybe you don't realize it, but you have been bullying me mercilessly since I arrived. From what I've seen, you aren't very nice to my coworkers either. I don't know why. I don't know what any of us have done to offend you so…" She interrupted him.

"Nothing….you've all done nothing. I just…I was just so angry," she said through more tears. "I was angry that I was assigned service, angry at myself for what I did…and I took it out on all of you." She sniffed and wiped her face. "When I saw…what they did to you…what I did to you Henry…I'm so sorry. I'm dead and I haven't learned my lesson. How stupid is that?" She stared at her purse and tissues. Henry began to feel sorry for her.

"Well, Astrid, Heaven is grand and all," Henry said sarcastically and waved his hand to indicate the room, "but uh…we still have free will. I think that if any of us is endowed with free will, we will continue to make mistakes. We are not perfect creatures, you know."

"Henry I….um," She took a deep breath. "I committed suicide, you know. That's why I'm in service." Henry was shocked. He sat there looking at her, speechless. "Are you surprised?" she asked.

"Yes, I'm very surprised, very surprised indeed. You…you had it all. You were successful, beautiful…" Henry frowned. "I am also a bit surprised that they weren't more…that you didn't get punished more severely for that. I thought that was a bigger sin," Henry said. Astrid nodded.

"Well, I…I did it because I had cancer. I was in a lot of pain most of the time. If I had been healthy it would have been a different story…with punishment…but I probably only had a year left or so anyway but I just…I didn't want to go through it alone. I just wanted it to be over with." She sniffed.

"Oh, Astrid, I am so sorry," Henry said and he meant it. There was an awkward pause. Henry cleared his throat.

"Well, you know my mistake. I walked right up to old St. Peter and said…." Henry blew a raspberry with his tongue. Astrid managed a smile.

"Yes, it must have been awful for you down there," she said. Henry was about to say that, no, it had been perfectly lovely and was actually much better than this place when he caught himself.

"Oh, yes, yes it was," he looked at the floor to avoid looking at her. "But now I am here and safe and I can help other people. I'd really like to help other people like me, in the Waiting Room, you know talk to them, reassure them, but…it seems like no one ever goes in there."

"We are supposed to stay out," Astrid said. "Before you and I worked there they used to open the shutters and talk to people, but they had to stop doing that. People have just gotten so…self-righteous and demanding in these last several years or they will…try to order food…climb through." She smiled. "Pavel has some great stories. He's been around awhile."

"Pavel?" Henry asked.

"Oh, he's the vice president," Astrid said.

"Ah".

"You know Henry, you could go in and talk to people if you wanted to. I don't think anyone would say anything to you about it, as long as you didn't stay in there all day. You probably could help some people. And anyway, then our numbers would go up and they would like that upstairs."

"Maybe I will." He smiled. Astrid smiled back at him, glanced down at his shoulders and chest then looked away.

"Well, I better get going. We've had the door open this whole time, but I still don't want to be accused of…fraternizing. It is frowned on." She stood up and held out her hand. Henry rose and shook it. "I will try, Henry, not to be such a bitch. Old habits die hard…but I will try. Thanks for listening."

"It's ok, Astrid. I don't mind. I'm glad. Have a good night," Henry said. She nodded and walked out the door. Henry closed it behind her.

"Well, I'll be damned…again," and he whistled.

*****

In the weeks that followed, Astrid backed off. If anything, Astrid's interactions with him became friendly, which was strange all by itself. It was as if a terrible dragon that breathed fire and wanted to destroy the town and eat all its virgins suddenly started serving tea and asking how everyone's day was going. It was utterly bizarre.

Henry relaxed a bit and turned his thoughts towards the Waiting Room. It had always been off limits to him. There was one door that led into it, presumably into the area with the sliding glass window and service bell, but it was always locked. No one ever told him to go in and service the room in any way and when he asked, he was always told not to worry about it. When he asked a second time, one of the office workers told him not to keep asking, that he would get into trouble. Once Astrid gave him the key, he found that the little room had been turned into storage and the light left on. The sliding glass door was padlocked. There was a little side door that entered the Waiting Room proper, but it also had a large lock on it that had to be removed with special lock cutters. When he had been in the Waiting Room for the first time, the woman who had shouted "Coffee Break" at him turned out to be a secretary from the Assignments department who was hiding in there while she ate donuts. She wasn't the only one, as the floor was littered with the crumbs of various guilty eaters.

Now that he had a free pass into the Waiting Room, he wasn't quite sure how to proceed. As he bustled about the office spaces delivering mail and coffee, he began to pay more attention to the real operation of the place and to the Wall.

There was a large operations floor near the Waiting Room where several of the Regional Coordinators worked at desks facing a large, dark grey, granite wall. Names and information for the recently deceased would appear on the Wall when a person stepped through the door to the Waiting Room. The Wall was not electronic. It was a real wall made of dark, smooth, granite blocks. Names of the dead appeared, as if carved, and scrolled down as new names came in at the top and old ones dropped off the bottom. The Wall listed their full name, age at death, cause of death, religion and area of origin. Religions were listed as symbols and only spelled out if they were rare. If the person was an atheist, a zero would come up in that space. If they were agnostic, a question mark would be there. Many zeros that popped up at the top of the Wall were changed to question marks as they scrolled down. This was a source of a lot of laughter in the office. It sometimes made Henry think of Marc Cabrera, sitting in the Waiting Room and asking if he didn't have a big green question mark on his forehead.

Whenever a zero or a question mark showed up on the Wall next to someone's name, Henry went out into the Waiting Room and sat down to have a chat with that person. Sometimes it worked, and the person miraculously became a Christian. Sometimes it didn't. Many agnostics reverted to the faith of their birth. There was a small up-tick in the number of Hindus and Buddhists that went through. This didn't really bother anyone working in the waiting room. If Henry had any success at all in bringing someone back to Christianity that was enough. Eventually he had a better track record than the missionaries. He also started to run low on the coins Ambustus had given him.

The very first day that he entered the waiting room, he found Marc Cabrera snoozing on a couch. Henry's jaw dropped. He went over to Marc and sat down next to him. As Henry sat down, Marc woke up.

166

"Hunh, what the h…" Recognition slowly ignited in Marc's eyes.

"Henry?" he asked, unsure.

"Yes, it's me," Henry said.

"My god, you look…I could hardly recognize you. You look like, Henry's grandson not the rickety old codger I know! What in the world…why are you here? What happened to you?" Marc asked as his eyes drifted up to his forehead, saw the wispy cross, and grew wide. "Henry, you're not…what happened? What's going on? Is it true?" he asked with wide eyes.

"Marc, relax old friend, it is me. I just can't believe it's you. Didn't someone come in to get you? I can't believe you have been in here this whole time." Marc was getting agitated and people were starting to stare. "Marc…relax, alright? Just play it cool and I will get you out of here." Henry looked around. "Marc, go back through the door and come in again. Marc looked at the door and frowned.

"I've played that game before. Nothing happens," he said.

"Now look, just trust me. Do it and then take a number. You'll go into judgment again and we can get you somewhere," Henry said. Marc nodded, got up, and sauntered over to the door and stepped through. Of course he appeared at the door again. Then he walked over and took a ticket.

"Crap on a stick, Doc, it says, 95," Marc said.

"That's alright. You have waited a long time, you can wait a bit longer. Now listen to me carefully. You have some choices to make."

Henry quietly explained to Marc about the coins, Heaven, Elysium, and the choices he had. Marc listened intently. When Henry finished, Marc shifted his large bulk and sat back on the couch making a face.

"So, what would you like to do?" Henry asked. Marc sighed.

"Well, judgment in a Christian way is not going to end well for me, Doc and I don't exactly want a new job. I better just go straight to the pagans. How can I do that?"

"Well, a Hindu or a Buddhist has an automatic ticket, no questions asked, as I've said. Or when he asks you, you could just say no and you will go to Elysium." Marc thought about it.

"My sister's a Buddhist, or at least she was for a while. Lots of dorks in America become Buddhists don't they. Mm, let's do this coin trick of yours, Doc. It kinda sounds fun," Marc said. Henry smiled. He fiddled around in his pocket until he felt the Buddhist coin. He palmed it and shook Marc's hand. As Marc took the coin and put it in his pocket, a dharmachakra, or an 8 spoked wheel, appeared on his forehead.

"Is it there?" Marc asked. Henry marveled at it.

"Yes, yes it is. Oh my, look at that."

"So, now what?" Marc asked.

"Well, you just wait until your number comes up. When it does, go through the door just there. You will enter a place that looks like a large, old church. Keep walking forward until you get to the other end where three people will be waiting. The two young ones are nice guys, but in there, they won't say anything to you. The old one, that's Peter, he will see your forehead, probably curse or sigh or something, and then stamp some papers. The next thing you know, you will be in Elysium and someone will greet you."

"Just like that, eh?" Marc said.

"Yup," Henry said, though in his mind he thought of the Flood. He looked at Marc and hoped he would see him again. Marc looked back at him quizzically.

"Alright then, Doc. We're set. But you gotta quit lookin at me like that. You're starting to creep me out a little." Marc smiled at him to let him know he was joking. Henry slapped him on the shoulder and stood up.

"I've got to go Marc. I'll see you later," Henry said and walked away. Marc waved at him, looked up at the digital counter and sighed.

*****

Henry kept at it. Everyone in the office thought he was trying to convert people to Christianity but in reality he was gently telling people what their real options were and giving them the appropriate coin. Peter didn't bother with Hindus and Buddhists and a few other religions, but he would occasionally give an agnostic a hard time. Few people went that direction. Many of the agnostics that Henry talked to just wanted to see their families again and took the Christian coin.

One morning Henry took 10am coffee orders from everyone and went outside to the stand. He handed Jared the order and talked with him about where the cream came from. Jared didn't know. Suddenly, Henry heard someone shout his name. He turned and saw a dark haired young woman being half dragged somewhere by two gruff looking members of the Guard. One of the Guardsmen backhanded her and said, "Quiet, whore." Slowly, recognition dawned on him. It was Lauren.

"Stop, please, just stop a minute...please stop!" Henry shouted at the men. They stopped and stared at him. One of them said, "Do you know this woman?" Henry looked at her face. It was Lauren, young again, not sick, not old, young and lovely. Henry's heart heaved in his chest. Tears started in his eyes.

"No,..." Lauren said quickly. "He's not...he's not who I thought he was." She looked him in the eyes and shook her head no, ever so slightly. One of the Guardsmen grunted and they dragged her away, around the side of the castle and through one of the garden doors. Henry watched them go. Lauren looked back at him, tears visible on her cheeks. She mouthed something to him. It looked like 'wait'. He nodded, turned, and went back to the coffee stand.

"That was rough," Jared said as he packed up Henry's large orders.

"Do you know where they'll take her?" Henry asked.

"Well, it depends. The way they took her like that...probably the tower," said Jared. "She called your name. Who was she?"

"My wife," Henry said. Jared's eyes opened wide but he said nothing. Henry grabbed the drink trays and went back into the offices.

Henry carried the trays of coffee back into the castle and stacked them carefully on the cart he had left by the door. It was his mail cart, but he used it to deliver coffee all the time. He stopped at Astrid's office first. She smiled and was about to say something else to him but he turned and walked out, distracted by something in the hall. He stopped and talked to Chloe.

"Hey Chloe, I was just outside getting the coffee order and I saw some Guardsmen bring in a woman. They had her handcuffed and she looked...like they'd beaten her. Do you know what that might be about?" he asked.

"Oh well, she must have done something wrong," Chloe answered.

"Chloe, I'm still new here and I...want to understand. I know the rules that we follow, but I've never seen something like that before. What could a normal citizen of Heaven have done, apprehended like that?"

"Oh yeah, Henry, I keep forgetting you haven't been here long. I'm sorry…um, well, if she talked openly against the Castle, that could do it. If she started a riot or tried to cause a rebellion somehow, that would put her in the same category as you know who," she pointed at the floor. "Any of the normal crimes…assault…murder."

"Whoa, whoa, hold on now. Those things happen?" Henry asked. Chloe shrugged.

"Well, yeah sometimes. I mean…I think it's usually an accident. People are less careful when they know they can't die…a little more reckless and people do get drunk and get into arguments. It has to be pretty bad before the Guard shows up though, usually the local police handle it. Actually someone has to complain first. The Guard doesn't investigate disturbances, they investigate complaints. That's really how it works." She looked down at her cubicle with an angry frown. "Somebody's always a snitch," she said. She sat down and went back to work with a dour face. Henry took that as his cue to leave.

He walked on and delivered a few more coffees. Inside, he was a thunderstorm of rage and worry. He wanted to beat up those Guardsmen. He wanted to find Lauren and save her, take her to Elysium right now, the Flood be damned. She would be alright eventually, wouldn't she? It took a constant effort to keep himself under control and go about his duties like he was his happy-go-lucky self. He couldn't really do it, so he just pretended to be in a rush. His mind raced with questions: 'What could she have done? Where would they hold her?' Henry realized he hadn't really been an efficient spy. He had infiltrated very well, but what information was he gathering? What did he have that they didn't already know? He knew all about the Waiting Room Department and the Judgment Hall. He had plumbed the depths of the system of bribes and could get just about anything he wanted, even Ambustus's coins. That surprised him at first, but through Jared the barista, he was able to get them. At this point though, he did not know how the executive branch worked. Who were the Guard? Where did they hold prisoners? What would they do with them? Henry stopped cold in the hallway when he was suddenly struck with an image in his mind of Lauren getting the gift of pain from the demon doctor, without the benefit of a protective berry cobbler.

170

Henry thought up some excuse to tell anyone who asked and immediately went down to the demon's office to see if she was in the waiting room. When he found the waiting room empty he breathed a small sigh of relief. He stood and listened for a minute and heard people talking but no screaming.

He wheeled his cart down a hallway and left it outside a door marked "Storage". He went inside the small closet and shut the door. There he tried to get himself under control. He whispered to himself, "You must not panic. You can do nothing if you panic. Damn you, Henry Hall, get yourself together." He stood there breathing deeply for a few seconds, mind racing. "Get information, that's what you need. Get information and then you can help her." He rubbed his face and head with his hands, took a deep breath, and left the closet.

Henry went about his duties. He told a few people about the woman he had seen and asked what would happen to her. Two different people said that they thought prisoners went to the tower. Henry was thinking about this when he stopped in the IT department. Henry asked Ian, a friendly and appropriately strange IT guy, about what he knew.

"Oh yeah, that girl. I knew they were looking for her. So they got her huh?" Ian asked as he sat at his computer.

"Well, I saw the Guard bring in a dark haired woman. That's all I know," Henry said.

"Oh yeah, dark hair, yeah that's probably her. Yeah, my friend in enforcement told me. He said they had security footage of her going through a missionary portal and coming out again. I mean weird, right? Like, why would you jump into a shark tank or ….a pit filled with…something…anyway…yeah…weird. Yeah, so they'll probably put her in the tower, interrogate her or something. Actually, that's my friend. He's an interrogator. He hates it…totally."

"Does this happen often?" Henry asked.

"Wait, like does he interrogate often or do they bring in girls a lot?" Ian asked while looking puzzled.

"Well both, I suppose," Henry said.

"Um…like…not a whole lot. I mean sometimes…yeah, she's probably in the tower. Like, there are other places that they can hold people, but if they want to keep someone…isolated like that...zoop" he made a high-pitched noise and pointed towards the celing. "The portal only works for the Guard and the stairs are insane…totally. I mean, it's not like we have to work out any more right…thank god? Otherwise I'd probably train on those stairs…train those gluts…but anyway…Henry can I like, put in a coffee order. I mean, no offense, but I totally associate you with a caramel macchiato half-caff."

"Sure thing," Henry said. I need to deliver a bit more mail, but I will come back shortly, maybe 20 minutes."

"Awesome…can't wait. Thanks man." Ian smiled and turned back towards his computer screen.

All Henry knew about the tower was that it was there, it was very tall, and it had some holes in it. During his walks on the beach or in the garden he had sometimes looked up at it, saw the damage and wondered why it hadn't been repaired. One of the books he had found in the library made passing reference to some ancient war in which some of the castle was destroyed. Henry intended to investigate further when the workday was done.

Chapter 28

The Tower

Henry finished work around 6 and he immediately walked back downstairs to the basement. He passed by the demonic doctor's office and saw that it was closed and dark. He passed by IT and saw Ian, still sitting at his computer typing away. No one else was there.

He began to worry as he walked further into the basement , past doors and hallways he had never seen before. The place was labyrinthine enough that he could see himself getting lost. He imagined running into some grey, old man who had been lost for hundreds of years down here in the basement maze. Though any man he found wouldn't be old, not here. St. Peter crept into his mind then, with his salt and pepper hair and wrinkled brow. 'How did he do that?' Henry wondered.

Henry passed many rooms, all dark with locked doors. He passed several janitors' closets, a room labeled medical supplies, which he found odd, and then a room ominously labeled "operations". He became hopeful when he passed rooms labeled "Interrogation 1" and then "2", but they appeared dark and unoccupied. Eventually he began to detect a foul and familiar smell and realized he must be near the kitchens of the S-Caf. "Blech," he said aloud. "It must be Salisbury Steak night."

He continued on, backtracked a bit when he hit a dead end, walked on a bit more and finally, during one of his backtracks, he discovered a small, dark hallway that led to an indoor portal of stone and a dilapidated old spiral staircase behind it. He went to the bottom of the stairs and looked up. Perspective disappeared into a black dot in a distant, distant darkness. Orange light streamed in through some holes in the wall, but they looked so small, it was hard to tell how far away they were. This was definitely a tower, though he wasn't sure if it was *the* tower.

Henry tried the portal. He said, "Tower" and walked through. Nothing happened. He said 'up', 'top', 'prison' and anything else he could think of related to a prison tower. "Fuck," he said in exasperation. That didn't work either. He went back to the stairs and looked up again. He sighed and started to climb.

Youth and health aside, anyone can get tired climbing story after story of stairs. After several iterations, Henry reckoned he was 10 stories up. His legs felt heavy and he sat down for a rest. So far he had passed several locked doors to empty rooms, by the lack of sound, and nothing else. Looking up he could see dim red light coming through the holes in the tower wall above him. The first hole wasn't that far above. He got up and climbed again. Something up there wasn't quite right. He quickly learned why.

On floor seventeen he stood on a landing of stone that led into what was a left of a room. The end of the room was gone, most of it open to the air. Broken stones littered the floor of the room but so did bits of grasses and scatterings of driftwood. There were also big splotches of black and white bird excrement everywhere. Henry walked to the open wall and looked out. The sun was setting, casting a dim red glow on the beach and the tower. He walked back to the stairs.

Above him on the landing, the stairs were missing for several floors. Disembodied wooden doors dotted the inside of the tunnel like chocolate chips in a big, tower-shaped cookie. A broken bit of the stairs hung down at a strange angle and moved gently in the breeze from one of the holes. Beyond that, the tower disappeared into darkness. He sat down on the steps and looked out through the bird room at the distant ocean.

As he sat, an idea floated up in his mind. The ghost form. He could kill himself somehow, it was already past sunset, and then maybe the attributes of that form would allow him to climb higher. He went back through the bird room and stood looking down at the black rocks seventeen stories below. "Yup, that should do it," he said and jumped.

He landed with a crunch and his body died. A few seconds went by and he rose up in the spirit form. He looked back up at the side of the tower. As he began to put his arms up to climb, a man ran over to him. He recognized him as one of the cafeteria workers. He lived on the same floor of the dormitory as Henry.

"Oh...what the hell are you doing?" he asked.

"I...fell." Henry found it hard to speak. His voice sounded strange, like wind through a pine tree.

"No shit, you fell. Why were you up in the tower? That is totally stupid. Look, you're lucky it's dark enough. No one will find your body, but you can't let people see you in the ghost form. You could get in serious trouble. Go back to your room or hide in a

closet somewhere. Someone's coming. Quick, go underground!"
Henry stood looking at him. He didn't understand what he meant.
The man, Henry thought his name was Bill, looked at him and
understood. "You can go underground," Bill whispered harshly at
Henry, "Just walk down. Keep your head up a little though, so you
know where you are. There, behind the rock. GO!"

Bill turned away and Henry tried to step down. It worked
but it was an odd sensation. In the ghost form, traveling through
the air was normal, but walking down into the earth was kind of
like walking down into a pool of mud. He could get through it but
it took a little more time. Henry worked his way down in the
ground until just his ghostly head was above the sand and behind a
rock. He felt like he was neck deep in a swimming pool. He could
move his arms around and feel the slight resistance of the liquid
earth and rock around him. It was utterly bizarre and yet not
unfamiliar because it was so like being in water.

A couple of women went walking by and Bill sat on one of
the rocks and waved at them. "Hey ladies. What's up?" They
waved back and kept walking. Bill turned around. He kneeled
down to talk to Henry. "You're name is Henry right?" The top of
Henry's head nodded. "Look, stay underground and go back into
the building. You can take the basement all the way to under the
dormitory, then get to your room. I'm going to try and move your
body to here, behind these rocks. Your body doesn't look too
heavy so I think I can do it."

"Thanks," Henry said in a wispy ghost voice. "I owe you
one." Bill nodded and turned away.

Henry turned around and walked right through the outer
wall of the tower and into the area at the bottom of the tower stairs.
He stood there for a moment looking up into the tower. 'There
must be a way,' he thought. Just then he heard the marching feet
of at least two Guardsmen. He panicked and ran through a nearby
door and then kept going. He passed through walls and empty
rooms and water for a few scary seconds until he popped into what
had to be a boiler room. A nearby door was labeled "Kitchen".
Now he knew where he was. Carefully, he made his way back to
his room in the dormitory.

175

Chapter 29

Office Party

In the morning Henry lay across his bed, waiting for the magic of resurrection. As the first rays of sunlight spread across the sky outside, Henry breathed air into real lungs. He got up, turned on his TV, and bustled about his room, getting ready for work.

For a change, the news anchors on H-News 1 actually had something interesting to say. Usually the news was a constant recap of dead celebrity activities. Elvis and Martha Stewart would make pancakes and bacon or some other breakfast food. Bill Shatner would crash a car into something and make a scene and Ben Franklin would be photographed grabbing asses in the bars downtown; the usual sort of thing. This time service worker identity badge photos flashed across the screen and the anchors asked anyone with information about the whereabouts of those people to contact the Heaven's Guard. A phone number flashed on the screen. "So, workers are disappearing," Henry said aloud to his room. "Hm. Wonder what that's about?" He turned off the TV and went to work.

Henry went about his regular duties that day but he couldn't quite stifle his distraction and worry. Astrid tried to talk to him about the cafeteria or some such thing but he only half listened to her. "Mmm, sounds good. Yes, definitely, great…should be fun." He walked off pushing his cart, having no idea what they had been talking about. His mind was on Lauren, the tower, and the way out.

He was delivering some coffee and a 'ream of paper' to the demon doctor's office when it hit him. He looked at the rock walls of the office and that stupid picture of the kitten hanging from a branch. 'Hang in there, baby,' was the picture's caption. 'I can go through the wall!' he thought. 'I can walk up and inside the wall just like I did when I walked into the ground! It would be like…like swimming!' "Ha, Ha!" he said out loud. A woman in the demon doctor's waiting room looked at him and frowned. Henry apologized. "Oh, sorry, sorry," he said. He practically skipped out of the room. 'Yes, I can die, then walk up and go through the wall. As long as I am careful no one will be able to see my ghost form from the outside, and no one will be there on the inside because the stairs are broken. Henry was giddy. He couldn't wait to try it.

The end of the work day finally arrived and Henry was gleefully on his way to climb the tower and fall to his death when Chloe stopped him.

"Hey, Henry, what time will you get there tonight? I was thinking I would get there a little late," Chloe asked.

"What are we talking about now?" he asked.

"The office party tonight in the S-Caf, it's for some made up service worker holiday but who cares right? We might even get some watered down booze. And, and we are taking bets on how disgusting the cake will be."

"Oh, I wasn't aware that…uh…I don't remember…" Henry fumbled.

"Henry, I stood there and watched you tell Astrid that you would be there. She was practically gushing…Henry are you ok? You seem kinda distracted lately."

"No, Chloe, I'm…fine… I just wasn't really listening to her when she was talking today and I must not have realized that I was giving up my evening. Oh, well. Guess I'm locked in now." Chloe gave him a strange look.

"Yeah, you kinda are. Better be there or boss lady will be sad. She might even shed a tiny… little... tear," Chloe said. She turned around and walked off. Henry thought that was odd, but he let it pass.

'Damn, damn, damn!' he thought. 'I hate bloody, buggery parties.' He sighed heavily and sauntered off, resigned to his party fate. He knew he couldn't go missing after he told Astrid he'd be there. She would send someone to look for him. 'I will get out of there as soon as I have stayed my polite hour," he thought as he headed home.

*****

The service worker's cafeteria or the S-Caf, as it was not so affectionately known, was a grey, white and tan marvel of boring efficiency and lack of décor. If someone had decided to suck the life and enjoyment out of the dining experience, the S-Caf represented the culmination of a very strange life-long dream.

As Henry arrived, some of his coworkers were mulling around the end of one of the long, picnic style tables. There appeared to be a punch bowl filled with a raspberry-red liquid. A little butterfly of hope began to flutter in Henry's stomach. 'Maybe, just maybe,' he thought, 'that punch won't taste like soap.'

At first Henry stood around by himself, eyeing the clock. Eventually, Todd, one of St. Peter's helpers, came over to say hello. At first, Henry didn't recognize him out of his brown monk clothes. Tonight he was wearing blue jeans and a grey t-shirt.

"Hey, Henry. What's up?"

"Oh…Todd. Wow. It's really you. I almost didn't recognize you outside of your…robe. How are you?"

"Oh, I'm better now. It's nice to get out, you know." At that point, Chloe walked by to get some more punch. Todd watched her go and kept watching. "One of these days Henry, I am going to get all up in that," he said as he watched Chloe fill her cup from the bowl. Henry chuckled. "Good luck, my friend."

"Hey, Henry, you got your eye on anybody?" Todd asked.

"Ah…no. I'm still…I often still think of myself as being old. I know it's silly but I do."

"Well I have news for you, my friend. You are not old and you may not have your eye on anybody but a body certainly has her eye on you."

"What?" Henry was confused. Todd turned his back to the crowd and faced Henry.

"You mean really don't know?" he asked. Henry shook his head.

"It's Astrid, Henry. Look at her. She's always trying to catch your eye, trying to talk to you. We don't know what you did but she likes you and she's being nice to everybody. Did you…?" He nodded his head towards Astrid. "You know…did you and she…?"

"No, no…I didn't….good god…I…" Henry looked at Astrid and she was indeed looking back at him. She smiled at him sensually and then turned back towards the woman she was talking to with a knowing smile. "Oh, no, no, no. This can't be happening," Henry whispered to himself as he looked down at the floor.

"Mm, so it's not mutual eh? I don't blame you. She's a dragon for sure…a sexy, hot dragon…but a dragon regardless. I think I just said dragon way too many times." Todd eyed Astrid and shook his head. "That is a shame. Hmm. Well, good luck my friend and you can wish me luck too. I'm going in." Todd walked off in Chloe's general direction.

Eventually a cake was brought out and it was thoroughly disgusting. It was some sort of banana flavored concoction with raisins. The frosting was an unpleasant layer of dried out marzipan. It was so terrible that it was hilarious. Chloe dared people to eat a whole slice and giggled when they couldn't do it. Henry had actually begun to enjoy himself. He talked for a long time with a regional coordinator named Sanjay and was even introduced to Pavel, the vice president, who turned out to be a pretty nice guy.

Henry was torn. Part of him wanted to stay at the party, chat with people and relax a little. He hadn't seen this side of his coworkers and it was intriguing to see them in clothes they chose, laughing, and telling jokes. If he let himself he would have fun, but he couldn't let himself. Somewhere nearby, Lauren was being held. Maybe she was being interrogated or maybe she was just alone in a cell, but Henry wanted desperately to see her again, to help her escape, to bring her back with him to Elysium where they could be truly free.

He excused himself from Pavel, Astrid, and the others in the group he had been talking with and headed over to the punch bowl. Todd was right. Now that Henry knew, it was quite obvious that Astrid had some sort of a crush on him. He wondered about that. Maybe she always had. Maybe she batted her eyelashes at him when she was his student all those years ago because she had a crush, not because she wanted an A. He shook his head and decided that he had to get out of Heaven as soon as possible. He poured himself another cup full. The punch wasn't half bad. Someone had spiked it with something, probably vodka. As he raised his cup to drink, a thought struck him. 'They think I have the gift of pain.' He downed the rest of his punch and walked off toward the bathroom.

No one was in there so he took a minute to lean against the counter and think. He started running water from the faucet and with cupped hands, began to toss the water onto the tile floor of the bathroom. He walked back and forth, quickly, trying to slip by making awkward pivots. It wasn't working so he began to make short runs across the wet tiles. He was rounding the corner for another go when someone pushed their way into the room and caught him in the shoulder with the door, hard. It was a man he didn't recognize.

"Oh, man I'm sorry. I didn't think anyone would be in here." The man said.

"No, it's alright," Henry said. The man nodded and hurried into a stall.

"Dude," he said from the stall, "do not eat that cake." Henry chuckled. As he left the bathroom he held his shoulder and scrunched up his face in pain. As he walked back to the section of the S-Caf where his co-workers were, Astrid came over to him.

"What happened Henry, are you ok?" she asked.

"Well…I…someone came into the bathroom just as I turned to come out and caught me in the shoulder with the door," Henry said. For a moment Astrid looked puzzled and then she remembered.

"Oh…I had forgotten that you had…Is there anything you need Henry? Anything I can do for you?"

"Oh, no thank you, Astrid that's kind of you, but I think I will just head home for the evening, get some rest. It'll all be well in the morning." He smiled at her and the others who had gathered round. "Good night all," he said as he walked away still holding his shoulder and wincing a little. Their eyes followed him as he left. Even out in the hallway he continued the charade in case he ran into anybody.

Chapter 30

The Tower Part II

Henry made his way down some stairs into the basement and walked until he began to see rooms and doors that he recognized. Soon he stood at the bottom of what had to be Heaven's longest set of stairs. "Well, here we go," he said to himself.

Knowing he would die soon, Henry pushed it and ran up the stairs. When he got up to the 17th floor, he walked through the bird room to the hole in the wall and took a quick look up and down the beach. The coast was clear, so he jumped, aiming for the black rocks at the base of the tower.

After a disconcerting crunch, Henry was a ghost again. He rose up out of his broken body and walked through the outer tower wall. There he was again at the base of the stairs, but in ghost form, the walk no longer intimidated him. He took the stairs up again, two or three at a time, and quickly came to the landing of the bird room. He looked up and saw nothing but vague shapes and darkness.

Now here was the tricky bit. He went towards the stairs and stood next to the wall, looking at it for a moment. He pushed both ghostly hands into its syrupy embrace. Ra-Neferu had described ghost form in terms of differing densities and surface tension. Could he climb the tower just like that, by sticking his hands and feet into the thick goop of the stone? He moved his arms up through the rock and then inserted his feet. It worked! The wall held him. Henry was elated. He moved his hands and feet in and out of the wall like an awkward spider crawling across gelatin. He climbed until he found another set of stairs. Then he climbed the stairs normally. When the stairs disappeared, he went back to the sticky climb. In this way he managed to get to the top of the tower.

Along the way, Henry passed many doors. He didn't know exactly where Lauren was, so he stuck his head through each door long enough to determine whether or not the room needed more investigation. He was surprised to find several beautifully decorated rooms. One of them had deep red velvet curtains, patterned rugs, polished, intricate wooden desks, chairs and brass candelabras. One even had a small fire place. None of the rooms were occupied, but all had windows and the light of the city flowed in, casting deep shadows.

Near the top of the tower, Henry stuck his head through a door and saw a portal and prison cells. He pulled back quickly in case there was anyone there. He waited and hearing no noise, walked through the door, staying close to the wall in case he needed to hide.

Whatever the room was, it was like a jail. There was a central walkway bordered on both sides by jail cells with old, rusty looking bars. There were no interior walls between the cells, it was just all bars, making the cells seem more like cages. The walkway down the center ended at a large hole in the outside tower wall. The wind whipped in and all around the large room.

Henry walked through the bars and into each cell looking for Lauren, or anything that could have given some evidence of her. He found them all empty. The last cell on the left was practically teetering on the edge of the tower wall. It would have been possible to sit in the corner of that cell and look almost straight down at the beach below. In that cell, one of the mattresses had been torn up from the metal grate on which it had rested. It lay, casually thrown over a metal toilet.

Henry stood at the end of the center walkway looking down at the beach. The light of New Jerusalem cast a yellow glow over everything. He could see the long, ivory line of the sand against the blackness of the ocean. "Wow", he said out loud. His ghostly voice was carried away on the wind. Something caught his eye and he thought he saw a light; some low, glimmering motion in the water below, but he couldn't be sure. Was it bioluminescence of some kind? 'Lauren would know,' he thought. 'If I find her, I'll ask her'. This last thought made him anxious to do just that and he turned away to explore the rest of the rooms.

There were two other doors on this level. He walked through the door and back out onto the landing, then through the other door. This room was a mirror image of the one he had just explored except that there was no giant hole in the wall. Instead, there was a small window with no glass and two bars in it. The room was cluttered and dusty and looked like it hadn't been used in years.

He walked back across the landing to the room with the hole in the wall and stepped through the door. There was nothing but the whistling wind and empty cells. 'Now what?' he thought as he looked around. 'Clearly, she isn't here anymore if she had ever been,' he thought. He walked back through the door out onto the landing and looked up. There was still quite a bit of tower above him. 'Might as well,' he thought.

He climbed up and up for what seemed like ages. He passed a horizontal layer of stone and above that, there were no more interior walls. There he was in the center of the open tower. It made the dilapidated stairs seem like a tiny, spiraled thread in the center, and he, a gloomy ant slowly crawling up. He looked up and he could see another floor not too far above him. The stairs ended right below a round hatch in the floor.

Henry slowly pushed himself up and through the hatch, pushing until he felt that small give as his ghost body went through the wood. He climbed through and stood in a large circular room. Henry's first impression of the room was that it was a storage area. Light from the city entered through a window and he was able to make out dim shapes. There was no furniture, just boxes, either stacked on one another, or loitering around the room. Other shapes littered the dark landscape; broken crates, piles of fabric, amorphous lumps of who-knows-what.

As he moved around the room he was startled by a soft light; a yellow-gold glow. He walked towards it. Sitting on a wooden box, with other boxes acting like a small amphitheater, was the strangest object that Henry had ever seen. It was a roughly spherical receptacle, almost like a round vase, and open at the top. It was made of some sort of filigreed metal. The metal seemed to have both gold and silver highlights and was not anything Henry could identify. The object was ornate and the metal strands were delicately twisted and warped. It almost looked as if it was a decorative stand for a glass container, but the glass was missing. Instead, the strange vase seemed to hold a glowing, diffuse, yellow-gold substance that behaved like a cloud. Henry watched it swirl in the vase, always moving but always maintaining that roughly spherical shape. Forgetting his ghost form, he tried to pick it up and found to his surprise that he could. He could feel the cool metal and the surprising weight of it. He could handle it just as if he were in his living body. He turned the vase in his hands and looked at it carefully. He placed it back on the box and dipped his cupped hand into the golden stuff. He pulled his hand out and it was just as if he had put his hand into water, except in slow-motion. The golden cloud-liquid pooled in his hand and streamed out slowly through his fingers. Instead of falling to the floor or anywhere else, it slowly streamed back into the vase and continued its spherical swirling.

Henry picked up the vase and placed it on a higher box so that he could use the light. He walked around the room, rummaging through everything as much as he could. He couldn't pick up anything or open the boxes but he stuck his hands inside of things hoping to run across more items that ghosts could touch. He found only one more item that received his diffuse hand. Leaning against a box towards the side of the room was a sword. It appeared to be made of the same metal as the vase. Henry reached down and picked it up easily. He felt the weight in his hand. It was ornate and beautiful, just like the vase. He romped around a cleared space of the room, jabbing and parrying at invisible foes. The sword felt natural, like a piece of himself that he had just forgotten somewhere.

Henry put the sword on a box and reached up to grab the vase. He put it on the box next to the sword and then stood looking at them, trying to decide what to do. He didn't think he could carry both items and make it home without being caught. The vase with its captivating glow would certainly attract attention and would be difficult to hide. The sword he could probably shove between the mattress and box spring of his bed and it would be safe enough. He looked around the rest of the room and sighed, wondering what treasures it contained that he might exploit if he were there in the flesh.

He picked up the sword again and walked towards the hatch in the floor. As he walked passed one of the many small windows in the room, a thought struck him. He approached the window and looked out. The sky was still dark, but looking at it made him remember that there was a hard time limit on his ghostly abilities. How much time had he spent climbing walls and stairs? How much time did he have left?

He approached one of the windows and stuck his head out. The windows were open to the air; no glass and no bars. A very distant glint of light gave the impression that there was an ocean somewhere down there. The wind whipped. Clouds above seemed like they were near enough to touch, like puffy bits of cotton stuck to the pointed roof above him. Henry sighed and looked down at the tiny beach below. 'Well, I'm already a ghost,' he thought,

'Let's see what happens.' He climbed up into the window awkwardly, grasping the sword in one hand. "Geronimo" he said with his wispy ghost voice. He jumped.

Everything about the fall was just like when he jumped off the tower in the flesh except that he seemed to fall a little more slowly, like he was a heavy feather instead of a man. He approached the earth with enough velocity that ghost butterflies began to flutter inside his stomach. He hit the ground and then, with an ethereal squish, went through it, as if he had dived into marshmallow crème. He felt the sword leave his hand as it hit the sand above him and skidded away. He traveled downward through the ground propelled by momentum until unknown resistance slowed him down and he came to a gradual stop. At this point, the butterflies were transforming into real panic. Everything around him was dark. He sensed that he was in the ground, felt the slow resistance of the dense earth around him. He also felt a slight vibration coming from just ahead of him. He climbed-swam toward it and to his great relief he found he could move. The vibration became stronger as he worked toward it. Soon his head popped up out of the sand into shallow water where waves were breaking. He worked his way up and out of the ground and walked back towards the tower, looking for the sword.

He found it lying in the sand a few feet away from where he fell. He picked up the sword and without thinking, tried to walk directly through the outside wall of the tower. The sword clanged on the outside wall and fell to the ground as he walked through the wall. "Damn it," he said aloud. He walked back out through the wall and picked up the sword again. 'Well, I suppose we must go the long way.'

He made his way back to the dormitory. He walked quickly, always hugging a stone wall and ready at any moment to drop the sword into a bush. Luckily, he saw no one. When he got to the doorway leading to his hallway, he used the hilt of the sword to press it open. In a similar manner he was able to open the door to his room. He was about to enter when he heard a voice behind him in the hallway.

"Dude, rockin' the ghost eh?" It was Steve, one of the office's missionaries. He stood leaning against his doorway, smoking a big joint. The smell of marijuana drifted by. Without thinking, Henry held the sword behind him.

"Hello, uh…Steve is it? Good …good to see you." Henry cleared his throat. Steve chuckled, took a big drag off the joint and pointed at him.

"Dude, you're a ghost. I can see what you're hiding. I can see right through you. Looks like a sword…That's weird. Hey…that's cool. How are you holding it?" Steve asked.

"I…uh…I…" Henry stammered.

"Whoa, look, dude…" Steve said putting his hands up in the air. "Look, Henry, I don't care if you have a sword…or whatever. I mean, look what I'm doing. Relax…it's not like, it's not like it's a box of donuts…right? Am I right? Ah…fucking donuts." Steve closed his eyes and smiled.

"Yes, well…good-bye then. Enjoy that," Henry said, indicating the joint. Steve held it out to Henry as if to offer him a drag. Henry shook his head.

"Oh yeah right…no lungs." Steve started giggling and then waved Henry off as he giggled into his room.

Once in his own room, Henry collapsed onto his bed with a long, ghostly sigh. He held the sword and looked at it, turning it over in his hands. He imagined himself bravely and easily fighting off the Guard while he and Lauren made their way to the portal to Elysium in the Judgment Hall. He would crash through the stained glass window with the sword and swing her through with him, his arm around her waist. He smiled at his silly fantasy.

He sat up and wedged the sword as much as he could between the mattress and box spring. Outside his window the first rays of the sun crept across the roofs of the city. He felt his ghost body dissolve into flesh and air entered his lungs. He looked around his room, at his work clothes hung neatly over the back of his desk chair. He sighed and got ready for work.

Chapter 31

Marc Cabrera, Buddhist

The digital counter turned over to 95. Marc sighed and heaved himself up from his comfy spot on the couch where he had apparently been napping for months. He felt like he had only been in there a few hours. With briefcase in hand and Henry's coin in his pocket he walked through the door.

The church was just like Henry described it: old and dimly lit except for the stained glass windows. Marc did not slow down and have a look. He walked straight down the center aisle towards the waiting monks. He came before them, put his briefcase down, and stood waiting.

Peter looked up from the paper he was reading and looked at Marc over his glasses. He was about to start talking when he saw the Buddhist wheel on Marc's forehead and stopped short. He stared at the symbol, at Marc, his clothes, and back at the symbol.

"You…have…got…to…joking," Peter said. Marc looked at Peter, back at the other monks, two young men, then back at Peter. He waited. "How in the hell are you a Buddhist?" Peter said asked loudly. One of the monks behind him startled and dropped a file he'd been holding.

"Whaddya mean?" Marc asked.

"Whaddya mean?" Peter mocked his accent. "What are you from Texas or something?" He paused to lean farther over the desk "I mean, how…are…you…a…Buddhist? You don't look like a Buddhist, you don't sound like one…you don't act like one…you don't even smell like one. Do you even know what a Buddhist is?" Peter asked.

"Sure I do." In his mind Marc tried to remember all the stuff that his sister had babbled on about when she went through her Buddhist phase. "I follow the eight-fold path, as best as I can. I meditate… I look at myself in the mirror and say…mantras and sometimes I cry….well, you know I get a little teary…because I'm so calm and happy…because of the inner peace." Marc cleared his throat. "Yup, lovin' that inner peace. So…that's what we Buddhists do…in America. I don't know what they do in other countries." Marc waited. Peter stared at him.

"You're not a Buddhist. You're just stupid," Peter said. He eyed the symbol on Marc's forehead. Marc looked back at him, at the other monks, and around the room. Peter sighed heavily. He opened a drawer in the large wooden table he sat behind and pulled out a stamp. He stamped a paper and handed it over his shoulder to one of the monks. "Fine," he said. "Have it your way." One of the young monks came out from behind the table and motioned for Marc to follow him.

"Thanks. See ya," Marc said. He followed the young monk to a stained glass window. The monk moved to push him and Marc blocked him and shoved him down to the floor.

"That's Tae Kwon Do, bitch," Marc said. He turned and put his hand through the glass. He smiled as he felt his hand push through the portal. He walked through.

Suddenly he was walking out into an open area that looked a lot like an airport terminal. A dark-haired, young man was holding a sign with Marc's name on it. Marc smiled and took the coin out of his pocket.

"That's a fun coin trick you guys are playin'. He said to the man. "I'd like to see what old Pete would do if I had some other symbol on my head. He'd probably pop his top." Marc stopped to shake hands with Burhan. "So, do you know Henry?" Marc asked. Burhan laughed.

Chapter 32

Henry and Lauren Hall

Henry bustled around his room getting ready for work. He listened to the news from the TV as he dressed. Apparently, there were food shortages. For the next few months, milk, butter, and beef would be scarce. They didn't say why but offered the alternatives of olive oil and goat meat. Henry grimaced. He thought about the S-Caf and the mystery meat that they often served. Was it beef? Was it goat? Whatever it was, it was unpleasant. Sautéed green peppers can only hide so much. The news continued,

"Tonight on Heaven News 7, our team investigates …Limbo. Why are the Unwanted trying to breach the missionary portals? What is the Kingdom's response? How can you protect your family? Tune in tonight at 7pm on Heaven News 7."

"Unwanted," Henry said as he put on his shirt, "That's interesting." He finished getting ready, turned off the TV and went to work.

Almost as soon as he got through the door, Astrid found him.

"Oh, Henry, I was so worried about you," she said as she looked him over. "Were you...were you able to sleep?"

"Yes, yes, thank you, Astrid. I was fine. My shoulder ached for a bit but I took a hot shower and went to bed. So I am fine and well. No worries at all."

"Well good, Henry. I guess we'll need to be more careful with you from now on," she said. She grinned and ran her finger along the collar of her shirt. Henry felt like a small mammal about to be devoured by some large jungle cat. He murmured a 'Thank You' and hurried away.

In the afternoon Henry was making rounds down in the basement. He stopped by the IT department to pick up and deliver mail and to take special coffee orders. Ian hopped up from his chair and walked over.

"Henry, you're like my favorite person in the world right now. I want the usual, you know the caramel machiatto half-caff, but I'm jones'ing for a vanilla shot." Henry was writing the order on a notepad. "Oh and also they released that girl you were talking about. Yeah it turns out, she didn't know anything. Everything she said checked out...I guess...so vanilla, v, a, n, i...oh you got it, okay good."

"Um, Ian, I'm afraid I missed that middle bit. Caramel machiatto half-caff with a vanilla shot and?"

"Oh, no that's it."

"Then, what else did you say? And Ian, why would you think I wouldn't know how to spell vanilla?"

"Cause you're foreign right? Anyway, they released that girl you were asking about. Yeah, I guess she didn't know anything so they let her go. So it was even weirder that she went through a portal...I mean...hello...death wish...well no, 'cause they rez too don't they?..., so maybe like...life-is-not-as-good wish...mmm, no. Oh well." Ian turned around and wondered off still mumbling about something. Henry stood next to his cart with the notepad in his hand processing what he'd just heard. 'She's free,' he thought. Henry had been planning on killing himself and spending another night combing the tower as ghost Henry, but not now. Now he needed a change of plans.

He spent the rest of the day mentally devising ways to find Lauren in Heaven. He hoped that if they had interrogated her, there would be a record of it somewhere. If he could find it, maybe he could find where she lived. He wasn't very familiar with the enforcement side of the castle but there again was another opportunity for effective spying.

Henry left work in the evening, carefully avoiding walking past the door to Astrid's office. She always left it open and always seemed to be looking out. Twice that day she had caught his eye and both times were disconcerting. Astrid's 'I like you' look was not that much different from her 'I'm going to send you to a demon,' look. Henry had been thinking recently of how to let her down without damning himself and everyone in the office to the fiery hell of a dragon scorned. Even if this problem was solved by his disappearance, he still felt for his long suffering coworkers. He shook his head and sighed. 'How is it that I'm in Heaven now and I'm still damned?' he wondered.

Henry walked into his room, kicked his shoes off, and collapsed onto his bed. As he shifted around finding a comfortable way to lie down, he felt the lump of the sword between the mattress and box spring. He had not seen it in daylight and decided to get it out and have a look at it in the sun. He felt under the mattress until his fingers made contact with the sword. As they did, he slumped over dead, lifeless on his bed with his arm still stuck under the mattress.

A good hour and a half later, after the sun set, Henry's ghost rose up out of his body. He reached into the bed and pulled the sword out from between the mattress and box spring. He sighed as he held the sword and looked at it. "Well now," he said, "this changes things a bit."

*****

The next morning when the sun rose, Henry resurrected. He took a couple of hand towels from the bathroom and used one of them to hold the sword. He sat straddling the bed and laid the sword out in front of him on one of the towels. In the sunlight, it was a beautiful color, a shifting combination of gold and silver highlights embedded in a metal which was both of those colors and neither of them. The sword was engraved and some of the flourishes contained small jewels. He carefully wrapped the sword in the towels and placed it back between the mattress and box spring.

He went to work and went through his daily routine. He delivered and picked up mail, made copies, took coffee orders, and delivered the result; he even emptied Chloe's trash can which had somehow been overlooked. After he had received all the 2:pm coffee orders, he pushed his cart outside to go to the coffee stand, and there she was. Lauren stood there at the coffee stand talking casually to Jared. She turned to him and smiled. Henry left the cart and strode right over to her. He embraced her, kissed her, embraced her again. There she was; her familiar height, arms, lips, even the smell of her hair. Henry dissolved into joy.

Their reunion was interrupted by Jared clearing his throat. Henry and Lauren looked at him. He nodded in the direction of some nearby Guardsmen. Henry frowned.

"What? I can't hug my wife?" he asked. Lauren stepped out of their embrace.

"No, he's right Henry. If I was just your wife, but I'm also a recent suspect and service workers …are always suspect," she said.

191

"Let them suspect, I don't care," Henry said. He took her in his arms again. A nearby Guardsman started to watch them with narrowed eyes. Henry let her go.

"Alright, alright. I see your point. Just a second," he said as he walked over by the building to retrieve the cart. He brought it over and started loading drinks on to the top and bottom shelves. Lauren helped. As they loaded, Henry whispered.

"Part of the beach is walled off for our use, but I'm certain that a young ocean-going girl I know could get around such obstacles and come visit me under cover of night?"

Lauren nodded. "As soon as it's dark enough. Wait for me in the open so I can see you. I'll come to you." She turned to Jared. "Thanks," she said. She touched Henry lightly on his arm and smiled at him as she walked away. Henry watched her walk away and finished loading the cart. Jared had a puzzled look on his face.

"What?" Henry said.

"I uh...I thought you were banging Astrid," he said. Henry snorted.

*****

After several days of quick coffee meetings and many secret nights together, Lauren and Henry sat together in the sand in the most secluded section of the beach that was bounded by the walls of the castle and reserved for service workers. They leaned together against some dark rocks.

"How long do we need to wait tonight before we can go to your room?" Lauren asked.

"Oh, weekends don't change things here but uh, things seem to get pretty quiet after midnight. I always get kicked out of the library around 11 or so."

"You go to the library often?"

"Oh, yes. I have got more reading done here in so many months than I did in many years at the university." He smiled at her and touched her hair.

"So you haven't been...you know...playing around?" she teased him.

"No, no, no. Don't worry. Since I've been here I have been too busy being a spy to be anyone's lover. I've been very absorbed in my task. Also, their rules for service workers...well you can get past them like you can any rules, but they do make everything difficult."

"Is it true that you're not supposed to eat during the day…at all?"

"Well, we may have coffee and tea, coffee drinks from Heaven's version of Starbucks. Also, there is the S-Caf, if one were…beyond desperate. But none of that matters. People are eating…just secretly…but if you get caught, they do get very upset about food, food and booze. Oddly though, they are not so much concerned with…affairs of the heart. They seem to look the other way in that respect. I have been trying to be a careful observer and…well let's just say that I probably won't be the only chap with a girl in his room tonight." He smiled and squeezed her. Lauren smiled but it faded quickly.

"So you haven't …?"

"Lauren, what is this really about?" She looked down at the sand. "Ah," Henry said. He put his arm around her and squeezed. "Listen, lovely, you were here for 13 years and some before I came…and even then you didn't know I was here…or that I would ever come here knowing my philosophy." He stroked her hair. "A person cannot be expected to enjoy Heaven without love can they? That wouldn't make much sense." He sat holding her for some time. She rested her head on his shoulder. "Actually Lauren, I…don't expect you to stay with me if you don't want to. The vow was 'till death do us part'. If you didn't want to stay with…" she interrupted him.

"Oh Henry, you big idiot. Stop it. Stop being a professor for two seconds. You know how I feel." They embraced and kissed and then sat quietly in each other's arms as they watched little wavelets creeping up the shore and sinking into the sand. Henry imagined himself and Lauren living freely together in a lovely house, enjoying meals, being served by ushabtis. His thoughts turned towards Elysium.

"I was sent here to recruit people and get information but all I really wanted was to find you somehow. Now that you're here and I have the sword, I think we should make plans to go back to Elysium. I'd like to get the vase of light down from the tower as well, but…mmm" He trailed off into thought. Lauren frowned.

"Henry, I…what about my family?" she asked.

"I think…that they, my people in Elysium, have figured something out with the portals in Elysium. I watch the news every morning and they post pictures of missing service workers. Something is certainly going on there in any case. With your family, we might be able to get them out or you might be able to visit. They were working on it when I left. Oh yes, here," Henry said and he reached into his back pocket. He pulled out a golden cross like the ones used by missionaries. "Do you have a bag, or a place you can carry this?" Henry asked. Lauren took the cross out of his hand. She turned it over and looked at it.

"So, this is it. You know Henry, any golden cross will work, you just have to have it touch the portal first."

"I don't know if that's true, at least from the Elysium side, but this one is the real deal. We took it from missionaries. We know it works."

"Shouldn't you keep it?"

"I don't plan on going anywhere without you, salty girl,"

"Henry, the Missionary Wells are guarded now. I saw them when I was waiting for you to come out and get coffee. There are more Guardsmen in the towns too. Do we really have to go back?" she asked.

"Well, not right away. I suppose I could smuggle the sword out. I could keep doing what I'm doing..."Henry scratched at his chin absently as he thought. Lauren watched him and smiled. "It's just that...I want to go back there. I want to live freely, eat good food,...experience the wonders of the world. The White City is beautiful and I think...I think I had only scratched the surface," Henry said. Lauren looked out at the ocean.

"Heaven is beautiful too. Don't you think you could be happy here, once you're done with service?" Lauren asked. Henry frowned. He had not told Lauren about his meeting with Osiris. He wrestled with himself over what he should or shouldn't tell her. He thought of the flood. Would Lauren still be Lauren after that?

"I know that face, Henry. That's your bad-news face. You made that face when Willa broke her arm," Lauren said.

"There is going to be a war, I think ," he said softly, "and I would like to have you safely in Elysium before that happens." Lauren searched his face.

"Why would I be safer there than here?" she asked.

"Well, for a start, in Elysium I was never aware of imprisonment and torture."

"Let's not start that again, please."

"How could you possibly want to stay here after what they did to you, Lauren? I get so angry when I think about it, it makes my teeth hurt. Are you sure you don't remember anything about them? No names or anything for me to go on?" he asked. Lauren shook her head 'no'. "I will find out who did it. There are pathways of information in the Castle and I will eventually find out."

"And then what? We rez. It doesn't matter what they did to me. I rezzed and I'm fine. Whatever you do to them, they will rez and be fine the next day too. Accuse them and your sentence will be extended. Just let it go," Lauren said. Henry scowled.

"In any case, the bottom line is that they do have the power to make people disappear. I have heard that if they really want to get rid of someone here they will send them to Hell. I have also heard that if they really want to get rid of someone in Hell, they throw them through the Lover's Door. They push people through it all the time and the rest are begging to go. No one chooses torture and death. Why on Earth would they? Here, in this place, they have the power to take you away from me again, and I might never find you."

"Is there a Lover's Door in Elysium?"

"Yes, it's at the terminal. Anyone can go through at any time...if they choose to," Henry answered. Lauren nodded. She leaned back on the rock and looked up at the sky. Stars were beginning to peek out from the twilight.

"You know what they say, Henry, they say that if a man and woman go through the gate holding hands, that they will be lovers in the Sorrowful World. And they say that if several people go through holding hands, they will be a family. Did you ever hear that?" Henry raised his eyebrows.

"No. That's news to me," he said. Lauren kept looking at the stars.

"Where is god in all this? I mean, I thought...I thought Heaven was about justice, at least a little bit. I don't understand how all of this could be happening. They shouldn't be able to send anyone to Hell who doesn't belong there and when I got here I thought the service worker thing was strange, but I had...faith that their judgment was right and fair. And Henry I...being here and living in Heaven, I feel the way I felt in the Sorrowful World about god...that he's here and I can connect with him on some level." She thought about her experience at the eternal flame and whether or not to tell him what happened. "It's just that…"she looked at him with a pained expression, "I'm sorry. I feel strange talking with you about this."

"No, it's alright. It's alright. You're safe now, love. No lectures from me. Go on."

"I was only going to say that even though I still feel that way, everything else is a colossal mess."

"Some things don't change, no matter where you are, eh?" Henry chuckled.

"Henry, I know about the coin, but what do you really feel?"

"About what?"

"About god?" Henry paused to gather his thoughts.

"Well…I feel that this place doesn't have much to do with god. This place is about people, their laws, their government …their silly rules…people have made all that. The portals, and the resurrection, works of clay… I don't know…I have been puzzled about how god fits into all that. Heaven, Elysium, all of this …has not really answered that many questions for me…I've just been presented with more mysteries."

"But you believe now don't you?" Lauren asked.

"Oh yes, I do. Don't worry about that. Unless I'm still alive and this is all …coma town, I believe…in fact it's more than that…I know." Lauren looked at him, puzzled.

"How do you know?" she asked. Henry shrugged. He thought of Osiris in the temple. "In Elysium, Osiris and Isis stand in the center of town by the fountains and hand out food and flowers. You can go right up to them, shake hands…have a nice chat. It feels…peaceful…like all your worries just melt away."

"Oh, Henry, they aren't god though. They're just…what you were telling me about…ushabti. They're not really god."

"Why not? Why can't they be god? Why can't all of the gods really be god? An omnipotent supreme being should be able to take any form or any…multitude of forms that it wants. Is it really so absurd?" Henry asked. Lauren frowned.

"It's just not…those other gods are not real. They are just animated statues or something like that. That's why all those people are down there instead of here in Heaven. God gives us free will but they made the wrong choice. That's why they can't be here." A small flower of doubt began to open in Lauren's chest.

She thought of the eternal flame and the strange woman. She assumed at the time that the woman was Mary.

"What about the people from before Christianity? Why are they separate?" Henry asked.

"They were given a choice too when the time came. That's what I've heard."

"You know, they aren't being punished. In fact, I think they have it easier than people here," Henry said.

"I just always assumed that if you were there, you couldn't …feel it anymore. You would feel the absence instead, like a hollow place in your heart. And really Henry, how much of it did you see? Maybe there are places there that you don't know about, where it is terrible like they say here. You weren't there very long, you didn't go very far or meet that many people. Maybe you were lied to." Henry was shaking his head no. Lauren continued, "Well, how do you really know…Mr., or no, no… Dr. Skeptical?" she asked. Henry put his arms around her again.

"Just like you, my salty girl, I just know." He stroked her hair again and squeezed her tight. Lauren sighed.

"I don't know what to do, Henry. I want to be with you, but I can't stand the thought of never seeing my family again. And I…as strange as it might sound to you…I don't want to turn my back on god."

"You shouldn't have to. You shouldn't have to choose or leave your family or any of it. I don't know what to do either. I just want to keep you safe and with me."

"We don't have to figure it all out tonight," she said. They embraced. Henry stroked the side of her face.

"True," he said and he kissed her.

Chapter 33

Astrid

By blackmailing Pavel, Astrid was able to get all sorts of contraband items forbidden to service workers. She thought it was very silly that service workers couldn't have alcohol, tobacco, good food, and that they couldn't mingle with the more blessed residents of Heaven. She also knew immediately, from her first day of working in the Castle, that there were ways to get forbidden items and accomplish certain tasks. There was always a way. This was how she had gotten her hands on a bottle of port; a sweet wine for a sweet night.

'Poor Pavel', she thought, 'but he really shouldn't have had that cafeteria worker bent over his desk like that…especially in the middle of the afternoon…and especially not a cafeteria worker named Matthew'. The Sorrowful World had been getting more tolerant for 60 years or so but it was not so much the case in Heaven. Heaven had more old people than young, more ancient people than modern. Astrid wasn't surprised at the fear in Pavel's face.

She walked along the hallway of the dormitory cradling the port under her jacket. Also, under her jacket, she wore lingerie; another rare set of items. She felt sexy and happy for the first time in years. 'Oh Henry,' she thought, 'you are going to get it.' He was a long realized dream for her. She had loved him when he was her professor so, so many years ago. Oddly, he didn't look quite as good being younger. She had loved his salt and pepper hair and the few, small lines around his brown eyes. She sat in the front row of his lectures with love and promises flowing from her eyes. She wanted Professor Henry Hall then and now. She wondered briefly if there was a way to age someone here, not for herself of course, but for others.

She stopped in front of Henry's door and knocked twice. There was no answer. She knocked again and listened. She looked up and down the hallway, opened his door and slipped in.

The room was dark. She shut the door softly behind her and flicked on the light. She set the bottle down on Henry's dresser and went to lie down on his bed. She stretched out, kicked off her high-heals, and nuzzled her head into his pillow.

She lay there for a few minutes and then decided to look around. Henry's room was a carbon copy of all the dormitory rooms. Hers was just like it. She had a different quilt from the Service Workers Relief Association but that was about all the difference there was. She even had the same green coffee mug next to her microwave. A few books were stacked neatly on his dresser. She read the titles aloud, "History of the Guard", "The Castle", and "The End of the Pagan World" by the emperor Constantine. "Yawn," Astrid said as she ran her fingers over the books and down their spines. She continued to look around and started to open drawers.

"Oh, he's a boxer's man…I think I knew that," she said as she went through his drawers. The drawers contained the usual; socks, boxers, t-shirts, folded pants, pajamas. The 5th drawer down was empty except for a bible. Astrid's eyebrows went up as she took it out of the drawer. "Hmm, he must really have taken it all to heart." She went to put it back in the drawer but felt the weight of the book shift strangely. She frowned and opened the cover. The center of the book was hollowed out and filled with strange coins. They shifted and began to spill out onto the floor. The coins were brass colored and bumpy, like pirate gold recovered from the sea. On each one, carved in relief, there was a religious symbol. Some coins had crosses, some had the Buddhist wheel or the Hindu 'Ohm' symbol. Some had symbols she did not recognize. On the back of each coin the words, 'Let them see' were engraved. Astrid frowned.

She picked up all the coins and put them back in the hollowed out book. She buttoned up her coat, gathered up the bottle of port and the bible, and went to leave the room. Before she left, she turned and looked at Henry's room. 'How sad,' she thought, 'I could have loved you, Henry.' Tears welled up in her eyes. She closed the door softly behind her and walked away down the hall.

Chapter 34

The Jig is Up

The next morning Henry got up and got ready for work in the usual way. Lauren left early to avoid being seen. Sunrise was a good time to be out and about. No one asked too many questions. It was a good bet that any one up and walking just after sunrise had just resurrected somewhere they didn't mean to. It was polite not to ask.

Henry arrived at work and said 'Hello' to Chloe and Sanjay as they came in. Other workers arrived but Astrid was not there. Her office door remained closed and dark. He found his cart in the mailroom and got started on his rounds, basement first.

Midmorning, Henry started taking coffee orders in the basement and headed back upstairs to take first floor orders. The only thing he noticed was that Ian was also missing from the IT department. Henry stopped next to Chloe's cubicle. Astrid strode out of her office and approached Henry. Something was wrong. Her puppy dog eyes were gone and her manner seemed cold and professional. "Henry, please come to my office next to get my coffee order. I have an important meeting that starts very soon."

"Sure thing," he said after her. She had already turned to walk away. Henry got his pen and note pad and turned his attention to Chloe.

"So Miss Chloe, what are you going to have today?" Henry asked. Chloe looked up at him with sad, pleading eyes.

"Henry, run," she whispered. "Run, now."

It took Henry a second to process that. He looked at Chloe's frightened face and then down the hall towards Astrid's office. There was someone in the office with her. He couldn't see who it was, but he thought he saw a gleam of metal, like the armor of the Guard. He turned and began to walk briskly towards the nearest exit. He wanted to make a run for the Judgment Hall and dive right through the portal to Elysium, but that door was caddy corner to Astrid's office and he knew he would never make it. His only hope was the missionary portal in the courtyard. He headed towards the door that went out by the coffee stand. Soon, he heard his name being called and cries of "Hold it!" and "Stop where you are or I'll shoot."

'Shoot?' Henry thought as he began to run down the hall that led to the exit. He burst through the door and out into the courtyard. It was about the right time for Steve and his cronies to come rising out of the well and get their 10am coffee. Henry's heart shuddered with fear and hope.

In the courtyard, several members of the Guard milled around. As Henry came through the door, he almost knocked over Lauren who was standing next to the coffee stand. He grabbed her arm and they ran for the well. The Guardsmen moved in around and behind them. Henry and Lauren moved towards the well and turned to face the approaching men.

"Do you have it?" Henry asked, breathless as the Guardsmen slowly closed in.

"Yes" she said, her voice shaking. Henry grabbed her hand and they turned to try and get over the rail and down into the missionary well. Just then Henry heard an odd sound. There was a rush of air, then a 'thunk'. He couldn't move. His side near his stomach was a fireball of burning pain. He felt wetness soaking into his shirt. He looked down and saw an arrow sticking out of his body. The arrow's feathers were black and there was a strange burn mark on the wooden shaft, as if someone had singed it just enough to blacken it. For a brief moment Henry wondered how they did it. Blood was oozing from around the wound and dripping down onto the paving stones. The pain was shocking and confusing. He looked up at Lauren and in that moment two Guardsmen grabbed her and hauled her off to the side. Tears streamed down her face as she watched him. Henry fell to his knees. He started to feel a little woozy. He didn't think that the arrow would kill him immediately, but he certainly wasn't going anywhere and it hurt like hell. If he could just fight past the pain, such intense, strangling pain.

The Guardsmen near him and a gathering crowd watched and waited for him to die. Henry took his coin out of his pocket and looked at it. His body shook slightly. He looked up at Lauren.

"I will come back for you,…I will come back," he said to her with a cracking, breathy voice. He tossed the coin up in the air behind him. Everyone in the courtyard watched the coin go up and up into the air and then watched it fall right into the missionary well. As the coin hit the bottom of the well Henry vanished. The crowd and Guardsmen in the courtyard gasped. Lauren screamed, "Henry!"

*****

Henry tumbled out of the missionary door in Elysium and rolled across the salmon colored paving stones. The coin popped out of the door as if thrown, hit the stones and rolled to a stop next to his leg. Henry looked at it and then at the arrow still lodged in his stomach. Steve, Chad and another missionary whom Henry did not recognize stopped shouting at two passers-by and turned to stare at him.

"Dude, Henry," said Steve. "Why do you have a demon-arrow sticking out of your...oh." For a moment Henry saw a look of understanding and panic in Steve's eyes that was very uncharacteristic of his personality. Henry picked up the coin and got up to stumble off towards the river, holding his side. The three missionaries watched Henry, looked at each other and fidgeted.

"Should we, ...should we go get him and bring him back?" asked the other missionary. Steve shrugged his shoulders as his eyes followed Henry until he could no longer see him. Chad shook his head.

"No, it's too dangerous. We missed him. Let's just go make the report." Chad pulled out his cross and the three of them marched up and through the portal.

Henry made an adrenaline fueled burst that took him down the path towards the river. It didn't last long. He stumbled by the palms that ran along the river-facing side of the terminal. He took a few steps, stumbled, got up and took a few more until he was close to the river's edge. He crawled the last few feet, the arrow burning in his side. He slid into the water and happily, blissfully allowed himself to drown.

Chapter 35

Swords and Angels

After Henry disappeared in front of the missionary well, all eyes turned to Lauren. An odd little moment of déjà vu hit her as the Guardsmen marched her along the castle, through a door in the stone wall, through the walled-off rose garden, and right up to the same tower cell she had previously occupied. Before they left her alone they searched her and found the cross. The two Guardsmen said nothing but for a moment their eyes burned into her.

Immediately after they left, Lauren sat down on one of the bunks and took off her shoe. Since her ordeal in the tower she always kept a broken piece of a kitchen knife wrapped in a thin bandage and tucked into the side of her shoe. Sometimes the slight bulge annoyed her, but she looked at it as an insurance policy. The Guardsmen hadn't bothered with her shoes at all when they searched her.

She took out the little bundle and unwrapped the blade. For a moment she hesitated, the stigma and taboo of suicide still ingrained in her mind. She took a deep breath and made lengthwise cuts along both arms. She slipped down off the bunk and crawled over to the corner of the cell that was so close to the open part of the wall. She held her arms out in front of her. Blood flowed from the cuts, ribbons of dark red, down onto the stone floor and out over the ledge. It took less than a minute for her to bleed out.

*****

That evening at sunset she rose up out of her corpse into ghost form. Her body and the cell were undisturbed. She thought it was odd that they would leave her alone for so long after what happened. She expected to go straight to the interrogation room, but instead they brought her here and left her. 'Are they really that stupid?' she thought.

She walked out of her cell, straight through the bars, and stood looking out at the red sunset. 'Red sky at night, sailor's delight' she thought and jumped.

Just as Henry said, her ghostly body made contact with the rocks below and then went through it as if it were just a thicker liquid than air. Everything was black all around her so she closed her eyes and listened. There it was! Henry said that underground he could hear the waves on the shore and that's how he knew what direction to walk. She could hear the muffled 'whoosh' sound of the waves. She could also feel the vibration as waves hit the beach. She slowly made her way through the rock and sand. Her ghostly head popped out into shallow water and she smiled, turning her head and looking around. Instead of walking towards the shore, she stayed in the water with just the top of her head and eyes sticking out. Two people, probably a couple, walked by on the beach. From under the water, their shapes were distorted. Other figures moved about on the beach in both directions. She would need to wait.

She turned and walked down into deeper water. Presently, she came to the big U and sat on it. She considered her options. How long before they came to her cell and found her body? Would they bring an angel to rez her? How long did she have before she could get to the dormitory unseen by men or angels? She had to leave but she needed to get Henry's sword first. The sword seemed too important to just leave it there, stuck in the mattress. She decided to go back to the dormitory, get the sword and then try for a portal. Maybe she could hide with the old ones like Rosie said. Maybe she could get a message to her mother. She sighed and looked at the dark stones of the portal resting on the sandy sea floor. 'I could go through there,' she thought, 'but then where would I be? Could I get back? What kind of portal rezzes you as you go through?' None she had ever heard of. She decided to stick with her first plan.

Lauren waited near the big U until it was dark and everyone left the beach. As she walked up through the water to the shore, she wondered if angels could swim. She pictured them getting wet and then carefully preening their wet feathers awkwardly with human mouths. The image made her giggle.

After some time, the beach was empty and she walked out of the water slowly, watching for people. She ran from the water to the tower wall and went straight through it into the basement. She hugged walls and ran in the general direction of the dormitory, stopping only to duck into a closet or a dark room and listen. The basement was quiet.

The dormitory presented its own problems. There wasn't really anyone up and about, but there was someone in every room. Lauren crept up the stairs and down Henry's hall. Ahead of her she heard the noise of someone coming and quickly ducked through the wall on her left. She froze. The TV was on in the room with the sound turned down. A man and a woman lay cuddled up together, sleeping. She relaxed. 'I guess Henry was right about everybody sleeping around,' she thought. The sound of footsteps went by in the hall so she kept going through the wall into the next room. This room was dark. A woman lay in the bed snoring softly. 'The next room should be Henry's,' she thought.

She went through the wall again into the next room. Dim moonlight allowed her to see the familiar trappings of Henry's room, but she was not alone. A woman lay sleeping in Henry's bed. She still wore what Lauren assumed were her work clothes. One of her black high heels was on the floor. The other still clung to one of her stocking feet. An empty bottle of the something lay on the floor next to the bed. The woman was very attractive, even laying there sleeping and in disarray. Lauren frowned at her and crept carefully around the side of the bed. She pushed her ghost hand through the mattress and soon felt the cool metal of the sword. How odd it was to feel something in ghost form, much less lift it and feel its weight. Slowly she pulled the sword out. The woman did not wake or even move. Lauren suspected that she had drunk herself into a stupor. As if to answer her question, she saw some vomit on the floor, near the head of the bed.

'Now what?' she thought. She looked down at the sleeping woman and a tinge of jealousy began to rise in her ghostly stomach. She knew it was stupid to feel that way, but the suspicion and anger rose none-the-less. The thought floated through her mind, after all, she was holding a sword…but to what end? She would only produce a confused ghost. Lauren turned and stepped through the outside wall. The half of her body carrying the sword went through the open window. She stepped off the wall and fell to the ground. This time she landed in the ground only up to her knees and was able to extricate her legs from the earth and keep walking.

She ran, taking cover periodically near a wall or under a tree, towards the center courtyard where she knew there was a portal. It was the closest one she could think of. Unfortunately, like most portals, it was out in the open, separated from any nearby buildings or trees. She would need to run for it.

Just before she made it to the portal she heard the familiar swish and rustle of angelic wings. She felt warm fingers on her ghostly arms, which immediately became flesh. The angel lifted her up. "Not this again," she said under her breath.

"You should drop your weapon. You can't hurt me," the angel said. His voice was pleasant and deep, calm and unmoved. Lauren watched the ground beneath them. The angel was flying her back up to the tower in the most direct route. He shifted her in his arms, as if he was having trouble holding her weight. Lauren watched the ground below and waited.

"Something is wrong with you. I must keep healing you to keep you alive."

"Well, you could just drop me. That would work."

"I have never felt this before. Are you human?" he asked. Lauren watched the buildings end and the moonlit shoreline begin. The angel turned and flew upward, aiming for the hole in the wall where her cell was. Directly beneath them was the little bit of shallow water and sand next to the rocks by the bottom of the tower. Gripping the sword with two hands she stabbed backward between her arm and body. The angel cried out in pain and let go of Lauren's arms. The sword instantly killed her. At the moment of death she let go of it.

Her body landed with a splash in shallow water. The sword lay nearby in the sand. Lauren's ghost got up and out of her body and raced to pick up the sword as the wounded angel approached her from the air. She grabbed the sword and ran back just as he landed in the same spot. He held his hand to his side where blood trickled out. He appeared to be in pain. Lauren stood facing him with the sword in her hand.

"That sword...where did you get it?" he asked. His breath was labored. Lauren began to feel sorry for him.

"You...do you feel that pain?" she asked. The angel nodded.

"Why, I mean...Don't you...you should have the same blessings that we do. Do angel's rez?" she asked, suddenly fearful.

"Do we what?" he asked. He went to his knees.

"Resurrect. Don't you resurrect when you die?"

"Yes, of course...but I don't want to do it here. It shouldn't...you can't hurt us... never hurt us. You're too weak."

He sat on the sand and let his legs go out in front of him. He held out his hand and a small, golden horn appeared in it. He blew one sharp blast which pained him even more. The sound bounced against the rock wall of the castle and reverberated against the nearby rocks. Lauren took a step back. The angel looked up at the sky. The bright half-moon shone through wispy clouds. After the trumpet blast, everything seemed very quiet. Curiosity got the better of her and she looked back at the angel and pointed up, towards the moon.

"Is god up there? Up on that floating island place where everybody says the angels are…where you live?" Lauren asked. The angel shook his head and looked at her, as if seeing her for the first time. He looked pale and a bit sad.

"No, there's no …island up there…just clouds. You don't know anything...about anything," he said as he removed his leather and gold armor and an ivory cloth tunic underneath. He lay down on the sand, his chest bare. Blood oozed from his wound and through his fingers where he held it, coloring them dark red. Blood soaked into the sand. Lauren came nearer to him and knelt in the sand.

"Then *tell* me something. I died and I came here and I still…I still don't understand. Where is god? Where is the real Jesus? I went to the eternal flame and it was in ruins and …Why…how can he let all these terrible things happen?" The angel laughed and smiled. His teeth were red with blood.

"So you've seen Jesus, have you? Oh that's funny." He panted and coughed. "You know what we say when humans ask questions? We say 'God works in mysterious ways.' You know what that means?" He sat up and spat blood. He frowned at the red spot in the sand and wiped his mouth. "It means stop asking questions that you are too stupid to understand the answers to." He lay back down. "My friends will be here soon and they will take you and your magic sword. You will go to hell for this. There." He pointed up as best he could. Lauren looked up and saw movement, a slight flutter. Gray-white shapes moved across the moon and down, closer and closer. The angel looked back at her.

"If you don't belong here you should go now," he whispered. Lauren looked up at the approaching host of angels and down at the wounded one.

"I'm sorry," she said. "I thought you would die and rez like we do. I didn't think I was hurting you. I'm sorry." The angel nodded but did not reply. He closed his eyes. She turned and ran into the water and through it, like it was air. As she approached the big U she heard the splashes of angels entering the water. In the moonlight, she could see their shadows on the sandy sea bottom. She ran to the U, hopped over the arch of the portal and went straight through. Her last thought before she went through the portal was, 'I guess they can swim'.

*****

No angels followed her through the portal. She tumbled into a small dark closet. Passing through the portal did resurrect her, but she only had enough time to realize that she was still holding the sword and dropped dead again. Her ghost rose up out of her body, sprawled on the floor. "This is really getting annoying," she said.

In front of her she could just make out a line of dim light coming from the crack under a door. She stepped through the door.

Chapter 36

Hurry Up and Wait...and Then Kill People

As Lauren stepped through the door of the closet, the sword would not come through along with her ghostly arm, so she came back through the door and laid it down on the floor next to her body. She turned, went back through the door and stood looking at an empty airplane terminal. To her right there were rows and rows of chairs. Beyond that, at the end of the terminal, was a large portal, much larger than the ones she'd found along beaches and in towns. Opposite from her there were more rows of chairs and a symmetrical door in the wall. There were many windows on both sides, all looking out on darkness. There also seemed to be vending machines of some sort. 'That's weird,' she thought. Further down the other side of the terminal there was a standard airport entry point. The whole place was lit with dim, fluorescent lights hanging from the ceiling. The center walkway of the terminal ended in a large, round staircase, open to the air. With a great, ghostly sigh of relief and elation she realized she was not in Hell, but in Elysium.

Henry told her that if they were ever separated and she managed to go through the gate in the Judgment Hall, to stay at the terminal until he came for her. He said that just coming through the terminal door would make her name appear on a stone wall downtown in the White City. She decided to wait, at least until morning when she rezzed, to try to go to town and find Henry.

She turned and went back into the closet. She examined the door handle and frowned. Unfortunately, it was a bulb type knob rather than a handle. There would be no way she could grip it with her ghostly hands. She tried anyway just to be sure, but her hand went right through it. She looked around the closet in the dim light. There were mops, buckets and rags, a sink, and even a buffing machine. Nothing looked useful except for the sword. She picked it up from the floor and, grasping it with two hands, brought it down, hilt first on the doorknob. The brass knob popped off easily and dropped to the floor with a soft thud. The door knob on the other side also popped off and rolled away somewhere in the terminal. She pushed the door open with the sword and walked out with a triumphant smile.

She walked across the building to the entry point she had seen earlier. There was a set of double doors which were propped open. There appeared to be a walkway there, just like the extendable ones used to funnel passengers on and off planes. Curious, Lauren walked through the doors and into the walkway. When she came to the end of the tunnel, there she was standing at the same double-door side entrance to the same terminal. She turned and walked back and it was the same. Apparently wormhole doors that bend time and space back on themselves were a common feature in the afterlife. Lauren chuckled.

As she stood at the entrance looking around, the vending machines caught her eye. She approached one to investigate. Rather than snacks or sodas the machines contained pamphlets. All the vending machines, there were three in all, contained the same trifold pamphlet. She couldn't really extricate one of the pamphlets without breaking the machine but she found one lying discarded on the floor. It read:

"LAST CHANCE for HEAVEN! Go to the missionaries and submit. Come to Heaven! Save yourself from a life of sadness and brutality."

It went on like that on all the pages and even had a few pictures of smiling people shaking hands with missionaries in their Island of Sanctity, or standing in front of palatial homes. In one picture a smiling man was shaking hands with an angel. The wings looked photo-shopped and the man, handsome maybe, but not angelic. She thought about the angel she had injured and how rude and condescending he was. 'Yup,' she thought with a smirk, 'He probably wouldn't shake a human's hand."

She left the vending machines and walked to the vast rows of chairs and had a seat. As she sat looking all around her she realized that the building had an interesting symmetry to it. At one end was the large set of stairs that led right out to the desert. Directly opposite, was the large portal that must be the Lover's Door. It hummed slightly. The center of it, the invisible membrane, seemed to have some color in it. It made the terminal wall behind it slightly pink.

On either side of the Lover's door, were the walls of the terminal. The broken door to the closet she came out of was ajar, the brass knob a few feet away on the gray carpet. Directly opposite that door, on the other side of the terminal, was another, identical door.

Intrigued, Lauren got up and went to investigate this door. She used the sword to bust off the door knob and then pulled it open with the blade of the sword. There was an identical closet inside. The same mop, bucket, brooms, and floor buffer sat in the dim closet in the same configuration. She held one hand out in front of her and walked cautiously forward. At a certain point she felt the silky, metallic sensation of a portal and the slight resistance as her ghostly fingers pushed through. She sensed heat on the other side and immediately pulled her hand back. As she did, a puff of air came through with her hand. It stunk of sulfur and something that had burned. She grimaced and backed out of the closet, closing the door as best she could with the sword.

Next in the line of symmetry was the jetway, which was apparently a one-way trip from the Judgment Hall. Directly across from that was a windowless section of wall. She lay the sword down on the carpet next to the wall and looked around. The terminal was still dark and quiet. She stepped through the wall. There was a space there, closet-sized but empty. Oddly, the secret room had a skylight. Moonlight shone down in a diffuse beam. Lauren stepped forward with her arms extended and the familiar feeling of the portal met her fingers. She wanted to step through and have a look but fear kept her back. She had no way to know if the portal was one-way or not. She turned and left the room. Back in the terminal, she picked up the sword.

The terminal was carpeted, which made the mops, brooms, and floor buffers that much sillier. The carpet ended near the large stone staircase that led directly outside. It didn't even end nicely and wasn't sealed. Free, little strands stuck out from a frayed edge. Lauren lifted the edge up with the sword and saw more stones underneath. She stood looking at the terminal, the doors and closets, the Lover's Door at the end. She began to get a sense in her mind that the terminal building was a later addition to some sort of stone structure with large, free standing portals. The Lover's Door at the end with Heaven on the right, Hell on the left, another part of Heaven and what else? What was the moonlit door? These mysteries would need to wait, a little longer anyway. The sun was coming up.

*****

211

As the sky began to lighten, Lauren sat down on the top step of the rounded stairs, put the sword down next to her on the step, and watched as the first red-orange rays of light crept across the sand dunes in the distance. "Oooo" she said out loud, and then giggled at the idea of herself being a ghost and saying "Ooo". As the light reached her, she rezzed into her whole, fleshy, fully clothed self. She started to rip the fabric of her dress along her hem. She also ripped off one of her sleeves to use to hold the sword as she wrapped it. It was a tricky business, painstaking and awkward. She chuckled at the idea of the missionaries finding her dead on the stairs and then touching the sword and dying one after the other on top of her. The missionaries were of course, Larry, Curly and Moe. She smiled as she worked. When she finished, she had an awkwardly ripped dress and a wrapped sword of instant death which she could wield without dropping dead herself. She felt very satisfied.

She wandered around the terminal. Other people began to arrive but they stayed well clear of her. Their eyes went wide when they saw the sword and they rushed to get away. She gave up trying to talk to any of them.

The sunrise turned into late morning and still no one came for her. She began to get anxious. She walked over by the missionary Island of Sanctity with its door-shaped portal, little pond, and ridiculous red velvet bank ropes. She ran her fingers over the ropes, faded and orangey from the sun. By the small pond nearby she saw delicate, blue and white lotuses resting on the water. There were lilies and other water plants around the pond. As she watched, a small green frog hopped from a lily pad into the dark water. The whole area was shaded by a couple of palm trees and a few bushes that she could not immediately identify. It was all quite pretty in the morning light.

Just then Lauren heard soft, murmuring voices and the scuffle of feet very nearby. Not knowing what to do, she crouched down behind some of the bushes near the pond and listened. She saw the backs of three missionaries standing behind the red velvet bank ropes.

"Chad, who's up first?" said a dark haired man. A blond, short haired man dressed in a white collared shirt, black tie, and black slacks looked over a clipboard that he held.

"Mmmm, unpronounceable Indian name, unpronounceable Indian name, Joe Smith…ha ha that's funny.

Yeah…we don't need to yell," Chad said as he looked down the list.

"But, dude, we always yell," said another man that Lauren couldn't quite see.

"Steve, I can't pronounce these names. Can you?" Chad showed him the clipboard. Steve read and looked confused.

"Those are names?" he asked.

"Exactly," said Chad. He frowned.

"Can't we… like, can't we just shout 'Hey Indian Dude…Glory of god over here…dude…or something?" pleaded Steve.

Chad shook his head and grimaced. The other dark haired man began to yell anyway.

"Come to Heaven with us! Accept the One True God! Come before it's too late," he shouted at some passing Indian men but they ignored him.

Lauren was getting angry as she listened. Even if Henry had been lied to by people here, people in Heaven were definitely being lied to every day. She stood up and walked out in front of them holding the sword. The three men stopped everything they were doing and stared at her, mouths agape.

"Do you tell them that if they do go with you that they'll have to do service for a hundred years or more?" Lauren asked. Anger rose within her and colored her cheeks pink. The three men stared at her, frozen in place. The dark-haired man eyed her sword. "Do you tell them that if they say the wrong thing in a public place they could be held prisoner…questioned…even tortured?" Chad frowned when she said this. He looked at Steve. Steve shrugged his shoulders. Lauren continued. "Do you tell them that they can't eat during the day? Or how about…how about this…do you tell them about the gift of pain?" She stepped forward and her leg brushed against the velvet bank ropes. She slashed at them with the sword. They disintegrated into ribbons and stuffing. She kicked over two of the brass stands. The three men cowered together and inched backwards. Chad looked at the missionary door. "Catch!" Lauren shouted and she tossed the sword at them.

Chad and the dark-haired missionary both made contact with the blade of the sword and fell dead, hunched over on the salmon-colored paving stones. The sword skittered away across the stones. Only Steve remained, looking at her with wide eyes and holding his hands in the air in surrender. Lauren came forward and picked up the sword. Steve took a step back.

"Lauren, you don't need to do…"

"Liars…you are all liars," she shouted. "None of you know what's going on. It's all just another…stupid game of power, just like it always was."

"I know," said Steve, his surfer accent and mannerisms gone. "I'm one of you…one of the rebels. I smuggle things. How do you think Henry got his coins?" Steve said. Lauren frowned at him.

"You know Henry? And you knew my name. How do you know Henry and my name?" she asked keeping the sword pointed at him.

"I know Henry and I've seen you too, getting coffee and talking to Jared. The missionary office and the Waiting Room are in the same department," he said. Lauren stared at him. She moved closer and looked into his eyes. "Look, if you don't believe me go look under that bush. There will be stuff there for me to take up." She continued to stare and say nothing. The anger left her face and was replaced with searching and confusion. "Look, it's okay if you kill me. It will look bad if you don't." She took another step towards him.

"Steve…" she said softly, "That's not…who you are… that's not your name…I know you, your name is…" Steve caught her as she dropped the sword and slumped to the ground.

"No, no, dammit, no! Don't know me…you don't know me…shit! HELP!" he shouted. "HELP!"

Steve picked her up and carried her to where the paving stones ended in sand. He arranged her so that both her arms were extended. He filled her hands with sand until they were almost buried in it. Lauren's body began to change, twisting and morphing in and out of other shapes of the people she had been in previous lives until her form became a vague blur. Steve knelt next to her on the sand and held her forearm. "Go back to the light. Go back to the light and remember who you are."

Chapter 37

Dave the Badass

Henry, Ra-Neferu, Burhan, and Marc Cabrera, now young and fighting fit, stepped out of the portal near the river docks at the terminal and ran up the path to the missionary island. Henry found Steve sitting on the sand next to a shifting, morphing person in the flood. Henry's sword lay nearby in the sand, though the handle was wrapped in a familiar fabric. Steve stood up and approached them. He looked nervously at the portal.

"Look, I don't have a lot of time. We were due back 10 minutes ago. With everything that has happened recently, they will send in Guardsmen to see what happened. You guys need to take her to the House and somebody needs to kill me before I lose my cover. Ra-Neferu, I won't be able to take what's there today," he said. Ra-Neferu reached out to touch his arm.

"Don't worry. I'll take care of it," she said. They all looked at Lauren's blurred form on the sand.

"She was here when we came through," Steve said. "She was angry. She killed the other two. I'm sorry…but she remembered me and that was it."

"It was not your fault, Steve. Good luck cannot last forever. Thank you for everything you have done," Ra-Neferu said. Steve nodded and started walking back to the portal. "Henry, would you please take the sword and kill Steve, over there with the others." Henry nodded and picked up the sword. Steve waited for him by the portal, eyeing the sword as Henry approached.

"It doesn't cause pain or anything does it?" Steve asked.

"No, just…instant death. The thing killed me a time or two." Henry smiled at the sword. Steve frowned.

"I hate ghost form," he said.

"Look Steve, I wanted to thank you. You've done so much for us and…at no small cost. I don't know how you do it. I never once suspected…" Steve nodded and smiled, then as if he had flipped a switch, he was 'dude Steve' again.

"Dude, righteous sword. Can I touch it?"

"Sure," Henry held it out to him. Steve touched the tip of the sword and slumped over dead, right on top of his fallen co-workers.

Henry looked at the pile of dead missionaries, what was left of the velvet bank ropes, and the overturned brass stands.

"Wow, she was angry," he said. He turned and walked back to Ra-Neferu, Burhan, and Marc. Ra-Neferu was giving orders.

"Burhan, please go to the House of the Lost and get a stretcher," she said. Burhan nodded and ran off. Ra-Neferu looked past Henry at the missionaries. "That will not go over well," she said.

"What? No harm done. They'll rez," Marc said. Ra-Neferu shook her head.

"When insult to the body does not matter, insult to honor does. Things are escalating. We must expect retaliation soon. " Her attention turned to Henry's sword. "Henry, will you hold that up for me." He complied and she examined the sword closely.

"I think...that this is the sword of Yama," she said.

"What, really?" Henry said with renewed wonder. Ra-Neferu nodded.

"Who's Yama?" Marc asked.

"Yama is an old god, the Hindu god of their underworld," Ra-Neferu explained. "There are many such weapons, divine weapons. This one is called, 'The Turning Hand'. It gives death, but also life, somehow. I do not know how it works."

"Well, the death part is pretty obvious," Marc said. He indicated the pile of dead missionaries. "Ah Henry, do you mind if I..." he pointed at the sword. Henry nodded and handed it to him. Marc sauntered off with the sword, testing the weight of it. Henry sat down in the sand next to Lauren. Ra-Neferu sat with him.

"So, what now?" Henry asked.

"Burhan will come back with the stretcher and we will take her to the House of the Lost." Henry frowned. "You remember, we went by it several times in the city. It is where people in the flood stay until they recover."

"Will it take long?"

"There is no way to tell. It is not good that we couldn't...bind her to the earth. It was good of Steven to fill her hands with sand, but that is probably not enough. It could take hours or weeks." Ra-Neferu ran her hand around the shifting form. Where she 'touched' Henry could see the constantly changing skin and clothes of the different people that Lauren had been in her many lives. Her form shifted through men, women, children, and infants. Henry felt sick for a moment and looked away.

"I was terrified when I had my flood, but it was over…so quickly….so wait, why hours and weeks? Mine was over in minutes, wasn't it?" Henry asked. Ra-Neferu shook her head.

"Your Flood took 11 hours. We started you in the morning and you came out of it that evening. That is about average. If it lasts longer than a day we transfer people to the House." She looked up at the missionaries and the portal. "She cannot stay here."

"I thought…I thought it only took a few minutes," he said.

"From your perspective, it did. You had no sense of time in the Flood and neither does she. It is worse for her that she had no preparation. You should have told her, Henry. You may not remember the lives in Heaven but you knew that you had them."

"I was afraid. I was afraid that if I told her, she wouldn't come here." Ra-Neferu pursed her lips.

"You must allow people their choices, Henry, even if you do not like them. Now, I am done scolding you. I know you just want her back and…she will find her way out of the flood eventually. No one stays forever." She gave him a reassuring smile. Henry continued to look dejected.

"What if she is not herself anymore? What if she chooses someone else?" Henry asked.

"Well, most people chose their most recent life, if only because they tend to be so much better educated and good with technology. It is a fifty-fifty kind of thing as you are fond of saying." Just then Burhan came running up carrying something that looked like two wooden poles wrapped in white canvas. Marc was standing by the missionaries poking them with the sword.

"Marc, come on," Burhan yelled to him as he unrolled the stretcher. Henry frowned at it. It looked flimsy.

"Will that hold her?" Henry asked.

"Yes," Burhan answered," when they are in the flood like this they shift and change…they weigh almost nothing. The trouble is getting them on the thing."

The four of them worked to put the stretcher down next to Lauren's form and shift her onto it. It was tricky. Henry would reach for a leg or a hand and it would shorten and disappear into an infant's leg or hand. Ra-Neferu was having the same trouble. Meanwhile Burhan tried to maneuver the stretcher underneath the

217

form. He grabbed at Lauren's arm and caught it. For an instant, Lauren became Lauren again. "Henry?" she said. "Burhan?, Burhan…why…why did you leave me?" Lauren dissolved and faded back into the flood of people. Henry glared at Burhan with burning eyes. Burhan took a step back and put his hands up defensively. Henry stood up.

"Henry please, I didn't know," Burhan said. Henry glared at him, looked at the sword on the sand where Marc had laid it down, and looked back at him. Burhan shook his head. "Not now, you need me now. You can punish me later if you want but not here. They'll take my body back and send me to hell. Don't kill me here." Henry clocked him right on the jaw. Burhan stumbled backwards.

"Enough!" Ra-Neferu said. "We have work to do. If you must act like children you can do it later, not now." Henry knelt down next to Marc who was working to get Lauren's form on the stretcher. Burhan got up from the sand and followed.

"It's okay," Marc said, "I managed. I scooted her on there before she faded out. We got her. Let's go before they come."

"They're here," Burhan said, looking towards the portal. Henry looked up to see three members of the Guard inspecting the dead missionaries. He picked up the sword.

"Take her. I'll be along shortly," Henry said. He turned and walked towards the men. As he approached, one of the Guardsmen saw Ra-Neferu and the others carrying the stretcher away and moved towards them, drawing his sword. Henry took his head off with a glide and a stroke. The sword made it easy, effortless. The other two Guardsmen pulled weapons from their belts and made ready. In that moment, Henry slashed at them both. He hit one, a glancing blow, but of course it was enough. The Guardsman dropped dead. The last Guardsman took a step back. He pulled a dagger out of his belt. Henry feinted left and when the Guardsman moved right, Henry thrust the sword into his stomach. The Guardsman slumped onto the step of the missionary portal, blood pouring out onto the paving stones. Henry stood quietly and looked at them, at Chad, and Steve, and the unknown others. Bitter anger rose in his throat. He searched Chad for his cross and used it to activate the nearby missionary portal. Then, as best as he could, he picked up each man and tossed him through. He picked up the golden cross and threw it hard through the portal. He envisioned the cross coming out the other side and pinging one of the Guardsmen in the head. Finally, he attacked the wooden portal itself with the sword, shattering it to pieces.

*****

Henry followed as Marc and Burhan carried the stretcher through the portal behind Ra-Neferu. She said 'House of the Lost' and instantly they all stood in the street in front of a tall building near the center of the White City. They ascended the stairs and entered.

The interior of the building was dim and cool compared to the bright light and heat outside. There were no interior walls. The roof was supported by large, round pillars. Colorful banners hung down from the ceiling, separating the interior into 'rooms' and 'corridors'. They were shiny, like silk, and white, golden yellow, burgundy and deep sapphire blue. Small windows dotted the exterior walls and allowed light to shine in rays from the left side of the building. The banners were never flush and often moved slightly in a breeze. The play of color and light was gorgeous.

In each of the bannered 'rooms', there was a stone pedestal. Ra-Neferu led them along until they found an empty one. Marc and Burhan carefully shifted Lauren's form onto the pedestal.

"Henry," Ra-Neferu said in the voice she used when she was giving orders, "you will stay here until evening, then someone else will take a shift." Henry lifted his hand to protest but she cut him off with a dangerous look. "Marc, I have work for you. Burhan, you will come with me as well." She turned again to Henry. "When she wakes up, we need to know how she came through and what else happened after you left. Even if she is…someone else…she will still have this information." Ra-Neferu approached Henry and gave him a sympathetic hug. As she did, she gently took the sword from his hand. He didn't protest. "We will send you dinner," she said and turned to leave with Burhan and Marc in tow. Henry sat on the edge of the pedestal.

"Lauren," he whispered, "come back to me."

*****

In every 'room' of the House of the Lost where a pedestal stood, there was also a small stone table with some candles. As the sun set, Henry lit these candles with some matches he found on the table. The fabric banners hanging near Lauren's pedestal were white and gold and the candlelight bathed everything in a comforting yellow glow. Henry felt tired. He sat on the floor with his back against the stone of the pedestal. In a strange way, this reminded him of waiting on Lauren the many times she was in the hospital. Over their lives together he had spent several days' worth of hours in hospital waiting rooms, patient rooms, and for a while, chemo rooms. He waited for them to deliver their daughter by C-section. He waited for them to diagnose her with diabetes, with cancer, to treat her, to remove her breast, to give her chemo, and later, in the end, to tell him she would never wake up. Now here he was again, waiting for her to wake up.

Henry heard footsteps and soft speech and was happy to see Ra-Neferu and Marc as they walked towards him. Marc was carrying a covered tray.

"Brought you some food, Doc," Marc said as he put the tray on the small table next to the candles. "And something to …drink." Marc smiled as he put a bottle of amber liquid on the table. Ra-Neferu sat on the edge of Lauren's pedestal. She seemed about to say something but stopped and turned instead. A slight breeze disturbed the candles and banners and then they became very still, almost as if they had frozen in time. The area became very quiet. Marc looked at Henry, his face full of questions.

The room was dark around the edges from candlelight. A figure approached them and resolved into a woman once she stepped into the light. She wore a white, pleated linen dress and a large necklace with many jewels. Her dark hair spilled out onto bare shoulders. She also wore a light crown, so thin it was almost a tiara. Her face was beautiful, flawless, and serene. In one hand she carried a delicate blue lotus flower. Henry felt the aura of peace descend on him and wash away all his petty worries. Now he recognized her as the goddess Isis. He and Ra-Neferu bowed to her. She nodded to them in return and stepped up to the pedestal. Marc watched everything with wide eyes but stayed silent.

Isis smiled as she looked at Lauren's form on the pedestal. She ran her hand over the changing, blurred form just as Ra-Neferu had done. Suddenly, they could all see Lauren, clear as day, lying on the pedestal in the midst of all that strange motion and chaos. Henry gasped. Isis continued until her hand came to Lauren's face. Lauren lay with her eyes closed, but wet tears ran down her cheeks. Isis ran her fingers over Lauren's cheeks and then rubbed her thumb and forefinger together. As soon as Isis' hand left Lauren's form, the chaos and strange motion returned to its former opacity. Henry suddenly felt very sad.

"They need the water," Isis said with a voice like honey. She looked at Henry. "The sea is their mother. Put them in the sea and they will remember how to be one," she said. Henry bowed to her again and again she nodded. She turned and left them. It took a few seconds for them to shake off the trance.

"*Who* was that?" Marc said with wide eyes. "I've never felt anything like that in my life…lives…any of them. Wow, Doc! What just happened?"

"That was Isis. She is one of our gods," Ra-Neferu said. Marc's eyes opened even wider.

"Shit on a shingle…oh sorry…" he cleared his throat and glanced at Ra-Neferu, "but Doc, I thought, I thought that was all myths. Hell, you said it was all myths," Marc said.

"It's worse than that, Marc. ALL gods are real here; all gods from all cultures and all mythologies. You don't know the half of it," Henry thought of his fireside chat with Osiris. "…or even the quarter of it." He turned to Ra-Neferu. "So Neffie, where's the nearest ocean?" Henry asked. Ra-Neferu smiled.

*****

Ra-Neferu, followed by Marc and Burhan carrying Lauren's stretcher and Henry behind them, stepped through a portal onto the golden sand of a lovely beach. The sun was just rising over the water. Henry and Marc brought the stretcher down to the water and lowered it into the wet sand and shallow wavelets that came and receded, came again. The amorphous form slowly took humanoid shape until finally it solidified into a man. Henry judged him to be a nearly 6 foot tall and well-muscled with short dark hair and a square jaw. He opened grey eyes and looked around. He sat up on the stretcher, looked out to sea, and smiled with a lopsided grin. He turned to look up at Henry, Burhan, Marc, and Ra-Neferu. He put his hand up casually and waved. "Hi there," he said. His voice was deep and friendly. Henry and Burhan both stared at him, speechless. Marc looked back and forth between them and the new man. Only Ra-Neferu smiled and walked forward.

"Welcome," she said. "My name is Ra-Neferu. You already know Henry and Burhan and Marc as well, I believe. They knew you when you were Lauren. Please tell us your name now." The man gave another lopsided grin. He was quite handsome in a rough, 9 o-clock shadow kind of way.

" Yeah, yeah I know you guys. My name is Dave…er David, but I go by Dave." Dave approached Henry and Burhan and extended his hand. Henry took it and shook it weakly, feeling as if the entire world had just been kicked off a nearby cliff. Burhan responded similarly.

"Hey you guys, lose the sad faces man, come on. It's all good," Dave said.

"You…you were my wife." Henry managed to choke out. Dave laughed heartily.

"And also his girlfriend." He pointed at Burhan and chuckled. "Look, I'm not your wife now. Lauren was. She's in here. Watch." In an instant Lauren stood before them, smiling in a summer dress. In a flash she was Dave again. "But I'm also this awesome guy." Dave smiled. "I know this is weird, but I think it's for the best. With everything that happened between you two and Lauren, I figured…well it was never going to be not awkward…kind of like what I just said there…you know…never not awkward." Dave chuckled again. Henry was getting annoyed with him. It didn't help that he was so friendly and handsome. "Besides, you're somebody's wife in another life," Dave pointed at Henry, "and you're somebody's girlfriend." He motioned to Burhan. "What are you going to do if those guys show up? Also, Lauren is an excellent marine biologist but I'm a Navy seal. I've got mad skills. With the war coming up and everything…" Dave scratched at his stubble as he looked from Henry to Burhan and back again. "Mmm, you guys still need some closure huh." Instantly, he turned into Lauren. She walked up to them both and tried to take a hand from each of them in hers. Ra-Neferu moved to intercept her. Lauren switched back to Dave and grinned.

"David…please stop changing back and forth. It is considered very rude and …it does not help," she said.

"Oh, hey..sorry," Dave said. "I didn't know."

"It is alright," Ra-Neferu said, but she made sure to meet his eyes to underscore her point. Dave nodded.

He took a step back and rubbed his hands together. He then turned to face the sea and breathed in deeply. When he turned back around he eyed Ra-Neferu up and down and whistled.

"So Princess, where can a guy get a beer around here?" He gave her his best dashing smile. Henry was astonished to see that Ra-Neferu had actually blushed.

Chapter 38

Dude... It's Steve

"Honestly, Neffie, I don't know how I did it or...why it worked. It was a Hail Mary pass if there ever was one," Henry said.

"A what?" she asked.

"Oh...er...it's a reference to football...American football. It just means that I threw the coin towards the missionary portal in desperation, hoping it would work. I didn't think it would work but I had nothing to lose at that point," Henry explained. Ra-Neferu frowned. She turned Henry's 'Christian' coin over in her hands and stared at it. The cross of light appeared briefly on her forehead.

They sat together in the fire pit area of her roof; Ra-Neferu, Henry and Burhan, who sat silently brooding on the end of the other sofa. In the weeks that had followed Henry's escape from Heaven and Lauren's transformation into Dave, Ra-Neferu's house had become a boarding house for liberated service workers. The whole place seemed to hum with activity. Henry heard a splash and looked out to see a few people swimming in the shallows of the river. Dave was one of them. Calf-deep in the water he threw a football to another man farther away down the shore. Henry rolled his eyes. The first thing Dave had wanted to make when he remembered works of clay was a football.

"We have tried everything," Ra-Neferu continued. "The only thing that works is native gold from Heaven. Perhaps it is a good thing that there are so many missionaries."

"Are there really so many?" Henry asked.

"Their numbers are almost as endless as ours," she said. On the end of the couch, Burhan was fidgeting.

"Ra-Neferu, has anyone ever died during their flood?" he asked. She looked up in surprise.

"Not...recently. There have been some instances that I remember. Once or twice someone has fallen into the flood and then fallen off of a barge, right into the river. One of them washed to shore, still flooding. Another of them, his body washed ashore. At sunset his ghost rose up and then ran off. We never found that one. Usually people are not trying to kill someone in the flood...before or after...yes, but not during. They change so much it is difficult to …get hold of them, to harm them. Why do you ask this, Burhan?" she asked.

"I was just trying to think of ways to deal with so many refugees, so many people in the flood. If we could cut the flood short somehow…" Burhan stared at the swimmers in the river.

Henry ignored Burhan. He was still angry with him. As much as he tried to suppress it, hide it, explain it away, his anger betrayed him. He and Lauren had spent barely a week together in Heaven before they were forced out. Now she was gone again, lost in the depths of a giant jackass named Dave. Henry's anger and grief rose and fell and rose again inside him, like little thunderstorms. Burhan only served to remind him of that loss.

Ra- Neferu stood up and went to the edge of the roof. She looked out over the river and at the distant White City. She waved and smiled at someone down near the river but her smile quickly faded to a look of concern.

"Henry," she said. Her voice betrayed a hint of alarm. "Come here, please." Henry stood and saw a man half-running, half-walking along by the river. Other people near the river ran to meet him. He wore a long, yellow robe and stumbled over it every so often. There was something wrong with him. He needed help to walk and seemed to be in pain. He pointed to the house.

"By god, Neffie, I think that's Steve," Henry said.

They all headed to the roof hatch and down the stairs. When they reached him, Steve was being supported by Dave and a woman that Henry didn't know. Steve's face was a grimace of pain. As they approached the woman said, "He's got three demon arrows in his back." Steve groaned and fell to his knees. The back of his robe was soaked with blood. He looked up at Ra-Neferu.

"It's started," he said, breathless. Blood began to trickle from his mouth. He tried to talk and spat out blood instead. "How about I…I'll tell ya about it tomorrow." He fell into the sand and died.

*****

That evening when Steve's ghost rose up out of his arrow ridden body, he and Ra-Neferu both agreed to wait until morning to talk about things. Ra-Neferu wouldn't say why. Henry watched Steve saunter off into the gathering darkness beyond the torches and lamps of Ra-Neferu's open courtyard. Steve, even in ghost form, looked heartbroken.

The next morning, breakfast was served in the courtyard, buffet style. This was becoming the norm as Ra-Neferu's guest list grew. Ushabtis shuttled to and fro, refilling heated trays and freshening drinks. Henry wondered where Ra-Neferu had conscripted them all. He also wondered how the ushabtis made ice from clay. Was it brick by brick? Was there a tray? Did they make a clay model of a freezer and have ice cube trays with water in them?

Steve showed up at breakfast and sat down to an overloaded plate with wide eyes and a big grin.

"Oh my gosh...food. It's been so long since I've had real, hot, food. This is excellent." Steve said as he shoveled food in his mouth. In between bites Steve said, "So I suppose...you want to hear...about..." Dave interrupted.

"Easy partner, you can eat. It's all good. We'll wait," Dave said. Steve paused to look around, one cheek bulging with something. He frowned. "Hey Henry, where's Lauren?" Henry and Ra-Neferu looked at each other and then at Dave. Dave put one hand on top of the other and wiggled his extruding thumbs.

"What are you doing?" Ra-Neferu asked him.

"Oh no, don't tell me you haven't seen the awkward turtle?" He said. Steve watched the scene with growing confusion.

"Steve, this is Dave...whom you once knew as Lauren," Henry said. Dave gave his trademark small wave and lopsided grin. Steve's eyes went wide and went from Henry, to Dave, and back to Henry. He swallowed his cheek-full of food and looked intently at Dave.

"Yes...I see you now, at least, I see who you were when I knew you." Dave's smile faded. Steve turned his attention back to Henry and gave him a sympathetic look. He looked back down at his plate which still had a substantial amount of breakfast foods piled on it. "I don't think...I don't think I will finish this...I just got so excited about real food...anyway, so do you folks want to have a meeting or what?" He looked at all the faces around the table. Ra-Neferu spoke first.

"Steven, I do not want to rush you. If there is something very critical yes, but otherwise it can wait," she said.

"Not so much," he said. "Things are moving in that direction, don't get me wrong, but they were not ready to...invade, when I left. I was forced to come through because they shut everything down. They recalled all the missionaries and shut down the Waiting Room operations. So many service workers were disappearing that there were problems taking in the harvest, processing the food...so they diverted all manpower. They won't use ushabti or works of clay. They think it's witchcraft." He shook his head. "Anyway, they were also sending some of us into the Guard for retraining. That was where I was ordered to go. I thought about continuing on from there but ...I'm not a good fighter...or at least Steve isn't. " Steve said. Henry looked at Steve and suddenly realized that surfer-dude-for-Jesus Steve had been replaced by this articulate, congenial man. 'What a wonderful actor he must be.' Henry thought. 'What an effective spy.' Henry was impressed.

"Where did you come through?" Henry asked.

"Well, after someone...ahem, " Steve nodded in Henry's direction, "destroyed our missionary portal in the central courtyard, I had to go to one in one of the other towns, but it was guarded. That's why I took those arrows in the back. After everything that happened with Henry and Lauren...they have an archer on every portal, 24-7."

"Hurts like hell doesn't it?" Henry asked seriously then he laughed at his own joke. "Ha ha, a demon arrow hurts like hell...fitting..." Henry chuckled. No one else laughed. Henry shrugged.

"Anyway, that was it...nothing special," Steve said. He shrugged his shoulders and looked down at his breakfast. Henry got the impression that Steve was either lying or leaving something out of his story

"Steve, what...what brought all this on? What made them shut everything down and reorganize?" Henry asked. "Did it start with my little disappearing act or...?"

"No, no...that was the talk of the Castle, no doubt, but what really riled everyone up was Lauren and the angel," Steve said. Everyone looked at Dave. He shrugged his shoulders.

"Well, apparently, after Lauren was captured she killed two Guardsmen while escaping from her cell, made rude gestures at an angel and dove through a portal to hell she found in the ocean. That was the official story anyway. There was a comical re-enactment on Heaven News 7. The actress flipped off the angel, which was blurred out of course, and then said 'I renounce heaven and I renounce Christ!' and dove gracefully into the ocean."

"Yup, that's what happened," Dave said.

"David." Ra-Neferu stared him down.

"Alright it wasn't exactly like that. I uh…I had a broken knife blade hidden in my shoe…they took the cross Henry had given me when they searched me, but they didn't check my shoes. So…I was surprised they left me alone so long. I was worried they might drag my body off somewhere and have an angel rez me but…nope…they are just really that arrogant…or bogged down with paperwork or something. So, as a ghost, I went back to Henry's room to get the sword…and there was a woman in your bed by the way…" he cleared his throat and gave Henry a look, "so I got the sword and tried to get to a portal…" Marc interrupted him.

"How did you get the sword as a ghost?" he asked. Dave shrugged.

"A ghost can hold it. It's…not an ordinary sword. Though it won't go through stuff like a ghost can. There was a few times when I went through a wall without thinking and the thing clanged out of my hand onto the ground. That made things difficult. So anyway…an angel did pick me up while I was running to a portal but I stabbed him with the sword and he dropped me, right on the beach there by the castle…and so I made a run for the big U. I told you guys about that…the big U…anyway I died and rezzed a few times in there but anyway… the angel blew some sort of war horn and others were coming so I had to beat feet."

"Was the angel hurt?" Steve asked.

"Oh yes. He had a wound in his side and he looked like it hurt him. We had a little chat about it. I mean, I did just stab an angel. I felt kinda bad about it," Dave said.

"The angel spoke to you?" Steve asked.

"Yeah. He said, 'If you don't belong here you should leave now,' and also he said that I would go to hell for what I'd done," Dave said. Steve's eyes were wide. He whispered a 'wow' under his breath.

"So I ran and then…swam for the big U," Dave said.

"How did you know there was a portal there?" Steve asked.

"I found it, well first I saw it…from up there in the tower cell the portal looks like a "U". I didn't know what it was when I first saw it but when the sun set and it was ghost busting time I needed a place to hide until the wee hours, ya know. So naturally I went into the water."

"Why didn't you just go through the portal then?" Henry asked.

"I didn't have the sword and…I didn't know where it went. That wasn't my plan at all. I was going to go home and then out to the islands. I was desperate. It was my only choice."

"And when the angels came, you still did not know where it led," Ra-Neferu said with a hint of scolding in her voice.

"I didn't have a choice, Nef. Sometimes the world doesn't give you one." Dave shrugged. "I didn't figure it for hell."

"Why not?" Ra-Neferu asked.

"Because I stuck my hand through and it wasn't hot and it didn't stink." Ra-Neferu frowned at him. Everyone at the table was silent.

"I have something else I need to tell you," Steve continued, "It doesn't really affect us that much yet but, it's something you all should know. They are planning to shut down the Judgment Hall. They hadn't done it yet when I left but preparations were underway. Everyone in the Waiting Room will be separated into two groups. Christians, Muslims, and Jews who agree to convert will go straight in to Heaven. Everybody else will go straight into service work on the farms. Nobody will come to Elysium any more…directly. They were getting ready to sort people based on what was on their forehead. I was setting up velvet ropes for lines when I left. Also, there was a rumor going around that they would start raiding," Steve said.

"What sort of raiding?" Henry asked.

"Raiding Elysium, for workers, to get them back," Steve said.

"That's ridiculous," said Burhan. "How could they keep them there?"

"They give them the gift of pain," Ra-Neferu said. "That has already happened in a few places. There have been reports of workers being subdued with pain." Everyone went quiet. Steve looked at Ra-Neferu.

"They know about the Water Door, that's what they call the portal in the ocean, Dave's big U. They are doing something with it," Steve said. "They blocked off the beach and had construction crews there. They put up big barriers. We couldn't walk on the beach anymore and I couldn't ever get out there to see what they were up to...even as a ghost...too many angels."

"David, did you say that portal is large?" Neffie asked.

"Yup. It's at least as big as the Lover's Door at the terminal," Dave said.

"This is worrying news," she said frowning, "We must investigate. We must also prepare for these raids. Burhan, send the word out. Tell people to block off the missionary portals...but not to destroy them...at least not yet. Some of them will anyway but...there is nothing we can do about that. As for the terminals..." she paused, thinking.

"I vote we burn them," Burhan said.

"We can't destroy them. We don't want to be cut off forever. We still need to get people out," Steve said. He looked frightened. Everyone nodded agreement.

"I don't think fire will destroy the stone portals, but it would burn down the terminal building. That would reveal the other portals," Dave said.

"Other portals?" Steve asked.

"When I came through the Water door it opened to a janitor's closet in the terminal. There are other portals in that building, hidden in the walls. I'm pretty sure one of them goes to hell," Dave said.

"I like the idea of burning them," Henry said, "burning the terminal building around the portals I mean, and ...exposing them again. I presume they were once exposed. I also don't believe they would be destroyed this way. Years and years of sea water have not shut down the...Water Door. We certainly can't destroy them, if such a thing is even possible. Also, the unknown portal bears investigation as well, don't you think? Even the one to Hell may come in handy ...or be very dangerous...depending on whether it's a one-way or not. We should devise some sort of test or expedition or something." He looked at Ra-Neferu. She was still frowning, her delicate brow wrinkled with thoughts and decisions.

"I remember the time before the terminal," she said, "but...it has changed." She said this more to herself than to anyone at the table.

"Then, you don't know where the other two portals go? You didn't know about them?" asked Dave. Ra-Neferu shook her head no but said nothing. She stared absently at Steve's breakfast plate then looked at Henry.

"Henry, you are right. We must investigate those portals and do something about them if we can. I do not think that destroying the terminal building will harm the portals. In fact, I know it will not. Let us burn the building around them."

"How?" asked Henry. "How do you know it won't destroy them?"

"Because I have tried to destroy them before. The Water Door is on the ocean floor because I put it there... more than 2000 years ago. At one time it was the main portal between Heaven and Elysium."

Chapter 39

Burn Baby, Burn

Henry, Burhan, Dave, Steve, Marc, Ra-Neferu and many others came through the portal near the river by the terminal. Henry carried the sword.

As they approached the terminal building, Burhan carried glass containers of a flammable liquid that Ra-Neferu called "Egyptian fire". They all carried similar containers and unlit torches. Ra-Neferu said that the liquid burned so hot, it would melt anything, except stone.

They gathered around the stairs that led into the open terminal. In addition to bottles of Egyptian fire and a torch, Marc carried a war hammer in a sling across his back. It appeared to be made almost completely from metal and looked heavy.

"Marc, where did you get that hammer and what are you going to do with it?" Henry asked. Marc removed it from the sling on his back and held it out to Henry.

"I made it, with clay. It came out great. It's not as heavy as you think. Here, try it," Marc said. Henry raised his eyebrows and eyed him. Marc laughed. "You know Doc, that look doesn't work quite so well when you don't have your glasses and when you're young. Anyway, here feel it," Marc said. Henry took the hammer and tested its weight. It was nicely balanced as well as beautiful.

"This is a nice...weapon, Marc. But what are you going to do with it?"

"War is coming, Doc. This isn't just going to peter out to nothing or go away. Pretty soon we are going to be in it and in it deep. I don't know how war is going to work here with rezzing and ghosts, angels and all that, but I want to be ready to fight. Besides, did you think you'd be the only one to have a cool weapon? Come on Doc, that's just not fair. We should all get to play. I'm going to take this beauty and just ruin everything in there, ruin it all." He pointed to the terminal. "Speaking of, I gotta go. I want to bust out the windows before somebody else does." Marc ran up the steps to the terminal, hammer in hand. A few seconds later, Henry heard the crash of glass from within.

Henry, Dave, and a few others joined Marc in the terminal. Dave carried a firehouse axe and used it to destroy the doors to all janitor closets. He threw out all the mops and brooms and other junk and started a pile on the terminal floor. Bent-Reshet went about the terminal tossing chairs onto the piles with enough force to break some of them. Henry went along cutting the carpet into long strips with the sword, exposing the stone below. When Dave was done with the janitor closets, he attacked the vending machines with a new fury. His face was red with anger. A small line of blood was smudged across his forehead. Fresh blood dripped from a shallow cut above his eye. Henry turned away. Lauren had never been quick to anger, but when she finally did succumb to it, she was like Dave in that moment, on fire with rage.

Once the physical destruction was over, they gathered together on the steps again. Weapons were put down in favor of Egyptian fire. Everyone gathered up the containers and went around the terminal, inside and out, dousing it with the harsh, sharp-smelling liquid. The air around the place became suffused with stinking vapor, ripe for fire.

They gathered again at the steps with their torches. There was no ceremony. There were no words. Dave lit Ra-Neferu's torch with a silver cigarette lighter. She walked around to everyone, lighting their torches with hers. When everyone's torch was lit, they dispersed and went about setting the terminal on fire.

Henry passed by Dave as he was setting a pile of chairs on fire. He was back to his easy-going, friendly self, though blood was still smeared across his forehead.

"Do you know what Egyptian fire is?" Henry asked. Dave shrugged.

"I don't know. It's something the little lady cooked up. It sure as hell isn't lighter fluid…but it smells like barbeque…well kind of." Dave walked by Henry and clapped him on the back. "Watch it now. We need to get out of here. Just the fumes are enough to kill us and I don't want to be a ghost tonight. I've got plans." Dave winked at him and continued on.

In spite of Henry's confusion and grief, he liked Dave. There had been many moments like this when Dave said or did something to Henry like clap him on the back or try an exploding fist bump. Part of him thought, "I miss my wife, you annoying jackass." The other part liked this rambunctious new friend. In every possible way, Dave was not Lauren and yet, in a few very critical ways, he was. Henry's heart went up and down with friendship for Dave, longing for Lauren, and sometimes anger at them both.

Enough of the terminal was now on fire that the whole place echoed with the "whoosh" of air as the fire sucked it in. Everyone left the terminal building and gathered in front to watch it burn. Henry felt the heat of the fire on his skin. In the building, some critical support had finally melted and given way and the whole roof came crashing down. The crowd cheered.

Ra-Neferu stood near Dave, clapping and smiling. Henry watched with growing horror as Dave reached out and put his arm around Ra-Neferu's waist. Without any hesitation, she returned the gesture and they stood there, arm in arm, like a couple.

Henry made eye contact with Burhan who was also watching with wide eyes. Burhan made a face and shrugged as if to say, "What can you do?" Henry shrugged back.

Somewhere in the ruined building there was a loud, muffled pop. Black smoke poured out of the broken windows and the roof. Soon the tops and then the sides of the hidden portals became visible as the walls burned away.

The crowd cheered and yelled once more. They hugged, kissed, and danced with joy. Dave picked up Ra-Neferu around her waist and lifted her in the air like she weighed nothing. As he brought her back down, they kissed.

Chapter 40

Portals and Doors

One evening, Henry found Steve on Ra-Neferu's garden roof top, leaning on a raised section of adobe, looking out at the dark desert, and smoking of all things. Henry smelled the sweet, mellow aroma of cloves. Steve was ripe with it. Henry coughed.

"Steve. Where are on earth did you get that?" Henry asked.

"They make them around here. The locals grow real cloves, no clay. You want to try it?" Steve held the cigarette out to Henry. He declined.

"No, but thank you. I'm just not a smoker," Henry said. Steve pulled on the cigarette and exhaled thick, white smoke from his nostrils. Henry smiled and thought of dragons.

"You know, in the Sorrowful World, you can't get these. They're illegal in most states, though clove oil is still around. It's got a pretty strong painkiller in it." Steve pulled again and the tip of the cigarette glowed orange, lighting up his face in the darkness. Henry saw sadness and pain, barely concealed, in his face.

"Well, we have made our plans," Henry said, "Now that the big portals are clear, we will go investigate tomorrow. Tomorrow night Dave and Marc will go through the Water Door…in wet gear as they call it." Steve nodded and stared out at the gathering darkness. The sun had already set and the sky was a deep red near the horizon. "Steve, will you come with us?" Henry asked.

"Come with you where?" Steve asked, still far away.

"To investigate the portals. They're exposed now. They cleared away all the burnt rubbish, now Neffie wants to investigate. We might need to brick them up or…something," Henry said. Steve smiled.

"Sure. I'll be there, Henry. No worries." He looked back out at the sunset. "Henry, I'm sorry…about Lauren. It must be hard to lose your wife and gain a jackass."

"Ha!" Henry laughed, a short, sharp bark which degraded into a chuckle. "Yes…good god, yes, it has been …difficult. I can't decide if I hate Dave or like him, or if I want him to stop…pawing on Neffie. That part is truly disturbing."

"Well, I wouldn't worry too much about that. Ra-Neferu is pretty smart. Plus, you know, time heals all wounds…well not really…but it's a nice lie that we tell each other." Steve exhaled more gray smoke through his nostrils.

This man was so very different from 'dude Steve'. Henry marveled at how he had transformed. Every expression, every stance, even the tenor of his voice was different. This man had more gravitas in his pinkie finger than 'dude Steve' had in his whole body.

"Steve…I wanted to ask you… How did you manage? It must have been so difficult to keep up that façade. I…had a bad time of it…I panicked a few times. But you…how long were you there?" Henry asked.

"You did fine, Henry. You're here aren't you? You got out. It was messy, but hey…sometimes that can't be helped." He paused to smoke. "It was never about doing it perfectly all the time. It was more about doing it perfectly when it mattered…like at the beginning. Once people have developed an expectation for you they stop paying so much attention. Also, it gets easier after a while…you just step into that role, become that person."

"How long you were there?"

"Well, I died in…1985…so fifty and some years, something like that." Steve said. Henry whistled. "Yeah, I died of a drug overdose. I know cliché, right? Especially in the 80s…and it was coke too. So, I went to Heaven and was assigned service of course. A drug overdose is considered… 'suicide-light' by the powers that be."

"Do you think anyone ever suspected you?" Henry asked.

"Nah, they should have, though. I should have been caught years ago, Henry but…people…people don't really care that much. Most people walking around, even in Heaven, are so caught up in their own minds that they don't pay attention to much. It's amazing what people miss or ignore. They fill in the blanks with what they want, believe what they want." Steve paused. "Only one person ever caught me."

"Oh, what happened? Who was it?"

"You wouldn't know him. He was gone from the Castle long before you got there and…nothing happened. He never spilled the beans or anything like that. He understood." Steve turned back to face the dead sunset and pulled deeply on his cigarette. For a moment in the orange glow, Steve looked so sad, Henry wanted to ask him if he was in pain, but thought better of it. He excused himself and left Steve to his grief.

*****

The next day Ra-Neferu led them to the burned-down terminal to investigate the exposed portals. Henry, Marc, Steve, Dave, and Bent-Reshet came along.

Now that the terminal building was cleared, all that remained was the set of round stairs, a stone platform, and 5 stone portals. The Lover's Door at the end of the platform and the two closest portals were equally large. The one-way conduit from the Judgment Hall and the portal opposite it were the same size as the portals in the White City and along the river path.

Dave led them to the portal to the right of the Lover's Door.

"This is it. This is the big U that I found lying flat on the sea floor," he said to Ra-Neferu.

"How much water is above it, David?" she asked.

"Oh maybe 30 feet or so." Ra-Neferu approached the portal and slowly reached through with her hand. She knelt down and reached further into the portal. When she brought her hand back through, it contained wet, white sand. She let it fall to the floor and frowned at it.

"David, the sand is wet and I felt water but…I think something is wrong. Perhaps you and Marc should take weapons when you go tonight."

"Don't worry," said Marc, "that was going to happen anyway." He grinned and thumped the hammer on his back. Henry laughed.

"For a physicist, you have strange tastes, Marc. I never took you for a warrior," Henry said.

"I never took you for one either, Doc, but there you go with your death-touch sword."

"No, it's called 'The Turning Hand', though I still don't know why."

"No, death touch…it's a thing from a card game…never mind. It's a gamer thing." Henry shrugged.

Dave walked over to the opposite portal. Steve followed him, but stopped in front of the Lover's Door. As Henry walked by, Steve caught his arm.

"Did you ever notice that before…that hum? Do you hear it?" Steve asked. Henry listened.

"Oh yes, there it is. I have heard that before…and it also…unlike the other portals, I think it has a bit of color to it…like a blush of pink," Henry said. Steve looked up the portal and smiled.

"Yeah, it does. I see it now," he said. "I forgot all about that." Steve continued to stand in front of the Lover's Door. Henry went to Dave in front of the opposite portal.

"I'm pretty sure this one goes to the hot place," Dave said. Ra-Neferu approached the portal and put her hand through again. When she brought it back out, they could all smell the burnt-sulfur, volcanic air that came with it. Bent-Reshet held her nose.

"You were right. That is Tartarus," Ra-Neferu said, frowning at her hand. "Portals to hell are usually one directional." She wrinkled her nose. "Excuse me, I must go and wash this." Bent-Reshet went with her.

Dave walked down to the one-way portal to the Judgment Hall and casually walked through it before anyone could stop him. Henry's heart leapt into his throat. Just as quickly, Dave reappeared in front of the portal.

"Jeez, Dave. Don't go traipsing through portals when you don't know where they go. What the hell?" Marc said. Dave laughed.

"No, that one down there is hell. Relax, Marcus, I knew where this one went," Dave said. Marc frowned at him. Steve walked up to them and made a face.

"Blech, what smells like hell?" Steve asked.

"Neffie put her hand through the left portal. She's just gone to wash it. Ah there she is," Henry said.

Ra-Neferu came back up the terminal stairs and saw them at the portal to the Judgment Hall. Dave shook his head 'no'. She frowned and walked over to the opposite portal. She put her arm through and moved it around. She brought it out and sniffed her fingers.

"It is not hell. It smells…musty. David, take my hand. I will put my head through."

"Are you sure that's a good idea?" Dave asked.

"I will be fine, please." She took his hand and put her head through, then stepped back quickly.

"I think it is safe to go in. It looks like a storage room of some kind. It also looks…untouched for years." She walked through again, holding Dave's hand. After a moment she let go of his hand and walked completely through. A moment of panic gripped Henry again, but Ra-Neferu popped back through, unharmed.

"It is just a storage room. Come in and see." The others followed. As Henry went through and saw the room he gasped.

"I know this place. Neffie, I was here. This is the tower, in NJ, the very top of the damn thing. This is where I found the swo…Marc, don't touch that!" Henry yelled at Marc, who was standing next to the metallic, filigreed vase of yellow light and reaching up to touch it. Marc brought his hands up as if he were under arrest.

"What? What?" he said.

"Marc, that…thing will kill you, instantly, just like the sword," Henry said. Marc put his hands down and stared at the vase.

"Makes sense," he said. "It looks just like the sword."

Ra-Neferu stepped forward and looked at the vase.

"Neffie, have any ideas?" Henry asked. Ra-Neferu shook her head.

"No, not…at all. This must be a …" she trailed off and went to a nearby window. Henry followed her. There he could see the ocean, the castle, and New Jerusalem bustling beneath them.

They poked around the room for a bit but did not find much. Except for the vase, there was just junk in the room; curtains, curtain rods, lamp shades, empty, cracked ceramic jars, and other little pots and containers. It was a treasure trove to Earthly archaeologists but useless, assorted junk to the residents of Heaven. Henry wondered how or why anyone ever bothered to take all of it up to this high room. The true treasures, the sword and vase, had not been hidden when he first entered the room.

Steve parked himself in front of the vase on a crate and was watching as Marc experimented with it. Marc picked it up, using a scrap of curtain, and tested the weight. He poked at the swirling, golden light with a metal curtain rod. He turned the vase upside down and watched as the golden fog streamed out and pooled on the floor. When Marc turned the vase upright, the golden fog flowed back into it, even from the floor. "Ooooh," said Marc with wide eyes.

Ra-Neferu continued to stand by the small window, looking out at New Jerusalem, her eyes busy with thought. Henry joined her.

"Penny for your thoughts?" he asked. She pointed at the castle and ocean below them.

"Henry, do you see...something is going on down there. There are vehicles on the beach. I can hear the noise of machinery as well. Do you hear it?" she asked. Henry heard a faint rhythmic noise, but didn't recognize it.

"I hear it, but I don't know what it is," he said. Ra-Neferu frowned.

"Part of the view is blocked. There is no way to see...directly underneath us." She turned to face the others. "We should go back now. I believe they are closer to invasion than we thought. We must prepare."

"Wait," said Marc. "Shouldn't we check the rest of the wall for portals? If that part of the wall could be a portal, than any part of it could be right?" he asked. Henry looked around the room at the walls. There was a suspicious pattern to the stone work.

"That will need to wait," she said. "If they take the terminal...it will not matter what is here." She motioned to Marc. "Bring the...vase." She stepped through the portal. Marc found a loose curtain and wrapped the vase.

Everyone stepped through the portal except Marc. Henry stuck his head through.

"What's going on?" he asked.

"I don't know. It won't come through. This thing hits the portal like it's a wall. Look." Marc attempted to bring the vase through but it wouldn't budge. Henry frowned.

"Leave it," Henry said. Marc protested.

"No, look, I can...how about I touch it and die...then I could bring it through,"

"Yes, at sunset. That's five hours from now, Marc. We can't take that risk," Henry said, looking around the room. "I know it looks like, just old storage...but I think that's a cover. I think this is a gatehouse for angels. I didn't bring any coins and that ...probably wouldn't matter anymore. Put it down, Marc. We'll try again later." Marc frowned and put the vase back on the crate were he had found it. He stepped through the portal.

"Where's the vase thing?" Dave asked as Marc came through.

"It won't come through the portal," Marc said. He looked at all their faces. "Hey, where's Steve?"

"He's down at the Lover's Door," Dave said. "He said he had an idea and wanted to check something."

"No," Henry said, almost a whisper. He ran to the Lover's Door. Steve looked back at them and shook his head. He gave a brief wave goodbye. Just as Henry got there, Steve stepped through. "Steve, no!" Henry yelled.

As Steve entered the portal his outline became a burst of silver-white light that faded quickly. The portal's hum increased in frequency for a brief moment, then cycled down to its former level. Henry's heart dropped in his chest. He thought about Steve killing his pain with clove cigarettes on Ra-Neferu's balcony. He had lost someone he loved and couldn't live without them. For the first time, Henry really understood why they called it the Lover's Door.

Chapter 41

Parts Won't Cut It

Close to midnight Dave and Marc stood before the Water door in the terminal in Elysium. They wore wetsuits and air tanks, fins and masks. Ra-Neferu and Henry stood nearby. Marc struggled with a swim fin on his foot. Henry handed Dave the Turning Hand, safely covered by a new, leather sheath with a belt attached. Dave cinched it around his waist.

"I don't think we'll need this," Dave said.

"Just in case," Ra-Neferu said as she checked his tanks. Henry noticed that Marc had his hammer but the air tanks prevented him from carrying it on his back.

"Marc, can you swim with the hammer? Won't it pull you right down?" Henry asked.

"Well, even if it does, the big U is not that far from shore. I'll just walk out if I have to," Marc said smiling. "I'm not leaving Althea behind."

"You named your hammer Althea?" Henry asked.

"*Lady* Althea. What? You think you're the only one that gets to have a fancy, named weapon? It's just not fair, Doc. We should all be able to play." Marc winked.

"Hmmm, that sounds familiar," Henry said. Ra-Neferu checked Marc's tanks and stepped back from the portal.

"All I am looking for is information. See what you can and get back quickly. We are not prepared for any…heroic battles now," she said, making eye contact with Dave.

"Yes, ma'am," Dave said and grinned. Then, deftly, before she could stop him, he swooped in and kissed her. Ra-Neferu looked embarrassed and turned a little pink. Henry was amused. A small kernel of jealously was still left inside him but it was slowly fading. Dave was a big, burly man and it was often difficult to associate him with Lauren. Henry wondered if he would get mad if he saw Lauren deftly kiss Ra-Neferu. It wasn't hard to imagine Lauren in scuba gear. He had seen her in it a million times. Henry smiled at the thought. Dave looked at him.

"Whaaaat?" Dave said.

"Nothing," Henry said and smiled. "Go get to work."

*****

Marc and Dave stepped through the portal into dry air and semi-darkness. As Dave's eyes adjusted, he looked up and could see stars. Except for the beach in front of them, they were surrounded by a high, dark wall. After several seconds of adjustment, it wasn't hard to see at all. New Jerusalem was never dark. The diffuse glow of the city permeated everything, even the beach where there were no decorative lights. For a few seconds, they stood perfectly still, waiting to see if anyone was nearby. They saw no moving lights and heard no sound except for the surf pounding the shore in the distance.

"Son of a bitch, they drained it," Dave whispered. Marc nodded and waddled over to the exposed stones of the Big U. He took off his tanks and fins and left them on the stones. Dave did the same.

"Well, now what?," Marc asked.

Dave looked around and spotted a generator, a couple of large machines with hoses attached, and other large plastic containers. The hoses ran over the walls and disappeared. The whole place smelled of gasoline and exhaust.

"Well, let's take a look around. She wants info, right?" Dave whispered. Marc walked off in the opposite direction and Dave headed towards the nearest part of the wall. It appeared to be made of thick, corrugated metal. In some places, leaks were plugged with tar or something like it.

"Dave, c'mere," Marc said. Near the opposite wall there were several wooden pallets lined up and stacked with something that was wrapped in clear plastic. At the end of the line of stacks, near the shore, a forklift sat, with its forks still sticking into the last pallet. Dave saw more dark, blocky shapes farther away on the shore.

Marc took out a knife and cut through the plastic wrapping. A puff or two of fine, tan dust was released into the air as he cut. Dave put his hand through the hole and felt around. He pulled out a small object with a very familiar heft and texture. Marc took out a small flashlight and shined it on Dave's hand. It was a small, clay vehicle, a jeep by the look of it. It was sculpted and dried, ready for the oven. Dave crushed the little clay jeep in his hand. He took out his knife and cut open other pallets. They found more jeeps, as well as other machines and tools of war:

243

automatic weapons, knives and swords, tanks, planes, small clay horses, grenades, missiles, rocket launchers, and small round devices that looked like mines.

Again Dave heard Marc's whisper. Marc was shining his flashlight on his hand. There, replicated carefully in miniature, was a pair of shackles. Marc reached into the hole in the plastic and pulled out handful after handful of shackles and dropped them to the ground. Anger flashed through them like fire. Marc raised his hammer, ready to bash the pallet to pieces. Dave caught the hammer before he struck. He stood glaring at the rest of the pallets.

"This stuff must be destroyed but not like that. We couldn't destroy enough of it before they got here," Dave said. Marc looked around.

"How? I think that's gas over there in those plastic things, but I didn't bring a lighter, did you?" Marc asked.

"No…but there's more than one way to make fire," Dave said. His eyes made their way back to the forklift at the end of the row of pallets. "I have an idea. Take the gasoline and douse everything…all the pallets," Dave said. Marc frowned.

"What are you going to do?"

"I'm going to take the battery out of the forklift and try to rig it so it will spark. Jumper cables would be perfect but we're not going to be that lucky. I just need the battery and some wire. I s'pose the generator would work too." Dave looked around. "If it works, these pallets will go up fast and the Guard will come. Be prepared to hit the portal."

"Worth a shot," Marc said as he walked off towards the plastic containers near the generators. Dave came to the forklift and got to work.

After several minutes Marc came back and said a breathless "Done." He was still carrying one of the plastic containers with a little gas in it. Dave had opened up the forklift and removed its battery. He was ripping wires out of the engine and cutting them with his knife.

"Seen anybody?" Dave asked.

"No, still quiet." Marc watched Dave strip the ends of the wires and carefully connect them to the battery.

"I wonder…" Marc whispered. "I wonder if they will just burn…or will they turn?"

"If they burn at all. I don't know how much it will help, but we can't stay here all night and smash them and we can't leave it for them….Got any gas left?" Marc nodded. "Pour it on this pallet, on the top." Marc Poured. "Either way, if it works there will be damage…but I'll probably get burned too. You might have to drag my corpse through the portal. That portal rezzes when you go through," Dave said. Marc was surprised.

"Well, alright then. I'll get into position." Marc turned to walk towards the portal. A few seconds later, Dave heard a faint noise and the familiar flutter of wings. He turned to see an angel facing him, holding a bloody sword in one hand and a limp, barely conscious Marc in the other.

"You cannot win," the angel said in a beautiful voice. The perfume of gasoline wavered around Dave in the air. The battery was sitting behind him on one wooden edge of the pallet. He had not quite finished wrapping the second wire around the negative terminal of the battery but it was close enough that he hoped there would be some sparks. He backed slowly into the pallet behind him, pushing the battery into the plastic wrapping, hoping that it would cause the wires to come near enough to each other to spark and ignite the gasoline fumes from the wood. Suddenly, the pallet behind him erupted into orange and yellow flames. Dave smiled.

"Maybe not, but we will die trying…probably several times." Dave reached for the naked hilt of the sword of Yama on his belt with his bare hand. As he dropped dead, the fire behind him erupted and spread along the line of wooden pallets. Shouts and the sound of people running could be heard in the distance.

The angel dropped Marc and came after Dave as his ghost rose up out of his body. Dave's ghost rose up, grabbed the sword and rolled away to stand near the portal. When the angel saw that Dave was holding a sword, even though he was a ghost, a look of confusion passed over his flawless face for the briefest second. In that moment Dave feinted left, turned right and separated Marc's head from his body on the sand. The sword parted flesh like it was nothing…air. He jabbed the sword into Marc's head enough to pick it up, like he was skewering some bit of meat, and then threw it and the sword through the portal. He jumped in after it.

*****

Ra-Neferu was telling Henry about Tutankhamen's murder when suddenly Henry's sword with something fuzzy stuck to it came tumbling through the portal. Dave came tumbling through right after.

"Dave! What's going on? Where's Marc?" Henry said frantically. Dave looked around.

"You mean, he's not here? But I threw his head in." Ra-Neferu walked over to the sword. Her face fell. Carefully, she picked up Marc's head. The sword fell from it and clanged on the floor.

"Oh, David….no…this is not enough. Parts…are not enough," she said sadly as she cradled Marc's head. Dave turned to jump right back through the portal.

"No!" Henry and Ra-Neferu both shouted at once, but as Dave turned to go back through, Marc came tumbling in and barreled through them all.

"We've got to go!" Marc said frantically. "They are coming now!"

Chapter 42

Old Gods Rejoice

"Neffie, remind me again why we are walking up this mountain," Henry puffed. "And also, I thought I was supposed to be in perfect shape," he said. "This doesn't feel like perfect." He wiped sweat from his brow. Ra-Neferu smiled.

They hiked together up a rocky path along the side of the mountains next to the city. As Henry walked he could see changing views of the sculpture of Osiris, carved out of the stone below them. Below Osiris and the other gods, the White City glinted and wavered in the shimmering, hot air.

"I want to look at their formations. I hear the reports, but I want to see for myself." A very large set of binoculars rested on her neck. "The battle golems we sent took out most of their air power when they smashed their field ovens. They have what they have...for now. This has become a ground war...which is good news for people of our times. We only ever had ground wars," she explained. Henry snorted.

"Field ovens...well, they took to works of clay fast enough didn't they?" She nodded.

"What is that saying you have...all is fair in love and war?" Henry sighed.

"Yes, that's one of them. The other one is, 'Do as I say, not as I do.'" Ra-Neferu chuckled.

"Hypocrisy never goes away, Henry. I have lived a very long time and I have never seen a people without it."

They hiked in silence for some time. Henry's thoughts turned back towards the coming battle. He looked back through the catalog of his lives. Had he been a soldier? Yes, many times. Had he ever been a general or a war chief of some kind? Not so much. He had been a clan chief in Scotland once, but that was ground warfare too; wild fighting in close quarters. He had died that way several times. He shook his head.

"What are you shaking your head about, Dr. Hall?" Ra-Neferu asked.

"I was...remembering. I've been a fighter, a soldier...but never a general or any sort of strategist. I am sorry about that."

247

"You cannot help your lives, Henry. We are what we are."
She stopped and used her binoculars, pointing them at the river and the blurry grey smudge on the horizon that Henry knew to be Heaven's Army. After Marc and Dave's impromptu burning of so many of their supplies, Heaven decided to advance their invasion. They had occupied the terminal platform and the desert plains behind it and along the river for weeks now. Soon they would advance on the city.

The path up the mountain split. One way went off to the left and appeared to end near Horus' ear. The other path went off to the right and up towards a lesser summit of the mountain. As Ra-Neferu watched the approaching host, something caught Henry's eye. There were stone statues further up the hill on either side of the path.

The first statue was of a woman. The surface of the stone was very worn and pitted in places but Henry could tell that it was a young woman, wearing a robe and holding something in her hand. Her hand and whatever it had held were long gone. Across from her there was a statue of a young man, also wearing a robe but carrying the handle of what had once been a weapon. Similar statues faced each other all the way up the path until it ended at one of the lesser summits of the mountain. Directly on the high summit, there was an altar that looked like a birdbath, but with a flat top. Ra-Neferu walked up to the summit and tried her binoculars again.

"It is difficult to see for all the smoke. I think they burn things just to obscure our view," she said.

"Mm…and to be a nuisance. We know they burn the houses…they probably burn the vegetation on either side of the river as well. They might think they are destroying our food," Henry said.

"Well, they are," Ra-Neferu said angrily. "We have works of clay but…we grew things there as well and…" she looked down into the city, her face drawn with sadness. Henry put his hand on her shoulder.

"Neffie, it will be alright. Plants grow back, homes are rebuilt and hopefully…invaders are vanquished in a storm of Egyptian fire and war golems. We are not defenseless."

"What will you do if they win?"

"Oh, I don't know. Maybe I'll turn into a bird and fly away. Maybe I will make a run for the Lover's Door. I hear India is quite nice these days, stable economy, low crime, nice climate."

Ra-Neferu frowned and looked out at the horizon again with her binoculars.

"So much is at stake. I will not see my way of life destroyed."

"Well, if you insist on being serious. Here, let me have a look," Henry said. She handed him the binoculars. Through the clouds of smoke and haze he could vaguely make out slow-moving convoys of large, loaded down vehicles. He thought he could also see groups of soldiers walking. He thought it odd that they would walk rather than ride, but there they were. Maybe the battle golems had destroyed more of their equipment than they first thought.

"Well, look at those amateurs. You had me worried there for a minute, lady, but now that I see them …bah…easy pickings, tenderfeet. We have the home field advantage. What do they know of the desert?" Henry handed her the binoculars. She took them and smiled up at Henry, but her face still carried worry and sadness. They began to walk back down the path.

"Neffie, what are these statues for? Who do they depict?" Henry asked. She shrugged her shoulders.

"I do not know."

"What? What do you mean you don't know? You know everything about this place. You've been here for ages…literally. How could you not know?" Henry asked. Ra-Neferu laughed.

"Henry, I do not know because no one here knows. They have always been here and I have never met anyone who knew them." She stopped to use her binoculars again.

"I don't understand," Henry said. "There is always someone who remembers, who lived in that time."

"Old gods are forgotten and new ones are made. There may be people that remember them but they are not here." She sighed. "Maybe they are in Heaven." She looked at the statues as they passed by. "They are beautiful." Henry looked at them too. She was right. Before they had been eaten away by wind and rain, they were beautiful.

They continued to walk down the path together. As they walked something changed in the air. The light seemed brighter and the colors of the sand, the stones, and the sparse bushes and scrub seemed deeper. Henry felt something inside himself lift and float. He and Ra-Neferu exchanged wide-eyed looks. She felt it as well. They stopped and turned, looking back up the path. Every statue was suddenly decorated with cut flowers. Roses of various colors, violets, carnations, humble daisies, elegant orchids, and many more kinds of flowers hung on the statues in lines or wreaths. The path itself was strewn with petals. Ra-Neferu gasped. Henry paced back up to the end of the path to the bird bath altar. There on the round stone of the altar was a single blue and white lotus. Ra-Neferu came up behind him. Henry picked up the flower and held it out to her.

"Do you know what all this means?" he asked. She shook her head.

"No, Henry. I have no idea."

Chapter 43

Smoke, Fire, and the Minions of Hell

Henry and Osiris stood together in a chariot on the field of battle in between the two great armies. Their one small chariot represented no threat, so no one from Heaven's army rode out to meet them. Those negotiations had already failed. The battle was inevitable, but it seemed that Heaven was reluctant to make the first move. This made Henry laugh. 'They don't want to be seen as the aggressor even as they invade and lay siege on a foreign city,' Henry thought. He watched the amassing ground forces through binoculars.

In the past two weeks, the White City had sent out squad after squad of giant battle golems, made in the great ovens in the heart of the city. Quite a bit of Heaven's heavy equipment was destroyed. It took them some time to finally find a weapon that would stop the golems. Nothing worked except mortars, which they had enough of to do the job. The path behind the army along the river was strewn with chunks of metal, damaged vehicles, sand dunes covered with broken glass and boulders from destroyed golems.

Now the two armies stood facing each other, ready for the final battle. If the White City's forces couldn't defeat them and push Heaven back, they would invade the city. If they got control of the great ovens, there would be no stopping them. Every great city in Elysium would fall, one after another.

Henry surveyed the enemy with binoculars. A flutter of white wings at the back of the ranks indicated angels. There were also strange, dark tents lined up on one side of the formation. As Henry watched, the angels flew up and away in the direction of the terminal. There hadn't been that many of them to begin with.

"The angels are leaving and there was only…twenty or so to begin with. Why would they leave?" Henry asked.

"The bird people refuse to fight with the Hellions," Osiris said.

"What?" Henry was confused. "Bird people?"

"Do you see those black tents?" Henry pointed his binoculars at them.

"Yes…I don't see any people nearby," Henry said. Osiris smiled.

"And you will not. Hellions do not have a pleasant odor, as you know, and their presence causes pain. They cannot tolerate sunlight. They will come out when it is dark…or when it is made to be dark. The bird people will not fight alongside their ancient enemy."

"Why 'bird people'? Henry asked.

"Because, Henry among others, that is what they are. Some day you will learn more, but not today. Today is about battle." Osiris said the word 'battle' with relish. He pounded his great fist against his golden chest armor and smiled at Henry in a way that was both beautiful and terrifying. Henry returned the binoculars to his eyes with shaky hands.

They were close enough to Heaven's army that with binoculars he could see individual faces of the fighters on the front lines. He saw in those faces fear, anger, sadness, and weariness. This also made Henry uneasy. As he looked at their faces a sinking feeling hit him right in the chest. What was he seeing? People. He saw people, not the faceless ranks of the enemy, not monsters who deserved a violent death. He saw people who were confused, sad, angry, and resentful yet committed. Yes, they would fight and die and resurrect but for how long? Did Heaven's army really intend to invade and conquer the whole of Elysium? How many years would these people spend fighting, dying, and resurrecting? Even though they were fighting for slave labor, they themselves had become slaves to war. He put the binoculars down and frowned.

"What troubles you, Henry among others?" Osiris asked.

"I feel…terrible for these people. They are as much slaves as any service worker," Henry said. Osiris pursed his lips and nodded.

"Do not pity them. They have made their choice and they must experience the consequences."

"Did they really have a choice though? Fight for Heaven or become a slave? Fight for Heaven or go to the Sorrowful World or even to Hell?" Henry asked.

"These are still choices," Osiris said without emotion. Henry stared out at the ranks.

"Henry among others, you worry too much." Osiris smiled and pulled the reigns of the horses to get the chariot going. A cloud of dust went up behind them. They went parallel to both armies on either side. Towards the end of the ranks, he wheeled the chariot around and had the horse run back the other way. From his waist he took a war horn and handed it to Henry as they rode.

"If they are slaves," he yelled against the wind, "let us free them!"

*****

Henry fought. He fought alongside Osiris. He fought in full armor and wielded the Turning Hand. Marc fought beside him with his hammer. Dave was never far away with an axe he had taken off of a dead soldier. Bent-Reshet joined them, but not as herself. She arrived as a muscle-bound fighter from one of her previous lives.

Ra-Neferu and Burhan stayed with the small and large catapults, loading them with Egyptian fire in big bottles and shooting burning arrows after discharging them. Burhan, who had been a long bowman in one of his other lives, dipped arrows into a fire pot and shot them a few seconds after every bottle went flying. Wherever the containers fell, whatever substance it touched, metal, wood, plastic or flesh, it burned. The smell of charred flesh and the screams of the dying permeated the battle field. Henry wondered why they screamed. How far did the painful influence of the Hellions reach? He still felt no pain.

There was smoke on the battlefield. This smoke grew thicker and greyer as the day went on. Henry soon realized that in addition to the smoke from the Egyptian fire, great piles of something were being burned at the edges of the battle field. They weren't there at the beginning of the battle, but as the day went on they sprung up, tended by women. Soon the sky was almost dark with smoke. A horn sounded. Heaven's forces retreated. The battlefield was covered with swirling, silent smoke.

"What's going on? What's with all the smoke?" Marc asked. He had a gash along one side of his face and part of his leg armor was damaged.

"I've no idea," Henry said. Bent-Reshet called to Henry from somewhere to his left. He followed the sound. She, as the warrior she had become, sat on the ground. Her leg was savagely bent. She beckoned to him.

"Henry, you must kill me," she pleaded.

"What? Why? We can pull you out of this. You'll be safe until tomorrow." She was shaking her head.

253

"No, no. Kill me now before they come. Henry, the smoke is for..." she leaned over and grunted reaching for her leg, but not daring to touch it. "Henry, they made it dark for the demons. The minions of hell...cannot be in the daylight. It is starting to hurt already. When they get here...the pain will be terrible. Please, do it now." Bent-Reshet the warrior transformed into Bent-Reshet the small Egyptian woman as she reached for the sword. Henry put the sword down for her to touch. Instantly she died. Henry picked up her small body and carried her back off the field and behind the catapults. He laid her gently on the sand next to countless other corpses.

Henry walked back over to where he thought the others were. He shouted once for Dave. After a second someone one grabbed him by the arm and lead him to a group of people. Marc sat on the ground, gritting his teeth.

"It hurts," he said through his teeth. "Why does it hurt?"

"Quiet!" Dave whispered harshly. They listened and heard nothing at first, then a kind of hum, in the distance. It was like the scuttling of thousands of little feet. It made Henry's blood run cold. He knelt down to Marc and held the sword out for him to touch.

"It's only going to get worse as they get closer, Marc," Henry said. "Demons. That's what all the smoke is for. Demons can't go out in daylight. Just being near them causes pain to come back. Just, go ahead and we'll see your ghost tonight." Marc was shaking his head no when a wave of pain suddenly went through him and he turned and vomited. When he turned back around he nodded, removed a gauntlet, touched the sword and died. Dave and Henry carried Marc's body away to the ever-growing lines of corpses in the sand.

"We can't do anything with all this damn smoke. The demons and those crawling things will incapacitate us with pain," Henry said. Dave frowned and peered into the smoke.

"I think I have an idea. They are making so much smoke with those fires...that's not normal. They must be keeping it wet or putting something special on it. It's not burning hot if you get me. I'm going to get Neffie and Burhan and see if we can't stoke those fires a bit. The heat of intense fire will actually drive off some of the smoke...and get rid of the smokers," Dave explained.

"They are tended by women. Do you think that they thought...?" Henry asked. Dave laughed.

"We are all women and men and children…and so were they. They just don't remember. Hey, why do ya suppose that is? Why don't they remember and flood out?" Dave asked. Henry shrugged his shoulders.

"If we could get them to all to flood, we would win, hands down. Perspective is the mother of tolerance," Henry said. Dave chuckled.

"I don't know how to do that, Hank, but first things first. It's time to start some fires." Dave's eyes gleamed with excitement.

"Alright then. I'll go get a couple of horses and we can go," Henry said and he turned to walk away but Dave caught his arm.

"No, no, sorry Hank. I know I'm not supposed to call you that…but I really like doing it," Dave said. He slapped Henry on the shoulder and laughed. "Look, let me be serious for a minute. The question is, what do you have that none of the rest of us have?" Dave asked.

"A PhD in philosophy?" Henry said.

"No, dammit, you big nerd," Dave said, grinning. "You've got the sword…the fucking Turning Hand! And you're marvelous with it, Hank. It's like you're a dance of death with that thing. So, I have this feeling…down here in my gut, that you are supposed to be out there fighting demons …and whatever the hell is making that creepy noise." Dave looked over his shoulder and shuddered in an exaggerated way. "Go get 'em. Find out what that sword can really do and send 'em back to hell." Dave grinned and ran off to disappear in the smoke before Henry could respond.

Henry stood alone in the smoke. Briefly he wondered where Osiris had gone. The silence nearby was slowly replaced by the clash of arms, the thunder of horses, and a new sound…the moans of the wounded. Henry went back behind the catapult lines until he found an armored warhorse. He mounted the horse and turned to gallop into the fray.

At first, he galloped blindly through smoke. His horse whinnied in protest but grudgingly followed his commands. When he came across wounded in pain, he reached down and tapped them with the sword. As he rode, he began to hear the screams of women and small popping sounds coming from one direction. He saw a large shadow in the haze and slowed his horse.

"Ah Henry, I thought I smelled you." The demon doctor appeared out of the smoke, walking along as if he had just come from his library into his living room. He didn't have on the doctor's coat. He was almost naked except for a leather square covering his pelvis. Henry's horse put his ears back and snorted, hooves scratching at the ground. The demon doctor came closer.

"Who'd have thought that berry cobbler would lead to such fun! Boy, are they mad at you. We haven't had this much fun in ages," he said and smiled. His smile was as unnerving in the doctor's office as it was on the battlefield in the smoke. "Oh by the way…hey sorry about your wife. No hard feelings I hope. If I had known…and Jerry…that guy is crazy. I've never seen anyone so cruel. That guy is messed up. So…uh I gotta kill you now…no offense, it's just what I'm here for…probably do it all again tomorrow with any luck."

"What if I could kill you?" Henry asked with real curiosity. "What if I had some magic weapon that could hurt you? Would you rez at sunset? Would you still be here? What would happen?" The demon doctor raised his eyebrows.

"Hmmm, I don't know really. Good question. I can ask around, find out later, after I kill you, and let you know. You'll probably be in Hell so you know…we could do lunch or something. " Henry pulled the sword from the sheath and held it out to the demon, as if to give it to him.

'Have you ever seen this sword before?" Henry asked. The demon doctor came closer and reached up to take the sword.

"Well, that is a nice…" As the sword made contact with the doctor's hands, he disappeared. The sword dropped from midair to ground. Henry dismounted and picked it up. For a moment he wondered what happened to the demon. As far as the minions of hell go, he didn't seem like a bad guy.

Henry moved to mount his horse but he paused. There it was again, that scuttling, creepy sound of so many tiny little feet. The sound grew louder and seemed to be approaching him on all sides. Fear surged in the pit of his stomach. His horse whinnied and galloped away. Soon, he saw them.

Small, grey, husk like things, creatures with claws and long teeth, but with the stunted, dog like, bodies of hunched over people, came crawling up to him. Henry slashed at them. The ones that touched the sword disappeared but there were so many, he couldn't stop them from climbing up his leg and overwhelming him. As they climbed, they bit or stung him, he wasn't sure which. He hunched over with the sword underneath him, meaning to touch it and end all the pain but a strange thing happened. As Henry disappeared into that swarming mass of stinging pain, he touched the sword against his bare arm, above his glove. Suddenly all motion stopped. Henry stood up uncovered and unharmed. The creatures were gone, replaced by little piles of light grey dust.

"Well alright then, "Henry smiled. "Let's go kill some demons."

Chapter 44

Burning Bush

After a bit of searching behind the catapults, Henry found his horse and rode back into battle, jabbing his sword at any demons he found. None of them expected anything to happen, so he often caught them off guard. They would reach up to block his attack and then, eyes wide with surprise, disappear. None of them wore armor. They fought with their hands, nails, and teeth.

The strange, crawling creatures were less easily dispatched, but he felt he was making a dent in their numbers. Every time he let them engulf him, he felt their sting, but every time he dispatched a group in this way, all his pain was reduced. As the soldiers and the wounded began to feel less pain, they cheered and rallied. Fighting began in earnest again.

Dave's plan was working somewhat and the smoke was lifting. Henry rode through a wash of smoke and found himself head to head with Osiris, also mounted and wielding a sword. When he saw Henry he smiled broadly. Henry rode up next to him and together they surveyed the scene. The army of the White City fought Heaven's soldiers all around them. Henry even saw some members of the Guard, their armor glinting in the smoke-orange rays of the sun.

"So…are we still in that room, that cozy room in the temple having a nice chat? Is that also where we are right now?" Henry yelled over the din.

"Of course! Where else would we be?" Osiris clapped Henry so hard on the back he almost fell off his horse.

Things continued like this for some time. Henry followed Osiris and together they fought demons, the horrible scuttling creatures, and soldiers. Word was starting to get around about the sword. Henry rode directly into a group of the Guard and with one long slash of his sword, caused them all to drop dead. When men saw Henry slash through ranks of men, they turned and ran. Men fled before Osiris as well, but for different reasons. Henry watched him hack a demon into pieces with a long axe. He didn't even get off his horse.

Osiris brought his horse around and sat looking at Heaven's army and the western horizon. Henry rode up, jubilant.

"If this isn't victory for us, I don't know what is," Henry said. Osiris's face showed no emotion.

"Today, yes. But what of tomorrow? All these men will be whole again and ready to fight. What then, Henry among others? Shall we do it all again?" Osiris asked. Henry's good mood melted away. It was true. Heaven's army was not going to turn around and go back through the gate with a tip of the hat to their military superiority. The whole thing would start again in the morning. They would fight and fight until the city was theirs. Then they would take the rest of Elysium, city by city, in the same way. Once they had control of the great ovens, there would be no stopping them.

The sun was setting. Long golden rays shone through the diminishing smoke. The fires had been put out and the smoke was starting to clear. Henry looked out on a sea of corpses. Retreating soldiers walked toward their camps, sometimes stumbling over bodies. Henry frowned at them.

"When the sun sets, all these ghosts will rise. What then? We can't stop them from entering the city," Henry said with renewed worry. Osiris was unmoved. As they sat and watched, the sun slowly descended below the western horizon.

"The sun is setting. Good. Let's fight," Osiris said, looking as jovial as ever.

"Who?" asked Henry, "The soldiers are retreating and I don't see any demons."

"You and I are going to fight," Osiris said.

"What? Why…would I fight you? We've been….you are…what?" Osiris brought his horse about.

"You and I will fight. The sun is setting, ghosts will rise and they will see. Let…them…see!" Osiris shouted as he rode off on his horse. Henry watched him go wondering what was going on.

All around Henry and all over the battlefield the ghost forms of the battle dead rose up out of their broken bodies. They stood, unsure, looking around. Henry sat on his horse and sheathed the sword.

From the direction that Osiris had ridden off in, a horse and rider were approaching again. It was not Osiris or at least it didn't look like him. Instead a muscly, hard looking brutish man was spurring on the horse. As he got closer his eyes locked on Henry and gleamed. He charged at Henry and with a good whack of his fist, knocked Henry off his horse. Henry stood up as fast as he could, catching his breath as he pulled out the sword. The man trotted back and hopped easily off the horse. He brought up his sword and postured aggressively towards Henry. Henry returned his stance. The man lunged forward. Henry parried and swirled out of the way. The big man growled.

"Fight!" he said with a deep, growly voice. At that moment, Henry realized that the man was Osiris, just in a bigger, meaner form. He had the same dark eyes, green skin, and dark hair. Henry thought of a comic book character and he chuckled.

"Do you find something funny?" Large Osiris asked. Henry dropped his fighting stance.

"You just, you look like…. Look, Osiris, I don't want to fight you. Why do you want…"He was interrupted by a brutal attack. Henry dodged but Osiris' sword caught his shoulder armor piece. Henry was propelled downward by that blow. Also, it hurt. The force and pain of the blow shocked him. He sat on the ground, sword in hand. Large Osiris moved to attack again. Henry rolled, hopped up and thrust the sword at him. He blocked it easily and set himself up for his next attack. He came at Henry again. Henry danced out of the way and managed to nick him on the back of his leg. Henry turned around to block the next lunge and found he was alone. He turned and looked around. Large or any other Osiris was nowhere to be seen. A gathering audience of shimmering ghosts watched him with blank, questioning faces.

Henry blinked and suddenly his surroundings changed. He was standing in a boxing ring, wearing shiny, long, silver shorts, big, red boxing gloves and no shirt. The boxing ring had just appeared in the center of the battlefield. In the opposite corner sat Osiris, or a man who looked like Osiris but who also looked different. A bell rang and Osiris danced into the center of the ring on light feet.

"Fight!" Osiris said. Henry could see his mouth guard. He put his gloves up and began to step back and forth.

"Not you, Henry. You're not a boxer," Osiris said. "Find somebody else in there. Come on!"

That took Henry a second to process. 'Find somebody else?' he thought as he stepped around the ring. Then it came to him. He skimmed through the pages of his many lives and found a man, a good boxer, named Tam. Henry became Tam. Osiris smiled and lunged. Tam easily avoided Osiris's jabs and upper cuts, dodging and bending like a dancer. They boxed.

Henry, as Tam, took one good hit and knelt to the ropes, but he got back up and fought viciously. In one, small, millisecond of time, Osiris left himself open on the side and Tam pounced. Tam gave him a liver punch which pulled Osiris down to his knees. Osiris held his side and looked up at Tam.

"Now, you're getting it," he said and disappeared, along with the ring and Tam's boxing gear. Henry, and he was Henry again, stood in the same spot on the battle field surrounded by the same army of perplexed ghosts. Here and there, the currently living also began to congregate and watch.

Henry became aware of a vibration in his feet, softly at first, and then more pronounced like an earthquake. The crowd was able to discern an epicenter, a direction of force, and moved away from a spot a near Henry. Suddenly, the earth there erupted in a stream of water. It burst from the ground and poured out. It did not spread and sink, but rather curled in on itself, bulging and pulsating. Henry could feel the spray on his face and looked down to see pools of water developing. He realized that it was salt water. The self-contained form of water gathering in front of him also looked like sea water. It was semi-transparent and held that characteristic blue-green color, darker now in the diminishing light. Henry saw seaweed swish by and thought he saw a fish. Unafraid, he stood and watched the water shape as it twisted and gathered in front of him. Though it was all sea water, it took on a vaguely humanoid form, with a blocky head and two arms. The water rose up and then seemed to look at him, menacingly. He took a step back. From somewhere he thought he heard a voice, a whisper on the wind.

"What have you been, Henry among others?" said the watery whisper. Henry blinked and had an idea. To the astonishment of the crowd he ran to the sea-water form and jumped in. As soon as he hit the water he became a fish. The water twisted. He twisted with it. The water bounced and flowed viciously and moved within itself. Henry, fish Henry, swam with the flow. The arms of the water form tried in vain to catch him and separate him from the water. He was so small that every crashing wave or twisting eddy within the waves was a freeway of space for him to travel through. The water began to retreat back into the crater in the earth from which it had burst forth. Fish Henry swam to the edge of the shape and jumped out, to squirm and flap in the dust, fish mouth opening and closing in a suffocating "O".

Suddenly, he was Henry again. The crowd cheered. He knew the game now. The question was, 'what was next?'

As if in answer, that now familiar vibration began in his feet. The epicenter of this disturbance was in the opposite direction of the first one. The crowd cleared the area. A stream of liquid came bursting up from the earth, but it was not water. Lava rose explosively from the earth, raining fire, ash and chunks of dirt. A few of the fleshy left on the battlefield were engulfed and died, only to rise as ghosts. Henry backed up out of the range of the falling lava and watched as again, a vaguely humanoid lava shape seemed to climb up out of the hole in the earth and charge at him aggressively.

Henry disappeared. The sun had set but the sky was still at lavender twilight. It began to get cloudy. The lava form looked around and chased after anyone still fleshy, burning them up in shapeless arms. A breeze blew, which transformed into a steady wind. The temperature plummeted. It began to rain and then to snow. More and more snow fell until it was almost a white out. Snow fell on the lava menace. At first it just melted. As the snow continued, dark spots began to appear on the lava form's body. The dark spots grew and spread. The darkening monster took one step awkwardly, another and then, it couldn't move anymore. Snow began to pile up on its shoulders. It moved its arms around angrily. Large chunks of cooling black basalt were flung from its arms as it moved and turned. Thick snow surrounded the lava form until all that was left was a black statue of a remotely humanoid, menacing shape.

And again, it was all gone. The statue was gone as well as the snow. Henry stood where he had been before, in his same battle gear holding the sword and looking rather smug. The crowd cheered and shouted his name.

Cheers and applause were replaced by silence, hushed whispers, and pointing towards the horizon. Henry heard a low familiar sound, though he couldn't see anything in the purpling sky. Then he spotted it: a plane, an old-fashioned quad-engine plane. As it came closer he thought he could just make out a large R in a circle on the tail. As it passed overhead he could barely make out the number 82 on the fuselage. Something triggered in

Henry's memory. He looked around for shelter but of course there was none. The sky filled with white fire.

No one who was still alive survived the blast. All flesh was destroyed, vaporized away by the nuclear blast. The field of battle was now completely ghosts and the charred, decimated remains of their bodies.

Henry picked up the sword and smiled, happy that he could still wield it in ghost form. He walked over to the ghosts of his friends, Ra-Neferu, Burhan, Dave, and others he knew. As he approached them he shrugged. They shrugged back.

"Has anything like this ever happened in your time here?" he asked. Ra-Neferu looked at him, her ghostly eyes wide in disbelief.

"Nope," she said.

Something caught Henry's attention and he looked up at the sky. Towards the east he saw a bright, yellow light moving across the backdrop of stars.

"Look at that," he said to those around him.

Soon the light began to take shape. As it got closer, Henry realized that it was an angel. She flew to the center of the battle field and dropped lightly to the ground. In her hands she held the filigreed vase of light that Henry had found in the tower room in Heaven. She placed the vase on an outthrust of rock, near where the lava form had emerged. She then stood, quietly waiting. For a while nothing happened. All the ghosts stood looking at each other, at the vase and at the angel. The angel almost looked bored.

Soon, Henry became aware of a low sound, like distant thunder. The other ghosts around him felt it too and looked around at each other and at the ground. The sound gradually grew louder and louder. He and the other ghosts exchanged looks of worry. Dust clouds began to appear on the horizon in all directions, floating lazily away in the twilight.

As they watched, a strange and beautiful menagerie of beings descended upon the battle field and gathered around the filigreed vase on its basalt pillar. Henry saw mounted warriors, warriors on chariots, beautiful women in varieties of clothing, and various multicolored animals. He also saw men and women who seemed to be partly an animal of some kind and part human. The beings were all attractive or noble or fierce or stunning in some way. The animals were oversized, decorated, and regal. At one

263

point, Henry saw Osiris walk to the crowd and stand among them. Isis joined him.

As they watched, Dave gasped. "It's her." He pointed at a dark-haired woman in the crowd of fantastic people. She wore a white dress with a pink ribbon tied at her waist. In her hand she held a blue and white lotus.

"Do you recognize someone among them?" Henry asked.

"Yes, I...Lauren saw her. Lauren went to see the eternal flame in Heaven and she saw that woman, except she looked older, but it was her. I just thought...Lauren thought she was Mary." Henry looked and suddenly realized that he had seen her as well.

"That's the girl from the temple!" Henry said. Dave and others nearby looked at him. "I went to talk to Osiris. She was there." Burhan stepped forward.

"I saw her too, but she was a child. She's the reason I left the missionary island," Burhan said. They stood and watched.

"I think," Ra-Neferu said, "that she is Nephthys, Isis's sister. She comes to people in different...ages. She can be a child or a woman, any age. It has partly to do with her message. " Henry frowned.

"What was she doing in Heaven? And why haven't we seen her here? I've never seen her in the courtyard," Henry said. Ra-Neferu shrugged.

"It seems that she has been busy." Henry was about to respond when he realized that a man and woman from the crowd had turned off to walk in Henry's direction. The man was dressed in gleaming armor. His skin was subtly blue. The woman's blue skin was so dark it was almost black. She wore a necklace of white skulls around her neck and not much else. The man addressed Henry.

"Please return my sword, Henry among others. You will not need it anymore." The man smiled broadly. Henry thought of Osiris when he saw that smile. He held it out to the man, hilt first.

"Thank you for letting us use it," Henry said. The man nodded and took the sword. The pair turned to leave but Henry stopped them.

"Wait, just one moment please," he said. "I have a question for if you don't mind." The pair stood waiting. Henry cleared his throat. "The vase over there...the container with the yellow cloud. Is that the source? Is that...what animates?" Henry asked. The pair laughed heartily. The bluish man shook his head. The dark woman said,

"It is just a device, a machine…like these swords…it is a tool."

"It is like…a microphone through which many may speak as one," said the bluish man. He grinned broadly and turned to leave. "Goodbye, Henry among others. We will see you again." The pair turned and walked off, headed toward the menagerie surrounding the vase. Henry exchanged looks with Burhan and Dave who shrugged their ghostly shoulders in return.

A hush fell over the crowd. All eyes turned toward the vase on the pillar.

The yellow, swirling cloud of light began to stream out of the filigreed vase. Long, thin whispers of yellow light slowly spread throughout the crowd, surrounding them with a phosphorescent fog. Thin streams of the fog hung in the air and circulated slowly around them. Here and there the fog shimmered as if it contained many small auroras. When the air around them was saturated, they all looked up and opened their mouths. With one voice they said:

"I am the first and the last.

I am the one and the many.

I give all and receive all.

There is no separation.

I am one light."

As if in a trance the crowd of ghosts answered, "As are we all." Henry shook his head as he came out of the trance and looked around to see others similarly confused and shaken. He felt weak and strange. He looked down and realized that he was back in his body again as was everyone around him.

Among the crowd of fantastic people and creatures, the yellow fog was receding back into the vase. When it was done, the angel picked up the vase and flew away, towards the terminal.

The crowd of gods dispersed in much the same way they had come, in large dusty trails heading off into the night. Henry stood watching the whole scene, dumbfounded, numb and filled with a strange glee. He heard an elephant trumpet and began to laugh. In the distance, he heard the sound of many engines starting. Headlights and other lights were lit among the army of Heaven. Jeeps, tanks, trucks and other vehicles drove off, also in the direction of the terminal. Henry could hear distant shouting and angry voices barking orders. The orders went unheeded as a mass exodus of soldiers, both on foot and in vehicles, or clinging to their sides, drove away. When the soldiers of the White City realized what was happening, cheers began to ring out all over the battlefield. All the wounded and dead were risen and whole and they began dancing and shouting. Henry and the others joined them.

Chapter 45

Portals and Doors Part II

Henry and Lauren walked along the beach near her mother's villa. It was evening and the sun shone almost horizontally across the deep blue ocean. The horizon was dotted with clouds and suffused with a pink-orange glow.

"Now you must admit that Dave was the right choice," Lauren said. Henry nodded and grinned but wouldn't say anything. "Come on now," Lauren teased, "admit it."

"Yes, yes…alright then…yes, he was the best suited for the war. He was confident and skilled and intelligent…he was also just such a jackass, Lani. He was… is goodhearted, but not enough to compensate for the rest. He kept calling me 'Hank' and he knew I hated it." Lauren giggled. They walked quietly for a time and Lauren began to fidget. She adjusted her hair and tugged on her ear. Henry looked at her and smiled.

"Out with it, woman."

"I uh…well with our past lives and everything…I um…Henry, this is hard to say but…at least for a while…I am going to…go my own way," she said in a small voice.

"What do you mean?" Henry asked. Lauren looked down at the sand.

"This whole time since I died, I was just…waiting for you. Now that you're here and we've had some time…Well, I…I'm not going to live with you in a villa somewhere and settle into some…mundane routine," she said, gathering strength. "I want to travel. I want to see what's out there. I want…"

"Is it Burhan?" Henry asked. Lauren looked surprised.

"Oh…no, no. Actually Henry, he…I knew him. He was my husband too…in a previous life. When I was Dave he stayed away from me and we never…connected. Recently we talked and we recognized each other. Once you remember spending 40 years with someone…And look…that's just what I'm talking about. I've had lots of husbands and wives too…and so have you. I remember you from other lives too…I remember," Lauren scrunched up her face and then frowned, "…well not here. Here in Heaven …I guess it's just us." She took Henry's hand and they sat down on the sand to watch the sunset. Henry put his arm around her. "Henry, I can

267

always come and see you. I can walk through a portal and, bam...I'll be there. It's not like I'll never see you again, and I do want to see you again. I just also want..."

"It's alright. It's alright, salty girl. I understand. I don't blame you at all." He smiled at her and caressed her face. "So, what will you do? What's your grand plan?" he asked.

"I want to travel...in Elysium. I want to find a coastline and just walk it...till I come back to the same spot. There's a real ecology there. These fish...they're not the same as Earth fish. It's not just a facsimile. I've seen...divergent evolution in action. I want to explore. Where I can't walk I will swim. And as a ghost...there's really nowhere I can't go." She turned and looked back at the house. "Before I leave I am bringing my mom and some others to Elysium. I told them about the flood and past lives and everything. I think mom wants to come because she doesn't want to be fat anymore."

"Well, that's silly. She's a perfectly lovely woman," Henry said.

"Yeah but...she just wants to know what it's like. I think when it happens her perspective will change."

"Absolutely," Henry said.

"So what about you, Dr. Hall. What are you going to do? You can come if you'd like but I didn't think you'd like to...look at fish with me," she said. Henry scrunched up his face.

"You know me too well, my dear. I would be lying if I said it sounded appealing." Lauren nodded then brightened.

"You know who else calls you Dr. Hall...Ra-Neferu," she said teasing.

"Lani, Lani...jealous girl...always suspicious of every woman." Henry sighed in an exaggerated manner.

"Well?"

"How can you ask me that when you...Dave was all over her. I mean I might as well be asking you 'what about Ra-Neferu?'"

"Mmmm...nope. She flirted with Dave but uh...she wouldn't have him. That's why I thought..."

"No, my dear. Neffie is my dear friend and my...mentor in a way."

"Oh...Bent-Reshet?"

"Lauren! She was my uncle. Good god! Do you think every woman in my life is a love interest?"

"Well, it's not like I don't have reason to worry. Yeesh. After remembering my past lives...men cheat...I cheated when I was a man. I...I was a ridiculous liar in a couple of my lives. And...and...what about Astrid? She still had the hots for you even after she died." Henry snorted.

"Astrid is a predator not a woman. I was just the bit of meat she hadn't caught yet. If I had let her have me, that would have been the end of it. She would have moved on to her next victim. Actually, Astrid is someone who would benefit from the flood. I have a feeling that she didn't like herself very much. Underneath it all she seemed very sad." Henry scratched absently at his chin.

"You could find her...help her," Lauren suggested. Henry shook his head.

"Though I think helping Astrid in that way would probably save many people in Heaven from suffering...it's not going to be me that saves her. I have other mysteries to solve, I think."

"Oh, like what?"

"Well for one thing, the portals. Remember the portal to the tower room and how the portal itself was disguised as part of the wall? I have a feeling that there are other portals in that room...also in the walls. I was talking to your Aunt Rosie about this. She spent time out on those islands you spoke of, with the old ones. Apparently they told her stories. She said that at one time there were portals all over the castle grounds before they walled off the garden and in other places as well, ruins in the ocean and such. I have a feeling that those hidden portals...that they go to more places than just the ones we know. There must be a reason that the Castle wanted to keep them secret. I think that this is where my line of investigation begins."

"Dave might like that," Lauren said.

"Well, he can come along," Henry said. Lauren looked up at him with an eyebrow raised.

"Do you really want Dave to come along, Henry?" she asked.

"Well no, not really but..." Henry shrugged his shoulders. "The truth is that I wouldn't like to do it alone. I'm not like you, salty girl. I need people around to talk to...but your Aunt Rosie might come, depending on who she is after she floods. Burhan might want to go...who knows? I want you to follow your heart, but you can always come with me, anywhere I go, you can come."

From the villa they heard Mahina's sonorous call. "Laaaaaaauuuuuuuuuurrrrrrrrren."

"What lungs that woman has," Henry said laughing.

"Dinner must be ready. Mahina's famous clam chowder. Let's go." Lauren stood up and brushed sand off of her legs. She held her hand out to Henry. He took it again and they walked to the house for dinner.

*****

While Heaven's Army had occupied the terminal in Elysium, they sealed all the portals except for the one to the Water Door. At one point a commander stuck his head through the portal to the tower room, shrugged his shoulders, and ordered it sealed without investigating any further.

During Heaven's massive retreat, they tried to destroy the portal on the Elysium side with a timed bomb. The bomb went off as planned, but all it did was blow part of the brick and mortar seal off of part of the Lover's Door. The rest of the brick seals were easily destroyed and the rubble removed by golems.

In Heaven, they re-flooded the Water Door and put up warning signs, and threatening signs, and signs about penalties and punishments but other than that, the door was free as it ever was, under 30 feet or so of water. Henry, Lauren, and the members of her family that wanted to come to Elysium, went for a swim off the coast of New Jerusalem one evening, drowned, and then ghost-walked to the Water Door and entered Elysium. Lauren left a few weeks later.

To Henry's surprise, Ra-Neferu wanted to go with him to investigate the portals. Along with them came Marc, Bent-Reshet, and Lauren's Aunt Rosie. They arrived at the terminal one afternoon and entered the portal to the tower room. The filigreed metal vase sat in its usual spot on a velvet-covered crate, its golden cloud gently swirling in on itself.

Rosie stood staring at the vase while Henry and Ra-Neferu marked portals on the walls with chalk. Marc and Bent-Reshet looked out the little window onto New Jerusalem.

"If it was sunset I would jump out of this window right now," Marc said. Bent-Reshet looked at him like he was crazy.

"Ok, which one shall we try first?" Henry asked after they had finished marking the portals.

"Let us investigate clockwise from the portal home," Ra-Neferu said.

"Ah, a very reasonable suggestion," Henry said. "Would you like to go first Nef?"

"No, no you go. I think it is safe. I felt cool air when I stuck my hand through. Put your face through first, then come back and describe what you see," she said. Henry stepped forward and carefully stuck his head through. The metallic membrane pushed ever so slightly on his face and he closed his eyes. When he opened them he saw a beach. White sand shone brightly under blue sky. The long green leaves of several nearby trees shook and shimmered in a slight breeze. Henry smelled salt water and heard breakers on a shore line. He pulled his head back through.

"It's a beach. Did we bring a picnic lunch?" Henry chuckled. "Come on." He went back through. The others followed.

They each walked through the portal and stepped onto the white sand of the beach. They all stood looking around and then gradually, at themselves. Henry realized that he felt different. There was something new in this body, a powerful pathway to something he could sense but couldn't quite grasp.

"Do you…Neffie, do you feel different here?" Henry asked. Ra-Neferu nodded. She looked at her own arm and hand.

"I do. I feel strange," she said.

"I feel strong…almost like, I could fly," Marc said. Everyone nodded and agreed.

"Well, what do you want to do now?" Ra-Neferu asked. Henry looked around at the beach and the trees. He saw no signs of people anywhere.

"I don't know. Let's go exploring," he said.

And they did.

Bonus Short Story

How Hypatia Started the Third War in Heaven

Elena Sands

This story is set in the same world with a few of the same characters.

The main character of this story, Hypatia, was a real Neo-Platonist philosopher and teacher in Alexandria, Egypt between 370 A.D. and her death in 415 A.D. She taught philosophy, astronomy, and mathematics and was highly regarded by her students and some political leaders at the time. She was caught up in rising political tensions between a secular governor and the Christian Bishop of Alexandria around 410 A.D. She was murdered by a Christian mob in the streets of Alexandria. The mob was led by a fanatic called Peter the Reader. Her death is often seen as a symbol of the downfall of paganism and the rise to power of Christianity in Ancient Rome.

Hypatia's last memories of her Earthly life were of a brown, dirty, stinking mob of angry men who were stabbing her to death. She felt the cuts of the shards of broken pottery they used to open her. She heard her own screams as if from far away. She felt a pool of warm, sticky blood spread underneath and around her naked body. In that fading moment when she lost consciousness, a childhood memory floated up out of the darkness. She remembered a sunny day at a public bath. She and her friends splashed water onto the sun-warmed concrete edge of the pool and then scrambled to get out of the pool and lay flat in that thin layer of warm water. Hypatia smiled in the memory and was gone from the living world.

A moment and an eternity passed and Hypatia found herself lying on a rectangular stone pedestal. The pedestal lay in the center of a small room with long, colorful silk banners extending down from a high ceiling in lieu of walls. She sat up and looked around. There was a marble table next to her pedestal which contained unlit oil lamps, a glass container of water, and a wooden bowl of bread and figs. The room was pretty but it was foreign to her and she was confused. In all the other lives she could remember, when she died she had gone somewhere that made sense. This place was new.

She hopped lightly off the pedestal and moved past the marble table. She held back a purple silk banner and walked out into a corridor. The corridor was only suggested by the placement of the banners. There appeared to be no interior walls in the building, only pillars. The banners swung lightly in a breeze and Hypatia saw between them more pedestals, pillars, tables, other banners, and the outer stone wall of the building, broken at regular intervals by narrow windows. Some of the pedestals contained a human form, others lay empty. It was hard to see clearly in the mix of shadows and light. The whole place had a feel of age to it, of dust and light and time. She thought she heard muffled voices and the soft sounds of bare feet on stone.

"Is anyone there?" she asked aloud. Her voice sounded small, swallowed up by the huge building. There was no answer, only the same muffled, distant sounds she had heard before. She walked cautiously along the corridor towards a distant doorway that ended in bright sunlight. As she approached, the light seemed to become brighter. It was so bright compared to the dimmer interior of the building that she could not resolve anything beyond the door. She stepped out into the sun and carefully down stone steps.

When her eyes adjusted, she saw spread out in front of her an endless, undulating plain of golden, brown sand dunes. A cloudless blue sky reigned over the world. She turned slowly around and saw the building she had just walked out of and the massive city that it belonged to. She stood staring, open-mouthed, at the beautiful, mostly white city and the high, stony mountains, several waterfalls and terraces, and the sculpted likenesses of gods, carved right into the mountain itself. She stood in awe and silence, forgetting for the moment to breathe.

Motion caught her eye and Hypatia became aware of a woman walking towards her from the road. She wore a clean, white dress, probably of linen by the way it moved, and jewelry appropriate to a patrician. The woman approached and then stood next to Hypatia, facing the city and mountains.

"Beautiful, do you think?" the woman said in Greek. Hypatia stared at her. She had dark hair and eyes. Her skin was a friendly caramel color. A gold necklace with green stones hung at her neck. She was lovely. She spoke Greek well but with a strange accent. There was something familiar about her pleated linen gown, her jewelry, and her hair. Then it came to her.

"Ah, you are…this is Egypt…Old Egypt…or one of your after worlds. Why am I here? Why didn't I just go to the usual place?" Hypatia asked as she stared more carefully at the mountainous stone gods. There appeared to be a waterfall between the two central statues.

"Which one?" the woman asked.

"The Elysian Fields. I have been there before many times."

The woman pursed her lips. "I am afraid that things have changed. The Elysian Fields are now ruled by the Christians. They call it the Kingdom. Pagans of any kind are not permitted there any longer. Now these lands are called Elysium and all pagans come here to us."

Hypatia turned slowly towards the strange woman. A million thoughts and questions ran through her mind. 'When? Why? How did they do it? Where was her father? Is there danger here?'

"I don't know why I'm here," Hypatia said. She was surprised by the shakiness in her own voice. "It is beautiful, but I am confused. I died. I was killed by a …filthy mob." Hypatia looked down at herself, thinking that she must be filthy as well. She was perfectly clean. She wore a simple, undyed linen shift. She wondered briefly where it came from. The woman turned to face her.

"You are the philosopher called, Hypatia?" she asked.

"Yes," Hypatia answered. The woman smiled.

"Welcome to Niwt Hedj which we call the White City. My name is Ra-Neferu. I have come today to the House of the Lost," she gestured at the building Hypatia had left, "to find you and guide you." Hypatia frowned.

"How did you know…to look for me?" she asked. Ra-Neferu smiled.

"Your name was on the Wall of the Dead. Come, I will show you." Ra-Neferu began to walk down the street and into the city but presently she stopped in front of a stone arch, a portal, on the side of the street. She turned and reached for Hypatia's hand. Ra-Neferu said, "The Center" and together they walked through the portal.

Instantly, they stood together in front of a very large fountain with a wading pool all around it. Men and women sat on the tan and ivory edges of the pool or waded through it. Children jumped through jets of water and blocked them with their hands. Hypatia's first thought was to join them in the water. It looked cool and clean and inviting. Ra-Neferu still held her hand and must have felt the almost-tug as Hypatia turned towards the fountain. Ra-Neferu waited while Hypatia looked at the pool but then led her gently away.

On the opposite side of the fountain there was what appeared to be a ruin. The remains of a thick wall made of large, slate grey stones cascaded down from a high, finished edge, to a whisper of rubble and a few out of place stones. A few loose stones sat randomly on the finished paving stones of the fountain area. They looked serenely out of place.

As they approached the wall, they passed a child who sat on one nearby grey stone, happily eating something and bouncing his heels off of its side. Hypatia chuckled at him. When she looked back towards the wall, Ra-Neferu was reading text that slowly scrolled from the bottom of the stone to the top, as if some invisible sculptor were carving it instantly and effortlessly. Hypatia watched as words scrolled by in Latin, Greek, Aramaic, Hebrew and other symbols she did not recognize. Suddenly she saw her own name. "Hypatia, daughter of Theon and Daphne- Renowned Philosopher of Alexandria –Platonist - murdered by a mob of Christians." That was all it said. It moved up the wall and disappeared at a height Hypatia could not see. After a few minutes it appeared again, coming up from the bottom. Ra-Neferu waited while Hypatia stood silently watching her death scroll up the wall.

"Can most people here read?" Hypatia asked softly.

"Yes. In one life or another they learn…or they learn here. We have many libraries and tutors," Ra-Neferu answered. Hypatia nodded. She turned and looked at the fountain and the waders. Even though she felt she should be happy, as if it were her duty to be happy in this moment, instead she felt sadness creep into her, seeping in slowly at the cracks until she began to feel heavy with it. Ra-Neferu stepped towards her and put a light hand on her shoulder.

"Here, come with me. It will get easier. Just give it time." Ra-Neferu took her hand again and led her back towards the stone arch through which they had arrived. Before they stepped through the portal Ra-Neferu said, "Home."

*****

A few weeks later, Hypatia sat on a lounge chair on the roof of Ra-Neferu's house enjoying the view. The golden desert stretched out to the horizon broken only by the wide, dark swath of the great river Havilah and its soft, green edges. To the south she could just make out the suggestion of the White City and its mountains. To be so far away and yet so easily traverse the distance through a mundane looking stone arch was a luxury and a puzzle. She wondered why the portals couldn't work on Earth. 'How do they work? Could we take one apart?' She sat in silence and thought.

Ra-Neferu was downstairs doing something. Hypatia mused that what Ra-Neferu was doing was leaving her alone. It did not take long for Ra-Neferu to figure out her habits. Hypatia wanted to be left alone most of the time. She wanted time to read and think, to write, and to idly scratch out geometric figures and sums on papyrus. In the Living World, or the Plane of Sorrow as they called it here, time was always in short supply. Maybe things would be different now, especially here in this new world. It was not on the Egyptian agenda to mandate belief and squash innovation and creativity, though she wondered. 'What is their agenda?' and 'Where is my father?' She heard steps coming up the stairs that led out onto the roof.

It wasn't Ra-Neferu, it was her bald little andrapodon; a mute, female slave made from stone. Hypatia had heard Ra-Neferu call them 'shabti' or something like that in her own language. The andrapodon brought her wine, water and food on a tray. She shook her head and waved it all away. The andrapodon bowed and left. A few minutes later Hypatia heard Ra-Neferu's light steps on the stairs that led up to the roof. She came to the sitting area where Hypatia had made herself at home and sat across from her on another lounge chair. Hypatia suddenly felt guilty about her behavior. Ra-Neferu had been a most gracious host. Hypatia sat up on the chair and faced her.

"Ra-Neferu, please forgive me for being…distant. You have been a wonderful host and I have been an unfriendly house guest. Thank you for all your help," Hypatia said. Ra-Neferu nodded.

"You are most welcome and…I understand," Ra-Neferu said. There was an awkward silence then she asked, "Do you find our food unpalatable?"

"What? Food? Oh…I am sure that there is nothing wrong with your food but I…even through my own death I am finding that I am a creature of habit. In life I never ate very much. Most food caused me some mild illness. As I got older my teeth…" Hypatia waved her hand away. "Here I know…every morning I am resurrected to perfect health but…honestly I saw that fact as my opportunity to avoid eating," Hypatia explained. "I had such an aversion to it."

"Do you think you will change? In one of your other lives could you have been…a more contented person?" Ra-Neferu asked. Hypatia thought about the question and stared out at the distant desert. Finally she shook her head 'no'.

"No, no. When a blind man is cured, no matter what he sees, he will never wish to be blind again. I lived…all those lives…an ocean of the mundane…rarely was I intelligent or educated… and even in those few lives in which I was…I was vain or dull or greedy. Hypatia, with all her faults, is my best so far." She said this as much to herself as to Ra-Neferu. She continued to look beyond the river at the endless dunes.

"Do think you will return to the Plane of Sorrow?" Ra-Neferu asked. Hypatia raised her eyebrows.

"Not anytime soon. Perhaps I will wait a few hundred years. I don't know how long Christianity will persist, but even if it doesn't last that long, the persecution of the Pagans will continue for some time. I would not like to be born a Christian. They abhor all our customs and so shun them, even the good ones! They have closed all the public baths. People don't even bathe properly, Ra-Neferu! It's disgusting." Hypatia made a face and then chuckled. Ra-Neferu smiled.

"Well, here you may bathe daily and be highly regarded," Ra-Neferu said still smiling. Something caught her attention by the river and she stood to look. Hypatia stood as well. Coming from a nearby portal a child was running towards the house.

"Is something wrong?" Hypatia asked. Ra-Neferu frowned as she watched the child approach.

"A messenger is coming," Ra-Neferu said softly.

278

"Andrapod-…or rather a shabti?" Hypatia asked.

"We say 'ushabti' but in this case…no, they have sent a person which is…bad news I am afraid to say. For routine things they send ushabtis with a written message. I know this child. He is a trusted man who has taken this form. Something must have happened," Ra-Neferu explained.

"Why does he take the form of child?" Hypatia asked. Ra-Neferu smiled a little.

"He says that it is his fastest and most anonymous form," she replied as she turned towards the hatch in the roof that led downstairs. Hypatia followed her. They walked down recessed stone stairs into the large house.

In the courtyard, the small boy was gone and a man stood waiting. The andrapodon hovered nearby, waiting to be called on.

"Princess," the man said as he bowed to Ra-Neferu. Hypatia raised her eyebrows. She had not been told that Ra-Neferu belonged to a royal family. Ra-Neferu nodded and the man continued, though he looked nervously at Hypatia.

"News has come to us that emissaries are coming to the city. They will demand to take custody of …" he looked nervously and apologetically at Hypatia, "the lady Hypatia. They say…please pardon me," he gestured at Hypatia, "that she is a sorceress and she must pay for her crimes." Hypatia's heart sank inside her chest. Ra-Neferu looked at her sympathetically and then back at the messenger. "Thank you," she said. "Nedjes, would you like to stay and eat?" It was customary to offer messengers food and drink. Nedjes shook his head no.

"Do you have anything to send in return?" he asked.

"Yes. Tell them that the Philosopher Hypatia was distraught at the manner of her death and so has gone through the Lover's Door and returned to the Plane of Sorrow and the loving arms of a new mother. She has been gone many weeks." Nedjes nodded and turned to leave. As Hypatia watched he began to run and to transform into a child at the same time. Soon he was just a small brown speck in the distance heading straight for the stone portal by the river.

"Will that work?" Hypatia asked. Ra-Neferu shook her head slightly.

"No, but it will give us time. My friends in the city sent Nedjes because he knows how to avoid being followed. Just by sending him it means that there are spies in the city looking for

279

you." Re-Neferu frowned and looked around at the courtyard absently. "Also, Hypatia, I am well known in the city for helping new arrivals, and in particular for helping pagan refugees who have fled the Kingdom."

"So, I am not safe here?" Hypatia asked. Ra-Neferu shook her head.

"No, not at all. There are other places, but Hypatia…you must change your form. Getting there is the problem. I cannot take you as Ra-Neferu and you cannot travel as Hypatia. Find someone else to be for a time. It will not be forever," Ra-Neferu explained. Then before her eyes Ra-Neferu slowly changed, dissolving into a young boy as she spoke. "This…hostility and coming into our lands to retrieve people is new. Before, when we told them that someone had gone through the Lover's Door, that was enough. Now they are trying to subvert us here in our own lands. They grow bolder every day. We may have to guard or block the gate but…"

"That would mean war," Hypatia finished for her. "I remember the other two wars. I fought in the first one, but I suppose…we all did." Hypatia then changed herself into a young girl. Ra-Neferu shook her head.

"No, no. Find a boy. They look suspiciously on girls. Two boys walking together is better…and not a white one…brown like me," Ra-Neferu said. Hypatia sighed and rolled her eyes. She then transformed into a young boy who looked enough like Ra-Neferu's boy to be his brother. She nodded her approval and smiled. "Were we ever brothers?" she asked and moved closer to Hypatia to look into her eyes. Hypatia shook her head.

"No, I have never known you," she said.

"And I have never known you," Ra-Neferu said, "but that is not so strange. I have been here a very long time."

"Why?" Hypatia asked.

"That is a story for another time. Now, we need to go."

"Right now?"

"Yes, right now." The two women, in the guise of two, sun-brown, pre-teen boys, walked towards the portal.

The portal wasn't that far from Ra-Neferu's house and they arrived quickly. Hypatia was about to ask Ra-Neferu where they would go when two men stepped casually out of the portal in front of them. They wore leather armor and were armed with swords. In the center of each of their breastplates was a small golden square. It glinted in the sun as the two men turned towards the two boys and looked at them intensely. The men stepped forward and one of them grabbed Ra-Neferu's arm. He spoke to her harshly. He spoke Latin, which Ra-Neferu understood, but she pretended not to. She shook her head and said in Egyptian, "What? What do you want?" The other man spoke up.

"Who are you and what are you doing here?" the man said in heavily accented Egyptian. Ra-Neferu thought fast.

"We are the workers…the apprentices of Ambustus," Ra-Neferu said. Her dark eyes were wide with fear. Hypatia wondered how much of it was real.

"What did you bring here? Why did you come here?" the man asked, still holding her arm tightly.

"A necklace. The princess receives many gifts. Now let me go! My master will be angry if we take too long." Ra-Neferu twisted her arm out of the man's grip. He smiled and let go of her. Ra-Neferu and Hypatia stepped past the men to the portal. The men stood waiting and listening to hear them say where they would go. "Ambustus," Ra-Neferu said quietly and they entered the portal.

Ambustus's compound was a series of buildings near the center of the city. Ambustus, the master smith, carver, engraver, and jeweler, was in charge of the great ovens of the city. He was an expert in works of clay but also in working all metals. It was not unusual for him to have apprentices and it was not unusual for his apprentices to take the form of children. Ambustus said that his apprentices should be young so that they might learn their crafts with small, nimble fingers. It was a good place to hide on short notice but unfortunately, it was not good enough. Almost as soon as Ra-Neferu and Hypatia exited the portal, more armed men seized them. The portal opened up on to a wide open area of paving stones and a series of forges and work benches. Many of the work areas were covered by wood and fabric shades. A couple of apprentices were busy hammering away on the glowing end of a long rod of metal. Ambustus was talking animatedly with a man who was dressed in the same leather armor as the other men who had stopped them at the portal near Ra-Neferu's house. When Ambustus saw the two boys come through the portal he raised his hands in the air. Two men on either side of the portal immediately grabbed Hypatia and Ra-Neferu.

"Ah, there you are…you naughty boys. You took too long. Where have you been? You are late for your appointment with Jaharis. Now, go, go, go…and go to the right place…I will know if you don't… now go!" Ambustus said. The two men holding them ignored Ambustus and looked to the man he had been talking to. Like the others he wore the same leather armor with the engraved golden square in the center of his chest. He approached Hypatia and Ra-Neferu and looked at them carefully. He turned to Ra-Neferu and looked deep into her eyes while the other man held her arm. After a moment he smiled.

"Ah, princess, you cannot hide from me. Go. Go and join your friend." He then grabbed Ra-Neferu roughly by the shoulder and pushed her towards Ambustus. Ambustus looked at her with anger and confusion. He stepped forward.

"Hey, hey, hey. You cannot treat my boys, my people like this. Get out of my place. Leave my apprentices alone." The man who had pushed Ra-Neferu looked briefly at Ambustus and then looked to his companion. He nodded his head in Ambustus' direction. Before Ambustus could react the second man had stepped to him and opened his throat with his blade. Ambustus went down. Ra-Neferu gasped in surprise and knelt to help him. Blood spurted with arterial rhythm from the big man's neck and gradually slowed. Ra-Neferu looked helplessly at Ambustus while he died. Ra-Neferu stood up and changed form, blurring slightly, until she was herself again. Blood stained her white linen gown.

"You cannot do this," she said angrily. The man, who appeared to be the leader, ignored Ra-Neferu and looked deep into Hypatia's eyes. For a moment there was silence. Hypatia resisted. She tried with her whole being to be this young boy whose body she inhabited. The man peered into the dark pupil of her eye and saw the boy, but behind the boy he saw Hypatia in all her grace and beauty; Hypatia lecturing to students, studying a conic section made of wood and smiling at her father.

"Ah!" the man said and broke the silence. "Here she is." He picked up Hypatia, still a young boy, and threw her over his shoulder like a sack of potatoes. The three men moved to go through the portal.

"You cannot do this!" Ra-Neferu said again, loudly. "You have no authority here. You cannot walk into our country and murder and kidnap people. You risk the start of war." The leader of

282

the three turned around and smiled. Hypatia wiggled on his shoulder, trying to escape his iron grip.

"Ah Princess, but you misunderstand. I welcome the start of war." He smiled and his companions smiled and nodded their heads in agreement. "The sooner this war starts and ends, the sooner you will all be in the arms of god's grace. Your fat friend there will be well and whole tomorrow and he will work for us and you will make a fine wife to an officer when we take this place. The King will rule."

"The King will rule!" the others parroted. Then they went through the portal.

*****

As soon as they stepped through the portal, the leader took Hypatia off of his shoulder and punched her in the head. She fell briefly to her knees and watched a drop of blood fall from her mouth into reddish-brown dirt.

"Not this again," she said softly and blacked out.

Hypatia woke up on the floor of a stone room. The room was huge and was lit by one small, high window. In one corner there was an orange-brown pot with a lid. The rest of the room was bare. Hypatia did not get up. She lay on the floor and listened. She heard high winds and a rhythmic noise…very far away. She thought it might be ocean waves breaking on a shore. She also heard the hum, the collective noise of people and houses and animals. 'Hmm…a city…by the sea,' she thought, 'I am in Elysium.'

They left her in the stone room overnight and into the next day. In a brief moment of despair she thought she might spend eternity in that terrible room, but she quickly realized that this would not be enough. She would be made an example of in some gruesome and public way. Daily resurrection: a torturer's dream.

In the afternoon, the one door to the room swung open and two leather clad guards came in and grabbed her by the arms. On the other side of the door, near a set of stairs, there was a small, stone portal. Without saying a word they stepped through this portal and out of another one into another dark, stone hallway. They marched her up some nearby stairs and out into bright sunlight. She turned her head from the glare. They continued to march her along, through wooden doors in stone walls and along pathways in what seemed to be a huge garden that had been sectioned off. With a gasp she realized that these were the Great Gardens of Elysium. Someone, in a crisis of power and tyranny, had built rough, stone walls all through it, hoarding and coveting its beauty for themselves. This alone was a terrible tragedy and Hypatia's heart was heavy in her chest.

Finally, they went through one more wooden door in a wall and came to a triangular shaped section of green grass and rosebushes, dotted with pink and white blooms. A stone bench sat in the center of the triangle. The two guards dragged her to the stone bench and forced her to sit on it, like a mother positioning a little child. During this little ordeal Hypatia was able to get a good look at the engraved golden square that all of these men wore attached to the front of their leather armor. Inscribed in the square was a circle. Inside the circle was a cross. The circle had little decorations all along the edge of it to make it look like a crown. In the space between the cross and the edge of the circle, lines of light spread out from the cross. In each of the four sections, doves flew in the light towards the cross. In the horizontal bar of the cross there was an inscription in Latin: "Rex imperabit." The King will rule. The guards left her on the bench.

She sat quietly and took a good look at her surroundings. She thought she could probably scale the wall and walk along it, but to what end? The Great Gardens were so big. Had they really enclosed all of it this way? She looked up in the direction she thought they had come from and sat in awe of the huge and sprawling castle that had been built in the city center. She saw men with bows and arrows on the many balconies and ramparts. One of them stood quietly and watched her, an arrow ready in his bow. She sighed.

After a few minutes Hypatia heard a door open and close, and down the length of the opposite wall, she saw a man walking towards her. He was a small man with brown hair and eyes. He looked slightly familiar and perhaps…Egyptian. He wore a simple, natural linen robe. He stopped a few feet away from her.

"Ah, Hypatia. We meet again." He smiled in a way that was both friendly and off-putting. Hypatia tasted something bitter in her mouth. She looked at his face but could not place it.

"Pardon me, but I don't remember you," Hypatia said politely. The man's face soured. Lines of disgust formed around his little mouth. He quickly recovered and went back to his terrible smile.

"Of course you do. I saved you from your sinful life. A few days later I also…well, no matter. I am here now in God's glorious kingdom and so are you." He gestured to her with a flourish of his hand. He then stood up straight and bowed slightly. "I was known as Peter the Reader. I saved you from the sin of your pagan existence. I will yet save you again." Peter had a lisp. When he said, "save" he reminded Hypatia of a snake. Hypatia still did not know him. If he was responsible for her death, he did not participate when it happened. She remained quiet on the bench but she looked up at him with daggers in her eyes.

"Oh, you wish me death do you?" He laughed. "What else can a woman wish for you when she looks at you like that?" He turned and shook his head softly. He approached the rose bush and brushed his hand over a nearby flower. He plucked it from the bush and brought it to his nose. He then approached her with the flower in his hand.

"You see this flower Hypatia…this flower is you. It has the essence of piety, here in the white…" he showed her the flower and pointed to the white petals, "but you have been tainted by sin…so you see the pink… around the edges there…and there." He pointed again. "All women are tainted thus." He shook his head sadly. "However, God in his great mercy still wishes to accept you and make you his own…but…you are unclean. So you see…you must be cleansed. I will help you with this." He bowed slightly. "I will save you but…you must accept my help." Peter paused to look at her. Hypatia looked down at the cement bench, working to control her anger.

"No?…Well that is sad news. Perhaps you will change your mind in time." He smiled that terrible smile again. "There are two paths here you may tread, dear Hypatia. One leads to salvation and the other…damnation. You will choose. Each path begins the same way. In the grand courtyard of the city we have made seven pyres. Every day for seven days you will be burned to death on each of those pyres and…all in the presence of one who would…ensure that you feel pain. Your penance must be real you see…so then on the morning of the 8th day you will either submit to god and become a faithful wife and servant here in the Kingdom or…" Peter let the flower fall from his hand. He stepped on the rose and rubbed his sandaled foot around until the flower was a ruined mess. "...a sad outcome indeed. So...what do you say?" Hypatia stood up and spat in Peter's face. As soon as she did this the archer on the wall let an arrow fly. Hypatia collapsed onto the grass as a dark red stain spread across the front of her dress. She heard Peter laughing as everything went dark.

*****

Hypatia spent a few more days in the empty stone room, though she was not left alone this time. Every day, three times a day, someone would come and implore her to accept Christianity and be baptized. Sometimes it was Peter. Sometimes it was a monk that she had never met before. Twice it was a woman who had been burned to death in life. Her appeals were real and ardent. Hypatia felt that she could see the fire in the woman's eyes when she spoke. Hypatia did not relent.

She had two reasons to hope. Based on her conversations with Ra-Neferu and what she knew of Christianity she believed there would be an opportunity for mercy. Before they burned her they might offer her the Lover's Door so that she might "be born of the correct faith" and live properly. Hypatia sighed. She did not want to go back to the dirty, stinking Plane of Sorrow, but it might be her only choice.

Her other hope was that there were now rumors of a Lover's Door in Tartarus. She wondered how that happened. The idea did not make sense. No one would choose to stay in a realm of torment if they could go back to Earth. Maybe Tartarus wouldn't be so bad if it was empty. Hypatia laughed at the thought. She imagined the hydra looking bored and sleepy, licking its chops with its many heads.

One dark question bothered her. Peter had said that she would feel pain and that someone would be there in whose presence she would feel pain. 'How?' she wondered. 'Who had such a power?' The residents of Elysium, or the Kingdom as they now insisted upon calling it, were not, as a rule, bothered by pain. So how could they do it? It didn't seem possible in any normal way. She hoped it was just an empty threat. Still something about the idea bothered her deeply, as if some long distant memory of pain and despair was approaching, just over the horizon of her mind.

*****

On the last night before Hypatia was to be burned alive in the city courtyard, one of her previous visitors came to her again. It was the woman who had herself been burned alive in her most recent life. Hypatia received her graciously though inwardly she laughed at the idea of receiving guests in an empty stone room. The woman, whose name was Messalina, seemed nervous and clutched at something in her robe.

"Hypatia, I know that you won't be baptized but I feel compelled…" she looked nervously over her shoulder at the door to the room and then moved close to Hypatia. "I feel I must help you," she whispered. Messalina took something from her robe and pressed it into Hypatia's hand. It was a glass vial filled with an amber liquid. "Drink this at dawn. Very soon after, they will come for you. The pyres are prepared and notices have been posted that you will perform your penance tomorrow. Drink it and your pain will be lessened. Someone else will come tomorrow with the same thing…that is if they don't offer you mercy. Oh, Hypatia, for your sake I hope they do." Messalina embraced her vigorously. When she came away, her eyes were wet. "You don't deserve this."

"Neither did you, Messalina," Hypatia said. Messalina looked grateful but said nothing. She embraced Hypatia again and then left quickly. Hypatia sat on the floor against the wall and looked at the glass vial. She wrapped it carefully in a section of her dress and then broke it against the wall. She opened up the fold of fabric and picked out a sharp edge of glass. She then carefully cut open the veins in her arms, lengthwise, so that she would bleed out very quickly. Her body slumped over and she died.

As it was night, she was then able to rise out of her body in ghost form. The past several nights alone in the prison she had been trying to choke herself, swallow her tongue or find some way to end her life and escape as a ghost, but she had not succeeded. Even the orange-brown pot in the corner had proven to be too tough to break into useful pieces. Tonight Messalina had provided her exit.

Hypatia's ghost, a subtle, bluish form, walked silently to the door of the room and slowly pushed her ethereal head through the substance of the door. She looked right and saw the guard standing against the wall with his eyes closed. He did not look like he was asleep at all but short, soft little snores came from his nose. Hypatia brought the rest of her body through the door and headed for the portal. She walked through and came out at the bottom of the stairs in the same building.

Her first thought was to exit the building and get away from the city center but that begged the question, how would she get back to the White City? Where was that central portal that she remembered? Once it had been attached to the central courtyard on a jetty that extended out into the ocean. Was that blocked off now too? Ghosts were subtle but not impossible to see. She would have to be very careful.

She walked slowly through the exterior wall of the building and into the city. She felt her ghost body and the stone wall merge and then separate, as if she were a net passing through muddy water. It was a strange sensation.

Out in the streets of the city it was not anywhere near as dark as she had hoped. Lamps and torches were lit everywhere. She had exited directly into the courtyard. Across the length of the place Hypatia could see vague pillars with what looked like bushes at the bottom. She counted seven of them and realized what they were. A spasm of fear seized her heart. She looked around, trying to see the portal to Ra-Neferu's world. The whole of the courtyard was walled in with exits in various places. She walked towards where she knew the ocean was and hoped.

The sound of the waves grew louder and Hypatia began to feel hopeful. Sometimes she heard another sound in the background, like the rustle of wings. She thought of sea birds flying over the ocean but she saw none in the sky.

Finally she turned a walled corner and there it was! The portal was still there at the end of the jetty. Through its center she could see the ocean and the dim remains of twilight on the horizon. Forgetting caution she began to run. She heard that rustle of wings again and saw a shadow on the ground. She felt strong hands grasp her shoulders and suddenly with a sharp inhalation of breath, she was alive again in her fleshy body. 'What sort of creature can resurrect you with a touch?' she thought as she looked up. Her head was jerked down again and she felt the creature lift her off the ground and carry her through the air as it flew. She struggled, but it was no use in the creature's steely grip. She was flown back to the castle and right back to the front entrance where guards stood. The creature dropped her roughly on the ground in front of the door and then said to the two guards, "Did you lose something?" Hypatia turned to see a winged man fly up and out of sight then the guards took her. They put her back in her cell, cleaned up the broken glass, and even ripped her linen shift from her body, leaving her completely naked.

*****

The next morning they came for her. Oddly, the first thing they did was dress her and apply cosmetics. They forced her into a ridiculously pompous and old-fashioned Roman dress. They then reddened her lips and darkened her eyebrows. She looked more like a whore than a philosopher. Perhaps that was the point. They even doused her with perfume which she viewed as an unnecessary extravagance. If she hadn't been about to die horribly she would have laughed at the whole situation.

She was then marched through the familiar portals and out into the courtyard. They starting walking to the farthest of the seven pyres where Peter the Reader was waiting with his terrible smile. As they passed the first pyre, Peter raised his hand in the air. The guards made her stop. He then indicated with a turn of his finger that she should turn and face the pyre. The guards forced her to do this. They then made her turn and walk forward and stop in this way at each of the seven pyres. A gathering crowd cheered. They cheered each time she stopped in front of a pyre and was forced to face it. Hypatia noticed that the crowd was unnaturally far away. She wondered why.

As they approached the final pyre, Hypatia began to feel nauseous. She was also aware of a soreness in her arm where the guards had held her down to apply the cosmetics. At the end of the row of pyres and against the stone wall that encircled the courtyard there was a black tent. The tent was quite small, only large enough for two people. Hypatia quickly realized that the tent was actually the top of a litter. The poles to carry the litter were stacked neatly nearby against the stone wall. The litter bearers were nowhere in sight. At the top of the tent there was a mesh section through which someone inside could look out. She could not see any more details but she detected movement inside the tent. There was also a smell; familiar but sickening. It smelled like sulphur and something else. Then finally she knew. It was the smell of Tartarus. Someone or something from the darkness of the pit was there in that tent. Anyone near it would feel pain and sickness. She looked back at

289

Peter, this time with real fear in her eyes. Peter watched her and smiled his terrible smile. Hypatia began to panic.

"No. No. NO! You don't know what you're doing! You can't do this." She began to struggle with the guards, desperately hitting them. They beat her down cruelly with short sticks and whips. She screamed in agony. In the background she could hear the crowd cheering. Battered and bleeding from wounds in her head, they tied her to the pyre. Peter was reading from a book and saying something but Hypatia couldn't hear him. Her ears were filled with blood.

Hypatia was vaguely aware that Peter had stopped talking. Her head thumped with pain and blood oozed from her wounds but she could see that something was dispersing the crowd. Large creatures had entered the courtyard and were picking up soldiers and throwing them over walls. People began screaming and fleeing the courtyard. Andrapodons! The stone slaves, bigger ones than she had ever seen before, were blazing a path to the pyres. Behind them came men and women dressed in the familiar garb of the inhabitants of the White City. Tears of happiness streamed down Hypatia's face. "I'm here," she said softly. "I'm here."

Big-armed Ambustus was among her saviors and Ra-Neferu glittered in the sunlight behind him. Ambustus came to the pyre, cut the ropes that held Hypatia, and picked her up as if she were made of cotton. All around them the large andropodons ripped the pyres out of the ground and threw them in all directions. Any armed men who approached them were also tossed away. Peter was nowhere in sight.

Ra-Neferu and Ambustus, carrying Hypatia, walked towards the portal to the White City. All around them the andrapodons held the line, repelling the soldiers who came to fight them. In this way they walked down the jetty to the portal and stopped briefly before it.

Ra-Neferu produced two small scrolls from a little purse that she carried. She then stood at the foot of a stone slave and with a hand signal bade it to lower its head and open its mouth. She inserted a scroll into the andrapodon's mouth. It stood up and bowed to her. She then repeated this procedure with another stone slave who also bowed. She then ushered all of her party back through the portal including several of the andrapodons. Then she stepped through herself leaving the two to whom she had given the scrolls.

After they walked through, the two stone slaves began to throw themselves against the portal. They rammed both sides of it until finally the mortar at the bases cracked and the entire portal fell into the ocean. The two andrapodons fell with it, disintegrating into dust that fell on the surface of the ocean like grey snow.

On the other side of the portal, at the edge of the desert, Ra-Neferu and Ambustus, still carrying Hypatia, waited and watched the portal. After a few seconds there was a snapping sound. Ra-Neferu walked forward and stuck her hand through the portal. Nothing happened. She walked through it completely and then stepped back through.

"It is done," she said flatly. Ambustus just nodded. All around them the crowd of people cheered and whooped. They began walking towards a nearby portal, near the river. Hypatia still in a fog reached out for Ra-Neferu.

"Is it over?" she asked. Ra-Neferu shook her head.

"No, my friend" she said sadly, "I am afraid it has just begun."

www.ingramcontent.com/pod-product-compliance
Lightning Source LLC
Chambersburg PA
CBHW030318200626
46816CB00006BA/1842